# Review

What makes *Proportional Response* a powerful novel is that it is realistic and convincing. Award-winning author Stefan Vučak, not only knows his subject well, but he also has an effective writing style. As global disaster seems inevitable, it is interesting to note the disparity between American and Chinese cultures, which ultimately directs the actions of the main protagonists in the story. This is a tale of international politics that sadly, seems all too familiar in our world today, except that in this case the reader gets to know what is really going on behind the news headlines. Fast paced and peppered with interesting technical details, *Proportional Response* is a book difficult to put down, especially because the events might well be happening in our midst right now!

Readers' Favorite

# Books by Stefan Vučak

**General Fiction:**
*Cry of Eagles*
*All the Evils*
*Towers of Darkness*
*Strike for Honor*
*Proportional Response*
*Legitimate Power*
*Autumn Leaves*
*All My Sunsets*
*F/X-26*
*28th Amendment*
*Night Sirens*
*Broken Rose*

**Shadow Gods Saga:**
*In the Shadow of Death*
*Against the Gods of Shadow*
*A Whisper from Shadow*
*Shadow Masters*
*Immortal in Shadow*
*With Shadow and Thunder*
*Through the Valley of Shadow*
*Guardians of Shadow*

**Science Fiction:**
*Fulfillment*
*Lifeliners*

**Non-Fiction:**
*Writing Tips for Authors*

Contact at:
www.stefanvucak.com

# PROPORTIONAL RESPONSE

By

Stefan Vučak

Stefan Vučak ©2014
ISBN-10: 0-9942923-6-8
ISBN-13: 978-0-9942923-6-0

# Dedication

*To Frank ... seeing through life's veils*

# Acknowledgments

My thanks to Dr. Gary M. McMurtry, Associate Professor at the Department of Oceanography, University of Hawaii, Manoa, for his contribution to my understanding of tsunamis.

Valuable information was provided by Dr. Jim Kauahikaua, Scientist-in-charge, Hawaiian Volcano Observatory, US Geological Survey, on Hawaiian volcanism, underwater landslides and slumps.

I also want to thank Ms Mary-Louise Hickey, Publications Editor, Department of International Relations, School of International, Political & Strategic Studies, Australian National University, for information on Chinese leadership.

I gained much understanding about China's culture and politics from Francis Fukuyama's book, *The Origins of Political Order*, Profile Books Ltd, 2012. Excerpts by permission from the author.

Special thanks to Bonnie Milani for her suggestions how to improve the book.

Cover art by Laura Shinn.
http://laurashinn.yolasite.com

"To see what is right and not do it is want of courage."

Confucius

# Chapter One

Zhou Yedong smiled broadly, turned slightly, and extended his right arm. Tall, his impeccably tailored dark blue gabardine suit that understated a taste for all things Western, he cut a dominating figure, authority etched on his hard featured face. President Samuel Walters returned the smile and clasped the proffered hand in a firm grip. The two leaders waited as camera flashes from the state-run *Xinhua* and the *People's Daily* tabloids recorded the event for local and international consumption.

Still wearing a friendly grin, Zhou leaned toward Walters, murmured something, and the two men laughed, obviously enjoying each other's company. Observing the proceedings, Keung Yang scowled, absently adjusted his rimless glasses and took a sip of orange-red Fujian rice wine, taking comfort from its delicate flavor. There wasn't much comfort coming from anywhere else. He looked around the opulent Diaoyutai Banquet Hall. Several fellow Standing Committee members, clutching crystal wine goblets, also wore frowns of concern. They had reason to be concerned. Instead of pressing China's economic and financial advantage to humble the Americans, Zhou advocated cooperation and appeasement, mindful of incurring negative world opinion should he tread too hard. It burned Keung to see his country still kowtowing to the West, despite forceful rhetoric to the contrary.

He turned his head, scanned the crowded hall, locked eyes with Chen Teng and gave a small nod. Chen's mouth twitched in return, but it wasn't with humor. They shared a similar outlook and philosophy, explored over numerous lengthy discussions, fortified with liquid lubricants. Keung clenched his teeth in frustration and waited as his friend moved unobtrusively toward him.

A ripple of subdued applause and shuffling of feet followed the two leaders as they made their way toward broad tables arranged on the far side of the hall, where an elaborate dinner would celebrate the meeting of the only two superpowers left. Usually, large state functions were held at the modern complex next to the Fang Fei Yuan villa on the Diaoyutai State Guesthouse grounds, or the Great Hall of the People at Tiananmen Square, but the American delegation was small, only forty State Department officials and trade hangers-on. Keung gave a forlorn sigh of resignation and glanced at his stocky friend.

"Damnable, that's all I've got to say," he growled in Cantonese, his black eyebrows coming together in disapproval, not afraid to voice his disquiet to a trusted comrade. The barbarian Westerners were hardly expected to understand a civilized language, which included some of his provincial colleagues attempting to eavesdrop, most of them knowing only Mandarin. He had to be careful voicing open dissent, even to a friend, and the walls had sharp ears.

Chen shook his head and chuckled. "Zhou's star burns bright, my indiscreet friend, and the elitist princelings rule—for now. You would be prudent to remember this."

Keung waved a hand in dismissal. "I haven't forgotten, but this was an opportunity lost. America is floundering and the venerated dollar isn't the world's powerhouse anymore. With our bond holdings we were in a position to dictate terms to the financial markets. Instead, Zhou has caved in to imperialist demands who now dare instruct us how we should run our country after the mess they made of their own, which incidentally plunged us into the Global Financial Crisis. Such gall. It's intolerable, I tell you."

Chen ruefully shook his head. "Ah, the pitfalls of free enterprise. Until we can project power with a navy capable of facing the Americans, all we have are our diplomatic and economic weapons."

"And we're using them, but it's not nearly enough."

"What do you want to do? Granted, we have the means to cripple them, but the resulting world chaos would hurt us just as badly, perhaps more."

"We'd be in a better position to weather it."

"Possibly, but at what cost? The diplomatic damage would be considerable, and maybe irretrievable, at least in the medium term. We'd alienate our export markets and seriously harm developing countries we're trying to bring into our sphere of influence. Without markets to sell our goods, the neon lights proclaiming our prosperity would soon shut down. Another thing; our fiscal position isn't as strong as we think."

Keung stared hard at his friend, taking in Chen's imposing 180-centimeter full frame. Bald, a ragged scar running down his left cheek—a remnant from a near-fatal car accident with a drunken fool—the man's cold black eyes were inscrutable. Depth lay behind that bland face, which many failed to recognize. It could also be fatalistic acceptance of a volatile domestic political climate, or simply a constant need to compromise, thereby avoiding confrontation that might threaten his position. Keung was still to decide.

"Don't tell me you agree with Zhou's policies?"

"They're not his policies. They are collective policies of the Standing Committee, of which you are chairman."

"That's sidestepping the issue and you know it. Anyway, I'm chairman only because Zhou's elitist princeling lackeys don't dare oust me. I still have power, you know."

"Fast diminishing. The Tuanpai are on the decline, my rebellious friend. I'd take another count of your alleged supporters and consider curbing those radical revolutionary tendencies of yours. They will land you in trouble one day. You have achieved much in a long career to the State and the Party. Savor the fruits of your labors instead of hatching dissenting plots. We're both past such foolishness. There are also our families to consider."

Keung stared at the Vice Chairman of the Central Military Commission, not believing he heard him right. Had Chen given up the fight to further the Tuanpai populist cause, unwilling to risk the privileges of his position? As a member of the ruling State Council, could his friend be one of those numbers he should be concerned about? No, it wasn't possible. Still, however unpleasant the thought, it might be worth delving into.

"My career isn't over yet, and I tell you this. We're entering a pivotal time for China. Zhou and his *taizidang* clique are squandering it, turning their backs on the people. I cannot allow that to happen."

Chen rubbed his scar and frowned. "You want to mount a coup? You'd be crushed and I'd lose a skilled mahjong opponent, or worse. They could come after *me* simply for talking to you. Not an optimum outcome for either of us."

Keung slapped his friend on the shoulder and laughed, which caused some heads to turn toward them. "That would be a shame, wouldn't it? Relax, I'm not plotting to immolate my career in some grand gesture of misguided ideological patriotism. However, Zhou and his liberal ideas are dangerous for our country, as is the creeping erosion of our social and moral fabric. We're selling our revolutionary values to Western conglomerates. You know that, don't you?"

"Those Western conglomerates which you so decry gave us the power to confront them using their own tools against them. Boardroom diplomacy and the stock exchanges, these are our battlegrounds now, but enough of such disturbing talk. We better start heading for our table before our absence becomes an unwelcome talking point."

Keung watched as Chen hurried after Dzhang Qishan, grabbing the premier of the State Council by his right arm in an intimate gesture. Chatting amiably, confident in their power, the two men walked casually toward elaborately decorated dining tables. In the crowded, noisy room, Keung suddenly felt alone, and the breeze of change whistled hollow through his bones. He gave an involuntary shudder and sighed. His right knee had begun to hurt again and he wanted to sit down and rub it, Chen's words haunting his thoughts.

A fellow populist, he was somewhat taken aback by his friend's casual dismissal of his concerns. Born in Baotou, Chen understood the plight common people labored under in the bleak northern reaches of the country. Inner Mongolia, with its deserts and harsh winters, provided a tough training ground for a rising young Party official and serving Army officer. Recognizing early the value of vast stretches of rare earth metals, almost half of Earth's known reserves, Chen formulated a policy of export quotas that helped propel his career. To grow in the twenty-first century, China needed those reserves for itself rather than squander them to its ideological and commercial competitors.

Had Chen become too comfortable in his position, no longer willing to push the interests of the country and the Tuanpai cause, lest the effort threatened his sunset years in the Party? As a Hun, his friend harbored deep suspicion of all foreigners, swallowing his resentment in pragmatic recognition that China needed Western investment to expand. He accepted the need, but didn't like having to compromise. Did Chen have information that made him acquiesce to Zhou's unrelenting push to turn China into a global economic power, sacrificing the national spirit along the way? Zhou could have it all, including global dominion by manipulation and control of the world's economic and financial levers, but the fool simply didn't get it. Keung hissed in frustration as he watched Zhou and the American president chatting amiably.

It seemed all so simple back in Hefei, he reflected; first running the prefecture, ending up as the Anhui Provincial Committee Secretary, being noticed by President Jiang Zamin, until he finally obtained a foothold in the Politburo Standing Committee. He longed for the simple, uncomplicated life he had in Hefei, but he knew too much, understood too much, and now he couldn't find peace; all because of one thing…power. He had it, understood its application, and intended to continue using it. Whatever demons now haunted his nights, he wouldn't change a day. Well, one or two, perhaps. If Chen was right and his power base had eroded—something to look into—he would see Zhou and his princeling coalition destroyed before that happened. The Shanghai Gang faction a spent force and not worth worrying about.

Chen's concern about a possible threat to their families unwarranted. The Politburo had moved on since Mao's days and business wasn't done that way anymore. Still…

"I hope I am not intruding, Mr. Chairman," a soft, but strong voice inquired beside him and Keung turned, affixing a political grin suitable for the occasion.

"Not at all, Mr. Secretary." Keung's English perfect, certain he could fence verbally with the American Secretary of State.

Larry Tanner appeared relieved, his icy blue eyes twinkling with amusement. They were eyes that gave nothing away and saw everything. Impeccably dressed as always, thick brown hair neatly combed, the tall foreigner looked imposing. Keung had dealt with the man before and within obvious limits trusted him, forgiving Tanner's barbaric penchant for plain talk so alien to eastern sensibilities, grounded in elaborate protocol, veiled nuances, and double meanings. He knew Tanner, all right, remembering him well as an exasperating and arrogant ambassador to his country in the previous American administration. Both had polished their technique since then. One learned by doing.

Keung found Americans amusing and irritating. They had a driving need to establish who was right in any argument when often there was no outright right or wrong, merely a tapestry of contradictions. They did not necessarily want to understand or appreciate another's point of view, but disprove it, replacing it with their own obdurate position. By comparison, the Chinese

psyche did not demand working through apparent contradictions, accepting that reality is multi-layered and unpredictable, in
a constant state of change. A workable compromise would do
fine. The Chinese dialectical approach more tolerant and avoided
confrontation in most situations, but it also meant that people
did not challenge the status quo and tended not to change much
over time, which explained their tolerance of the Party's harsh
rule and of past tyrannies. Were it not for this almost phlegmatic
attitude, the vast masses out there would have swallowed them
long ago.

As they walked slowly toward the tables, Tanner cleared his
throat. "I couldn't help noticing, sir, your intense conversation
with Chen Teng, although jovial at times."

Keung smiled, comfortable dancing around important state
matters, which by their very significance could not be broached
directly. Behavior he understood and appreciated. Plain speaking
had its place, but the subtle maneuvering around a subject exercised his mental flexibility and generated genuine pleasure when
a skilled opponent responded in kind.

"Discussing a fruitful agreement between our two countries,
Mr. Secretary," he murmured suavely.

"I dare say," Tanner replied dryly, conveying his skepticism
in no uncertain terms, and Keung chuckled.

"You don't believe me? Agreeing to float the yuan not an
easy decision for us. Despite misinformation from some quarters,
we do understand the need to do so and the impact this will have
on our mutual trade positions."

"In exchange for an additional seat on the IMF Executive
Board. I cannot help wonder who got the better of the bargain."

"As a major global economic power, Mr. Secretary, it's a seat
we deserve. Curbing patent and intellectual property violations
so dear to your heart also a significant concession."

"Welcomed, certainly, but your expansion into the Pacific is
of concern, as is the undermining of some of its island states."

Keung laughed, vastly entertained by the American's parochial black-and-white attitude. He felt mildly peeved at Tanner's assumed air of superiority, demanding deference by his mere presence, which perhaps unconsciously reflected a degree of condescension toward all people not white. Tanner would probably be appalled if this were pointed out to him. A product of what he considered a superior social order, his attitude axiomatic.

"Hardly accurate, sir. China is merely extending a helping hand to new friends; friends the United States and Europe have neglected. You can hardly blame us if Polynesia and Micronesia are now turning to us to form lasting partnerships."

"That's what I was saying," Tanner murmured.

Keung nodded, allowing himself a small smile. In this case, using their vernacular, America had dropped the ball. The subtlety of the English language and rich American idioms in many respects rivaled Mandarin silkiness.

"I must say, however, your acknowledgment of China's sovereignty over the Diaoyutai Islands as per the Potsdam Declaration a gratifying shift in your foreign policy, something we appreciated. Japan has no legal claim over those islands, having occupied them during the first Sino-Japanese war in 1894."

Tanner shrugged. "The President had to overcome Congressional resistance over that decision. He recognized, and something which I support, unless checked, disputes over energy sources are likely to become more common, Mr. Chairman, and that's what this one is about. Your willingness to jointly exploit gas and oil reserves around the Senkaku Islands was a generous gesture on your behalf. You could have taken a hard line over the issue."

Keung felt amused at Tanner's use of Senkaku as the name for the islands. Japan no longer the economic power of old, facing a crippling national debt—more than double its GDP—declining balance of trade, shrinking manufacturing base, and a falling birthrate. Those were all warning indicators of a country in trouble. As an island nation, it could no longer claim unrestricted access to the world's natural resources to support its security as it did in the past, which explained its alarming diplomatic and military reaction to China's claim over the Diaoyutai Islands. National pride forbade them bowing to international pressure, but however unwilling, they were forced to do precisely that as the price for being part of the world community. Japanese leaders still clung to the outmoded samurai Bushido code, refusing to acknowledge the impediment this code presented when dealing with international disputes, something the younger generation recognized, but were powerless to change for now in the current domestic political climate.

"It's a matter of perspective, Mr. Secretary. Tolerating and accepting a historical difference will benefit Japan as much as us. However, this weighty talk, sir, threatens to spoil what promises to be an auspicious dinner, something disagreeable to my sensitive constitution. Perhaps we can pick this up later over brandy and cigars?"

"A decadent indulgence?" Tanner queried with a raised eyebrow.

"Merely civilized enjoyment," Keung said with a disarming shrug.

Tanner grinned and nodded in capitulation. "I shall look forward to sampling again your fine brandies." With a small bow, he strode purposefully after Chen Teng and Dzhang Qishan, leaving Keung bemused. Although a barbarian lacking refinement, Tanner could be wily when he wanted to, and it wouldn't do to underestimate the man.

Keung negotiated waving hands and closed groups, and strode quickly across the exquisitely laid brown marble floor glittering under four brilliant crystal chandeliers, his Italian leather shoes hardly making a sound. When fully packed, the hall could entertain 200 guests, but this evening there were scarcely over a hundred and fifty. Every visit by the Americans represented an important occasion, but despite the attached trade delegation that provided a public facade, President Walters used this one to hold some very private talks with Zhou Yedong. Dressed in dark suits, trying to appear inconspicuous, special Ministry of Public Security operatives watched for any disturbance; another facade.

Politburo luminaries, most of the Standing Committee members with a sprinkling of Central Military Commission generals and admirals, were slowly taking their seats, the places arranged along strict protocol lines. Seated at the long central table, with Mao's large portrait hanging prominently on the wall behind them, Zhou Yedong, State Council heavyweights and, of course, President Walters and Secretary Tanner, looked relaxed, relishing the evening. They had cause to be cheerful, Keung reflected morosely.

Soft traditional zither music drifted over the assembly, complementing a wash of voices and occasional hearty laughter. Local red and white wines were already flowing freely. Keung nodded knowingly. When those who overindulged woke tomorrow, they'd be wishing for oblivion. He had seen it all before. Behind their polished veneer, many of his colleagues were really little better than provincial peasants, having risen to power through graft, bribery, kickbacks and backstabbing—sometimes literally.

Premier Dzhang Qishan looked relaxed as he sat next to Zhou. Indisposed, the State Council President not able to attend this function, and Qishan filled in for him. Han Yunshan, the CMC Chairman, said something to the premier and Dzhang laughed. They were polished operators and their veneer of sophistication very genuine. The three princelings dominated the elitist coalition. They were all Keung's enemies.

He didn't resent their promotion of China's Go Global Strategy *per se*. His country needed modernization to compete in the world marketplace and eventually control it. He understood all that. He detested the radical shifting into unchecked privatization, market liberalization and open foreign investment. Although China had prospered under these policies, first advocated by Deng Xiaoping, along the way the Party had forgotten the Revolution and the need to promote health, social welfare, justice and the rule of law. The growing rift between the wealth of cities and the rural multitude had turned into a festering and growing sore within the Party. Keung found it troubling that no one seemed to mind this destabilizing development, erroneously assuming that wealth would trickle down to the masses. Perhaps he was simply old-fashioned, acknowledging that growing complexity of modern world politics sometimes overwhelmed him. However, his focus to correct what he felt to be a wrong turning for his country clear, his determination remained unwavering.

Didn't Confucius say, *In a country well governed, poverty is something to be ashamed of. In a country badly governed, wealth is something to be ashamed of.* Perhaps the old man had it right.

Sighing, he deposited his goblet on a tray wielded by one of the invisible attendants and walked slowly toward the central table, allowing the media to follow him, but refusing to take questions. Keung seated himself next to Walters as befitted his rank, and nodded to the American.

"Mr. President, a delightful evening."

"A pleasure to have you with us, Mr. Chairman," Walters said, smiling broadly.

"You must forgive Yang's tardiness, sir," Zhou interjected, using the familiar first name, "but he is a rule unto himself."

Tanner chuckled and leaned forward. "I'm the one to blame, gentlemen. The Chairman and I were discussing matters of state."

Walters shook his head in resignation. "Can't you leave your baggage behind for one night, Larry?"

Zhou laughed with genuine humor. "Once a diplomat, Mr. President, always a manipulator. It comes with the portfolio."

"I'm afraid you're right, sir," Walters agreed regretfully.

Keung nodded politely and raised a glass of Shaoxing pale yellow *Hua Diao* wine in a sign of contrition.

"No more politics. At least not tonight."

He caught Zhou looking at him thoughtfully. *No, not tonight, my princeling friend, but you can look forward to a reckoning soon.*

Inevitable as their reckoning would be, he recalled another Confucius saying, *Before you embark on a journey of revenge, dig two graves.* To fulfill a dream, sometimes even death wasn't too high a price to pay.

"It is regrettable, Mr. President, that your short stay does not permit you to visit some of our more notable attractions," Zhou said smoothly, and Walters nodded.

"Something I also regret. My chief of staff can run the White House quite efficiently without me, but should I extend my visit, he might want to make my absence permanent."

"Unfortunately, I know exactly what you mean," Zhou agreed, glancing pointedly at Keung, who smiled faintly and broke eye contact after a few seconds of clashing wills.

"I sometimes bemoan not having the option of sending a recalcitrant Congressman or two to a correctional farm," Walters mused. "It would solve a lot of my problems."

"Your democratic system, Mr. President, lends itself to chaotic behavior," Zhou remarked suavely.

"Perhaps if we met somewhere halfway…" Walters looked pointedly at Zhou.

They had met halfway, Keung reflected, but the Americans were already standing on the dividing line.

Despite false smiles and some forced laughter, everyone appeared to have a good time. As the evening wore on, the Americans groaning from an endless procession of dishes representing every Chinese province, diplomatic protocol discarded—at least lowered a little—allowing real discourse to develop. These functions also acted as legitimate cultural exchanges, the Americans always walking away actually surprised to discover warm, yet serious personalities in their counterparts who genuinely did not seek conflict. Keung wasn't surprised at all, needing to re-educate processions of their officials every time the U.S. administration changed.

By ten, the dinner had run its course and people were starting to fidget, but no one dared walk out until Zhou Yedong officially called it a night. The delicate wine had begun to clog Keung's head. He also wanted to get away, stroll around the Zhonghai—the Central Sea—shore and take in some crisp air. Not much fresh air in Beijing these days, the city usually covered by an impenetrable blanket of gray smog. When the Communist Party of China president stood up and finally announced an end to the evening's activities, he was greeted with enthusiastic applause. Everyone still faced a full day of talks likely to be intense before the American diplomatic delegation took their leave. Keung desperately wanted to know what Zhou and Walters had to say to each other, but planting bugs in their private meeting room would be foolish in the extreme. Given the security measures in force, including the sweeps by the White House Secret Service, the gambit wasn't workable anyway. Had he been tempted, he would have needlessly alerted prowling Ministry of State Security agents and the exterminators would have been called in.

Shen Lei followed him a few paces behind as Keung made his way out of the Diaoyutai State Guesthouse. Shen a bit old for his duties as a front line bodyguard, but Keung never dreamed of replacing his formidable taciturn friend, and he did consider him a friend despite the enormous social divide between them. They'd been together for fifteen years now, since Keung's appointment as the Anhui Provincial Committee Secretary. Shen had stood by his side, a bodyguard and sometimes trusted confidant, while Keung maneuvered his career up the promotional ladder through the Central Military Commission, and finally into the Standing Committee. He knew Shen to be a Ministry of State Security agent tasked to keep an eye on his activities, but Keung never doubted Shen's loyalty to him.

A luxury black, specially modified, armored BMW 7 pulled up beside the curb and his shadow quickly opened the rear door. Uniformed police had the road blocked, keeping the curious out of the way. Keung glanced at his colleagues waiting for their transports and eased himself into the back seat, the fine beige calf leather squeaking under his bulk. Shen got into the front seat and the car eased onto Fucheng Road. The Americans didn't have to go anywhere, occupying the entire State Guesthouse hotel for the duration of their visit.

Despite the relentless traffic, it didn't take long to reach the western gate of the Zhongnanhai compound nestled against the Forbidden City's western wall. Once through the security check, the guards standing stiffly at attention, the car entered what Keung called his sanctuary, an oasis of sanity in a city that knew no peace.

Built as an imperial retreat by Jin and Yuan emperors, the compound now served as headquarters for the Communist Party and State Council administrative arm. It also provided residences for high-ranking Party officials. Surrounded by immaculate lawns and groves, Qing Dynasty palaces and drab gray brick office buildings from Mao's time lay scattered around two lakes—the South and Central Sea. Inaccessible to tourists and the general public, the compound exuded tranquility by its very presence, engendering contemplation and reflection.

The BMW neared a complex of residential buildings, brightly lit from discreetly placed lampposts, capped by traditional curved red-tiled roofs, and elaborate carvings painted in prominent colors. Keung needed reflection. He wondered how Confucius would regard China's headlong rush to embrace all things material, stripping the soul bare.

Some of his *taizidang* opponents called Confucianism an intensely backward-looking philosophy, emphasizing family and kinship over loyalty to the State, which now meant loyalty to the dollar. During the heady days of the Cultural Revolution, Mao Tse-tung and his elitists sought to eradicate such counterrevolutionary thinking, but his efforts were given lip service by the population at large, determined to guard their independence against political authority. Kinship networks were a direct hindrance to accumulation of political power, but Mao's efforts to implement policies that tied individuals directly to the State was nothing more than Legalism practiced since the Zhou Dynasty—never entirely successful, and largely explained why China had always been ruled by an iron hand.

Someone had to provide leadership and vision, Keung mused, or nothing would ever get done. Local parochial interests would otherwise paralyze the country as cities and provinces sought to manipulate the state's bureaucratic machinery to further their own ends. What Westerners regarded as nepotism, graft and corruption was in reality filial and village loyalty expressed writ large. Keung knew he painted with a broad brush here, as genuine corruption existed, but it helped unravel the underpinning machinations. The plain fact, Westerners simply did not understand China and its people, automatically assuming that their version of uncoordinated democracy and dubious morality represented the ultimate social model for all mankind. Such arrogance made him snort with derision. The one exception was Tanner. Despite obvious character flaws, he understood the Chinese psyche all too well. Keung wondered if President Walters shared that understanding.

Slowing, the car pulled up to his two-story residence and stopped. Shen immediately leaped out and opened the rear door. Keung nodded to him and walked toward the broad entrance, two stylized lion statues guarding the path. The heavy lacquered wooden door opened as he stepped under the elaborately carved portico and a slim figure emerged. Lian bowed, her patterned blue silk gown shimmering under subdued lighting.

"I trust you had a successful evening, sir?" she said softly, closing the door after him.

Graceful and willowy, long hair cascading down her back, her smoky black eyes regarded him frankly. Lian ran his household with unobtrusive efficiency, a product of her People's Liberation Army training, no doubt. Security supposedly impenetrable within Zhongnanhai, but Keung knew, as did the State Council and Standing Committee members, absolute security did not exist. He didn't resent this level of intrusion into his personal life, careful not to reveal his inner thoughts to Lian and others of his household staff. They were undoubtedly all Ministry of State Security operatives. Trust was a coin he spent frugally.

"I did, but these functions are always unsettling, and this one was no exception."

"Do you want me to get you something?"

"Tea. Have someone bring it upstairs. I'll be retiring immediately."

"A pleasant night, sir."

He slowly mounted the curved staircase, lightly holding onto the balustrade, favoring his right leg. Feet sinking into thick maroon carpet, he opened the last door at the end of a short corridor. Entering the brightly lit lounge room, he closed the door with a backward shove of his hand. He pulled at his tie and strode to an antique coffee table, picked up the remote and switched on the large LED TV mounted into a ceiling-high bookcase. Glancing at rows of bound volumes, tempted to pull one out to read in bed, he decided he'd had enough of heavy thinking for the day.

About to change channels, the unfolding image of an enormous wave rolling toward a line of skyscrapers froze him. The column of green water crashed against the shore, smashing buildings, drowning everything in its path, sending people scurrying in panicked frenzy trying to escape the surging wall bearing down on them.

The special effects and computer animation were superb,

and Keung shook his head at the wonders delivered by the inexorable march of technology. In a fade, the image merged into a map of the Pacific showing expanding rings originating from the western side of the big island of Hawaii. He turned up the volume and groped for his pipe and tin of delicately blended rum-flavored tobacco.

*"—is only an estimate should the 4,000 cubic miles of the Hilina Slump, part of the Kilauea protrusion, break away from the main island, but extensive computer modeling supports what you just saw. All Pacific rim landmasses would face extensive inundation and infrastructure damage, not only from the resulting tsunami, but from a possible magnitude nine quake generated by the slide."*

The suave presenter looked concerned. *"Professor Degard, how likely is this scenario?"*

The middle-aged scientist sat back in his chair, brushed back a lock of white hair above his right ear, and smiled. *"Your viewers have no need to be alarmed. Such a catastrophic event isn't expected to occur for hundreds of thousands of years."*

*"But isn't it true, Professor, that in 1975 a 37-mile-wide section of the Hilina Slump suddenly dropped eleven-and-a-half feet and slid seaward twenty-six feet, generating a 7.2 magnitude quake and a 48-foot-high tsunami?"*

*"Which demonstrates that the Kilauea eastern slope has a tendency to relieve internal stresses through periodic slumps rather than a single catastrophic slide such as happened some 115 thousand years ago with the Alika debris avalanche. All volcanic islands are prone to periodic slumps and landslides, but in human lifetimes, these are extremely rare events."*

*"Tell me. What part of the world is most vulnerable right now?"*

*"Well…without being alarmist, the collapse of the Cumbre Vieja Volcano's western flank in the Canary Islands off Morocco represents a genuine and immediate threat, counted in hundreds of years. The entire region is particularly unstable and a displacement slide of 100 to 400 cubic miles is theoretically possible. Such an event would cause cataclysmic damage along the entire North Atlantic basin, including the United States' eastern seaboard."*

*"Damage from tsunami waves?"*

*"That's right. Portugal and the western African coastlines would suffer the greatest impact, but a tsunami front with peaks of up to sixty feet or more would devastate everything from Florida to New York."*

Staring directly at the camera, the presenter looked suitably grave. *"We'll take a short break before resuming—"*

Keung exhaled and clicked off the TV. He didn't need to watch disasters likely to come in some unknown future. There were enough man-made ones happening right now to worry about. He filled the pipe, lit it and sighed as aromatic smoke leaked through his nostrils.

A knock on the door made him turn, the image of a giant wave toppling skyscrapers fresh in his mind.

"Yes?"

"Your tea, sir," one of the servants announced.

"Very well."

He left his glasses on the coffee table, walked into the bedroom, and began to undress. The outer door closed and the pervading scent of rosehip tea filled the room, making his mouth water. Barefooted, he padded into the lounge room, poured tea into a genuine jade cup, added honey and a squirt of lemon juice. He took a thirsty sip and nodded with satisfaction. The *Hua Diao* wine excellent, but he shouldn't have had that last glass. He picked up the pipe, took a couple of puffs and placed it in the tray.

After a shower, he finished his toilet and slipped under navy blue silk covers of his king-size bed. He pressed the master switch on the night table console beside him, which plunged the apartment into darkness. No one to shared his bed these days, Juan having died two years ago from a liver infection that even Western medicine failed to overcome. Although he prided himself for having a strong libido, he did not use the services of readily available women provided by the state, wary of honey traps and emotional entanglements. After Juan, love like hers would never be his again, and he had little interest in mere diversions of the flesh.

The only family he had was a son, a Navy commander with his own *Jiangwei II*-class frigate attached to the North Sea Fleet. The Qingdao naval base a long way from Beijing, but his son could call sometimes. That he didn't, said something about their relationship. Having a powerful parent couldn't have been easy for the boy keen to make it without his father's shadow hanging over him. Admirable, but naïve. Keung had power and used it to advance his son's career, which generated the ensuing rift between them. He consoled himself with the thought that with maturity and greater understanding how the system worked, his son might see fit to pick up a phone one day. Beset with introspection, which happened occasionally, Keung wondered why he didn't pick up that phone himself. A question he could not bring himself to answer.

With no one to share his bed, share his confidences, aspirations and frustrations, all he had to fill his days now was his work. Sometimes even that wasn't enough.

The day's events crowding his mind, he drifted into sleep.

* * *

Keung woke in the depths of night, images of giant waves wreaking destruction had haunted his dreams. With sleep deserting him, he lay with hands clasped behind his head, gazing at the impenetrable blackness of the ceiling. A chill spring breeze stirred the gauzy curtain, making the hairs on his arms twitch. April should normally be warmer. He fancied he could hear the incessant rumble of traffic from a city that never slept, but it was only his imagination working in overdrive. Inured against the outside world, protected by high stone walls, the grounds were silent.

Were the scenes racing through his mind an omen, a portent of things to come? He considered himself sophisticated, above influence from something crass like old wives' superstitions, but he never ignored such warnings. Zhou Yedong and his starched business suit cronies were steering China over hazardous ground toward a questionable objective, turning people into faceless Western-type consumers, and in the process, creating serious social tension between the emerging corporate elite and the vast peasantry. Of course, that same peasantry also wanted their cut of wealth represented by ultramodern skyscrapers, dazzling neon displays, shops crammed with goods beyond reach even ten years ago, resulting in an unstoppable migration into cities already groaning under the strain to provide basic services and support infrastructure. This in turn had led to a measurable reduction in agricultural production, a disturbing threat to national food supplies should the trend continue. Foreign assets were procured to counter the threat, not enough to guarantee food and resources security, and governments around the world were increasingly blocking such acquisitions, mindful of their own strategic needs.

Keung sighed. A merely a manifestation of human nature, he decided. Like people everywhere, the Chinese were good small business operators who sought to maximize their fortunes, which only exacerbated the problem. Fortunes these days were made in cities and corporate boardrooms. However good they might be at running small enterprises, his people were terrible at managing conglomerates, something the Westerners excelled at. The explanation was simple. Multinational corporations were too complex to be run as an autocratic family fiefdom. Authority had to be delegated, behavior that ran contrary to the Chinese psyche firmly rooted in Confucian loyalty to the family and its internal hierarchy.

The mold was nevertheless slowly being broken as wealthy families sent their sons to American universities where they learned to adopt the corporate mindset, which over the last twenty years had transformed the Chinese economic landscape from a primary producer to a global manufacturing and financial powerhouse. Instead of using this strength to exert influence on the world's economic and political stage, Zhou had squandered China's competitive advantage by bowing to the West, especially the Americans. An intolerable state of affairs.

Keung clearly understood the strategy and tactics behind Zhou's rationale and of his elitist supporters: buy up Western resource-producing assets, infiltrate and eventually control their financial institutions, modernize the military to project power, and in time, China would chart the world's course. Laudable goals which he supported, but he wondered if Zhou realized that by achieving his objective, China would be transformed into a model of Western imperialism, governed by an unfeeling corporate conscience. A conscience that would subvert the government apparatus itself, bending it into just another tool in the service of generating profits, as already happened in the West, the Global Financial Crisis being a textbook case.

Keung did not want such a future for China.

Soulless corporations must be tempered with responsible socioeconomic policies as advocated by Hu Jintao. If the Party became a commercial machine, everything Keung had fought for, everything the Tuanpai movement and Jiang Zamin fought for, would be swept away, replaced by the credit card. Greed and self-interest would conquer his vast country where emperors over millennia had failed.

His mind churning, he slowly closed his eyes.

He woke with a start and blinked at bright sunshine streaming through the windows. Amazed to see blue sky not shrouded by its usual blanket of smog, he shook his head. Energized, he sprang out of bed and did his usual seventy pushups, sit-ups and tai chi moves. He might be pushing the end run of sixty-three, but his body was still that of a forty-year-old and he intended it to remain that way. He hated the idea of turning into a portly, waddling parasite that unfortunately many of his colleagues had become. Giving his right knee a vigorous massage, it worked out some of the stiffness.

After a simple breakfast of ci fan tuan, baozi—the roasted pork in the steamed buns particularly tasty—topped off with a soup of fried tofu and noodles with assorted vegetables, he walked out, Shen Lei already standing beside the BMW, the rear door open. Glancing up at the clear sky, Keung took a deep breath and exhaled with satisfaction.

"Great day, Lei."

"Yes, sir," Shen replied gravely, his damaged throat making his voice rough, causing Keung to sigh. He couldn't remember ever seeing Shen smile. Then again, his job did not give him much to smile about.

"The Guesthouse, sir?"

"No. Take me to the office."

Keung settled into the luxurious leather and sat back as the car pulled away. Having Party and government complexes inside Zhognanhai had invaluable advantages, sparing him the daily commuter crush he would otherwise have to endure on the open road, not to mention the resulting security problems guaranteed to make his paranoid guard detail go pale. Situated near the Hall of Longevity on the western side of the South Sea, the plain gray brick six-story building housing the State Council headquarters appeared among tall oak, birch and pine, surrounded by flawlessly kept lawns and flowerbeds.

As Keung walked up the white marble steps, the two guards standing watch at the entrance snapped to attention, their AK-47 rifles held before them in salute. Shen opened the heavy wooden door and Keung strode through. After taking the elevator to the fourth floor, he quickly looked around. Most of his staff were already at their desks, careful to look busy. He ignored them as he walked briskly toward his office, which occupied a substantial part of the entire floor. Inside the reception antechamber, his personal aide looked up from his computer screen and jumped up.

"Good morning, sir! Tea?"

"With a dash of lime," Keung growled, waited for Shen to unlock the door to his private office and walked in.

Shen produced what looked like a black smartphone from his pocket and spent several minutes slowly moving around the room. As Keung waited for him run the bug sweep, he bit his lower lip and absently glanced about. The polished parquet floor glittered in the morning light, turning the sliding glass bookshelf panels into mirrors. He glanced at Mao's portrait hanging prominently above the desk and frowned. Even though the old leader's policies were now thoroughly discredited, like favorite socks, the Party couldn't bring itself to discard him completely. It still harbored nostalgic sentiment for revolutionary days that swept Chiang Kai-shek's Nationalists off the mainland, heralding a period of unprecedented brutality and destruction of priceless cultural treasures. Those were dark days from which his country was still slowly recovering.

As he stood there waiting for Shen to finish the sweep, Keung suddenly felt cold and his skin prickled, finally understanding the meaning of his dream. He dug out his pipe and stoked it to life, clutching the warm bowl.

Shen pocketed the detector and nodded. "All clear, sir."

"What? Oh, right. Lei, I have a job for you," he said quietly, astonished at the audacity of his idea. Could he pursue it seriously?

On top of a flagging economy saddled with burgeoning debt, a seemingly natural disaster would cripple America, leaving China to pick over the remains at its leisure. The human cost? The tens of thousands who might be lost hardly bothered him. It was obliteration of vital infrastructure and possible breakdown of local civilian authority that mattered here. Besides, the vast masses everywhere were merely ants in the service of the state. However, ants or not, they still had to be kept happy and productive.

The idea he harbored bordered on sheer lunacy, but what if it could be made to work? Lunacy or not, he saw no harm in finding out more. It could also serve as a trigger to remove Zhou, a most satisfactory outcome. That angle though, would need careful handling. The president was a wily political mechanic, and not to be underestimated. Titillated by the prospect, he needed to confirm its feasibility. A puff of white smoke drifted above his head as he tugged at his glasses.

"Yes, sir?"

"I need to talk to a geophysicist, one of the top men we have, but not the top. Check with Peking University. Once you find him, bring him somewhere discreet where we can talk."

Shen's forehead creased in thought. "My apartment is totally secure, sir."

Keung shook his head. "No. It might be watched. I got it. Book a room at the Grand Hyatt and bring him there at twelve."

"Presumably, you'll be having lunch at Da Giorgio's?"

"I have got a sudden craving for Italian food if anyone cares to ask," Keung said dryly, his eyes cold. "While you're at the university, stop by their library and copy whatever technical articles you can dig up on the Cumbre Vieja Volcano. Don't use their computer or the Internet, and no paper request slips."

"Understood. After you finish with the professor…"

"I'll let you know."

What he contemplated doing could never surface, even if the concept turned impossible to implement. Shen's subtle hint to silence the academic not only wise, but necessary. There must not be any evidence trail back to him. He pushed aside images of a wife and child who might never see its father again, but the high stakes he played for would demand more than one sacrifice before this was done.

Shen didn't say anything, nodding in understanding. "Very good, sir."

"Pick me up at eleven-thirty."

Keung waited as Shen softly closed the carved wooden door after him, then sat down behind his spacious matte black desk.

His eyes strayed to the blue-green jade figurine of the Buddha holding down a stack of loose papers, and pulled at his chin. Sometimes, to get things done required an unorthodox approach. However, what he contemplated went way beyond the unorthodox.

He logged onto his computer and quickly checked the email Inbox, but his mind wasn't on work. He could have Googled all the information he needed, the Internet not restricted to high Party officials and ranking military officers, but that would have been foolish in the extreme. Although assured that surveillance protocols didn't apply to him, the Ministry of State Security reported to the premier of the State Council, which meant the president, and Zhou Yedong hadn't climbed to his present position by trusting his adversaries...or friends. At the level Keung operated, they all had acquaintances of opportunity, nothing more. A fellow Standing Committee member was a competitor and potential enemy, and he wasn't about to give them any ammunition.

A hell of a way to run a country, wondering how the Westerners did it. From what he knew of the American NSA, they did it very well indeed. Were *his* communications monitored by that ELINT monster? Probably, but they wouldn't get much change from the random key encryption codes the Chinese government and military organs employed. China hadn't sent some of its brightest talent to MIT and Caltech for nothing; the MSS and the CMC General Staff Department becoming very good at all forms of espionage and network hacking as a result of that foresight. China needed Western intellectual input, its philosophical outlook not suited to application of the scientific method, but they were learning. His country owed a lot to those faceless men for its economic might.

* * *

The driver brought the BMW to a stop under the hotel's portico and Shen Lei immediately scrambled out. He held the rear door open and waited as Keung heaved himself out with a grunt, the traffic noises suddenly loud. His nose wrinkled at the sharp stink of raw pollution as he absently cast his eyes over cars streaming along Chang An Avenue. Noting the official vehicle, the concierge tugged at his navy blue jacket and hurried toward them, but Shen waved him away, slamming the door shut. The BMW instantly pulled away.

Keung had dined at the Hyatt a number of times and liked the variety of its restaurants, especially relishing its exotic Italian food, a welcome change from his regular domestic fare. A favorite for a number of his colleagues. As he passed through the glass revolving door, the foyer blocked out external noises, its subdued atmosphere filled with soft instrumental Western music. Pink marble glittered beneath an enormous chandelier. A transparent column touching the fifteen-meter ceiling was alive with exotically colored fish. Keung ignored the crowded registration desk, Westerners and wealthy locals rolling suitcases and extension handle carryon bags, and followed Shen toward an alcove of elevators. With a soft *ting*, the center elevator doors opened and an impatient group surged in. Keung waited as another elevator came down and he walked in. Shen pressed the eleventh floor button and stood protectively in front of him, his eyes staring pointedly at four business suits talking animatedly. A pleasant female voice announced the sixth floor in Mandarin and English, and the four got out.

"I have the material you requested, sir," Shen said when the door panels closed.

"Excellent. Any trouble?"

"No trouble. How was the meeting with Secretary Tanner, if I may ask?"

Keung rarely shared confidences with anyone, but Shen wasn't just anybody, and he needed to vent his frustrations to someone. A good listener, Shen sometimes came up with surprisingly astute observations and comments. Anyway, revealing what he discussed with Tanner wasn't going to betray a state secret.

"Unexpectedly productive. The United States is getting tired of its Taiwan policy and President Walters wouldn't mind if the whole problem simply went away. Tanner didn't say it outright, but it appears they won't stand in our way if we absorbed that haven of Nationalist subversives, provided we don't do it militarily."

"Isn't that what we've been doing already?"

"To an extent. However, this shift in American policy will enable us to formalize and accelerate the process."

"And what did the Secretary want in return?"

The lush voice announced the eleventh floor and the doors hissed open.

Keung glanced at his friend. "That we lift export quotas off our rare earths." Seeing Shen's raised eyebrows, he nodded. "Not a small ask, as it impacts a range of vital modern manufacturing processes, ours as well as theirs."

Always a professional, Shen peered out and walked briskly along the brightly lit corridor, his feet sinking into rich light brown pile. When they reached room 1123, he dug out a keycard and inserted it into a slot. When the lock clicked, he opened the door and waited for Keung to walk in. A slender balding man sporting heavy black-rimmed glasses, stood up. He might have been in his late thirties, but it was hard to say. All the Chinese looked young until they were suddenly old.

"Professor Chuan Jianbo from the School of Earth and Space Sciences, Peking University," Shen announced gravely. "I'll be outside, sir," he said, and softly closed the door after him.

Studying the man, Keung could tell Chuan was curious about this strange meeting, knowing he faced an important official, but didn't seem at all intimidated. Although unimportant, the professor did not appear to recognize him.

Well appointed with two double beds, a computer, flat TV screen, and a writing desk, the room otherwise unspectacular. Keung could have been in any hotel in the world. Without offering to shake hands, he strode to the desk, pulled back a padded chair and sat down. Glancing up, he swept a hand at an empty chair.

"Make yourself comfortable, Professor."

Chuan unbuttoned his jacket, sat down and crossed his legs. "An unusual meeting, Mr…"

"Keung Yang."

The professor's eyes widened and some color drained from his fleshy face. Clearing his throat, a faint smile played at the corner of his mouth.

"Everything is clear to me now, Mr. Chairman."

"Does anyone know that you are here?"

"No, sir. Mr. Shen Lei called me on my cellphone and asked me to meet him at the parking lot, a matter of state security, he said."

"And it is."

"He drove me here from the campus, told me to wait and not make any calls."

"Did you make any calls?" Keung asked softly, fiddling with his pipe. "We can check, you know."

"I called our departmental secretary on my cell, telling her I'd be away for a couple of hours. I didn't tell her where I was."

Keung nodded. He believed the man, but Shen would still check the hotel's phone records and Chuan's cellphone.

"Professor, this conversation is very much a matter of state security, and you will not divulge or refer to it in any way, written or verbal, to anyone. Is that clear?" He puffed out a cloud of white aromatic smoke. He had no need to elaborate. Chuan knew what would happen to him and his family if he said anything.

"Absolutely, sir."

"Are you married? Children?"

"I have a wife and a twelve-year-old daughter. She wants to be an astronaut," Chuan added proudly.

Keung pondered whether to continue with this, but somewhat late for second thoughts. Perhaps something could be done for the daughter—if he survived. He tapped the desk with his fingers, exhaled and sat back, deciding to push this to its limit, but indirectly.

"Last night, I saw part of a documentary on the Discovery channel about a tsunami and how they're generated. It disturbed me and I couldn't sleep afterward."

Chuan grinned broadly. "I also saw that program, but if you're worried about a likely threat to China in the event of a Kilauea flank collapse, sir, there is no reason for concern. Such an event is not likely to happen for hundreds of thousands of years. Not likely."

Keung puffed and nodded. "That's what the narrator said. Are there other vulnerable zones capable of triggering a massive tsunami?"

Chuan looked thoughtful. "Collapse events could and have occurred in the Caribbean Volcanic Island Arc. It's a very active tectonic region, a result of the Caribbean Plate moving in relation to the North and South American plates. As stratovolcanoes, they're prone to slope failure as an ejecta layer built from successive eruptions fails. These islands are more or less conical, although you often cannot tell by simply looking at above surface features. Gravity invariably weakens any fault line paralleling the rift zone, causing either a slump along the boundary or a total structural collapse. Both generate a quake and a tsunami, but of different magnitudes. Definitely different. The Montserrat Soufriere Hills and St. Vincent volcanoes pose a significant future threat. However, a tsunami event there would not be a threat to China. Tongatapu is quite active, but its effects are localized. It poses no danger, none."

"Last night's program mentioned another type of volcano."

"Yes, sir, shield volcanoes. The Hawaiian chain is an excellent example of the type, formed entirely by periodic lava flooding, the mounds resembling a warrior's upraised shield. Curious reference, don't you think? It's also a very unusual chain, created by a giant magma plume, which accounts for their enormous size, rising as they do from the ocean floor. Fascinating geology, that. Fascinating. No one understands how that plume functions or why it lasted several million years."

Keung regarded the scientist with interest. Undoubtedly, he was dealing with a character here. "Just for my information, how vulnerable is Cumbre Vieja?"

"To a slump?" Chuan pulled at his chin, his eyes vacant as he ordered his thoughts. "In geological timescales, very. The island of La Palma is one of the most unstable formations on Earth, and experiences regular earthquakes almost on a daily basis. A large part of the western flank is constructed from the scar of a previous collapse, which today forms the Caldera de Taburiente mountain, and sits on an unstable debris layer deposited by that collapse. I wouldn't want to live there. It is speculated that even a small eruption along the Cumbre Vieja ridge could trigger a collapse of the entire western flank ranging from 150 to 500 cubic kilometers."

"Cubic *kilometers*?" Keung stared at the scientist in disbelief.

Chuan smiled. "We're dealing with enormous forces here, sir. Enormous. However, slope failures generally occur in phases and not necessarily as a single large-scale massive collapse. Lucky for us. The Kilauea flank failure in 1975 is a typical example, displacing less than three cubic kilometers, resulting in moderate near-field destruction, with insignificant far field effects. Quite insignificant."

"What would be the effect of a large Cumbre Vieja collapse?"

"A large collapse? You have to think big here. A slide block of 500 cubic kilometers might be some twenty-two kilometers long, fifteen wide and up to one and a half deep, moving at 100 meters per second. Such a mass might displace a water dome 900 meters high, inundating the Canary Islands to a hundred meters or more. Within one hour, stacked short frequency waves of up to ten meters would sweep across the African coastline. Europe could have seven meter waves, and South America would be swept with twenty meter waves. Along the shallow continental shelf of eastern North America, twenty to twenty-five meter waves might hit after seven hours. The effects would be similar to the 2011 Tohoku tsunami off Japan. Very similar.

"Of course, this is a worst-case scenario. The most likely event would probably displace less than 200 cubic kilometers. Although only forty percent the size, the resulting tsunami would still be enormously destructive, on the order of the 2010 Sumatra earthquake. On the La Palma island itself, all towns on the western flank would be destroyed: Puntagorda, Tijarafe and La Punta, to name a few. On the eastern flank, Santa Cruz de la Palma, Los Cauces and others would probably be inundated. The entire population of some 90,000 might be lost. When nature speaks, it is always on a grand scale, Mr. Chairman. Grand scale."

"You paint a terrible scenario, Professor," Keung murmured, clearly visualizing the destruction, and took a puff.

"It's not that bad really. Since the establishment of the North Atlantic, Mediterranean, and Connected Seas Tsunami Warning System—NEAMTWS—in 2005, everybody is keeping a close eye on Cumbre Vieja, including Mount Etna and Vesuvius, a very underrated volcano. Very. Those sites are littered with remote sensing instruments, which should provide ample warning of any upcoming event, allowing time for evacuation. Naples is extremely vulnerable as people don't appreciate the danger Vesuvius represents. We generally refuse to learn from history, sir."

"This is truly fascinating, Professor. I don't envy our children their future. Tell me. Could a landslide be triggered artificially?"

Chuan opened his mouth, then closed it with a snap. He cleared his throat and uncrossed his legs. He bit his lower lip and

Stefan Vučak

stared at Keung.

"The forces involved—"

"Is it possible?"

"Well, a multi-megaton underwater detonation positioned at the base of a fault line could theoretically trigger a slump. I couldn't tell you the required energy release or the size of the resulting displacement mass without doing some detailed THETIS-FUNWAVE modeling, the solution dependent on specific site parameters. But the idea…"

Undecided, Keung weighed the risks involved. Chuan would probably keep his mouth shut, fear would make sure of that, but using university computer facilities would leave an evidence trail, which someone could later pick up. Still, records can be wiped, and he needed accurate data to determine the feasibility of his scheme.

"How long would it take to model a number of scenarios?"

"Not long. The basic data on every active volcano is readily available from ongoing studies, and Cumbre Vieja was modeled exhaustively. I've done some work on it myself for my graduate students. The unknown parameter is the effect of energy transfer to the slope from a transverse shock caused by a specific detonation, and whether such a shockwave would be powerful enough to trigger a slump. That's the unknown."

"Can you give me a guess?"

Chuan pulled at his chin and shook his head. "Not without detailed modeling, sir, but a five megaton blast could probably trigger a moderate slide. Although such an event is theoretically feasible, a thermonuclear detonation would leave incriminating radiation."

Keung puffed, sighed and nodded. "You're right." He tapped the pipe against the ashtray and pocketed it. "When can you start?"

"Well…I can run several scenarios this afternoon." Chuan shifted in his seat, clearly uncomfortable. "Mr. Chairman…you are not seriously considering—"

"Setting off a tsunami?" Keung laughed at the man's goggling expression. "Hardly, but the Party must be vigilant and explore all possibilities. China is a growing power and the West is jealous of our prosperity and economic might. There is no telling what someone in Washington might come up with, blaming the event on us. We must be prepared."

Relieved, Chuan smiled. "Yes, I understand, but no one could contemplate doing such a monstrous thing. The appalling loss of life and damage to infrastructure—"

"You're correct, of course. But as I said, we must be prepared."

"Definitely, and you have given me an idea for a paper I'm preparing. A great idea."

"What paper, Professor?"

"I'm invited to attend a symposium of volcanologists and geophysicists at the University of Hawaii, Manoa, next month. Induced slope slumps would make an interesting discussion topic. Yes, very interesting."

Keung stood up and stared hard at the academic. Whatever misgivings he might have had about getting rid of him, Chuan's rash remark removed them. The man might be brilliant in his field, but he had no concept of security. His bad luck that he lived in an innocent academic world. Bad luck or simply the first collateral casualty of a fantastic scheme? It didn't matter really.

"Our discussion must remain strictly confidential, for reasons I am sure you can appreciate. I cannot stress this too highly, Professor."

Chuan cleared his throat and nodded once as he rose. "Only a thought, sir. Of course, I would never—"

"Shen Lei will take you back to the university. It will not be necessary for me to see you again. Once you finish your modeling runs, please summarize your findings to him and give him all printouts. And, Professor? No record of your work in any form must exist anywhere."

"I understand."

"Good. Thank you for your time. It was most instructive."

"Ah, glad to help the State, sir," Chuan said weakly.

Keung walked to the door and opened it. Shen immediately stepped in.

"The professor has some work to do for me." He stared at Shen and gave a single small nod. After a moment, Shen returned it.

"Very good, sir."

Without looking back, Keung strode briskly toward the elevators, his head buzzing with images his audacious plan would wreak on the imperialists. Totally crazy, he knew it, and the risks frightfully real, as were the technical challenges, but if he could pull it off even partially, the results would vindicate him. A crippled America would be far too busy dealing with internal problems to be concerned with China's economic and geopolitical expansion, opening a door to turn around Zhou Yedong's appeasement policies, getting rid of him at the same time.

More likely, Keung figured, he would end up assassinated if this ever leaked. As the operation grew, the likelihood of betrayal would increase exponentially. Somehow, that risk needed to be mitigated and all activities compartmentalized. No one individual could have sufficient information to link all the pieces together. Sun Tzu was right when he said all war was based on deception. Subdue an enemy without fighting the ultimate offensive strategy, something the Americans found difficult to grasp, demonstrated so vividly by dismal failures in Iraq and Afghanistan. They needed to cultivate diplomacy instead of relying on technology and raw might to solve everything.

As the elevator doors opened, he wondered if he could actually execute his plan.

The plump girl at the booking desk flashed him a polite smile as he walked into Da Giorgio's. Enticing smells of cooking and good food made his mouth water. She bowed slightly and ush-ered him past noisy patrons toward a corner table next to floor-to-ceiling windows overlooking the green-tiled rooftops of an old royal residence. Knowing that important Party and government officials frequented the restaurant, the manager wisely held one or two tables always available. Over a weekend though, even the premier would need to make a courtesy reservation, not that Keung expected Dzhang Qishan to be dining here. It was be-neath him to be seen slumming with commoners.

"Garlic bread and a glass of chianti, sir?"

Keung seated himself and nodded. "Make sure the wine is chilled," he growled, casting his eyes over the crowded tables and harried waiters. The atmosphere noisy, but he didn't mind.

"Of course," she said, handing him a leather-bound menu. He waved it aside.

"Pork ravioli and gnocchi with your special veal and mush-room sauce."

"Excellent choice, sir. I shall only be a moment."

He watched her walk away, the tight skirt clinging to her curves. Not beautiful in the traditional sense, the handsome girl had character. Most young women had it these days. Discovering that they were in demand, the shortage resulting from a failed, although well intentioned one child policy, girls became inde-pendent and choosy, something boys found intimidating, reared in a culture where women were expected to defer to men. He swept his eyes around the subdued yet elegant décor. Embroi-dered cloth covered comfortably large tables laid with classy cut-lery and accessories, reflecting the quality of women patronizing the establishment. No doubting that here, men deferred to women, and by the satisfied looks on their faces the women liked it that way. Without a car, a good job and an apartment, a young man had little hope of attracting a bride or keeping one.

His bread and wine came and he munched with relish, allow-ing his mind to drift. As he dipped the strong garlic bread into a bowl of olive oil and balsamic vinegar, he wondered why Tanner chose to announce a shift in the U.S. administration's Taiwan policy to him. Surely, someone addressed this during one of the more formal talks between Walters and Zhou Yedong. Not only that, he found it difficult to accept that America would make such a radical policy shift merely to secure a supply of rare earth metals, especially when they were bringing more of their own mines back into production and securing imports from the likes of Australia. He would need to raise this with Jie Lao, the wily Commerce minister and a neutral friend; neutral in the sense that Jie wasn't an opponent. Perhaps Walters *had* hashed this with Zhou, and Tanner may be giving him a heads-up. If true, it exhibited a level of subtlety he did not normally associate with the American. Why did Tanner feel that he had a need-to-know? Whether he wanted to or not, a session with Zhou was in order. After all, as a loyal Party member, he could rise above parochial factional interests for the good of the people.

The thought made him chuckle.

His steaming plate of ravioli and gnocchi arrived, brought by the manager himself, and he dug in with undisguised gusto. Freshly made, the gnocchi were slightly chewy, just the way he liked it. When he finished the meal, he was tempted to lick the plate clean like he used to as a small boy. With two brothers and a sister sharing the table, they never enough to go around. Life in Hefei was nonetheless comfortable, if not prosperous. The Anhui province had always been a poor relation to the eastern lands, something he helped turn around with the establishment of technological and industrial development zones. They had a texture and density in their lives, an element lacking in today's rush into materialism, displacing the soul-filling teachings of the Buddha. Then again, the vast majority of his people had little else to cling to as they eked out a meager living from a harsh land.

Sipping fragrant tea, pipe clamped comfortably between his teeth, Keung declined a second glass of wine. Making a decision, he dug out his cellphone. In his position, he could not afford introspection and overt sentimentality.

"How are you doing, my friend?" Chen Teng responded after two rings on his secure cell.

"Just finished lunch at Hyatt's Da Giorgio's. You should try it sometimes." Keung laughed when he heard Chen's sigh, unable to resist the small barb.

"We're still wading through ours. After last night, I could have skipped it. It's supposed to be a working lunch, but nobody is in the mood for work. Having already dealt with the important stuff, President Walters and his party are ready to depart. At least you and I won't have to deal with their trade delegation. You're coming back to the Guesthouse?"

"Within the hour. Plenty of time to pay my respects to Walters and Tanner."

"Your absence was painfully conspicuous, you know."

"I felt like eating out, and I had nothing on the agenda that needed my presence. I didn't call to talk about your lunch. We need to meet. There is a developmental shift in the American Taiwan policy."

"Oh? Something serious?"

"Curious, more than anything."

"When and where?"

"Eight o'clock tomorrow. Your office."

"Done." The line went dead.

Shen Lei's substitute bodyguard appeared at the entrance, spotted him, nodded and withdrew. Keung patted his stomach, cleaned out the pipe and absently tugged at his glasses. Favoring his right leg, he walked toward the entrance.

"I trust you found everything satisfactory, sir?" The girl at the booking desk smiled brightly at him.

"Superb as always. Thank you."

Outside, he sniffed the raw air and walked toward his car idling beside the curb. At least the sun still shone, but the smog had started to roll in.

"The Guesthouse, sir?" the bodyguard inquired diffidently as Keung climbed in.

"Yes."

The bodyguard slammed the door shut, took his seat up front and the BMW eased into the traffic.

* * *

Shen Lei watched Keung's retreating back as the Standing Committee chairman walked briskly down the corridor, his right leg not moving quite naturally. He hoped the old injury wasn't bothering the chairman too much. The limp tended to be more noticeable during winter, but according to the specialists, a purely a psychosomatic reaction. That's what Keung told him. Psycho-somatic or not, the old gentleman hobbled in winter months, not that it impaired his movement in any way. Still uncomfortable, the pulled tendon never healed right. A simple jump off a tank and Keung now had a bum leg. Karma.

When the chairman disappeared into the elevator, Shen turned and gave Chuan an appraising stare. He didn't want to know what transpired in the room that demanded this man's death, and he didn't particularly care. Curious, of course, and would find out eventually from the chairman, but perhaps not. Whatever the plan, it had to be big. Strictly speaking, he should report this incident to his Ministry of State Security handler, but his loyalties were clear. To keep them happy, his report would read that the chairman had lunch at Da Giorgio's, and that was all. No need to burden them with unnecessary details.

Keung had always been a considerate master and never abused the power of his position, unlike some he knew, but that's how Party politics was done in Beijing, and the rest of China, for that matter. Being a simple man, although his horizons had ex-panded under Keung's persistent tutelage, Shen had no desire to accumulate power. He held the rank of Sergeant First Class in the People's Liberation Army, more than sufficient for his needs. As the chairman's principal bodyguard, it gave him authority far beyond the strict interpretation of the regulations. Given a paid apartment in the Zuojiazhuang residential district, practically in the CBD, a prize beyond measure, living space being so scarce and waiting time counted in years. It only had a single bedroom, but as he didn't have the weight of family, it adequately sufficed his needs. Besides, having a family would only distract him from his work and the chairman wouldn't be pleased. When he wanted female companionship, there were plenty available to satisfy his needs. He had nothing to complain about.

"Wait here, Professor," he said soberly, rubbed his throat, and walked into the room.

Shen stepped into the bathroom, moistened the face washcloth under the tap and carefully wiped down the bench top, bowl, fittings and toilet. Working his way from the writing desk, he slowly went through the room, carefully cleaning the ashtray. Probably unnecessary, but hotel cleaners would not be this thorough, and Shen disliked relying on random factors to cover his trail, not when a simple precaution ensured anonymity. He left the washcloth on the bathroom bench and strode out, wiping the inner and outer door handles with the corner of his jacket.

Chuan looked amused as Shen locked the door shut. "A bit of James Bond intrigue?"

"Perhaps, but you cannot be too careful. Some people would pay a lot to know what went on in this room, or worse. This is for your safety as much as it is for the Chairman's."

"I did not mean—"

"Let's get going, Professor."

Shen led his charge to the service elevator to avoid surveillance cameras mounted in the lobby. They got out through the emergency exit door behind the hotel, and he steered the bemused scientist toward a narrow street where he left his car, not wanting to use the hotel's underground parking lot where cameras would record his entry and departure.

Old rundown cottages lined the opposite side of the neatly swept street, now empty, waiting to be demolished and replaced by a new condominium. The few squatters rarely showed themselves and local kids took advantage of this playground, smashing in windows and doors. Progress had slowly eaten away traditional architecture residential districts, replacing them with soulless concrete and steel. He didn't much care for it.

Shen waited for a gap in traffic moving too fast along the narrow roadway, then scrambled across the street, pursued by blowing horns. He unlocked his scratched dark gray Honda Civic, climbed in and slammed the door. Chuan slid in beside him and buckled his seatbelt. Shen slipped on a pair a black leather driving gloves, started the engine and eased into the traffic. The chairman had offered to get him a new car, a 'be my wife' BMW, which he appreciated, but declined. The Honda now eleven years old—amazing how the years marched on—but it served him well.

From the 109 National Road, he turned right onto the West 2nd Ring Road heading north. Although heavy, the traffic moved steadily. Approaching the university along Xinxi Road, he turned right, maneuvering the car into the visitors parking lot behind the Earth and Space Sciences building. The rear entrance crowded with students returning from lunch. Several of them recognized Chuan and waved. Shen looked around, but couldn't see any cameras. Still, they might be there anyway. Once inside, he casually wiped his face as the young professor steered him toward a bank of two elevators.

When they got out on the fourth floor, brightly lit from tall windows, Chuan strode quickly down the broad corridor exchanging brief pleasantries with several colleagues. Shen wrinkled his nose at the pervading odor of books and chalk, reminding him of his schooldays, although he had never seen the inside of a university. The Army provided whatever education he had. Chuan entered his office and motioned at a cloth-covered chair.

"This will take a couple of hours at least, Mr. Shen. If you like, you can visit the cafeteria while I run the models."

"Thank you, Professor. I'll wait here, if you don't mind." He would have relished a meal and something to drink, but his indulgence would create unnecessary exposure. Somebody might remember him, and that would never do. He also wanted to make sure the professor did not talk to anyone.

"As you wish."

The small office packed with bookshelves, spilled periodicals, file folders, and stacked books. Two large flat computer screens crowding the cluttered desk made it appear cramped. The place also had a somewhat musty smell common to libraries. Shen made himself comfortable and watched Chuan power up the screens. The professor shifted his glasses, leaned over the keyboard and began typing. Sunlight streamed in through a smeared window.

He didn't have a bad life, Shen reflected. Certainly better than being yelled at by incompetent officers when he first joined the Army. Mindless abuse he and others were forced to swallow. Any sign of rebellion would have been dealt with harshly. Off duty, packed into cold barracks, he and his friends would talk without voicing open dissent. He had seen a colleague snatched in the middle of the night after being betrayed by a stooge. Still, army life had its compensations and Shen became a very proficient soldier. When picked for the Snow Leopard Commando Unit, his training in security and anti-terrorism techniques brought him to the attention of the Ministry of State Security. Not long afterward, they placed him in charge of Keung Yang's bodyguard detail. Life became very easy then and his loyalties slowly shifted as he began to know his master.

The phone rang, but Chuan ignored it. An hour or so later, he nodded, tapped a key, and Shen watched a wave simulation play itself on one of the screens. The purple wave front rippled from the African coastline, breaking up as it struck western Europe, moving rapidly toward the American eastern seaboard. Noting Shen's reaction, Chuan smiled.

"Without our high speed computer, simulations like these would not be possible."

"How fast is the tsunami moving?"

"The wave train moves at roughly 900 kilometers per hour...airliner speed."

Shen blinked, fascinated by the image.

The large color printer beside the desk came to life, producing two A3 sheets. Chuan glanced through the printouts and frowned. Fifteen minutes later, another simulation rippled across the screen and the printer churned out more paper.

Chuan completed two more runs, switched off the screens, sighed, and sat back. He gathered the printouts, folded them and inserted them into a cardboard folder. After glancing at Shen, he removed his glasses and rubbed his eyes.

"I'm done. A most interesting exercise."

"The execution programs—"

"I wouldn't worry about them, Mr. Shen. I ran a number of simulations for different locations. The Cumbre Vieja runs won't stand out. The Chairman need not be concerned about a breach in security. No concern."

"Nevertheless, I insist that any trace of these runs be deleted."

Frowning, Chuan nodded. "Very well."

He switched on a screen and ran a program that wiped all log entries generated by the simulations. Finished, he clasped his hands and leaned forward. "The printouts in the folder will show four simulations, each triggered by varying degrees of explosive force. The first two runs simulate detonations of two and four megatons respectively. Although a two-megaton blast will trigger a flank collapse, it would be moderate, on the order of twenty to forty cubic kilometers displacement, and would generate a minimal wave train of less than one meter along the United States eastern seaboard. Clear so far?"

Shen nodded. "Clear enough."

"I would prefer to discuss this with the Chairman, but never mind. A four-megaton detonation will trigger a slide of some ninety to 120 cubic kilometers, creating waves of up to eight meters. The last two runs represent equivalent forces from multiple detonations using conventional explosives. Each detonation assumes a yield of 500 metric tons of TNT. My calculations show that twelve such charges would be sufficient. Yes, twelve." Seeing Shen's puzzled expression, Chuan chuckled.

"How can so many individual explosions achieve an equivalent yield of a single thermonuclear device? Simple wave mechanics. When two standing wave fronts occur at the same time and are in phase, called antinode points, they reinforce each other and the resulting energy yield is magnified. Of course, the detonation sequence must be timed precisely, but that's covered in the printouts. Do you understand?"

"Not quite, but I'll remember what you said."

"Good. In that case—"

"In that case, the Chairman has everything he needs," Shen rasped and stood up, feeling his heart beat a little faster. He clenched his fists and took two deep breaths, waiting for the ideal moment to strike.

"Glad to help." Chuan switched off the computer and rose. "An induced collapse, a fascinating concept. Truly fascinating. Please assure the Chairman of my confidentiality."

"He'll be relieved to hear that."

Turning, Chuan reached for the folder.

Recognizing the moment had come, Shen's training took over. He grabbed the professor's head and in a fluid motion drove it against the desk's sharp corner. The neck bones snapped with a sharp crack. He stepped back and allowed the body to slide to the floor in a loose heap. Shen bent over the scientist, pulled off his right glove, and checked the neck for a pulse. Satisfied, he flexed his fingers and picked up the professor's cellphone lying on the desk. He quickly scanned the incoming calls log and deleted the call he made to the professor, then wiped the touchscreen and the phone. Finished, he slid his hand into the glove and took the folder. As he stood in the room, he slowed his breathing, allowing himself to relax. In the corridor, no one paid him any attention as he closed the door after him and walked briskly toward the elevators. When they found the body, it would look like the professor had slipped—a regrettable accident.

He slid into his car, dragged out his cellphone, and pressed the encryption key. "It's Shen, sir…I'm on my way back now…No, no problems…Very good, sir."

He pocketed the instrument, engaged first gear and pressed down the accelerator. He had plenty of time to park his car at the State Guesthouse, pick up the official BMW and get the chairman. There wouldn't be time to grab a quick sandwich, but working for the chairman, he had skipped meals before. Anyway, the Guesthouse kitchen will have something for him. As the car pulled out, he reminded himself to wipe down the passenger seat and have the car thoroughly washed.

With the comforting noises of traffic around him, he switched on the radio. He really should replace the thing with a CD player, the old cassette motor having packed up on him. Nodding, he placed his mind into neutral, not wanting to think about the computer simulations he had seen and what they implied.

Did the chairman actually consider setting off an induced flank collapse at La Palma? It wasn't any of his concern. What about the afterward? Provided no trail led back to the chairman, there would not be any afterward, and Shen made sure no trail remained.

# Chapter Two

With a bloated sun hanging above the jagged city skyline, the stark Soviet-style rectangular Ministry of National Defense building emerged out of its blanket of gray smog. Keung's BMW slowed as it approached the main entrance, stopping beside the broad steps. Shen jumped out and hurried to open the rear door. Keung absently twitched his glasses into place and climbed out, the city's morning noises washing over him. Looking up at the imposing orange façade, he mounted the steps under the watchful gaze of grim uniformed guards.

He knew what he wanted to do and why, but climbing the steps felt like entering a dragon's mouth, the sharp fangs ready to clamp shut on him. Not a pleasant image. What he contemplated doing wasn't like campaigning for his chairmanship. He risked the wrath of an aroused eagle, not something he relished seeing should things go badly wrong. As one of the Party's Tuanpai policy makers, he would not rise higher in the current Administration, and time to take a stand. Power was there to be used, not merely enjoy its trappings. That was the problem with many of his colleagues. They had grown too comfortable, forgetting their obligation to the Party and the people. Had he grown sentimental with age? Perhaps, but definitely more introspective.

Still, walking into the dragon's mouth willingly wasn't exactly what he envisaged.

Chen Teng greeted him with obvious pleasure, ordering his assistant that he cannot be disturbed. Keung allowed the chair's soft brown leather to mold itself around him and cast a quick glance over the spacious office befitting the Central Military Commission Vice Chairman. Functional, that's how he saw it.

Then again, Chen had always been economical in all things. A genuine four-star general, not a political appointee, Chen's sometimes severe manner reflected an organized and fastidious man. He had been offered a position within the Standing Committee, but declined, enjoying more power now than he would as a junior Committee member. Pushing sixty-three, age limitations meant that he would never receive the offer again, but he seemed content, although he would not have minded being the CMC chairman. As a Tuanpai populist, there were also ideological considerations that precluded his advancement within the current political climate.

"This place is getting more like an armed fortress all the time," Keung growled amiably as he crossed his legs.

"Hah! This is not the White House, my friend. So, Walters and his troublesome Secretary of State are finally gone," Chen commented affably, resting his arms on the desk. "I can now sit back and pretend I'm doing something constructive for the people."

"That would be a startling change," Keung said dryly and raised a finger. "A useful exchange, and Walters handled himself well. Although young, he managed the diplomatic nuances with surprising skill."

"Agreed, but you're not happy with the outcome. Our brief talk the other night…"

"The visit clearly successful from their point of view, not ours."

"What did you expect? Brokering an agreement with Japan over the Diaoyutai Islands will benefit us and has defused a potentially dangerous standoff. Denying Japan access to energy supplies drove them into World War II. Nobody wants to repeat that mistake."

"We're not a paper dragon we were then and the world is no longer free for the taking," Keung pointed out sternly as he dragged out his pipe. "But you are right. There is enough oil and gas there for everybody. There is no need to resort to aggression in the face of a mutually beneficial agreement." He took out a gold plated Dunhill lighter and puffed the pipe into life.

Chen touched his scar and nodded. "There certainly isn't. We also have a deal on the table over the Spratly Islands. By relinquishing our territorial claims, it made us look statesmanlike. In return, the Philippine government gave us exclusive rights to develop and exploit any oil reserves on an equal share basis. That's got to be good for us, no?"

"I suppose, but don't forget. To get at that oil, we'll have to put in drilling platforms and extraction infrastructure."

"The Americans will build them for us. A win-win for everybody."

Keung stared at his friend. "You understand why the Americans pushed these deals through, don't you? It wasn't because of any concern over our welfare or willingness to chart the middle ground to maintain regional stability."

Chen's mouth twitched in a stillborn grin. "Of course I do. America has grown tired of its Cold War foreign policy and the drain on its resources required to maintain it. The cost of keeping the 7th Fleet at Yokosuka, and bases in Guam and Korea, to name a few, must be staggering."

"The deal Walters struck with Pyongyang last year well executed—"

"Our misguided North Korean brethren didn't really need those nuclear warheads or the long range missiles, and he finally closed a chapter on a failed American foreign policy."

"True, but the driver behind that deal not entirely political, but economic."

"Helped along by Admiral Pacino's strike against Incheon and Yongbyon."

"An audacious application of surgical military power, I must say," Keung agreed thoughtfully. "I am still undecided whether Pacino acted alone or had tacit White House approval."

"A man of honor," Chen said solemnly.

"Agreed, but as I said, domestic economic pressure drove Walters into action. Their defense posture is unsustainable and will remain so until their fiscal position recovers."

Chen leaned forward. "Did you know that Walters is considering pulling out of NATO, or at least drastically scaling down the U.S. presence?"

Keung blanched, taken aback by the revelation. "Pulling out of NATO? Where did you hear that?"

Chen smiled. "I have my sources, my friend."

"I am sure you do, but that merely proves my point. Maintaining a presence in Europe is an outdated anachronism, a posture against an enemy that no longer exists."

"The old Soviet Union was never a genuine threat to the West."

Keung exhaled a cloud of aromatic smoke. "I know. A clash of ideologies and paranoia on both sides kept the world on the brink of annihilation for forty years."

"Which destroyed Russia when its economy could no longer compete in the arms race."

"The Soviets pursued flawed political and economic models anyway," Keung grumbled. "Ones we wisely abandoned."

"After considerable social dislocation. Never mind. When you called, you mentioned a shift in the American position on Taiwan."

Keung waved a hand. "That was for the benefit of our Ministry of State Security eavesdroppers, but now that you mention it, the reason for their change of heart is also obvious."

"Lack of material and financial capacity to sustain another armed standoff?"

"Exactly. Taiwan is ours in all but name. It took Walters courage to acknowledge that, but it's part of a pattern. Military doctrine has changed over the last twenty years, and standing armies are no longer weapons of choice. Something you understand well."

Chen sat back and grinned. "I do. Boardroom diplomacy and the stock markets are the new weapons. I told you that before, but everybody is still arming, as are we."

"Not in preparation for war, but because armaments industries everywhere have a momentum, playing on politicians' fears with doomsday scenarios. Our generals aren't any better. Terrorism and guerilla warfare are today's conflicts, and they can't be won using conventional tactics. American experiences in Iraq and Afghanistan should be salutary lessons for everybody."

"If you're not here to talk about Taiwan, why are you here? Or do you just like bending my ear?"

"Are we utterly secure?" Keung demanded softly.

"Rest easy, my friend. My position does give me some privileges."

"I never doubted it, but if this were to leak out…"

"You can speak freely."

Keung smiled faintly and inclined his head at the desk. "That Sony pocket recorder you keep there, I really wouldn't want to use it. I really wouldn't."

Chuckling, Chen opened the drawer, pulled out the recorder and extracted the SanDisk chip.

"I never had it on."

Keung nodded and pushed back his glasses, having made his point. Friends or not, one can never be too careful.

"You know, America never ceases to amaze me. To have allowed their financial barons to take over fiscal and national interest policies…Never mind. They're recovering from the Global Financial Crisis they created. Albeit slowly, but it won't take them long before they are again the dominant world force. I want to deny them that opportunity."

"I wouldn't mind seeing that either, but how do you propose doing it?"

"Cripple them economically."

"We're already squeezing hard, my rash friend."

"Not hard enough."

"Didn't we discuss this the other night? If I remember correctly, I told you that any such move would also mean crippling the world's economy, which in turn would harm us just as badly."

"You did tell me. However, I have a plan that would produce so much infrastructure damage it would take America decades to recover, if at all, leaving us to step into the resulting economic and political vacuum, emerging as the only viable world superpower without incurring any international wrath."

Chen chuckled. "You have a fire-breathing dragon tucked in a basement somewhere?"

Keung nodded, understanding how absurd the idea sounded, and chilling in its potential. An inner voice told him to consider carefully what he contemplated, but he would not be swayed.

"Not quite, but something equally effective."

"Okay, I'll humor you. What do you have in mind?"

"A tsunami that will sweep their eastern seaboard."

Chen frowned and stared. "A tsunami? You'll wave your hand—"

"I *will* need some help to bring this off. That's why I'm here."

"You're serious, aren't you, or you wouldn't be wasting my time with fantasy."

"You know about the Hawaiian Kilauea volcano and the slippage of its western flank?"

"I know the volcano has been active for decades, but I didn't know about any slippage. Not my area of interest." Chen's eyes widened. "Wait a minute. You want to induce a flank collapse?"

"Yes, but not in Hawaii. We do something like that there and we'd get smeared as well. No, the place we want is the Cumbre Vieja Volcano on La Palma, part of the Canary Islands off Morocco. Its west flank is very unstable and it wouldn't take much to get it moving. A displacement of 120 cubic kilometers would create a sufficiently powerful tsunami to cause severe damage to the American eastern seaboard."

"And Europe," Chen added dryly. "And South America, and western Africa. You can't be really considering this. The forces involved—"

"I'm considering it, all right. We place charges at the bottom of La Palma's western flank, set them off, and let nature take its course."

"You're talking about moving 120 cubic kilometers of rock!"

"I know what you're thinking, but this is not like shifting a standing mass. Cumbre Vieja is what they call a stratovolcano. The entire island chain is built from successive underwater eruptions, adding material with each event. This generated rifts and faults along boundary layers, and gravity is exerting enormous stresses on those faults. La Palma island is basically a cone. You keep piling up material, and sooner or later, something will give way. All I want to do is help the process along. I'm told that a four megaton blast should do it."

That's what Chuan's printouts and Shen's papers showed, if he interpreted them correctly. They made for heavy reading before he shredded them, going to bed late, hoping the professor was right, as he could not afford to duplicate the simulations. He would have preferred a lot more research, but that would only have added to an already formidable list of risks.

"And a larger blast would obviously be better," Chen said thoughtfully and slid his hand over his bald head.

"Obviously."

"You have clearly studied up on this."

Keung drew on his pipe, noted that it had gone out, and relit it.

"It's doable, I tell you. There are lots of unknowns, certainly, but the concept is sound." Keung refrained from mentioning Chuan Jianbo. Not something Chen needed to know. Compartmentalizing information came naturally to him.

"Four megatons, eh? If we set off a thermonuclear detonation, everyone would know that it wasn't a natural event."

"Of course. We'll have to use conventional explosives," Keung said simply.

"Even a conventional detonation will leave some identifiable residue."

"Buried under thousands of tonnes of rock? Do we have something powerful enough for this?"

Chen pulled at his chin. "Mmm. We're talking about CL-20 or a naval variant of a thermobaric cruise missile. Even then, we won't come close to four megatons."

"What's this CL-20 stuff?"

"Like all good things, it was initially developed in 1987 at the China Lake facility, a naval air weapons station in California, as a rocket propellant. We have a variant, but India claims their ICL-20 is better. It isn't. For what you have in mind a thermobaric mine might be more suitable."

"That's a fuel-air bomb, right?"

"That's right. It's the best thing short of setting off a tactical nuke. We designed the thing to take out heavy naval vessels like aircraft carriers and offshore installations. On a weight-for-weight ratio, they are considerably more energetic than normal condensed explosives. Ordinarily, their reliance on atmospheric oxygen makes them unsuitable for underwater application, but our scientists have overcome that limitation. A typical weapon consists of a container packed with a fuel substance, and there are several types. In the center is a conventional scatter charge used to disperse the fuel element. Once the fuel is released, atmospheric oxygen completes the combustion cycle. Damage is done by the generated pressure wave, which is what you want in this case. In our naval variants we encased the fuel cell with a layer of liquid oxygen and drastically reduced the scatter charge, making it suitable for underwater application."

"What's the yield?"

"The largest one we ever tested was equivalent to about 400 metric tons of TNT."

"Four hundred tonnes! We need four *megatons*!"

Chen shrugged. "It's the best I can do. Keep in mind though, setting off a series of mines would reinforce the blast waves in constructive interference, producing a much higher yield—provided it's timed right. If the Cumbre Vieja flank is so unstable, does it really need four megatons to get it moving?"

Keung chewed his bottom lip, trying to suppress his frustration. His grand vision had run against the immovable wall of reality and he hated being thwarted. According to Shen, Chuan also talked about constructive interference, but working with several weapons was always trickier than using one. It looked like he wouldn't be given a choice.

"The information I have, four megatons is the minimum yield that would set off a 120 cubic kilometer slide, but there are a lot of variables. Let's say we use your thermobaric mine. Can it be deployed from a submarine?"

"We designed our inventory with that objective in mind. The new T/SL-109 can be launched from a standard 65-centimeter torpedo tube, weighs almost six tonnes and is eleven meters long. It's self-propelled and capable of swimming for up to twenty kilometers in pursuit of its target—not a requirement here. It can also be set to sink to the seabed where it acts like a conventional influence mine."

"Sounds like it could work," Keung admitted grudgingly.

"How many would we need?"

"The simulation runs I had done were based on twelve 500-tonne charges. In view of what you told me we'll need to have this recalculated, something I'm not keen on doing as it means involving more people."

"A *Shang* SSN can carry sixteen." Chen chewed his lip. "Mind you, the thing is still experimental and they haven't worked out all the bugs, but short of using a nuclear depth charge or two, it's the only thing that will produce a yield even close to what you need. How accurately do they need to be placed?"

"There are some specific tolerances, but basically we need to have them spaced evenly along the slope."

"Mmm. That simplifies things, all right. How deep is the ocean there?"

"Quite deep, about 4,000 meters, but we don't need to set off the mines on the bottom. Four hundred meters should be enough."

Chen shook his head. "That's way beyond their crush depth. They weren't designed for deep water operations."

"How deep can they go?"

"Two hundred, maybe. I'll have to check."

"It's always the little things," Keung hissed, then frowned. "Getting a *Shang* to sortie on a long voyage is bound to be noticed." The practical constraints were mounting and he wondered whether this was actually doable.

"That's the easy part, my rebellious friend. We could do it during the upcoming *Jing Long* naval exercise, and one has been assigned to it."

Keung brightened. "I forgot about that exercise. It's ideal and would eliminate a lot of risk factors, but how would you divert one?"

"All I need to do is issue an authenticated operations order to the submarine commander and it's done. Not through the usual channels, of course. Unless you want to do more yield modeling, which is what I presume you did, we won't need to involve other people, which would be good."

"I'd like to do more checking, but it's too risky, and you're right about not involving more people. You know, of course, the submarine and its crew would have to be disposed of afterward. We cannot possibly allow it to return."

"Agreed. We could dispose of it there and then."

Keung raised his eyebrows. "And how do you convince the

crew that setting off the mines would mean their own destruction? I wouldn't do it, no matter what orders I had."

"Neither would I." Chen chewed his lower lip. "Mmm. We *could* give them a software patch for their firecontrol computer, instructing the mines to detonate when they receive the arming order. I can have one of the Wushiht'ala research center software engineers cut a CD. Of course, he would have to be disposed of also."

"Neat, and I have just the man for the job," Keung said softly, thinking of Sean's quiet, efficient way of doing things. *But not right away, not right away.* "How will you account for the loss of the submarine?"

"Vanished in the Pacific deeps during the exercise. It also eliminates any trail back to us."

"Plausible. I like it, but there will be an investigation afterward."

"And they'll find nothing." Chen snorted and shook his head. "This is a dangerous, dangerous thing we're contemplating. More than that. It's madness, you know that, don't you? Even if we manage to set off the mines without the submarine being detected, there is no guarantee that the resulting flank collapse will generate a sufficiently powerful tsunami."

Keung shrugged. "No, there isn't, but that's the data I've got."

"It is, eh? Who did the analysis for you?"

"Do you really want to know?"

Chen waved a hand. "Forget it. Idle curiosity. Okay, let's say I buy into this harebrained scheme. Despite what I said about issuing an authenticated ops order, we would still face a serious security problem." He stood up, clasped his hands behind his back and paced. Stopping, he glared at Keung. "If the submarine commander queries the order, which would be his right as he would be departing from the published exercise program, we'd be joining our ancestors. I have a few more useful years left in me, you know. If I had any sense, I'd throw you out of here," Chen growled and sat down, clearly agitated.

Keung knew what his friend felt, and didn't hold the outburst against him. The implication of actually going through with this would shake anybody. It helped if he thought of it as an elaborate game of mahjong.

"Naturally, the whole thing will need to be tightly compartmented. Nobody must know the end objective, and apart from the submarine commander we shouldn't need to involve anybody else anyway."

"Admiral Fang Youxia would have to know that I'm giving one of his sub drivers special orders, but he doesn't have to know what they are. I can probably manage that. Your researcher…he'll be taken care of?"

"Already done."

Chen ran a hand over his head and touched his scar. "How the hell did you come up with this idea anyhow?"

"When I got home the other night, I saw part of a documentary on tsunamis and how they're generated. Interesting, but I didn't think much of it then. Still, it kept me tossing and turning during the night. I figured I was bothered about the meeting with the Americans. It wasn't until yesterday morning that the idea hit me."

"Somebody hit you over the head, you old fool. That's what did it," Chen snapped, exhaled and squared his shoulders. "You know what would happen if the Americans ever found out that we were behind this? Remember the repercussions when Israel sabotaged that Galveston refinery, hoping America would blame it on Iran?"

"I'm not underestimating the risks. That's why this will have to be handled with exceptional delicacy. Even if the operation is moderately successful, it would add that much more pressure on them."

"We have dismissed them as a declining power, as has the

entire world, forgetting that they are still the premier economic powerhouse backed by unmatched military capability. Our propaganda machine has made much of our rising ascendancy, decrying Western imperialism, without mentioning that our increasing influence was bought using the dollar. Zhou Yedong and his princelings know this well, my friend. That's why they're pursuing the Go Global Strategy. By exercising some patience, China could achieve all its objectives without resorting to a drastic measure you propose."

"We could, but at what cost, Teng?" Keung demanded harshly. "Zhou doesn't see it, or refuses to see that his policies are turning us into another version of American capitalism. I don't decry our economic progress, but along the way we have neglected our social institutions, paying lip service to the rule of law. China is reverting to the autocratic imperialism of old, where the powerful ruled over the ignorant masses. Social dislocation is growing and the Party is pretending that it doesn't exist. When unrest does flare up, it is stamped out in the most brutal fashion. If we're not careful another Mao could rise up somewhere, setting off a revolution that could destroy everything we have created. If that happened, there might not be anything left to pick over. Zhou and his coalition must be made to realize this."

"And you think devastating America would do it?"

"Of course not. We're fighting on two fronts: keeping America at bay and forcing the Party to focus on institutional justice and fair opportunity for all."

Chen shook his head. "Your idealism has prevented you from becoming President, my disillusioned friend. *Somebody* has to work the land or we'd all starve. We simply don't have enough factories, cities and infrastructure for everyone to have a condo and a car."

"And those who did bought it on the back of industrial pollution and serious environmental degradation. It took the West two hundred years to become the power they are today. We're trying to do it in fifty, and serious cracks are appearing in the system. Zhou is pushing us too hard, I tell you. There must be time to consolidate and reflect on how we really want our society to look like."

"Setting off a tsunami won't change his policies. Even if we're successful, it would only play into his hands. The elitist princeling coalition dominates the Party and he's riding high."

Keung crossed his arms. "How did Walters strike you as a man?"

Chen frowned. "As a man? Compassionate, honest, but above all a realist and a pragmatist. He is prepared to accept that every side has flaws and virtues, that life is full of contradictions."

"Exactly, and he does not immediately descend into blame. He is very rational and won't overreact."

"What are you getting at?"

"Once the Cumbre Vieja operation is done, I'll have a quiet fireside chat with Zhou. He and his cronies will be asked to change their policies or I will reveal to the Americans that Cumbre Vieja was Zhou's plot."

Chen gaped then closed his mouth with a snap. "America would retaliate most vigorously."

"Of course. They would have to, but it will likely be economic retaliation only, not military, no matter how much Congress might howl for blood. Remember what you said about Walters? He'll seek the middle ground."

"You hope."

Keung shrugged and puffed. "In life, nothing is certain."

"If you did that, the whole world would turn against us. You're fond of Confucius. Remember the one where he says, *When anger rises, think of the consequences.*"

"There will be political damage, certainly, but the Western mindset is capitalistic and profit driven. Far too many of their industries are now based in our country. Their economic and po-

litical health is too tightly interlinked with ours for them to extri-
cate themselves without incurring serious long term damage.
There will be protests and marches and public vitriol, but the factories they have here would remain and continue to produce.
They have consumers and we produce the products they buy.
Western corporations will make sure that any retaliation is symbolic. War is a very messy thing and just gets in the way of doing
business."

"What if they stop buying, my friend?"

"The man on the street protesting against us purchased his
Nikes made here. As was his LED TV and cellphone. Anyway, I
doubt Zhou would allow things to deteriorate that far. He'll make
a deal. He is also a pragmatist."

"Pragmatic enough to make both of us disappear."

"Steps will be taken to make sure that doesn't happen. Now,
are you with me?"

Chen's expression turned quizzical. "I could tell Zhou everything, you know."

Keung sat back and smiled. "Do you think I haven't considered that possibility?"

"And covered yourself against possible treachery. I know
how you operate, but you have nothing to fear from me."

"And I know why you won't betray me. Because you're also
a frustrated idealist who dislikes what the Party has become and
what Zhou is doing."

"Mmm. This is mad. Totally mad, and I'm a fool for getting
involved."

* * *

Chen Teng walked to the liquor cabinet, rubbed the scar on
his left cheek, and sighed. He had looked forward to a quiet day
and a relaxing evening, perhaps dinner at the Lan Club, but
Keung's visit had spoiled it all. As a Tuanpai himself, although

he supported a number of elitist economic liberalization schemes, he shared his friend's frustration and disliked some of Zhou's policies, but the winds of change were fickle. Zhou might stumble and his *taizidang* coalition would be swept aside, making way for a more socially acceptable transition into the technological age. The problem, of course, no one could properly define what socially acceptable actually meant. The Chinese cultural fabric was a tapestry of mutually conflicting interests, which made it difficult to execute national goals. Still, some things were clear. Zhou and his technocrats were squeezing the country too quickly into a Western mold, neglecting the vast multitude along the way. He agreed with Keung on that. However, that did not necessarily mean Zhou was entirely wrong, or that he should be swept aside. Life was a book of change, exemplified by the writings of I Ching, and everyone had to bend to its winds or break.

He pulled out a bottle of *Mao Tai jiu* and poured a double measure of the clear yellow wine into a crystal goblet. Sniffing the delicate bouquet, he nodded and took a sip, relishing the sensation as his belly warmed. He sat down behind his desk and the leather chair creaked beneath his bulk. As he leaned back, his brow furrowed in thought.

He found nothing intrinsically wrong with the concept behind his friend's plan as such, regardless of its outrageous audacity, but coming up with the idea was the easy part. Executing it was something else, a problem that Keung had casually laid at his feet. Beyond the obvious technical challenges, overcoming security obstacles would be a major issue. Unquestioning obedience by the People's Liberation Army organs to the state, and fear of retribution for any failure or transgression, eliminated some difficulties, but not all. On the other hand, if he accepted his friend's challenge, he didn't really need to tell anyone anything. Like he told Keung, he only had to issue orders. In the end, it didn't matter whether the technical calculations underpinning the scheme were accurate or not. If everything went as planned, he would still lose a valuable tactical submarine and its crew, but that would be the Navy's problem, not his, at least not directly.

Did he want to do this? It wasn't too late to walk away. He had a wife, although in name only, two grown daughters successfully married to prominent Party luminaries, their future assured, a comfortable house in the Diaoyutai District, power, wealth and the respect of his colleagues. A lifetime of achievement and he could lose it all, the probability not negligible. Facing a firing squad wouldn't be pleasant, but better than the prospect of spending the remainder of his years withering at some remote correctional farm. His wife and daughters might not suffer physical harm, but life for them and their children would be permanently blighted. Not an enticing thought.

As he reflected on his wife's increasingly shrewish behavior, he decided it might be worth scuttling the plan and being banished somewhere simply to rid himself of her and her never-ending nagging. Since the onset of her menopause, some warmth had gone out of her. They still slept in the same bed, but it wasn't shared with love. He had been tempted more than once to take a mistress, but in his position, that would have been far too dangerous. One unwise indiscretion and the career he had carefully built over the decades would be torn down by his enemies. He reminded himself that his Zhongnanhai house had more than one bedroom, and his wife could have any one of them.

Getting his mind back to the problem at hand, he agreed that somebody had to do something, as Keung pointed out, or China would indeed descend into soulless capitalism. Besides, the idea of toppling Zhou appealed to his predator instincts. Still, the forces this could unleash, political as well as geological, might easily destroy his country in the aftermath. He did not doubt Keung's ability as a strategic thinker, but this plan transcended everything his friend had done so far. The problem he had, Keung loved to play his games of intrigue, perhaps more than the ensuing results. But if they pulled this off...

Stefan Vučak

The flutter he felt crawling in his stomach wasn't excitement, but trepidation of a dark future.

*Decide, Mr. Vice Chairman!*

He took a sip of wine, placed the goblet on the desk, and frowned as he considered his options. He sighed, reached for the phone, and pressed a direct dial button, then waited as the exchange chirped. Finally, he got the ringtone on the secure line.

"Rear Admiral Fang Youxia."

Hearing the strong, confident voice, used to command and instant obedience, Chen felt reassured, feeling some of the load shift off his shoulders. Commanding the PLAN submarine fleet at Yulin Naval Base, at forty-six, Fang was destined for great things and Chen was prepared to further a promising career. Sympathetic to elitist and populist policies, both factions thought highly of the young commander, neither considering him an immediate threat to their power. However, as Fang gained seniority, he would have to choose sides. To remain neutral simply wasn't an option; something comfortably far in the future and probably didn't concern him right now.

"It's Chen Teng, Admiral. Do you have a moment?"

"Of course, sir."

Although the admiral couldn't say anything else when talking to the CMC vice chairman, in this case, Chen knew the response to be genuine. What he wanted done might reflect badly on his protégé, but a risk he could mitigate, and some collateral damage had to be accepted.

"How's the weather at Hainan Island?"

"Warm. My Met boys are telling me the monsoon season might start early this year. I hope they're wrong. It would make things unpleasant for the *Jing Long*."

"A bit of rough weather will settle them down," Chen said callously, but meant it. "Our new Navy was designed to be an all-weather proposition. All preparations completed for deployment?"

"We can shove off tomorrow, Mr. Vice Chairman. Although *Peaceful Dragon* will be primarily a littoral deployment, the two *Tang* SSBNs and a *Shang* SSN should give the surface boys some excitement. Might as well build proficiency into our blue water sailors, I say. They certainly won't get it sitting bottled up in harbor."

"I agree."

"You must know, sir, Taiwan and Japan are accusing us of needlessly increasing international tension with this exercise."

"I wouldn't worry too much about them, my friend. They don't consider it provocative when *they* parade their navy up and down the East China Sea."

"Live fire exercises are the only way to test our inventory and evaluate doctrine."

"Agreed, but I didn't call you about the exercise, Admiral. Not directly anyway. The *Shang*, it will carry a full warshot load?"

"Torpedoes, anti-ship and land attack missiles, and mines. Non-nuclear, as per orders."

"What type of mines?"

"Some acoustic, but we'll be using the exercise to test a new thermobaric variant. General Armaments Department jumped at the chance to observe how their toys work under field conditions."

"The T/SL-109s?"

"Yes. We had some flap when the planned tests using one of our new Type 097 missile attack boats were shelved because of the *Jing Long* exercise, but we made it up to the Wushiht'ala boys by giving them a *Shang*."

"How many mines will it carry?"

"Sixteen, a full load."

Chen was very relieved to hear that. It removed the need to issue a special frag order to load the new weapons, something bound to be noticed by Admiral Xhal Shenglai, the PLAN commander, and the Politburo busies. It also made Keung's plan not only feasible, but eliminated several important risk factors, containing the number of people in the execution loop. This could be done.

"I hope they work better than their T/SL-95s," he growled, perfectly serious.

To create a naval version of the conventional fuel-air device had presented Wushiht'ala center researchers with multiple headaches, demonstrated by repeated test failures. The problem wasn't with surface vessel versions, but weight and size limitations imposed on all submarine-launched munitions. A submarine had only so much space available to pack an explosive charge able to fit into a torpedo tube. The mines *could* have been mounted on external ejection hardpoints, but it would have seriously degraded the submarine's acoustic characteristics, rendering them almost useless in a tactical environment. They would have clattered like a bunch of hanging pans.

The *Shang* would also face a tactical problem trying to break into the Pacific—the American CHIJAP sound surveillance system, a line of sophisticated hydrophone arrays strung along China's continental shelf designed to track all submarine activity, friendly or otherwise. Had Russia or China attempted to install a SOSUS line off either American seaboard, the action would have led to war, but they thought nothing doing it to others, another example of blind Western arrogance and sublime belief in the righteousness of their decadent cause. However, there were ways to beat their SOSUS system.

"Why the interest, Mr. Vice Chairman?"

Chen smiled. Fang was nobody's fool. He would expect the Central Military Commission to consider the broader political impact of the *Jing Long* exercise, but not be concerned with operational orders of a single submarine.

"I want it to sink the *Liaoning*," he said softly, the simplicity of his idea surprising him, and heard a sharp hiss. "Simulated, of course."

"I'd love nothing better, but the tactical evolutions are already published and my commanders have their orders."

"Wouldn't you like to put one over on Admiral Liao Keshi by sinking his precious aircraft carrier?"

In charge of the South Sea Fleet based in Zhanjiang, Vice Admiral Liao understandably proud of his new inventory, especially the refurbished Russian *Kuznetsov*-class carrier China purchased from them, paying lip service to Fang's sewer pipe drivers. He and several other surface commanders had some justification for their view. The submarine force, although in the process of rapid modernization, had been sadly neglected and the assets inadequate for strategic power projection. Inadequate against the American *Virginia*-class attack boats anyway, something the CMC intended to rectify, but it wouldn't be soon. The technology underpinning the manufacture of such submarines beyond China's near-term capability.

Fang chuckled. "You're right. I wouldn't mind seeing his pride and joy sent to the bottom."

"Mmm. I thought so. Like you said, the exercise has limited ASW evolutions and your boys deserve to have some of the fun."

"However attractive the idea, sir, deviating from operational orders—"

"You will be acting under my instructions, Admiral, and you'll be protected in case Liao Keshi raises a stink. Do you have anyone with enough balls to carry this out?"

"I've got just the man."

"Good. Please inform the *Shang* commander that he'll be getting special sortie orders on commencement of the exercise. He is to run his deployment under wartime conditions. No one is to know about this. Is that clear?"

"Understood."

"How's the family?"

"Missing the excitement of Shanghai. Yulin is too peaceful

for their taste, especially my daughter who's been hopelessly contaminated by Western music and fashion."

"Yes, I know what that's like. It's a creeping corruption of our national values."

"Something our younger generation seems happy to embrace."

"Hang in there, my friend. You're still on top of my list to take over the East Sea Fleet. Living in Ningbo would suit your daughter better."

"It would suit *me* better as well, and thank you for your confidence, sir."

"Good luck with the exercise, Admiral."

Chen replaced the receiver, reached for the wine goblet and nodded thoughtfully. Harebrained it might be, but this could actually work.

* * *

When the knock came, Commander Vang Kai paused, hands hovering above the keyboard, and looked up, secretly glad for the interruption. Managing the administrative requirements of command confounded him, not understanding the need for all the forms and reports, which often demanded the same information. With the *Jing Long* exercise, that demand seemed to have tripled. Were a real war to break out, the fleet would never leave port, everybody too busy filling out forms! He longed to be at sea again. Things were simpler there. Life was simpler...and much more satisfying. Nevertheless, any opportunity to take his boat out worth all the paperwork. The submarine force, especially the SSNs, spent far too much time in port polishing equipment and conducting drills rarely put into actual practice, which was no way to run a navy, careful not to say that aloud to anyone.

He sighed and sat back. "Come in."

Lieutenant Commander Chol Caihou opened the heavy steel

door, smiled sheepishly, and nodded.

"Sorry for the interruption, Captain, but—"

Vang laughed. "You saved me, XO. One more report and I'd have been a basket case. What is it?"

"There's a staff lieutenant on the pier demanding to see you. Claims to have orders from Commander, Submarine, South Sea Fleet."

"Admiral Fang Youxia? We have our orders."

"I'm only the messenger. What do you want me to do with him?"

"Hell, bring him on board. I don't like this, XO. Last minute changes always means trouble."

"I also wanted to let you know that we're ready to shove off at 0900 as per orders. Reactor temperature is nominal and the tugs are tied on to pull us clear. The maneuvering watch is set and all lines are singled up."

"That's very good, Chol. How about you? Glad to be going out?"

"I don't mind. Mishi has that look in her eyes. You know the one I mean."

"She's got her anchors into you, my boy, and there is no escape. She'll be good for you, settle you down," Vang said in his Old Man fatherly voice.

Married, an eleven-year-old daughter starting to become a handful, at thirty-six, he knew what having a family meant. It wasn't all smooth sailing, but Lina's head nestled on his chest at night, her supple body warm against him, talking softly beneath the blanket of night, made up for the rest. The sea his first love and his submarine a mistress. Accepting it, she was content to share what he gave her.

Chol raised an eyebrow. "And leave the rest of them mourning?"

"Relieved, I would say," Vang growled good-naturedly.

The executive officer leaned against the doorframe. "Seriously, I look forward to going for a sail. Carrying out training maneuvers while you're tied up to a post just isn't the same thing."

"I know you like your training done live, and this exercise should satisfy you. Get the lieutenant. The sooner we find out what he wants, the sooner we'll be out of here. I don't want to be caught in a tide rush."

"Aye aye, Captain."

As the exec closed the door after him, Vang momentarily stared at the naked bulkhead, then shook his head and snorted softly. Chol was a good officer with an astonishing capacity for organization and detail. He managed the submarine, making sure that everything worked; from propulsion, weapons, sensors, stores, and the ninety-five officers and men who served her. He had a relaxed command style and didn't bother himself with the small stuff, allowing the crew a lot of slack, but he made them work for the privilege. Nothing short of perfection in every department and every evolution satisfied him, and Vang liked it that way. He would hate losing Chol when he came up for his own command, probably one of the new *Qin*-class Type 097s that uses magnetic fluid water jet propulsion without a screw, but that won't be for a couple of years at least. Vang wanted one of those for himself, and Chol would just have to stand in line.

Van glanced at the flat computer screen, bit his lower lip, and started typing. If he didn't finish the damn report, the Yulin base weenies would give him a hard time, which would probably earn him a black mark on his fitness report. There were lots of commanders waiting for their own boat and he didn't want to give anybody an excuse to take *ChangZheng 4*—affectionately named *Jian* by the crew—their sword—from him. It wasn't worth aggravating his faceless masters.

Another knock and Chol opened the door wide.

"Lieutenant Tsua, Captain."

Wearing an admiral's aiguillette on his left shoulder, the kid looked like he hadn't started shaving yet. Still, the smart summer white uniform set off his clean features. Vang's eyes flickered to Chol, who shrugged.

The young officer snapped to attention and saluted with parade flourish.

"You have something for me, Lieutenant?" Vang prompted gently.

"Yes, sir! Orders from COMSUBSSF." The youngster reached into his jacket and held out a plain brown A4 envelope with the attached pink flimsy and a receipt tear-off.

Vang took the proffered envelope, dashed off his signature, and ripped off the receipt.

"XO, get him off the boat, then come back here."

"Aye, sir. Come along, Lieutenant."

The youngster saluted and strode out, Vang hardly noticing as the door closed. Frowning, he tore open the envelope and extracted a single sheet of white paper. His frown deepened as he pulled out a small A5 unmarked yellow envelope. By its feel, it contained a CD case. Placing the two envelopes on his desk, he began to read. Finishing, he pursed his lips and nodded twice. Orders were orders, no matter how crazy they sounded, and these were unusual to say the least. If it weren't for the impressive CMC seal and the eyebrow-rising signature, he would have considered the orders a practical joke.

When Chol returned, Vang waved him to a chair and held out the sheet.

The exec sat down and reached for the paper. "The kid had a staff car waiting for him, can you believe it? A staff car! Our new orders?"

Vang saw the XO's features freeze and almost grinned in sympathy. When the executive officer looked up, all traces of geniality were gone, replaced by grim professionalism.

"Canary Islands? That's a hell of a long way to sail, and what are we supposed to do once we get there? It's nothing but a bunch of bare rocks and seagulls."

Vang inclined his head at the desk. "Presumably the second envelope will tell us once we get there. Are you ready for a sixty-day cruise, because that's how long the round trip will take."

"Probably more. Breaking out through the Strait of Malacca will be a pain, Captain. That waterway is busier than a freeway and it's only twenty-five meters deep in places. We'll be scraping bottom."

"No choice, XO, but it won't be that bad. We'll latch onto a tanker or something and motor in its wake."

"What about our promotions? COMSUBSSF must have flipped his lid."

Vang smiled broadly. "That's treasonous talk, my friend. You don't like the idea of being a full commander?"

"I like the idea, all right, but not the price I have to pay to get it."

"You'll look good with three stripes on your shoulder boards. Mishi will be pleased."

"And you with four…Captain, confirmed only on successful completion of our mission," Chol said darkly and exhaled loudly.

"What did you expect? They want to keep us honest."

"This thing about maintaining total EMCON until we return to Hainan is scary. Beijing will think that we've defected."

"Somebody there knows what we're up to. Did you check the signature? Break out the authenticator, XO, and we'll find out if this is for real," Vang ordered briskly, dug into his pants pocket and held up a red key.

Chol took it and stepped to a small wall safe next to the desk. He extracted a clear plastic case half the size of a CD disk and broke it. Taking out a red card, he began to read.

"Zulu, star, Tango, Romeo, hash, hash, star, Alpha, Sierra."

Vang slowly nodded. "Authenticated."

"Well, that's that, then," Chol said and winced. "Sixty days of canned tofu? I'll expire! Besides, I told Mishi I'll see her in fifteen days. She'll think I ran off with somebody else."

Chuckling, Vang stood up. "My sympathies. Do we need to load additional stores?"

"The fresh stuff will run out, but with judicious management, we'll last the distance with the rest. The evolution to load more stores would only raise attention, and those orders say we shouldn't do that."

"Toasted sandwiches on the way back it is."

"Captain, given the unusual nature of these orders, I think we should have them confirmed."

"They've been authenticated, and that's good enough for me. Besides, if we queried, somebody would start asking questions to which I have no answers. I'll be on the sail bridge. You have the control room."

"Aye aye, sir."

As Vang walked out of the cabin, he didn't mention that he also told Lina he'd be home in fifteen days, or that he would miss celebrating his daughter's birthday. At eleven, these things were important. Liqiu simply won't understand why her daddy wasn't there. She'll only know he wasn't, and Lina would not be able to make it right. He wondered whether the fourth stripe made up for the wounded look in his daughter's eyes.

Lina of silken hair, his black swan, laughing almond eyes, alabaster skin, sinuous figure, delicate features that time had not touched. It still surprised him that she chose to marry him, a naval officer, accepting that there would be many lonely nights for both of them. Given his infrequent sorties, there hadn't been *all* that many. With the passage of years, her love blossomed as they discovered each other and became one. She understood him and did not begrudge his passion for the sea, knowing that he loved her unreservedly. He did, which made it all the more difficult when she realized he wasn't coming home, deriving cold comfort from an official notice that he was on an extended mission.

He preferred not to think about it too much.

Climbing through the pressure hull hatch, he took two rungs at a time as he scrambled up the tube to the sail's cockpit. A warm salt-laden sea breeze greeted him when he climbed out and Vang blinked, the bright sunshine almost painful. The watch officer nodded and shifted to the port side of the sail.

"In all respects ready to get underway, Captain."

"Very good. Remove the gangway, Lieutenant."

"Aye, sir." The youngster picked up the megaphone and leaned against the coaming. "Take off the plank!"

On the pier, the crane operator waved and black smoke belched from the diesel engine as the gangway lifted off the deck and swung back. Idling dock workers stopped to watch the submarine depart.

"Shift your pumps," Vang ordered.

"Maneuvering, bridge. Shift reactor pumps to fast speed," the lieutenant passed on the command.

"Bridge, maneuvering, aye. Shift main coolant pumps to fast," the speakerbox announced.

Vang glanced at the two tugs waiting off the submarine's starboard side, lines hooked and winched tight, ready to pull the 110-meter-long, 6,000-tonne submarine from the pier. He could have taken the boat out without help, and did—once—under Admiral Fang's goggling expression. The sub had emerged unscathed and Vang got a personal signal from COMSUBSSF complimenting him on the evolution, hinting that a five billion yuan people's asset wasn't a racing car. He got the message and hadn't repeated the maneuver.

Across the water some six kilometers away, he could clearly see the luxury hotels and high-rise buildings of the Yalong Bay National Resort District. Certain that wealthy international tourists and well-to-do locals were observing the morning's deployment with interest, as no doubt were American satellites. Beijing wanted the West to observe the *Jing Long* exercise, not bashful showing the capitalists China's growing naval power.

Around him, surface ships of all sizes and types lay moored to the piers, protected by hovering gantry cranes. Some would be part of the coming exercise. Warehouses and stacked containers crowded the shore, with trucks moving everywhere in endless processions. Opposite him, a *Yuan* Type 041 belched diesel smoke above its rudder, also making ready to get underway, as were two *Song* Type 039s. A *Yuan* had steamed out about an hour ago, the diesel subs forming part of the littoral defense screen for the surface combatants. With the soothing breeze brushing his cheek, Vang breathed deeply of the scented air, satisfied with the world. This is where he was meant to be, master under no one. Well…almost, but he wasn't going to be picky.

The years he spent at the Dalian Naval Academy, then serving in various classes of boats, paid off when he got an appointment as executive officer to a *Yuan*-class conventional diesel, a sign of approval from command. After a stint at the Naval Submarine Academy at Qingdao, which put him in line for an SSN, provided he didn't screw things up in between, they gave him a creaky old *Song*-class, but he loved the cranky, aging boat, leaks, stinks and all. No, he had nothing to complain about, paperwork notwithstanding.

He looked at the watch officer. "Cast off."

The lieutenant immediately stepped to the aft part of the cockpit. "Deck there! Take in lines two, three and four!"

Under the watchful gaze of a chief petty officer, the line-handlers waited as the pier gang tossed over the thick ropes that tied the sub to the shore. The deck gang coiled them and packed them into the lockers, rotating the cleats into the hull, which made a smooth surface in the black anechoic covering. Satisfied, the lieutenant touched the microphone dangling at his throat.

"Con, bridge. Signal the tugs that we're free to maneuver."

"Bridge, con, eye. Free to maneuver."

The lieutenant hurried to the front of the cockpit and yelled into the megaphone. "Deck there! Take in line one! Ease off line five!"

As the water boiled under the stern of the small harbor tugs, the submarine slowly drew away from the pier.

"Take in line five! Helm, bridge. Left full rudder! All back one-third."

"Bridge, helm, aye. Rudder is left full. Indicating turns for all back one-third."

Vang leaned over the cockpit coaming and looked aft, wanting to make sure the rudder had shifted to the correct position. The angle between the boat and pier slowly opened, *Jian* maintaining its place against the ebbing tidal current, the seven-blade screw churning brown water at the stern. At fifty meters from the pier, the deck crew cast off the tug lines.

"Shift your rudder. Make turns for six knots," he ordered quietly.

"Maneuvering, bridge. All ahead one-third."

"Bridge, navigator. Recommend course one-one-zero."

"Bridge, navigator, aye," the lieutenant snapped. "Helm, bridge. Steer course one-one-zero."

Vang turned to the youngster and nodded. "Nice work, Lieutenant. I'm going below."

"Sir!" The watch officer snapped to attention.

Vang took a last look at the deep blue sky, the smooth sea, reconciling himself to sixty days or more of reprocessed air, set his mouth, and slid down the ladder. Below, the control room was rigged for white. The electric smell of the ship, mixed with the aroma of lube oil, diesel, cooking and warm bodies, washed over him and his nose twitched. They were familiar odors, and after a moment his brain ignored them.

Surrounded by exposed overhead piping and cable runs, consoles and displays, in the center space stood the elevated periscope stand where the officer of the deck conned the ship. The OOD raised the nav periscope and pressed his face against the eyepiece module. Strapped into their seats, the two planesmen had their eyes fixed on the navigation screens, holding the boat on its designated bearing.

"Captain, ship is on course and the tugs have pulled back. We're clear to maneuver."

"Very well, XO. Maneuvering, con. All ahead standard."

"Con, maneuvering, aye. Turns set for all ahead standard."

"Mark the sounding," Vang ordered.

"Twenty-five meters," the navigation officer responded.

"Time to the forty-meter line?"

"Eleven minutes, Captain."

"Very well. XO, you have the watch."

"I have the watch, aye, sir," Chol acknowledged, and clasped his hands behind his back as he stood at parade rest.

Standing in front of the weapons console, Vang nodded. The ship smart and the crew alert, all due to the exec's hard work. There were a minimum of orders, the watchstanders knowing their business. He stood there, listening to the hum of machinery and a multitude of familiar ship noises.

"Coming up to the forty-meter line, Captain. Permission to submerge the boat."

"Very well. Submerge the boat."

"OOD, clear the sail!"

A moment later, the surface watch lieutenant slid down the ladder. Vang heard a sharp clang as the upper hatch slammed shut, followed by another clang from the pressure hull hatch. The rating dogged it and disappeared below.

"Sir, sail cockpit rigged for dive. All external openings secured."

"Very well, XO. Take her down to thirty meters."

"Thirty meters, aye." Chol picked up the 1MC microphone, his voice ringing throughout the ship. "Dive! Dive!" he announced and pressed the diving alarm button. Immediately, a deep *oog-aah* reverberated through the ship.

"Helm, ten degrees dive on the bowplanes."

"Ten degrees dive, aye," the helmsman responded.

"Sail's under…scope's awash," the deck officer announced.

"Helm, maintain ten degrees down bubble," Chol ordered.

"XO, call me when we reach the shelf. I'll be in my stateroom."

"Silent routine, sir?"

Vang paused then shook his head. "No. Run at flank," he said softly and strode toward the hatch.

Chol frowned at the unusual order, then nodded. Normally they would seek to run silent to avoid detection. "Aye aye, Captain."

In his cabin, Vang kicked off the shoes and sprawled into the bunk. Hands clasped behind his head, he stared at the ceiling. It would take them some three hours to reach the continental shelf hugging the Hainan Island. Some of the control room officers would wonder why they weren't steaming toward the exercise engagement area and running at flank. He would give them the word before going deep to clear the American SOSUS line.

His orders on that were specific. His penetration into the Pacific must remain undetected. A shadowing *Virginia*-class or *Los Angeles* attack boat, which COMSUBSSF knew always lurked about when the PLAN put on a show, could not be allowed to latch onto Vang's boat. At the first sign of detection, orders said to follow the published *Jing Long* program. Detection would also mean the end of his temporary promotion and probably loss of command as well. His orders didn't say that, but they didn't have to. COMPLAN desk weenies in Beijing had no sense of humor. With everybody focused on the exercise, it was unlikely the Americans had stationed one of their principal assets off the shelf waiting for someone to motor by.

His orders told him to avoid detection, but neglected to say how he was supposed to do that against an invisible *Virginia* boat. Even a *Los Angeles*, drifting silent, would be a hole in the water.

That was the problem with brass. They expected the impossible regardless of any practical difficulties. Well, he considered himself a sharp sub driver. Running at flank toward the shelf might be counterintuitive, but it should make any prowling American sub write him off as uninteresting—he hoped.

He allowed his mind to wander for several minutes, then swung his legs out and slid off the bunk. He still hadn't finished all the reports, and log entries had to be initialed. Sitting at his desk, he smiled and chuckled. With EMCON in force, he would not be able to transmit his reports anyway, but training and discipline made him switch on the computer. He had nothing better to do until Chol called him.

Sometime later a knock on the door startled him and he looked up. "Come in."

The diminutive steward entered bearing a loaded tray. "Your lunch, sir. Seeing how you didn't come to the wardroom…"

"That's fine, Bao. Set it down."

The youngster smiled sheepishly, placed the tray on the desk, nodded, and padded out, closing the door softly behind him. Vang glanced at the chronometer readout and raised his eyebrows, realizing that he spent almost three hours staring at the damn computer screen. No wonder he felt stiff. He stood up, poured himself a cup of herbal tea, mixed in sugar, and took two thirsty sips, his stomach relishing the invasion. After an appreciative sniff at the steaming food, he wasted no time digging in.

The phone rang and he picked up. "Captain."

"XO here. We're approaching the shelf, sir."

"Very well. I'll be right there."

Vang splashed water on his face and ran a comb through his thick black hair. As he pulled down the front of his shirt, he reminded himself to change the collar insignia. He slammed the cabin door shut and walked briskly down the narrow corridor toward the control room.

Chol looked up from the sonar repeater screen. "Crossing

the shelf now, Captain."

"Very well. Rig for ultra quiet, XO." The command indicated that Vang had taken the con.

"OOD, pass the word to rig for ultra quiet."

"Aye aye, sir."

"Maneuvering, con. Recycle pumps to slow and ease down the turbine to stop."

"Con, maneuvering, aye. Easing down."

"Mark the sounding," Vang ordered.

"Four hundred and twenty meters…approaching the 900-meter intermediate boundary layer," the navigation officer replied. From there, the continental shelf dropped steeply to almost 5,000 meters.

"Sonar, con. Report contacts."

"Con, sonar. All clear within fifteen kilometers."

"OOD, take her down to 300 meters."

"Make your depth three zero zero meters, aye, sir! Helm, ten degrees down bubble. Watch your trim."

Vang straightened his right leg, taking the weight as the boat slanted down. The SOSUS line sensors worked only if the target emitted a noise transient and moved, the Doppler change providing information on position, course and speed. By going totally silent, drifting down into the southwesterly flowing Guangdong Coastal Current, he would deny the sensors that information. After twenty kilometers or so, he would be able to maneuver, still running slow until out of range. The Americans were aware of this tactic, but there was little they could do about it, short of enclosing the entire Chinese coastline with a ring of submarines, clearly not a practical option. Besides, apart from maintaining a passive SOSUS line because they were paranoid, the Americans had nothing to fear from the PLAN. A diverting game everybody played, albeit a dangerous one.

*Jian* quietly sank through the 120-meter thermocline layer into the cold ocean water circulating down from Japan, devoid of life. Doing this demanded very accurate underwater charts and the PLAN had them, thanks to all the hard work done by Japan and the Americans. Hacking into their military and civilian ocean-ographic websites saved the Chinese navy millions of yuan.

"Three hundred meters, Captain," the nav officer announced.

"Very well. Check your trim."

"Zero bubble on trim."

Chol took a step to stand beside him. "Do you want to clear baffles?"

Vang shook his head. It would be a waste of time against a silent opponent. Besides, they hadn't detected anyone.

"That would require us to maneuver, which will generate unnecessary noise. No, let the current take her."

"And we drift…"

"Four hours should be enough."

In the black deeps, SSN *ChangZheng 4* became another silent, invisible ghost.

* * *

Chen Teng let out a long sigh, swept both hands across his face, and winced at the oily film sticking to his palms. The paper-work of his job threatened to demoralize him. Every day, he cleared his desk, and every day a new pile materialized; reports, briefs, analyses, attention memos, and plain trivia. Damn it all, his staff were supposed to handle the trivia for him. His frown deepened as he glanced at the computer screen.

A great tool and labor saver, but the email system had gotten out of hand. He spent far too much time culling CC mail, and not enough dealing with policy and directives. By including him in the recipients list, did his underlings think that he would be impressed by their efficiency? Like all office underlings, they practiced the cover-your-ass game. His name added authority and encouraged compliance, but it did not mean he needed to see the damned things. His people were meant to make decisions and take action without using his name to grease the bureaucratic wheels. Definitely time for another chat and a warning. This crap simply had to stop or somebody would likely find himself in a Mongolian correctional farm.

He reached for the cup, took a sip, and grimaced. The tea had gone cold, taking the fun out of his moment of rest. He should have stayed in Baotou, a plodding Party hack with suffi-cient power to enjoy the privileges of his position without being a threat to his superiors. Like an addict, he craved more. Now that he had it, why did he complain? He faced the realization that he was nervous. Keung's operation had kicked off, but not know-ing what was happening gnawed at him and his resolve.

*Suck it up, General!*

His direct line went off, the sound unusually shrill. Placing down the cup, he pressed a glowing white button and picked up.

"What is it?"

"It's Rear Admiral Fang, Mr. Vice Chairman. My apologies for disturbing you, but I have a situation."

Chen's shoulder's sagged, wishing for just one day without situations, yet Fang wouldn't be calling if it weren't important. Had the *Shang* been detected?

"Oh, and what would that be, Admiral?"

"The *Shang* you sent out with special orders, it disappeared."

"Disappeared? What are you talking about?" Chen de-manded, feigning surprise, his administrative problems momen-tarily sidelined.

Not entirely unexpected, but nevertheless, something hard knotted in his stomach. He had a fleeting image of grim MSS types barging into the office, hauling him away for some very unpleasant interrogations. From here on the weight of the PLA Navy, the Central Military Commission and the Politburo Standing Committee would be bearing down on him. As vice chairman, all military operations fell under his umbrella, including the screw-ups. The pointy end of Keung's plan had just stabbed him in the butt and he didn't like it. He covered himself and no information trail existed to implicate him, but there could always be some little detail lurking somewhere that he overlooked and might spoil his day. Would Keung feel the same pressure? Probably not, he decided, envying his friend's unflappable demeanor. The man pissed iced refrigerant.

"I mean it disappeared. It never entered the designated engagement area and it hadn't reported in since leaving Yulin. Admiral Liao just finished chewing my ass after Admiral Xhal Shenglai took out a piece. I don't like that kind of attention, Mr. Vice Chairman, especially from the Commander, PLA Navy. I want to know what orders you gave my boat skipper."

Chen sympathized. In charge of the PLA Navy, Xhal had jurisdiction over *Peaceful Dragon* and understandably wanted to know what was going on. Loss of an SSN wouldn't look good on his record and he wanted to make sure he wasn't smeared in stink. Right now, Fang probably regretted his impulse to score points against Liao. Not that he really had much of a choice. Saying no to the CMC vice chairman not career enhancing. Raw power did get things done occasionally.

"A routine sortie to sink the *Liaoning* like we discussed, Admiral, maintaining a total comms blackout until he did so."

"I hate to do this, sir, but I need a copy of those orders."

"No need to apologize, my friend. My office will fax them to you within the hour. Isn't everybody overreacting? It's only been two days."

"It's not like Commander Vang Kai not to report in. If he had problems with his comms gear, standard procedure demanded that he surface. Admiral Xhal is about to launch a full scale search, suspecting the sub has gone down."

"His reactor could have crapped in, you know. If it went over the continental shelf, we'll never find it."

"I admit our early boats did have reactor problems, but not Vang's *Shang*. It's a top-of-the-line unit. Besides, he shouldn't have been anywhere near the shelf."

"He could be lying on the bottom waiting for *Liaoning* to pass over him. It would be a perfect test for the new thermobaric mine, and his orders were to run under EMCON, remember?"

"I hope you're right, Mr. Vice Chairman. I hope you're right."

Chen exhaled softly and nodded with satisfaction. It looked like the *Shang* had made it out and appeared to have evaded the American SOSUS line. If all went well, no one would ever hear from it again. More importantly, no one would find it looking along the Yellow Sea coastline.

"If we lost it, I wouldn't worry about any fallout. Accidents do happen, and besides, you were acting under my orders."

"I appreciate your support, sir, but you know how the system works."

Chen knew all too well how the system worked. He had used that very knowledge to launch this operation.

"Keep me posted, Admiral," he said briskly and hung up.

He didn't blame Fang at all for calling him, mildly surprised the call hadn't come sooner. The man simply sought to protect himself, and understandably so. Admiral Xhal was not someone to cross. Sitting back, the day had turned out not to be so bad after all.

*Keung, you sly devil, we may get away with this yet.*

They may get away with it, but he had grave reservations about the wisdom to reveal the operation to Zhou Yedong. Perhaps he should have a long talk with his scheming friend. Sometimes Keung pushed the mental games envelope beyond prudence, and dealing with Zhou, one always had to be prudent.

\* \* \*

# PROPORTIONAL RESPONSE

A harsh, pealing blare reverberated over the placid Yokosuka harbor, sending swarms of white gulls screeching into the air in protest. By its distinct sound, Vice Admiral David Owen knew it was an *Arleigh Burke*-class guided missile destroyer heading out on routine patrol in the Yellow Sea. Towering over the base buildings, tied portside at Berth 12, the aircraft carrier USS *George Washington*, CVN-73, also getting ready to sail. His deputy, Rear Admiral Rick Haddon, didn't believe that 7th Fleet vessels should rot at their moorings, and neither did Owen. In his book, if the American Navy wanted to project power, it had to be out there, daring somebody to mess with them.

Haddon wasn't Kenneth Pacino, but so far, he had no complaints. Nobody was like Pacino, he thought morosely. The two of them still kept in touch, although infrequently. Owen didn't hold a grudge. As one of President Walters' policy advisors, Pacino had his hands full and Owen wished him well. Following Pacino's attack on Incheon and the North Korean Yongbyon nuclear facility last year, the subsequent court-martial could have resulted in a lengthy rest at Leavenworth, but the White House didn't relish having some Navy dirty laundry publically aired, or its own, and he got off with an administrative discharge. After all the excitement, Pacino avoided getting cashiered and managed to get a plum White House appointment, courtesy of the president.

Owen sighed. He understood what Pacino did and why, but to sacrifice a third star simply to make a political point was incomprehensible. To him the Navy meant everything, even if it did have an odd smelly sheet tucked away in places. Right or wrong the system must be used, not abused. He can bend it, but not break it. The way Owen looked at it, the Navy was never wrong, although sometimes it was a bit weak at being right. He doubted that any other flag officer would be prepared to follow Pacino's example, but then, he doubted such an officer existed out there.

However radical, Pacino's unorthodox action had been a

contributing factor to normalizing relations between the two Koreas, and between Pyongyang and Washington. After reaching an agreement with Supreme Leader Tong In-san, the United States withdrew thirty percent of its forces from South Korea, and logistical preparations to withdraw a further thirty percent by next year were well advanced. A masterful and extremely popular coup for Walters. Even the Republicans were making approving noises after accepting that protesting the agreement only cost them votes. The Cold War over, nobody really wanted the Americans in Korea, least of all the South Koreans.

It was also a shrewd economic move, freeing billions of dollars spent annually supporting bases, military assets and personnel. Owen felt certain the boys were relieved to be going home, as were their families. The withdrawal meant a reduction in manpower and appropriation allocations, which had not pleased some of the Joint Chiefs, undermining their cushy positions, but you bent with the wind or were broken.

Right now, he didn't give a rat's toss about Washington policy or what his old friend Pacino was up to. His concern these days, and had been for a while, centered around the rapid modernization of the PLA, particularly the navy. Within five years their presence in the Pacific would be tangible, although not comparable to the 7th Fleet—yet. However, at the rate the PLA was replacing aging and obsolete inventory, that day not so far off. Foreign policy had always been a matter of power projection and the U.S. enjoyed its supremacy, jealous of any upcoming upstarts. If Washington wasn't careful, it could wake up one day to find its presence in the Pacific relegated to secondary status, with all the regional problems that would ensue. Owen hoped that he would be long retired before that happened, and somebody else's worry, he thought comfortably. At the moment, he had a tactical situation to deal with. Well, monitor anyway. The nuts and bolts of keeping an eye on *Peaceful Dragon* firmly in Admiral Haddon's court, Owen felt more at ease when he kept an eye on things.

Besides, it was his duty.

The intercom buzzer went off. Reaching across the desk, he pressed a button. "Talk to me."

"Captain Ronald Briggs is here to see you, sir," his aide's hesitant voice announced, and Owen smiled. Always correctly dressed, holding himself as though in review with a dirk up his butt, the young lieutenant had turned into a very efficient office gofer, but he needed to relax more. Admittedly, somehow difficult when dealing with a three-star admiral. The experience won't do the boy any permanent emotional harm.

"Show him in."

Briggs opened the heavy wooden door and strode casually into the office. Not bothered with protocol too much, or overawed dealing with the 7th Fleet commander. Then again, all intelligence types seemed to be a rule onto themselves, Owen mused. Only five-foot-nine, he looked shorter on account of his impressive bulk, which no amount of dieting or exercise seemed to affect. Briggs didn't appear to notice or cared about his waistline.

"What's up, Ron?"

"Just got a heads-up from COMSUBGRU Seven, sir, relayed from NAVFAC Guam. Admiral Haddon has the dope and thought you should know about it."

"And…"

"The Chinese navy is all riled up. Most of the South Sea Fleet surface assets have sortied from Zhanjiang—"

"It's their *Jing Long* maneuvers," Owen growled. "We expected them to get excited. It's been a while since they mounted an all-forces outing. They're not shooting up anybody, are they?"

Owen projected a crusty exterior, matched by his sharp bark and dry sense of humor, which sometimes made it difficult for his subordinates to know if he was simply sarcastic. In this case, yes.

"I don't see no reason why the Chinese navy shouldn't be

free to squirt off some missiles or pop off a round or two from their guns. All good, clean fun."

Briggs gave a slow grin. "Yes, sir."

"So, what are they doing that's got Haddon bothered?"

"They have destroyers and anti-sub aircraft buzzing all Hainan Island approaches and the exercise area, with sonars banging away loud enough to scare off anything living. Remember the *Shang* SSN that sortied a couple of days ago? It powered out of Yulin like on a highway, approached the continental shelf and disappeared. We got a faint trace on the 110-decibel line from CHIJAP, then nothing."

"They pulled a dim sum on us, you told me. You also told me the thing went silent and allowed the Guangdong Coastal Current to take her. Damn it, Ron, I asked Admiral Rochester to keep Yulin covered. It's their premier submarine base, for Chrissake."

"You can't blame COMSUBGRU Seven, sir. He's only got five boats, and all were positioned to watch the exercise. We relied on the SOSUS line to tell us if anything broke into the Pacific. That's what it's for."

"And it's not doing its job," Owen said, clearly peeved. "Those hydrophones are obsolete technology, Ron, and not up to it. Washington is simply ignoring a serious strategic threat in China's new navy. I'll talk to the CNO again about it."

"Money is scarce these days, Admiral, and upgrading the CHIJAP line would be costly."

"Yeah, but how costly if China decided to interdict its entire coastline, denying us access to our subs? If shit happens we'd have no tactical warning." Before Briggs could protest, Owen raised a hand. "You don't have to tell me, Ron. Things aren't that bad and we have other assets to keep track of our yellow friends. Not that they're planning anything anyway…that we know of."

"President Walters is engaged in heavy talks with Zhou Yedong, sir. We'd be upsetting the Chinese if we upgraded

CHIJAP, and that isn't what he's looking for right now."

"I know about those talks. Window dressing, if you asked me. Damn it, he must know China is pissing in his ear with those talks. Smiles all around, nodding politely while they keep rolling out state-of-the-art destroyers and submarines, using technology they stole from us and the Europeans! Never mind. You think the PLAN is searching for their missing *Shang*?"

"Admiral Haddon thinks so and the Chinese are making all the right noises like they are. Of course, it *could* all be part of the exercise. However, if the sub suffered some sort of power plant failure and went down, no one will ever find it. The water off the shelf runs to sixteen thousand feet or more."

"What if it didn't sink, Ron?" Owen demanded quietly.

Captain Briggs shrugged. "If it broke into the Pacific, where would it go? And why would it go there anyway? The Chinese naval command keeps a tight rein on its assets, demanding regular calls home, and sub commanders were selected for their loyalty to the Party and unquestioning obedience. All sewer pipe drivers are mavericks, Admiral, it's their nature, but you won't get one of theirs doing something radical."

Owen sighed and nodded. "You're probably right and the damn thing will surface somewhere, wondering what all the fuss was about. Tell Haddon to keep me posted."

"Aye aye, sir."

When Briggs left, Owen pulled at his chin. Why the hell should he care if the PLAN lost one of their attack subs? One less for the U.S. Navy to keep track of.

\* \* \*

Professor Shaun Degard stared at the wide computer screen and absently reached for his coffee mug. He took a sip and winced. The thing had gone cold and tasted gritty. He placed the mug beside the keyboard, sighed and sat back. Rubbing his eyes, he glanced out the broad window. At least the University of Hawaii had the excellent taste to locate the Department of Oceanography in a congenial setting. Somebody must have made a mistake and it'll get fixed, he decided uncharitably.

Gentle surf creamed over golden Waikiki sands, reaching toward beachgoers sprawled on colorful towels or resting under slanting umbrellas. The shoreline crowded, people enjoying the mild tropical air, scented winds and a few days away from their mainland jobs. Shortly, as spring gave way to early summer in the northern states, Waikiki and other resorts in the Hawaiian chain would be left to international visitors taking advantage of cheap low-season rates. Beyond the breakwater, a large catamaran set up like a native outrigger slowly made its way toward Diamond Head, those on board waving at the shore, sipping tall drinks and laughing without cares. He wouldn't have minded being with them, laughing his cares away.

Watching from his third floor office, Degard felt a stab of envy. He lived in Honolulu, had for the last six years, but never seemed to find time to enjoy its many attractions. His fault, of course. After the divorce, the only time he saw Judy was when he picked up Rosalyn for weekend visiting rights. Then Judy moved to San Francisco and that ended it. An executive recruitment manager, she knew what a demanding job can do to a relationship, but he didn't hold the failed marriage against her.

The last three years for him were brutal. Field trips, seminars, international conferences, lectures, all took their toll. When he started sleeping at the campus occasionally, Judy hadn't liked it, but didn't complain. Perhaps if she had, if they'd argued, tossed it around, it might have prevented the inevitable. One evening after another silent dinner, she produced a sheaf of papers and told him to find someplace else to live.

Stunned, he stared at her, groping for something appropriate to say. What might be appropriate at a time like this, he wasn't entirely sure.

"You're emotional and overreacting," he told her at length. "Damn it, you know how hard I fought to get tenure and a full professorship."

What she said next had stuck with him, cutting deep. She said, "Shaun, I know what your job means to you, but it was all for yourself. It had nothing to do with me or Rosalyn. For a long time now, this house became somewhere you came to eat and sleep. We have no relationship, and I sometimes wonder if we ever did. Well, you got your professorship and I hope you're satisfied."

"What about *your* job?" he lashed back. "What about the long days and working on weekends? I didn't complain when you broke an outing with me and Rosalyn to attend a meeting or an interview. We were both nurturing careers and sacrifices had to be made."

"The difference between us, Shaun, you sacrificed everything for your career and you knew exactly what you were doing. You didn't need me and I wonder if you ever did."

She hadn't even raised her voice.

Life sucks, he decided.

The strange thing, he hadn't missed her. *I really must be a bastard*, he told himself glumly.

Downtown Honolulu skyscrapers beckoned, but the ocean deeps beckoned more strongly, as did their mysteries. They were his true love and Judy recognized it when they met, drawn to him because of it. He had been a good father to Rosalyn—when he had time for her. What the hell could he talk about to a seven-year-old kid! Sighing, he realized he should have made an effort—for the three of them. Too late now.

His phone rang and he picked up, glad to tune out his yesterdays.

"Yes, Canny?" he muttered, reading the CLI name in the display.

The department secretary sniffed and cleared her throat. She always sniffed, he reflected moodily. How the hell can she have a perpetual cold when it was always eighty degrees outside? Some things were beyond explanation and Canny one of them.

He should have spent more time with Judy, damn it.

"We just got an email from the School of Earth and Space Sciences, Peking University, Professor Degard. It looks like Professor Chuan Jianbo won't be attending the symposium next week. He's dead."

Shaun got his mind into gear, his thoughts on Judy, the cruise catamaran, and the laughing girls. "Dead?"

"He apparently slipped in his office and cracked his skull. The university is sending Professor Wei Xhulai in his place to present Chuan's paper."

"Wei Xhulai? Never heard of him. Okay, thanks for the heads-up, Canny. You better have the name tags and place cards changed."

"Will do."

"Oh, and let the hotel know—"

"I'm on top of it, Professor."

When she hung up, Shaun gently replaced the receiver. Chuan dead? He had met the quirky Chinese academic twice, the last time in Beijing while attending a conference on Pacific plate tectonics. Chuan hadn't published many papers, at least not in Western scientific journals, but those Shaun had seen were thoughtful, sometimes provocative, and always thoroughly researched. He had a paper to present on wave harmonics induced by underwater earthquakes and fault shifts. Shaun didn't know Wei and hoped the individual knew his stuff, but the Chinese were generally good and quick learners, having picked up the finer points at American universities, he reminded himself. As he scribbled a note on a pad to check up on Wei and his work, he wasn't sure if America made a mistake opening its learning centers to the Chinese.

As one of the symposium organizers, in conjunction with the

# PROPORTIONAL RESPONSE

Volcano Hazard Program of the U.S. Geological Survey, Shaun had managed to collect the cream of international luminaries, all experts in geophysics, plate tectonics, volcanism, tsunamis, and hazard mitigation. The four-day event would be a clash of brilliant minds, an exchange of radical ideas, tearing down cherished theories, and generally having a good time with colleagues they hadn't seen for a while. Shaun reveled in the cut and thrust of academic politics and character assassination, and looked forward to setting off a few verbal grenades, deriving sardonic pleasure from the resulting confusion. Judy had remarked more than once that he had an evil streak.

The plain fact, he liked his work more than he liked her, and that's all there was to it. Was there ever real love or merely a physiological hormonal response to a biological urge? There must have been *some* love along the way.

Rather than get up and get a fresh cup of coffee, he reached for the mug and drained the cold, bitter brew.

Life sucks, all right.

The phone rang and he groped for the receiver. "Degard," he growled sourly.

"Is that any way to greet a friend?" Johan Thorne demanded brightly and Degard's worries melted at hearing the familiar voice.

A brilliant geophysicist at the Hawaii Volcano Observatory, and an expert on slumps and slope slides, Thorne had written several provocative papers that challenged a number of assumptions underlying current methodology for analyzing and predicting tsunamis generated by shifts in tectonic plates. Degard remained undecided whether to support his friend's radical ideas, but looked forward to debating a paper Thorne would present at the upcoming conference.

"Sorry, Johan. You caught me at a bad time. Woolgathering."

"Well, gather it someplace else. I just got an advisory that Chuan Jianbo won't be attending our get-together. The man had

91

the bad taste to get himself dead."

"Yeah, I heard. By the way, how the hell did you happen to know this?"

"I have my sources," Thorne said mysteriously. "Are they sending a replacement?"

"Professor Wei Xhulai. I meant to check on his pedigree."

"Wei? Doesn't ring a bell. At least the Chinese are covering their butt."

"Have you decided to join my expedition to Tongatapu in the fall? My analysis tells me that it's about to blow big-time and I want to be there, but I could use your input. The thing is a living lab and it'll give you unprecedented opportunity to test your new prediction model. In case I haven't mentioned it, the university will be paying."

"The timeframe is tight, but I haven't forgotten and you did tell me," Thorne replied crisply. "I'll have to get back to you."

"Don't wait too long. The window to saying 'yes' is shrinking."

"You should have been a used car salesman," Thorne grumbled and Degard chuckled.

"Call me." About to hang up, he cleared his throat. "Johan?"

"What is it?"

"When you and Wendy split up, how did you handle it?"

After several seconds of silence, Shaun feared he had ripped scabs on an old wound.

"I loved her, but I wasn't there for her, Shaun. The thing is, I loved something more…my work."

"Yeah." Degard nodded and slowly replaced the receiver.

He sat back and gazed at the curling Waikiki surf.

# Chapter Three

"The Standing Committee wanted to *censure* me?" Chen demanded in outrage.

Keung puffed out a cloud of smoke and took the warm pipe out of his mouth. "Someone had to get blamed," he said soothingly. "Han Yunshan wanted to censure Admiral Fang Youxia, but he followed orders—your orders. Seeing an opportunity to discredit you for bypassing the chain of command, Han didn't waste time unsheathing his knife, claiming that you were unfit to hold the post of Vice Chairman. Nobody took it seriously and I wouldn't worry about it."

Chen snorted and shook his head. "*Taizidang* bastard. He's not fit to be *Chairman*! What about Fang?"

"They placed a letter of admonition in his record. After this, I doubt he'll get command of the East Sea Fleet. Not under the current political structure anyway."

"The investigation concluded that the *Shang* is presumed lost due to some onboard malfunction. They cannot blame Fang for that."

"As I said, someone had to get canned and he did violate the published exercise orders. He picked sides and Han wasn't about to forget it. Don't complain. It diverted attention from you."

"When the dust settles we'll have to do something for him, my friend," Chen said, his face grim. "We cannot have men of his caliber sidelined."

Keung adjusted his glasses and raised an eyebrow. "Don't tell me you didn't expect something like this?"

"Well…"

"I thought so. He got off lightly, if you asked me. The Navy thinks they've lost a five billion yuan asset, a full weapons load, and a valuable crew. They were more worried about the weapons load than the crew. As it is, both of you were out to score points, at least that's how it looked to Han and some of the Committee. In the end, losing the *Shang* was written off as a case of plain bad luck. Admiral Xhal Shenglai recalled all the SSNs and ordered a total systems check."

"Yes, I know. Your meeting went for quite a while."

"Our action caused a major flap, but it wasn't the only topic of discussion," Keung said, picked up his cup and took a sip. "*Jing Long* canceled—"

"To be rescheduled," Chen pointed out.

"—a costly search and an even more costly investigation. There is also an international dimension to consider. We gave Xhal a black eye and his pal Han wanted to bail him out. There is talk to make Xhal the next minister for National Defense. This flap won't enhance his chances."

"You won't see me shedding any tears," Chen growled. "Xhal is a greaser—"

"And an open elitist supporter, I know; which immediately makes him Han's pal...and Dzhang Qishan's. The Premier has an eye on both of them. You know what's going on, of course. The princelings are slowly weeding out anyone holding populist views and you're a Tuanpai. I'm not surprised they went after you, but I made sure nothing stuck."

"I appreciate your support, and we expected some reaction over our little operation," Chen admitted.

Keung puffed on his pipe. "Remarkably little, all things considered, and there will be far more...if the *Shang* makes it."

Chen ran a hand over his head. "Mmm. We'll know in twelve days' time. If it makes it, are you still determined to confront Zhou Yedong? Blackmailing him is not a good idea, my conspiring friend. You'll be playing a very dangerous game. There must be another way to bring him down."

"We'll see what happens at La Palma and how everybody reacts to the aftermath, but I won't do anything foolish, if that's what's worrying you."

"You have never been foolish—"

"But…"

Chen chuckled. "You must admit, setting off a tsunami to cripple America isn't something a rational person would do. Then again, since I'm an involved party, I cannot be considered rational either. Nevertheless, confronting Zhou…"

"He is a man like any other with weaknesses we can exploit, but I'll talk to you before doing anything," Keung assured him and took another sip.

"Han Yunshan…he has visions of greatness, my rebellious friend. Zhou Yedong made a mistake relinquishing his position as CMC Chairman and its given Han dangerous ideas."

"Oh, I don't know," Keung mused, sucking on his pipe. "They might be dangerous for Zhou and Qishan, but not for the Tuanpai movement."

Chen frowned then pointed a stiff finger. "It was *you*! You talked Zhou into relinquishing his position, wasn't it? The State Council meeting a year ago, I remember the look of surprise on Han's face when appointed Chairman."

"Too much power rested in Zhou's hands. It needed to be diluted."

"As a prelude to toppling the princeling coalition?"

"A large meal can only be eaten one bite at a time."

"And the La Palma operation one of those bites?"

Keung shrugged. "An unexpected opportunity to achieve two objectives."

"And fracturing the *taizidang* by setting Han against Zhou another planned bite? It won't work, you know. Zhou is far too powerful to be sidelined by someone like Han."

"I know, but if we can damage Han, it would be a step in the right direction."

"And how do you plan to do that?"

"Let's see how events unfold, shall we?"

"You play a devious and convoluted game, my friend. Whichever way this goes, we had a good time along the way."

Keung nodded as he sucked on his pipe. No, it had not been a bad time. He had been too young to appreciate the destructiveness of Mao's Cultural Revolution, but old enough to know that he and his country could only advance through science, technology, liberalization and the rule of law, discarding unworkable ideology never applied properly even in the old Soviet Union. Education helped him rise through the Party ranks, and when he joined the Communist Youth League, the Tuanpai, his growing circle of influential populists ensured his advancement as the Anhui Provincial Committee Secretary. He never really had any choice. To gain power, he had to choose sides, simple as that.

Deng Xiaoping then launched his Second Revolution, and with it, slowly began to transform a backward agricultural country into a growing world power. Easing economic restrictions gave people incentive to gather personal wealth, to the chagrin of diehard revolutionary conservatives who believed in subjugation of the masses and rule by an iron hand. Zhou Enlai and Deng retired many of them, allowing the Tuanpai to infiltrate provincial seats of power and assume important Politburo positions. The conservative descendants still managed to hold a majority in the Standing Committee, but not the Central Military Commission, the apparatus that really controlled the government, demonstrated so vividly by Deng Xiaoping.

Keung puffed out a cloud of smoke. Things got tough for the Tuanpai under Jiang Zemin, but that evened out when Hu Jintao became premier. These things come in cycles, he reflected stoically. Today the elitists ruled, but the reforms made by the Tuanpai had stayed. However, those reforms were now threatened by Zhou Yedong's rush to make China more capitalist than the West.

"We stumbled in places," Keung said softly, "but we made progress."

"You're referring to the 1989 Tiananmen Square protest?"

"That example comes to mind. A singular event that soured our relations with the United States."

Chen waved a hand in dismissal. "They talk loudly about human rights and the rule of law, not recognizing the damage they did to themselves with Guantanamo Bay detainees. Even *we* don't do that!"

"No, we simply shoot our prisoners. The Americans are a curious people, though. Dogmatic, intolerant, fantastically advanced, but still to learn the subtleties of diplomacy."

"Something you hope to teach them, my friend?" Chen murmured quizzically, and Keung smiled.

"Them and Zhou Yedong...jin and jang."

* * *

Capped by billowing white thunderheads, the fuzzy headland of Cape Agulhas had vanished below the dawn's horizon some hours ago as the warship turned south to avoid the notoriously shallow Agulhas Banks jutting 250 kilometers into the southern ocean; a graveyard for countless unwary ships over the centuries. Overhead, a bright sun made the smooth water shimmer and glisten like molten silver, forcing the watchstanders to squint against the glare. Creamy water broke on either side of SAS *Amatola's* sharp bow, racing along the hull to merge with the broad swath left by the two screws, the white trail stretching straight behind the South African *Valour*-class missile frigate.

Relaxed in his padded chair, Commander Masego allowed himself to be lulled into a semi-dream state by the ship's gentle motion. Usually, the confluence of the Agulhas Current meeting the Benguela Current and the frigid Antarctic Circumpolar Current churned the seas here, whipping up twenty meter waves under roaring winds. With the sun warm, the skies clear and deep blue, the elements were having a rest. Not for long though, judging by a dark band hovering above the southern horizon. Weather fickle in these latitudes, able to turn into a raging storm within minutes, but his ship would be long gone before the low pressure front reached his area.

He didn't mind this moment of respite. It might be pleasant in the sealed confines of the bridge, but according to the thermometer, the outside temperature struggled to top nine degrees C. The wind-chill factor induced by ship's motion made it decidedly uncomfortable for anyone venturing on the weather decks without their arctic gear. Around him, the afternoon watch stood at their stations quietly talking to each other lest they disturb his contemplation of life's mysteries—his daydreaming.

Masego had held his command for two years now and hoped to get one of the new upgraded frigates soon, but there were more commanding officers in the South African navy than available frigates, and competition ruthless. All it took was a single mistake to beach an otherwise promising career. He didn't intend to make one. So far, he had been lucky and all his efficiency reports read 'recommend for promotion'. His inane sense of honesty reared its head, reminding him firmly that competence also contributed to his measure of luck. Whatever it took, he decided. Anyway, he did not want promotion, not if it meant a shore billet.

The officer of the deck glanced at the GPS readout and looked up.

"Eleven kilometers off the continental shelf, Captain."

"Very well. Steer two-seven-zero. All ahead standard," Masego ordered.

"Two-seven-zero, all ahead standard, aye, sir."

He would need to make another course change to clear the Cape of Good Hope—over nine hours away at twenty knots—to run up the Cape Peninsula coast on his way home at Cape

Town. They won't reach it until tomorrow, but he wasn't anxious. After fifteen days at sea running anti-piracy and smuggling patrols, coming across nothing more than the usual traffic of lumbering tankers and bulk carriers, and an oceangoing tug hoping to snag one of those floating piles of dollars should it get into trouble, he looked forward to some R&R, as did the crew. Once he tied up, somebody would get a blast about the portside Umkhonto surface-to-air missile launcher. The damned thing had acted up again. He told the yard technicians that his problems started after they installed a software update to the firecontrol computer, but they didn't believe him. Preferring not to get upset right now thinking about it, he gazed absently at the sea. He would get upset at them once he tied up.

"Captain, we have a faint surface contact, bearing two-seven-zero. Distance, 4,200 meters."

Masego regarded the eager OOD. "What sort of contact?"

"Hard to say, sir. It's too small to be a boat...It's gone, sir."

"Reflection off a wave crest?"

"Negative." The OOD stared hard at Masego. "If I didn't know better, Captain, I'd say it was a search scope or radar mast. Shall I launch the SuperLynx to investigate?"

Masego exhaled loudly, not wanting his reverie to be disturbed, and heaved himself out of his seat. He strode to the instrument console and glanced at the RTS 6400 monopulse X-band Optical Radar Tracker screen. It was clear. A submarine out here? Possible. Russian and American attack and missile boats were known to come up in these waters to check their position as they rounded Cape Agulhas, but they weren't threats. Should he launch a helicopter to take a look? It would give the flight crew something to do, but by the time they made the Lynx and it took off, the contact—if a submarine—would be long gone. It wasn't worth the excitement. Still...

"You don't have anything definite, Lieutenant. No, we won't launch, but we might as well have a bit of fun, and it's a nice day.

All ahead flank. Make turns for twenty-eight knots and ready underwater search gear."

"Aye aye, sir!" the OOD replied brightly and turned to the helmsman. "You heard the order. Ring up flank speed."

"All ahead flank, eye, sir," the helmsman replied mechanically and shifted the enunciator to FLANK with a soft clang.

Water boiled off *Amatola's* stern as the twin screws bit hard and the frigate surged forward, leaning into the swell.

"Sir, shall I announce general quarters?" the OOD ventured hopefully. Masego shook his head.

"That won't be necessary. We're not shooting up anybody that I know of. This is simply an exercise."

"Yes, sir."

Two kilometers from the initial contact point, *Amatola* began active sonar search. Masego didn't want to linger too long prosecuting the unknown contact, but long enough to satisfy his fire-eating OOD. Besides, they weren't doing anything else and it gave the crew some excitement.

"Bridge, sonar. I have a positive contact. Range, six thousand meters and opening fast. Must be doing thirty knots. She's holding her bearing, but going deep. Now passing 350 meters."

"Sonar, bridge. Can you identify?" the OOD demanded.

"I have tonals on the 110-decibels line. Could be a Victor III, sir."

"Secure underwater search, Lieutenant," Masego ordered immediately. "All ahead standard."

"Aye, aye, sir."

A Russian Victor out on a cruise, Masego mused. Now that everybody had their bit of fun, he could back off. Pursuing the Victor would have been futile anyway, given it could outrun him. Besides, they were both in international waters minding their own business. Further pursuit would generate stern letters of protest from Moscow, and Pretoria would dish him a reprimand at best, which wouldn't do much for his career.

"Good pickup, Lieutenant," he said as he made his way to his comfortable seat to resume his pondering.

After logging the incident, the watch settled back into routine like nothing had happened.

* * *

Commander Chol Caihou checked the virtual positioning navigation display and the passive sonar repeater screen, nodded with satisfaction and turned. His face had a film of sweat, having spent the watch checking the boat's status, making sure it stood ready to execute the captain's orders in the final phase of their mission, whatever that might be. A big part of his job also meant bringing the boat to its designated position; strictly speaking the captain's responsibility if they ended up at the wrong place, but all crap flowed downhill.

"Captain, the ship is at 200 meters, running all ahead one-third on course zero-three-zero. Plot shows we have reached $28^0$ 35' North, $18^0$ 19' West."

Standing with his hands clasped behind his back, showing no expression, Vang Kai nodded. After such a long voyage, easily the longest of his career, he'd had plenty of time to evaluate the performance and character of his officers and men. Some had failed to meet his exacting standards and would be replaced. On the whole, he felt satisfied with them and his ship.

"Very well, XO. All stop. Bring her up to periscope depth."

"Periscope depth, aye. Maneuvering, con. Ease turbine to stop."

"Con, maneuvering, aye. Easing turbine to zero revolutions."

"OOD, raise the ship. Periscope depth," Chol ordered.

"Periscope depth, eye, sir."

*ChangZheng 4* drifted to a stop, then slowly rose, breaking through the thermal layer. Trimmed to neutral buoyancy for deep Atlantic, as the ship entered the warmer water above the layer the hull expanded, making it more buoyant. Additional ballast had to be taken on to prevent the ship coming up like a cork.

They just cleared baffles—turning the boat in a circle to allow the passive sonar to check for any contacts—not that Vang expected a trailing submarine, but this was standard operating procedure when entering unknown waters. After thirty-two days at sea—their passage through the Strait of Malacca turning out to be more problematic than anticipated, almost run over twice by unwieldy tankers while hugging the bottom—clearing baffles was a maneuver the crew practiced regularly. With nothing else to do, Chol drilled them mercilessly, with Vang's approval, turning them into a humming, coordinated team. High crew morale reflected the pride in their proficiency.

"Ninety meters," the XO said quietly, watching everything.

Relieved from the enormous pressure, the hull creaked and popped. Unwelcome noise, but Vang accepted it as a low risk transient. Taking her up more slowly would have used up time and he wanted to see if they'd hit their target.

The angle of the deck eased as the planesmen shifted their control wheel forward.

"Eight zero meters," the OOD announced. "Six five meters...four zero meters. Flood negative to the mark! Zero bubble!"

The ship slowed its ascent, avoiding broaching, which would not have pleased Vang at all. He could clearly imagine his boat popping up like a startled dolphin, water cascading down its sail and sides, naked to the world. It didn't bear thinking about.

"Three zero meters. Check your trim. Scope's clear." The OOD turned to Chol. "Periscope depth, sir."

"Good. Nav?"

The navigator already stood glued to the search scope looking for close surface contacts and checking their bearings. As Vang stared at the repeater screen, he could see the island of La Palma hugging the horizon, the Caldera de Taburiente mountain arch climbing 2,400 meters into the overhanging cloud layer, its brown face lit by the afternoon sun.

The control room completely silent, but an undercurrent of understandable excitement and satisfaction at what they had achieved hung palpably in the air, coming almost 22,000 kilometers without detection. They had one tense moment with a raised radar mast 280 kilometers south off Cape Agulhas to check their position before turning northwest, only to see a South African *Valour*-class frigate, probably out of Simons Town naval base, heading directly for them. When it went flank, Vang's mouth turned dry and his palms were clammy. He ordered flank speed and hoped this wouldn't turn into a confrontation. They were six thousand meters from IP when the frigate started pinging. A few seconds later it stopped its charge and fell back, to his intense relief. The frigate likely mistook him for a Russian Victor III, the *Shang's* acoustic signature almost identical, based on its design.

A postmortem by the XO revealed the sonar watch at the time had goofed off to take a leak, not bothering to get a relief. The rating lost a stripe for that fubar, a month's pay and five days in the brig. Sailing under what were virtually wartime conditions, Vang could have shot him. Perhaps he should have, but the looks of intense disdain from the rating's crewmates sufficient additional punishment. The only blemish in an otherwise perfect execution of his orders.

The crew had something else to be proud of—their ship. Apart from several minor breakdowns, always inevitable, the submarine had performed flawlessly, a testament to workers at the Bohai Shipyard. Even the temperamental reactor hummed quietly, thanks to the engineering gang babysitting it along.

"No close contacts. La Palma island is on our starboard beam. Distance, forty-six kilometers. Showing minor inshore traffic."

Vang exhaled with relief and looked approvingly at Chol. "Very well done, XO. A textbook evolution. Take her down to one hundred meters, then come to my stateroom."

"Aye, Captain."

In his small cabin, Vang splashed cold water on his face and ran a comb through his hair. He had done it! Well, almost. The hardest part of his mission may yet be ahead of him. Nevertheless, he was pleased, relishing the prospect of heading home and seeing Lina, making it up to Liqiu for missing her birthday. His 'beautiful autumn' would first pout in disappointment, then break out into a sunny smile and hug his neck, chattering about everything that had happened while away, demanding he tell her about submarines and sailing under the sea, calling him her 'Captain Nemo'. Well, there weren't many Chinese naval heroes...

He unlocked his safe and took out the plain yellow envelope, wondering what secrets it contained. Tempted to open it many times as the submarine cleaved its way south through the chilly Indian Ocean, his orders demanded the presence of his executive officer once they reached their designated coordinates. The XO wouldn't have minded taking a peek either, but it would have been contrary to discipline, breeding undesirable familiarity. He pulled back a chair, sat beside the desk, and tapped his fingers against the armrest.

The soft submarine noises talked to him, their voices very familiar now.

After knocking once, Chol opened the door and walked in.

"We're hovering at one hundred meters, Captain."

"Very good. Take a seat."

Chol eyed the envelope in Vang's hand. "Okay, I'm ready to hear the bad news. The suspense has been killing me. I like something to happen once in a while."

Without saying anything, Vang tore open the envelope and extracted a CD case and a single sheet of paper.

"Now we'll know," he said amiably.

His frown turned into a deep scowl as he scanned the page, not believing what he read, chills running down his spine. He understood instantly what those orders meant, but the Politburo must be totally insane! Surely they cannot expect to get away with this? Despite the initial rise of outraged indignation, he felt a surge of pride that Admiral Fang sought fit to select him for this mission. Without looking up, he held out the paper.

After a moment, Chol cleared his throat, face ashen. "This can't be real."

"I'm afraid it's real, all right. Real as it gets."

"But—"

"But nothing. We have authenticated orders, XO. I don't ask policy questions. That'll only give me a headache and I have enough on my mind already, like getting home undetected. I suggest you do the same."

Chol's concerned expression reflected Vang's disquiet, but he needed to project an aura of confidence even before his friend. The XO could speak out freely, but he didn't have the crushing responsibility of command, having to press the button that would annihilate thousands and unleash horrific destruction. Then again, was this any different from launching a nuclear missile? Hard as he might to justify his orders, there *was* a difference and he knew it. In time of total war, his country's very survival at stake, annihilating an enemy by any means the only option, but his country was not at war. The orders asked him to commit murder, plain and simple, and for what? To further someone's political ambitions? Could he look Lina in the eye and tell himself what he did preserved the integrity of his country?

He clamped his mouth and glared. He was a naval officer in the People's Liberation Army and a loyal Party member. The Party knew what it was doing, and his role did not include questioning orders, but carry them out with honor. What staggered him wasn't necessarily the cost of human lives this would entail, but the unimaginable audacity to harness nature's power as an instrument of national policy. *You don't question policy*, he reminded himself.

"If this works, all towns on the western side of the island will be obliterated!" Chol declared hotly. "We're talking about tens of thousands of people!"

"Not counting those the tsunami will wipe out elsewhere, I know."

"Captain—"

"There is nothing to discuss, XO!"

Chol bit his lip and nodded, aware that further protest might earn him a reprimand. "Once we get home, what then? If what we do here were to leak out—"

"It won't leak, and you know why."

"Yeah. We'd be dead men, as would our families."

"If we're lucky. There are worse things than death," Vang said softly. "You ready for this?"

Chol shrugged. "Deploying the mines will be simple enough. We launch them and let them swim out to their detonation points. I wasn't sure how we'd achieve the necessary synchronized firing sequence, but the firecontrol computer patch will apparently do that job for us. It's the required target depth that's a worry. Two hundred meters is way over their crush depth. They weren't designed to go deep. I don't know."

"We'll have to position them at the next fault line, then. They should handle 120 meters. Double-check the specs. I'm more worried about maneuvering close to the island's underwater wall."

"We'll run soundings to get the exact topographical layout."

Vang wagged a finger. "No good. Sonar pulses are bound to be detected by instruments strung all around this place. We'll use the search radar."

"That'll work." He raised a finger. "Wait a minute. Won't those sensors detect us when we launch?"

"We'll use minimal pressure to eject the weapons."

"When do we do this?"

"At start of the last dog watch. It will give everybody a

chance to settle down and relax. Deploying sixteen mines will keep the crew occupied for a while. Besides, I need a shower and something to eat."

"All important reasons not to rush things, sir," Chol said with a straight face.

"You don't exactly smell like an apple blossom yourself," Vang growled.

"I'll do something about that, Captain." Chol slid the sheet of paper onto the desk and stood up. "Well, the General Armaments Department wanted to have the T/SL-109s tested under live fire conditions. They'll certainly get that, although we won't be able to tell them how it went. Not directly anyway. By the way, how will we explain the missing mines when we get back? The bean counters will give us hell."

"Not my problem," Vang said, and Chol chuckled.

"You know, I joined the Navy because I wanted adventure and glamour that went with it. I don't know about the glamour part, but I've certainly got my adventure." Shaking his head, he walked out.

Vang sat back and stared at the closed door, wishing he had his executive officer's phlegmatic attitude. Life was uncomplicated for him, dealing with each moment as it came. It did not mean that Chol lacked depth or complexity; he simply had the ability to compartmentalize issues, concentrating on things relevant to him and the ship at any given moment. Maybe he had the right approach.

Vang skimmed over the orders again, amazed that someone could come up with such a crazy scheme, then actually have it executed. That took real balls. He meant it when he said he didn't ask policy questions. What was there to ask? He had his orders. Worrying about what might happen afterward an exercise in futility. Whatever happened, it wouldn't affect him, his crew or his ship. He had his promotion and could look forward to a flourishing career. Perhaps a little shore leave might be in order. A hint to Admiral Fang that a gesture of appreciation for a job well done was expected—provided he made it back undetected.

One thing did bother him. How would Fang explain his lengthy absence and sudden return? No doubt there would be tortuous debriefs and he would be told what to do, but he already knew what to do: keep his mouth shut forever.

He could live with that.

Of course, Fang had one sure way to keep everybody's mouth shut permanently, but the admiral wouldn't do that to him, would he?

With the air-conditioning fan whispering in the background, he reflected on the change command had inflicted on him. He could have turned into another Chol, taking simple pleasure being at sea, totally in control of his environment, the problems of shore life a distant memory. He had been innocent then, and more than a little naïve, he decided, but happier. Command of his own boat fulfilled a burning ambition, but it also exacted a price—he couldn't rest. His world had expanded, opening his eyes to the workings of strategic decision-making. An exciting world, but also dangerous, making him mindful of his political choices, something he hadn't bothered about before.

At precisely 1800, Vang Kai walked into the almost silent control room. There were small machinery noises, from the air blower to the hum of fans keeping the instrument racks cool. Chol looked up from the passive sonar waterfall display and straightened.

"Ship is ready, Captain."

Vang swept his eyes across the manned stations, the attentive officers and watchstanders, and nodded approvingly.

"I can see that. All right, let's get this done." He picked up the 1MC microphone. "This is the Captain. You all heard that we have been hovering for a while near La Palma in the Canary Islands group. *Jian* has an important mission critical to the security of our country, and I intend that we carry it out. If we all do our jobs properly, you can expect to see us heading home by end of the first watch. That is all." He replaced the mike. "Maneuvering, con. All ahead standard."

"Con, maneuvering, eye. All ahead standard."

"XO, make your depth one two zero meters. Steer east on the 28⁰ 35' line."

As Chol gave the orders, the submarine canted down slightly and began to move.

"Torpedo room, con. Ready to load all T/SL-109s. Check tubes one to six."

"Con, torpedo room, aye. Prelaunch check already completed."

Vang glanced at Chol, who appeared not to have heard, and frowned. He appreciated initiative, but he wanted the last watch rested. Clearly, his executive officer didn't feel they needed rest. Who did he think ran the ship? He opened his mouth to give the XO a blast, then checked himself. What the hell was he thinking of? He should be complimenting him, not voicing a reprimand.

*That's what happens when you think too much*, he told himself sternly, and he brooded in his cabin, so unlike him. He should follow his own advice: carry out orders and don't think.

He nodded to Chol and strode to the firecontrol console. The weapons officer looked up.

"All units read green, Captain."

"Very well." Vang dragged the CD case out of his pocket and held it out. "Get this uploaded."

"Aye aye, sir."

After loading the software patch and rebooting the computer, the lieutenant stared at the cascade of messages appearing on the screen.

"Begging your pardon, sir. What is it doing?"

Vang smiled and patted the youngster on the shoulder. "Synchronizing all units and setting the detonation sequence for remote command. This will not be your usual fire and forget launch."

"I…see." Clearly, he did not, but he did not need to know more.

At sixteen knots, it took *ChangZheng 4* ninety-five minutes to reach its position between El Remo and Puerto de Naos, a kilometer from shore.

"Maneuvering, con. All stop."

"Con, maneuvering, aye."

"Sonar, con. Report all contacts."

"Small surface traffic only, con."

"Can you identify type?"

"Two fishing trawlers due south of us heading west, and what sounds like a cargo tramp making into Puerto de Naos."

Vang did not concern himself with commercial traffic, but a prowling Spanish warship, then realized the absurdity of the idea. The Canary Islands chain had no military significance and the Spanish navy only had a handful of patrol boats in the group, the nearest base located on the other side of the island at Santa Cruz de la Palma. It was simply his training making him cautious.

"Very well. XO, let's get some data on what the slope looks like."

"Aye, aye, sir. OOD, begin the radar sweep."

The officer of the deck raised the search scope. On the navigation station repeater display, the contours of the Cumbre Vieja flank cleared to TV quality resolution. Although steep, the slope slanting down almost forty degrees, there were plenty of ledges along the fault line for a mine to land on, but not enough to allow them to swim out and simply sink to the bottom without guidance.

"We'll have to drop them individually, Captain," Chol said softly, echoing Vang's thoughts.

"Looks like it."

"This will take a while."

"Can't be helped. Without guidance, the things could roll and break their back on an outcrop."

"Or detonate."

"That would not be desirable, XO."

"No, sir. It wouldn't."

"Okay, we'll do this the hard way, then. Maneuvering, con. Transfer propulsion control to helm."

"Con, maneuvering, aye."

Chol turned to the two planesmen sitting on their padded couches and nodded. Vang needed to maneuver the boat along the slope, dropping each mine exactly where it needed to be. There wouldn't be time to issue normal steering commands and wait for a delayed response.

"You control the helm," Vang told him, "and I'll give you course bearings."

"Aye aye, sir," Chol said, and immediately moved to sit behind the planesmen.

"Torpedo room, con. Load tubes one to six."

Getting an acknowledgment, Vang looked up. "XO, take us to fifty meters off the slope and turn the ship to parallel the face, bow pointing north."

"Aye, Captain."

Relying on its radar, the submarine approached the jagged slope. One careless move and it might bump against unforgiving rock, possibly rupturing a ballast tank compartment. With water flooding in uncontrollably, unable to maintain trim, the ship would grind down the island's face, probably setting off a rockslide as it banged its way into the deeps beyond crush depth, registering as a minor underwater disturbance on the island's monitoring instruments. An ignoble way to finish the mission. At least he would avoid a court-martial, Vang mused sardonically.

The 110-meter-long ship hovered as it hung ten meters above a wide ledge that marked the fault line interface.

"In position, Captain," Chol announced.

"Very well. Torpedo room, con. Open outer doors to tubes

one to six."

"Torpedo room, aye."

"Confirm outer doors open, sir," the weapons officer said. "Ready to launch."

"Firing point procedures," Vang snapped.

"Ship ready," the OOD replied.

"Weapons ready," the weapons officer added crisply.

"Tube one, eject mine," Vang ordered.

The weapons officer rotated the trigger to the FIRE position. A soft thump forward barely registered as the air slug pushed the torpedo-like mine out of the tube. Clearing the bow, it immediately sank without engaging its motor, raising a plume of sediment as it settled.

"All systems read green, Captain," the weapons officer stated.

"Very well. XO, take us to the next position."

The mines had to be placed at fifty meter intervals, taking almost three hours to complete the evolution, well into the first watch. By that time, everybody was visibly fatigued, the intense concentration demanded by each launch draining their energy. Vang felt an ache in his legs and his eyes burned from staring at harsh screens, having been on continuous watch for over sixteen hours. When the last mine dropped into place, he stretched his back and groaned as the spine cracked. Looking around, he nodded.

"Well done, everyone." He looked at the weapons officer. "Arm the units and set for delayed detonation."

"Aye, sir." The lieutenant bent over the keyboard and began typing. "All units armed and read green. Delay interval?"

"Twelve hours."

Vang's orders told him the tsunami wave train moved at 900 kilometers per hour. Under water the *Shang* wouldn't be in any real danger, but no one knew for certain what effect the passing pressure fronts would have on the hull. After twelve hours at twenty knots they'd be almost 450 kilometers from the epicenter, a sufficient safety margin even for Vang. Of course, the whole thing could turn out to be one big dud.

"Delay interval set, sir. Ready to enable."

"Execute!"

The young lieutenant pressed the Enter key.

Vang heard a deafening explosion and the submarine lurched savagely to starboard, flinging him over the plot table. He felt his shoulder and collarbone go, and screamed. A scream of pain and rage at being betrayed like this, regret that he would never see his Lina and precious Liqiu again. The air around him became a kiln and he saw the skin on his hands turn red and blister. Before he could scream again, he heard the hull rip, the steel groaning in agony. High pressure water slammed into him and darkness brought with it merciful relief.

* * *

When T/SL-109 units eight and nine received the detonation signal, a voltage surge shot to the CL-20 priming charge. The sudden energy release ignited the surrounding nanofuel and self-contained starter oxidant. Four milliseconds later the expanding fireball vaporized the aluminum shield of the liquid oxygen chamber, flashing it instantly into super-pressurized gas, allowing the exothermic recombination reaction to reach its peak. Still confined within the mine's reinforced casing, the fireball set up reflective shockwaves which prolonged the reaction by six milliseconds, raising the reaction temperature to 3,400 degrees Celsius. When the casing finally flashed into vapor, an overpressure wave slammed into the Cumbre Vieja western flank at three point-four kilometers per second.

Five milliseconds later, units seven and ten detonated, followed by others in a timed sequence, generating perfectly synchronized standing wave fronts. The antinode points reinforced each other, resulting in a combined energy release equivalent to a two megaton blast. The sudden release of so much energy instantly turned four cubic kilometers of water into superheated steam, which added to the shockwave impacting the island's wall as surrounding water collapsed the hole.

The expanding white-hot fireball front enveloped *Chang-Zheng 4*, vaporizing the sail, the anechoic hull coating and ballast tanks, turning the tough pressure hull steel bright red. The hull lost its structural integrity and warped, then failed from the rebounding shockwave. Water promptly rushed into the stricken submarine, flooding the open spaces, not giving the crew a chance.

During the 1949 eruption from the San Juan Volcano, it opened a two point-five kilometer Duraznero rift one meter wide near the town of Jedey, running roughly east to west, causing the western part of the Cumbre Vieja ridge to slip several meters. In 1971, the Teneguia vent on the south side of the volcano opened additional fractures not visible from the surface.

As the transverse shockwave from the mines hit the flank, existing fissures along the fault opened farther, allowing the superheated water trapped within the edifice to expand rapidly. It dislodged an eight-kilometer-wide section of the southwestern slope, which cleaved at the base of the island's volcanic ridge, causing it to slide nine meters into the Atlantic. This generated a magnitude 6.8 quake that submerged most of El Remo and Puerto de Naos waterfronts, creating a water dome forty meters high, setting into motion an expanding two meter wave train.

Caught in the slump, the submarine was instantly crushed and torn to bits by the resulting avalanche. Most of the submarine lay buried under thousands of tonnes of rock, but some remains were swept into the deeps with the rest of the debris.

On the surface, the surging water rushed up the black volcanic sands of the western coastline inundating everything in its path, the inhabitants along the shoreline hardly having time to realize what was happening when death reached them, their screams of terror drowned out in the surging surf. The waves smashed over jetties and piers, sweeping across the coastal road, tumbling pedestrians, cars and motorcycles against shop fronts, hotels, warehouses, and apartment blocks.

After nine minutes the tsunami front had expanded to 240 kilometers in diameter and had already struck other islands in the Canary group. It continued to race toward the coastlines of western Africa and Europe.

NEAMTWS warning centers at CENALT France, KOERI Turkey and IPMA Portugal, immediately issued tsunami alerts to member countries, advising them that half meter offshore waves would hit their coastlines, generating two to three meter surges. A flash message also went to NOAA's—National Oceanic and Atmospheric Administration—tsunami warning center in Palmer, Alaska, alerting them to an event along the eastern seaboard of the United States. New York would be hit in six hours and forty minutes, with Florida fifteen minutes later.

Twenty minutes from the start of the slide, a set of hissing half-meter-high waves hit northern Morocco. Along Casablanca and Rabat beaches, seeing the white water, bathers scrambled to get out, but they couldn't outrun it. Nearing the shore, the wave grew, peaking at two meters, sweeping the beachfronts, causing considerable destruction, the surge much larger than most winter storms. Almost simultaneously, Nouakchott in Mauritania, and Dakar in Senegal were hit. Straddling the Cap-Vert Peninsula, exposed to the Atlantic, Dakar suffered only minor damage.

Unimpeded by any landmass, the wave train sped across the Atlantic toward the continental United States.

\* \* \*

President Samuel Walters pointed a finger at his chief of staff. "I tell you, Manfred, I really thought Zhou Yedong was trying to pull something over on me, but if he has, I haven't seen it."

The evening had long fallen and he knew that his chief of staff hoped he would get away to his Georgetown residence early for once, but a late night at the White House nothing unusual. A price his friend paid for power, and paid willingly. That dedication cost him a marriage, but in life you sometimes have to make choices, and Manfred had chosen.

Cars streamed along the brightly lit Pennsylvania Avenue, adding their smelly exhaust to the spring air. The fountain in Lafayette Square squirted soundlessly, making pretty patterns. Nothing to get excited about, Walters observed. Despite his own grueling daily schedule, Cathy always stood by him. Without her support and understanding, life as president would have descended into weary drudgery. He considered himself fortunate.

Cottard rubbed the underside of his nose with his thumb in a characteristic gesture.

"He gave in too easily, Mr. President," he remarked in a deep voice, fitting his chunky, powerful body, standing easily in front of the carved *Resolute* desk. On either side of the great seal, two beige, blue-green striped sofas guarded a polished wood coffee table. A silver carafe, cups and sundries lay littered on it, the smell of freshly brewed coffee strong in the air.

"China has an agenda to become the dominant military power in the Pacific and the world's premier economic engine. The concessions he made in no way impedes those objectives. The international press gave Zhou high marks for statesmanship after your meeting, but it's window dressing."

Walters bit his lip, picked up the cup and saucer and stood up, waving Manfred toward the sofas. He placed his cup on the coffee table, sat down, crossed his legs and sighed. Cottard sat and took a sip from his cup, the portrait of a grim-faced Lincoln hanging on the wall behind him.

"I don't read it that way," Walters said crisply. "We gave him

Taiwan and we're pulling out of South Korea. I even mentioned scaling down our NATO presence, much to Larry's consternation. As I said before, NATO is a Cold War relic, and one that's bleeding us dry. It's time the Europeans financed their own defense posture."

"They don't have much to finance it with," Cottard said wryly. "They're still recovering from the Global Financial Crisis."

"And we're not? The billions we'll save every year would help *our* economic position. The Germans especially will be glad to see us go, as will the Russians. We helped create the Iron Curtain, you know. We enclosed the old Soviet Union with a ring of missiles which only added to their historical paranoia. Modern tactical warfare doesn't need standing armies anymore, Manfred."

"Perhaps not, Mr. President, but it still takes troops to hold the ground."

Walters raised a quizzical eyebrow. "And you think the Russians are about to swarm over the Rhine?"

Cottard chuckled. "Unlikely, I admit."

"Damn right. The Russian Federation is a new ballgame, and they have resources we could use. We play it straight with them and everybody will profit."

"I would still be careful, sir. They have a fine constitution, but their rule of law is a smokescreen, applied when it suits the Kremlin. You only have to look at what Putin did to Ukraine."

"Change takes time and the electorate is weary of our global policeman image. Everybody wants us to put out the spot fires, but when it comes to material support, they are nowhere to be seen. Anyway, our strategic threats are no longer political, but economic."

"Water, resources and energy. You told me that already."

"And I'll keep telling you. Lack of water is a growing problem around the world, and our squabble with Mexico is a typical example. If you control the water your neighbor needs, he damn well better be polite to you or he's had it."

"Or he tries to take it away from you, I know. About Taiwan, sir, have you spoken to President Hain Lou Shin?"

"Not yet. I'm letting Larry lay down the initial groundwork first. From what he tells me, we're getting symbolic protests only. Gen Y over there don't particularly care who's in charge as long as there are jobs and money to buy Western consumer goods."

Cottard nodded. "So I gather, but it's not the Gen Y we need to worry about. It's the old diehards who still hold power. They're the ones we'll have to deal with when we formally announce the shift in our position."

Walters waved a hand. "That place is another example of a bankrupt Cold War policy and our paranoia about communism. It is high time that we disengaged ourselves from both. Our current foreign policy posture is merely propping up our vanity. Anyway, Zhou Yedong won't be making any sudden moves vis-à-vis Taiwan. By exercising patience, he'll get it all. No need to do things the hard way by saber-rattling his navy and popping off missiles."

"China isn't short on patience, Mr. President. That is a reflection of their dialectical reasoning, but it's something they need to apply to international diplomacy. Instead of seeking workable compromises, they have aped our reactionary tactics and we don't like it."

"So Larry told me," Walters agreed thoughtfully. "Our economic and military strength made us arrogant and we have reaped the reward for our arrogance, thinking we knew everything, allowing a deregulated market to bring us to our knees."

"Wall Street howled loud enough when you introduced the Marketing Instruments Bill."

"The Securities and Exchange Commission needed the teeth past Administrations on both sides of the aisle pulled out. China also howled when we trotted out the Foreign Ownership Bill, but after almost a year, that policy is bearing fruit. It was madness selling them our strategic industrial and agricultural assets, regardless of any profit considerations. The MIB will do the same for the financial market, and in a few years the people will thank us."

"They have already thanked us. We gained seats in the mid-term elections," Cottard pointed out, "and with a job approval rating of sixty-seven percent, most of the country likes what you're doing."

"Nice to know I'm doing something right. The mid-term results strengthened our hold on both Houses and gave us muscle to pursue our legislative agenda," Walters acknowledged, "but we cannot become complacent. We still have some hard fights ahead of us, which Admiral Pacino keeps pointing out. His voice is like a nagging conscience, prodding me to right the wrongs of the world. Bastard. I ought to fire him."

Cottard smiled. "You picked a hard man there, Mr. President. A man of principle, and they're never easy to deal with."

"He *does* tell me what I need to know even if I don't like hearing it, but he doesn't have to ram it down my throat every day!"

"That's why you got him on board. The Foreign Ownership Bill, Mr. President, it went through, but a number of Democrats voted against it."

"They did and I canned some of them, but not all. I don't mind healthy debate, Manfred, but when one of our own bows to lobby pressure and breaks ranks, I aim to have his butt."

"We'll ease them out come the next elections, and there are measures we can take against them in the meantime."

"Good. Getting back to China, we didn't leave empty-handed."

"On paper. Give them six months and we'll see if Zhou has honored his promises," Cottard said and took a sip of coffee. "I still don't trust him."

"Tough man to figure out," Walters mused and uncrossed

his legs. "One moment, he is jovial and open, the next, I have the feeling that he is silently making fun of me."

"Probably was. He is backed by 4,000 years of cultural history, Mr. President. To him, our three centuries must be a source of amusement."

"Larry said the same thing, but that's not stopping Zhou from aping our business practices and stealing our technology."

"China is not stealing our technology. We're giving it to them every time one of our companies sets up a manufacturing plant over there to reduce production costs and maximize profits."

Walters shrugged. "Not much we can do about that. At least I have a secretary of state who understands Zhou and China."

"Very useful that is too."

"Damnation! Tanner makes me so mad sometimes, I'm tempted to fire *his* ass."

Cottard grinned. "Like you're tempted to fire mine?"

Walters laughed with delight, enjoying sparring with his friend. "*After* you get me reelected. I found that I like being leader of the free world, and I haven't finished my job yet."

"At least the power didn't go to your head…sir," Cottard growled, a mischievous sparkle lighting his eyes.

"I have good men who keep my feet firmly on the ground," Walters said seriously, and meant it. "Men like you. At times you can be a monumental pain, pointing out things I don't necessarily want to deal with, but I cannot fault your keen political insight and commitment, directed solely to the interests of the United States, even when that meant bucking me. I don't pretend to know everything and you made sure I had all the facts and options available when an issue is debated to make a decision."

"Now you're making me blush."

"It's true, and what's more, you know it. Without your drive and organization, I would never be sitting in this office."

"Appointing Larry Tanner as your SecState helped you keep it."

"We had a row when I asked you to get him on board," Walters reminded him with a wry smile.

"We did, and I was glad to be proven wrong. He is a maverick, disrespectful and irreverent—and a Republican."

"A bad deal all around."

Tanner's commitment complemented with unmatched understanding of global events and political leaders who shaped them. Walters relied heavily on him for advice and execution of his foreign policy agenda, now needed more than ever. Tanner often grumbled how he could make lots more money on the outside, threatening to resign when Walters refused to follow his advice, but he never did. Money wasn't the tune Tanner danced to, already comfortably wealthy in his own right. He simply enjoyed power that shaped policy for the whole world. Few men were prepared to walk away from that.

"Graham Stone another good choice," Cottard said, and Walters nodded.

"Stone is carved from the same block of unyielding granite as Tanner. He never ceases to astound me with his grasp of all things military, and he has a rare ability to correlate that knowledge with broader policies. That makes him an invaluable member of my White House team, as is Kenneth Pacino, although I could strangle him sometimes."

Cottard wagged a finger. "I warned you about Pacino, but you refused to listen. He is another Stone, a man of principle and conscience who tells it like it is."

"You did warn me and now I'm paying the price. Has Stone talked to you about retiring?"

"Are you considering Pacino as a replacement?"

"It's possible." Walters cocked an eyebrow at his chief of staff. "I hope *you* don't have any ideas about retiring?"

They were all rebels at heart, he decided, wanting such men around him, having no patience with professional obfuscating bureaucrats whose goal in life was to maintain the status quo.

There were far too many such parasites in his administration, and were slowly being weeded out, including duplication of government agencies—a well-intentioned monster that had grown far too many tentacles—designed to proliferate more obfuscating bureaucrats, like the Department of Homeland Security.

He had to ease Ed Bishop out when the DHS director baulked at having his growing empire dismantled, installing one of his deputies, retired Lieutenant General Colin Forbes who used to boss the DHS Office of Operations Coordination. Discussing the restructure with Mark Price, one of Forbes' protégés, now heading the CIA, many DHS functions were handed over to the FBI who had the charter to protect the internal security of the United States. He needed to rid himself of people who merely hung around shuffling the same piece of paper, producing more paper.

The job of amalgamating and demolishing several intelligence agencies still had a way to go, but the process had already yielded results in increased efficiency, effectiveness and information reliability. Some of that due to Price's efforts, streamlining cooperation with the National Security Agency director, Trent Bruster, eliminating a lot of wasteful replication. The effort had saved the Administration almost two billion dollars so far and promised more, which made the Government Accountability Office and Congress smile approvingly.

"I serve at the pleasure of the President," Cottard said seriously and Walters cocked an eyebrow.

"At the pleasure of the President, is it? You serve because you like bending my ear and terrorizing Congress. You're a manipulator, Manfred. A born political mechanic."

"It got you the White House."

Before Walters could answer, a knock on the heavy wooden door that led to the working part of the West Wing opened and Unice peered in, holding the door handle.

"Excuse me, Mr. President, Admiral Stone is here to see

you."

Walters glanced at Manfred, who shrugged. As far as he knew, there weren't any immediate security issues needing his attention.

"Show him in."

She stood aside and Stone strode in, carrying his tall, trim frame with unmistakable military bearing.

"Sorry to interrupt your evening, Mr. President, but we have a situation," he said bluntly, nodding to Cottard.

"That approach is not going to win you any brownie points with me, Graham. Specifics?"

"At 10:50 p.m. central European time, a magnitude 6.8 quake struck the island of La Palma in the Canary Islands group. A partial slump of Cumbre Vieja Volcano's western flank caused the quake. We don't have too many details yet, but what's important for us, a tsunami is heading for the eastern seaboard of the United States and South America."

Walters sat up, China forgotten, doing a quick sum. "That was over an hour ago. Why am I hearing this now?"

"By the time NOAA got it, made an assessment and passed it to us—"

"When and how big?"

"In five hours it will hit DC and New York. Fifteen minutes later, Florida and South America. As for how big, I'm told twenty inches."

"Twenty inches? That's not even surf waves. What's the problem?"

"Mr. President, the wave crests are twenty inches in the open ocean. Once they cross the continental shelf and reach shallow water, they will pile up. We could see seven footers hitting the coast."

"I still don't see the problem, Graham. Seven footers are nothing. We get worse than that in an ordinary gale."

"These are not ordinary waves you see on the beach, Mr.

President. Those things travel at four or five yards per second. A tsunami train is going at 250 yards per second. It cannot go that fast when it hits shallow water and it stacks up, packed with energy. Remember hurricane Sandy in 2012? The surge swept up the Potomac and flooded Old Town. It did the same thing to New York, running up the Hudson and the estuaries. I'm not saying this will be that bad, but I recommend we alert the relevant state governors."

Walters stared thoughtfully at his national security advisor then turned to Cottard.

"What do you think?"

The White House chief of staff glanced at his watch. "It will hit before midnight…not much traffic around…most people will be in bed. Still, there will be traffic along coastal roads, and there is maritime shipping to consider. Those in the anchorage won't be affected, but anything tied to a pier could be in trouble. There is bound to be some flooding of low lying land. It's a sensible precaution, Mr. President. We simply don't know the level of impact this thing will have."

"Okay, call the governors and give FEMA a heads-up. I don't want them rushing around making a nuisance of themselves. Nobody moves until we have an actual emergency declaration on our hands. You better tell Forbes what's going on. Drag Granger out of his hole and tell him to alert the papers and the networks."

"Yes, sir." Cottard stood and hurried across the floor to a door that led to his office.

Walters nodded at the empty sofa opposite him. "Have a seat and pour yourself some coffee."

Stone got himself organized and sat down. He sniffed at the delicate brew and sipped.

"Good enough?" Walters mused. He had tried the navy java Stone favored. All he could say about it, it cleaned out the cylinders.

"Needs body," Stone remarked gruffly, but it didn't stop him from drinking.

"Suffer," Walters said, topping up his own cup. "Five hours doesn't give us much time to prepare."

Stone shrugged. "It will be enough to clear the waterfronts. Lucky it's night or we'd have a more serious problem on our hands. You know, Mr. President, no matter what we tell the people, some will ignore the warning and hang around to watch."

"We can't protect fools. What set the thing off? An eruption?"

"Part of the western Cumbre Vieja flank simply gave way. There are monitoring stations all over the island, but it will take a couple of days before we get detailed analysis."

"This happened without any warning?"

"It appears so."

"How bad is La Palma hit?"

"We don't have anything on that, but there is bound to be significant damage and loss of life."

Walters had seen images of the Sendai tsunami that hit Japan in 2011 and Sumatra in 2010, the wall of unstoppable water and debris sweeping everything before it, people floundering, grasping desperately at anything to keep themselves afloat, their cries unheard. The aftermath worse: homes and villages reduced to matchsticks, women wandering in a daze through piles of rubbish looking for family members, or cradling the dead in their arms, rescue workers searching for the trapped…

He couldn't bring back the dead, but he could help those still living. He rose, strode to his desk and pressed a button on the multifunction phone.

"Unice? Get hold of the Spanish Ambassador for me, will you? While you're at it, call the SecState."

"Yes, sir."

Tempted to tell her to go home, he refrained. For one thing, she would ignore him, and he hated giving unnecessary orders.

He leaned against the desk and looked at Stone.

"Strictly speaking, this isn't a national security matter, but I would like you to stay in the loop with Forbes."

"Of course, sir. What about Brazil, Mexico and the Caribbean countries? We should let them know."

"NOAA will take care of that. I don't want to start calling anybody directly unless this turns out to be a relief scenario, which doesn't seem likely from what you're telling me. You know, of course, you have ruined a perfectly good evening for me. Cathy is going to hate you. We had something special planned for tonight."

He had looked forward to a quiet evening with his wife, a rare opportunity, as they didn't come around often. Alone, presidential problems pushed aside for a time, sharing good wine, some intimate conversation, simply being close, it would help further glue their otherwise solid relationship. Something they needed to do more often. Cathy was understanding, knowing how his job consumed him, but she was also a woman who wanted to see her husband outside the Oval Office once in a while. His two girls safely married with lives of their own, he would talk to Unice about scheduling more personal time. Life used to be simpler and more enjoyable when he'd been an ordinary Michigan senator. Simpler perhaps, but not as intellectually rewarding. Anyway, Cathy enjoyed the power that came from being married to him.

Stone's expression remained neutral. "My apologies to the First Lady, but this time, she'll have to blame nature."

"They always shoot the messenger, Graham," Walters said darkly as he sat down.

The national security advisor smiled. "In that case, I'm safe."

Startled, Walters chuckled. "You mean, she'll take it out on *me*?"

"There is no justice, Mr. President."

Walters grinned when he saw the sparkle of amusement in

Stone's eyes. "I suppose not, but it's not something you tell your President."

"No, sir."

Walters pulled at his chin. "I was talking to Manfred about my Beijing visit. He thinks Zhou Yedong has given in too easily to our demands."

"He has."

"In what way?"

"China is playing from a position of strength and we have a weak hand. Your move to disentangle ourselves from South Korea and Taiwan is a sound policy, but it's one we were forced into."

"Yes, you told me that already."

"The economic weakness of the free world has required everyone to consolidate, giving China an opportunity to fill the gap. Their economic surge and significant fiscal reserves enables them to play a deeper game, making us concede geopolitical advantages, strengthening their position, which in turn forces us to give up more advantages. That's how you lose initiative. I'm certain Tanner has already discussed this with you."

"We talked about it, but I wanted your view. Tell me this. How would Zhou and the Standing Committee react if I told him we're dismantling the CHIJAP SOSUS line?"

"It reinforces what I just said, Mr. President," Stone said immediately. "Because we're fiscally weak we cannot afford to upgrade or replace it, even though in my view, its tactical value is questionable. However, Beijing would welcome it. China is in an interesting phase, emerging from Mao's period of totalitarianism into authoritarianism as modern external political and economic forces compelled it to adjust as it integrates itself into the global system. Although still very much a police state, the Confucian idea that a government should rule in the interest of its people has evolved into a fledgling sense of accountability. Partly to preserve its own existence by suppressing populist unrest, and to

127

project power on the scale it enjoyed during the Han Dynasty. It also reflects their penchant for compromise, looking for solutions that move both sides toward the middle. Having established a strong central government, Beijing is seeking to extend its global influence and regain the self-respect they commanded centuries before."

"In the same way the United States extended its influence across the world after the Second World War," Walter murmured, nodding slowly.

"Exactly. It's not necessarily a conscious policy on their part, but a natural byproduct of an expanding economy and a sense of national pride. They want to show us that they are our equals, and all their efforts to modernize the PLA are pursued with that objective in mind. From a straight brown water navy, they are evolving into a true blue water force. They're not doing it to create an instrument of aggression, in the same way we didn't with ours, but when the 7th Fleet parades off Taiwan the world takes notice. China wants to be noticed, Mr. President.

"Like the GIUK line, CHIJAP was created in an atmosphere of communist hysteria, and maintained against non-existent enemies. I'm not saying the SOSUS systems haven't given us a tactical advantage, but we have been preparing for a war that would never come. The military everywhere likes to fight wars," Stone added wryly and Walters chuckled.

"Good thing they're subordinate to civilian authority," Walters mused.

"Every system needs oversight. Getting back to my point, the specter of mutual annihilation won't be nuclear, but economic, as the Global Financial Crisis so vividly demonstrated. CHIJAP is an irritant, needlessly annoying the Chinese, giving us little in return. Dismantling it, or better still, making it available to them for peaceful oceanographic research, would gain us respect and help counteract a bankrupt Cold War mentality."

"Damnation! You're telling me that everything I learned at

the Air Force Academy was flawed?"

Stone grinned. "I was taught the same thing at Annapolis. It's in the military establishment's interest to promulgate fear and exaggerate strategic threats, the scenario supported by weapons contractors who of course, have their own agenda. This is something I am sure Admiral Pacino mentioned once or twice."

"He has, damn him. The Navy will howl if I chop CHIJAP."

"Certainly, but it will be a natural reflex reaction only. It's a net with far too many holes and is mostly ineffective. You heard about the missing SSN during the *Jing Long* exercise? It didn't even bother hiding its acoustic signature from us. It probably went over the continental shelf, went deep and allowed the Guangdong Coastal Current to take it soundlessly past the SOSUS line. Shutting it down would annoy some of the Joint Chiefs, but it will save this Administration a truckload of money."

"And get us some smiles from Zhou Yedong," Walters said.

"Ticking off another item from his to-do list," Stone added dryly.

* * *

Keung Yang pushed back his glasses and puffed on his pipe, the aromatic smoke drifting around his head. Washed sunshine struggled to break through the thick smog layer, making the sky look wintry and bleak. Allowing the soft leather chair to cradle him, he stared intently at the flat TV screen mounted into the bookshelf cabinet, only half listening to the commentary from the CNN presenter. With the actual event about to transpire, he was amazed to see the seeds of his audacious plan germinate into reality.

Given the considerable obstacles, he never really thought it would happen. Apart from technical unknowns about the Cumbre Vieja slope and unfavorable yield data on the thermobaric mines, procuring a suitable submarine and then have it carry out the insane mission, seemed an almost impossible task. Had the *Shang* commander queried his orders it would have unraveled the whole scheme. No way Chen Teng could have escaped exposure, and under some positive persuasion by the Ministry of State Security interrogators, his own involvement would have been revealed. There was much to be said about unquestioning obedience by the military.

As he watched the Manhattan skyscrapers claw into midnight darkness, towers of glittering light and prosperity, he felt a moment of apprehension. In the next few moments, he might be unleashing a different kind of tsunami against China, a catastrophe from which it might not recover. It is always dangerous playing with forces one did not fully understand or control. As a politician, he appreciated that maxim very well. His failure to abide by it may turn out to be very costly, and not only for him.

On Liberty Island the eerily green statue proudly held her glowing torch aloft in defiance. Somewhat fitting, Keung figured, admiring the symbol of American might. A helicopter cast its powerful searchlight at the black water below, focusing on a churning white wall advancing toward land.

*"It is now 11:57 p.m. on an otherwise fine Saturday evening, and the first tsunami wave is already in the Upper Bay, approaching Governors Island. It will hit lower Manhattan in a couple of minutes, where it will push into the Hudson and East River. The wave front isn't expected to top six feet..."* The picture shifted to the waterfront along Battery Park and the Whitehall Terminal. *"We can see it!"*

The picture shifted to a crowd waiting expectantly on ferry piers, lining the quay along South Street and the park. They started shouting excitedly as the band of white water approached, waving arms in a festive mood. Some, realizing that hanging around might not be very smart, began to run, but they had nowhere to go. Manhattan didn't have hills to climb and most buildings were locked for the weekend. Police used megaphones to urge the crowd back, but it was hopeless.

The hissing crest reared up and slammed against the quay and piers, sending a curtain of white water shooting into the air, inundating everyone standing there. Amid panicked shouting, people desperately scrambled back from the deluge, getting in each other's way. Swirling water washed over sidewalks, along South Street, flooding the park. The overhead helicopter showed the water cascading back into the sea, leaving drenched individuals picking themselves up, looking around in a daze. Those packing the wall and piers were swept into the sea as the water receded, along with litter and assorted debris, their piercing cries cutting through the darkness.

Thankfully, the CNN commentator wasn't saying much, the vivid images doing the talking for him. Forty seconds later another wave front crashed into lower Manhattan. By then, most of the crowd had managed to clear the waterfront. As the drama unfolded, Keung clicked his tongue and shook his head, wondering how Westerners could feel that they were invulnerable even in the face of clear danger. But then, the world was full of fools.

The commentary started again, shifting to Boston, Washington and Norfolk, the scenes showing the same thing: white water, minor flooding, wrecked boats hurled against jetties, but no overwhelming damage he hoped would subdue America. He wiped clammy hands against his trousers and sighed, forcing himself to relax and breathe normally. Picking up the remote, he switched off the TV. He had seen enough.

When he saw the aftermath earlier in the morning of Lisbon hit, the surge sweeping past several French ports, he realized that his grand plan had failed. The *Shang* clearly succeeded in its task, but not on the scale he planned. Even though La Palma suffered severe damage and loss of life, America managed to escape his wrath. The gods had stayed their hand and the capitalist blight survived yet again. Now, the eagle would unclench its talons and cry out in wounded anger.

He took a puff and wondered what happened to the submarine, praying fervently that it lay at the bottom of the ocean. Chen told him it would probably be vaporized by the thermobaric reaction, but some debris may have remained. Scientists from all over the world would swarm on La Palma, dissecting data gathered by monitoring instruments. If pieces of the *Shang* remained somewhere shallow and were found...Keung didn't want to think about that.

Then again, what if debris *were* found? Apart from some bits of metal, the investigators wouldn't be able to tell if they came from a Chinese submarine. Could they? If somehow they did identify the remains, there would be international outrage and condemnation, and America would be asking Zhou Yedong some very pointed questions, backed by missiles, which wouldn't be a bad outcome, and Keung made sure nothing led back to him. Shen Lei had seen to that. Frowning, he realized he worried himself needlessly over the unknown. He would deal with things as they came, in the same way he had dealt with other problems during his turbulent career. Nevertheless, some preparations needed to be made. America may have escaped destruction, but that didn't invalidate the other part of his plan.

*Zhou, my friend, the time of reckoning has come. Perhaps for both of us.*

The phone rang and he glanced at the blinking white light below the keypad. He picked up the receiver and pressed the button to his encrypted private line.

"Keung Yang."

"It's Chen Teng. We need to talk."

Keung nodded, not surprised by the call. "Come on over, if you don't mind having cold tea."

"Twenty minutes, and I'd prefer something stronger," Chen said briskly, and the line went dead.

Somewhat disturbed by his friend's evident anxiety, he wondered if Chen was cracking under the pressure of imagined worst-case scenarios, then decided not. Chen had not risen to his position by being jittery or indecisive. He was understandably concerned, a perfectly natural reaction, as was his desire to pick over recent events. For some reason, this calmed Keung down, giving him strength. Chen was reliable, ready to follow where Keung led, but he wasn't an idea man, not in the sense of having grand visions, and Keung was prepared to be an island of stability for his friend, providing guidance and reassurance. However, should Chen look like becoming a liability, steps would be taken.

As he waited for the Central Military Commission vice chairman to arrive, he ordered his thoughts and turned to the computer. Might as well get some routine work cleared up.

When the knock came and the door opened, he looked up.

"CMC Vice Chairman, sir," his assistant announced gravely.

"Show him in, and bring fresh tea."

"Yes, sir."

Chen strode into the room like a puff of wind. Without any preamble, he dragged a visitor chair closer to the desk and sat down with a grunt. When the door closed, he sighed.

"Damn smog. We really ought to do something about it."

"You could always move back to Baotou. I hear the air is very bracing there," Keung mused and Chen chuckled.

"You have an evil sense of humor, did you know that? Besides, both of us might end up there working in the mines…if we're lucky. Things are not going well with Hong."

Keung squinted. "What's your wife been up to now?"

"It's the same old thing, and that's the problem; grind, grind. She never stops. We had a row last night when I suggested that she use the spare bedroom from now on. It wasn't pretty, but I was also relieved when she stomped out of my study. I'm hoping the move is permanent."

"I am sorry, my friend."

"Ah, it was inevitable. After marrying off my two daughters, Hong lost interest in our relationship, and our house became a place where both of us just came to sleep. My long working hours haven't helped either." Chen took a deep breath and shrugged. "And you?"

A wave of pleasure swept through Keung and he beamed. "Meng called me last night."

"Your son?"

"His ship is in port and I suppose he got to thinking that calling his repentant father might do both of us some good. I was surprised and pleased to hear from him. He is a son to be proud of."

"You haven't exactly gone out of your way to keep in touch," Chen pointed out mildly.

"Thank you for that revealing insight, but you're right. I haven't been a dutiful father."

"Perhaps this is a turning point for both of you." Chen sighed and sat back. "Children…just as you think that you have them figured out, they do the oddest thing. I'm not here to rake over our mutual family troubles. You've seen the broadcasts?"

"I've seen them. Disappointing."

"Disappointing? Is that all you can say?"

"What do you expect me to say? Things didn't go as planned, simple as that."

Snorting, Chen crossed his legs. "Mmm. You're certainly cool about it, I'll give you that."

Keung folded his arms over the desk and leaned forward. "There was always a margin of uncertainty, but the plan did work and the *Shang* is on the bottom."

"You hope."

"There is room for doubt, granted, but it couldn't have survived. You told me that yourself."

"I also told you that there might be debris left on the slope."

"A distinct possibility, but there is nothing we can do about it. We need to sit tight and see what happens. Worrying about things out of our control is futile and a waste of energy. Even if they do discover the *Shang's* remains and identify it, we cannot be implicated. It will become Zhou's problem, which will be to our advantage."

"The other part of your plan?"

"The only incriminating evidence is the special order you sent to the submarine commander, and you wiped all traces of that. Did you?"

"It was a temp file, and I defragged the hard drive afterward," Chen confirmed. "I never thought it would work even with sixteen mines. When I looked at the TV this morning and saw the gash in La Palma's side, it's incredible that such a large section of the flank actually moved."

"I told you it was unstable. Too bad it didn't slide all the way to the bottom."

"But America escaped."

"Yes, it did. We may have failed, but the situation is not irretrievable."

Chen's eyes grew round and he tilted his head. "You want to try again?"

Keung adjusted his glasses and shrugged. "The thought did cross my mind."

Shocked, Chen gaped. "You can't be serious!"

"Think about it. We have set off a minor slide, which must have destabilized the entire side of the island even more. The broadcasts showed new vents belching steam along both central ridge slopes. It shouldn't take much to set off the whole thing. Even if the entire slope doesn't move, the section that did may need just a little nudge to send it to the bottom."

"Forget it. The thermobaric mines simply aren't powerful enough for the job. If that weren't sufficient reason to dampen your rampant imagination, my impetuous friend, there is no way I could procure another *Shang*. The *Jing Long* exercise covered our butts this time. We'd have no operational excuse to sortie another submarine. Besides, with the remaining *Shangs* being checked out, it will be some time before they're in commission again."

After a knock, the door opened and Keung's assistant walked in bearing a tray. He left it on the desk and hurried out. Keung spent a couple of minutes filling cups and adding sugar to his herbal tea, thinking what another set of explosions could do, but Chen was right. It would be impossible to orchestrate. He took a sip and sighed.

Cup in lap, Chen relaxed and his eyes strayed out the window.

"We achieved economic prosperity, but we also got its ills. The way things are going we won't be around to enjoy the prosperity. We'll suffocate ourselves. How did the West clean up its mess?"

Keung laughed. "By moving their factories here!"

Chen smiled. "Mmm. They did, didn't they. I wonder if it was a plot to slowly poison us."

"I'm afraid it was nothing so grandiose or clever. Western businesses wanted to maximize profits by using our cheap labor and we wanted their technology. I think we got the better of the deal, smog and all. Now they're dependent on us for their goods and we can start dictating terms."

Chen ran a hand over his bald head and touched his scar. "The rare earths quotas."

"That example comes to mind, but there are others, like securing strategic resource and food supplies. We'll need them if we're to grow."

"The West is waking up to what we're doing. Look what President Walters did last year with his Foreign Ownership Bill. Europe and Australia didn't waste time introducing their own restrictive legislation."

"We don't have to gobble when we can nibble," Keung pointed out softly, confident in his position. "But I agree. It has become more difficult. However, there are other places we can look at, like India."

"India? In case you have forgotten your history, India hasn't exactly been a friend."

Keung shrugged. "Our fault mostly. We have the money they need and they have the land we need. Handled right, both our countries could benefit. Economic power, that's the key to world domination, and America has shown us how it's done."

Chen bit his lip. "Let's table that for a while. I'm only a dumb general, and high strategy is beyond me. What do you intend doing now? You're still determined to confront Zhou?"

The idea of his friend considering himself dumb amused Keung. "Not directly, but the initial parameters haven't changed. He needs to become more receptive to Tuanpai populist policies. The Party is there to rule for all, something he seems to have forgotten."

"Ignored, more likely. If you confront him directly and attempt to blackmail him, you would expose your hand and he'd have a clear target. He would string you along pretending to accede to your demands while plotting to get rid of you."

"I know. This will require subtlety. Tell me. Those orders you gave the *Shang* commander. I presume they were printed on standard CMC stationery?"

"Of course. With my signature, stamps, and authentication code. They were genuine orders, which the sub commander was compelled to obey."

Keung slowly nodded. "Could you get hold of a blank sheet with Han Yunshan's signature?"

"Han…" Chen lost all expression then a slow smile creased his face. "No need. I have signed orders using his name—with his distinctive blue ink pen—including the distinguishing flourish at the end. It's more real than his own signature."

"No, we cannot run the risk having you incriminated. It's got to be his signature."

"What do you have in mind?"

"When it's obvious that the goals cannot be reached, don't

137

adjust the goals, adjust the action steps."

"Another Confucius quote?"

"Write a new set of orders tasking the sub commander to mine La Palma."

"You want to confront Zhou with it?"

"If it becomes necessary. Think about it. One of his closest supporters and allies commits treason. It would shake the whole Politburo elitist coalition—"

"And the Tuanpai would step into the vacuum once the dust settles."

"*We* would step in. The CMC chairmanship could be yours if you want it."

"Wait a minute. That won't work. Admiral Fang already testified that he received special orders from me, which he did."

"His sub skipper received orders to sink the *Liaoning*. Who is to say that Han hadn't issued special orders of his own without telling Fang? He could have used the *Jing Long* exercise for his own purpose, just as you did. As the CMC Chairman, his orders would take precedence."

After a moment, Chen shook his head and took a sip of tea. "Mmm. You are very devious, my friend, and that bothers me sometimes. Even Sun Tzu wouldn't have thought of this. Of course, Han will deny everything."

"Naturally, but the cancer of suspicion and doubt would start to grow. Once planted the roots cannot be pulled out."

"Hopefully, this may also infect our mutual pain, Dzhang Qishan."

"The Premier is young and ambitious, with an eye for greater things in his life. Zhou has power, likes it, and wants to keep it. He built his whole political career on the back of power grabbing. If he hadn't been educated in America, he would have made a fine Tuanpai. He is ruthless and not above eliminating an impediment, even if it means removing one or two of his own."

"With a bit of help from you," Chen murmured.

"We all serve the Party in our humble way." Keung raised his cup in a salute.

"If you do this, Zhou will know that only I could have given you Han's orders and he'll suspect a forgery."

"Whatever Zhou may suspect, he cannot move against you without evidence. He's not that powerful. That's why those orders must be signed by Han's hand. It's a matter of perception. You were doing your duty by giving me those orders, that's all."

"I wonder if it is wise to confront Zhou at all. You'll be exposing yourself…and me. Why not send them to him anonymously?"

"I have another objective in mind besides giving him those orders."

Chen touched the scar running down his left cheek. "I was just thinking. Why do we need to go after Han? He is a powerful figure, and what you're proposing carries a lot of risk. Why don't we take down a softer target, someone like Admiral Xhal Shenglai. He is tapped to be the next minister for National Defense and his removal would cause the princeling coalition considerable pain."

"But not as much pain as removing Han."

"You love your little games too much, my friend. Perhaps we should stop meeting for a while. We don't need to add to Zhou's suspicions."

Keung studied his colleague feeling deep disappointment. Chen wasn't thinking straight, worried about unlikely events instead of looking how to profit from the situation. He hadn't expected this character flaw.

"Coming back to my question. Can you get hold of a blank sheet with Han's signature?"

"Mmm, that might be difficult. He has an annoying habit of scrutinizing every document that comes across his desk, but in this case, we won't need an original. I can paste Han's signature to a set of orders and create a composite photocopy."

"Good. Make one copy for yourself and bring one to me. Make sure you destroy your working copy." Keung sipped his tea, regarding Chen over the rim of the cup. "There is a way we can finish the job, you know."

"La Palma? We're back on that? It's impossible, I tell you. No *Shangs*."

"I wasn't thinking about using a *Shang*, but the new *Qin*-class Type 097."

Chen's jaw sagged. "A *Qin*? Do you have any idea how much one of those things costs? We only have two, and you want to waste one on a scheme that failed, even if I could sortie it? Security surrounding those things is impenetrable."

"The General Armaments Department had a *Qin* scheduled to test their T/SL-109s, and the Navy wanted to shake down a *Qin*. The plan was scuttled because of the *Jing Long* exercise. Dust it off and sortie the *Qin*. General Armaments will kiss your feet, as will Admiral Xhal Shenglai."

"You're crazy! You know that, don't you? You want to tell Zhou Yedong that Han Yunshan is responsible for La Palma, which would set off the largest covert investigation in history that might compromise *us*, and you're planning to give Zhou more ammunition?"

"If you cool down and think about it for a moment, Teng, the plan is workable. All the pieces are in place, and having the *Qin* sortie will be totally official and beyond challenge. Instead of having it test the thermobaric mines off Taiwan, it will do it at La Palma. Given its instability, a little extra nudge will collapse the western flank totally and we would have wiped out America. It's worth one *Qin* for such an objective."

"And I'm supposed to write the orders for the sub's commander? He is bound to query them, and when he does, we'll be dead men."

Keung glared. "He won't query them if you tell him that he, his family, his crew and their families, will all be executed if he

140

contravenes his orders."

Chen sighed and shook his head. "Listen to me, Yang. I wrote the initial orders for the T/SL-109s test. The *Qin* was supposed to participate in a set of war games, escorted by destroyers and two *Shangs*. The same conditions will apply this time. Admiral Xhal won't let the *Qin* out of his sight."

"Yes, he will. The rescheduled *Jing Long* exercise, remember? The *Qin* will be expected to run stealthy, which means not getting detected. It won't get detected once it breaks into the Pacific."

"With the whole Navy combing our coastline looking for it? Having two submarines disappear off the continental shelf would stretch credibility."

"I don't care if it stretches somebody's credibility!" Keung roared and crashed his fist against the desk. "Don't you get it yet? Having started this, we must finish it! We covered ourselves last time, and we'll cover ourselves this time, but that is no guarantee that some loose end somewhere won't undo everything. I want America crippled and Zhou Yedong overthrown, even if it costs us our lives! And I would pay far more to rid our country of two of its most dangerous enemies. Understand me?"

Chen rubbed his scar, his lips pursed. After a long moment, he slowly nodded. "You are a driven man, my scheming friend. By rights, I should tell Zhou everything. Should America ever learn what we have done, there could be an actual shooting war, not merely economic and political posturing. Do you really want to risk that?"

"We won't be risking anything more than we already have."

"I suppose. Our plan worked once, and I don't see any theoretical reason why it shouldn't work again, provided the *Qin* commander keeps his mouth shut. We do have a problem, though."

"Oh?"

"You eliminated my Wushiht'ala software engineer who cut us the *Shang* firecontrol computer CD. Two disappearances would be hard to explain away."

Keung gave a thin smile. "Your engineer is safe...for now."

Chen blanched, his eyes round in surprise. "You considered having to use him again even then?"

"I always have a backup plan, Teng. Always."

\* \* \*

TSUNAMI LEAVES THE UNITED STATES UNMOVED
MINIMAL DESTRUCTION ALONG THE EASTERN
SEABOARD
TSUNAMI CAUSES LITTLE DAMAGE IN EUROPE
EXTENSIVE LOSS OF LIFE IN CANARY ISLANDS
SCIENTISTS PERPLEXED

Tom Meecham took a sip of espresso, his eyes fixed firmly on Melissa's animated features, oblivious to guests around them. The Blue Duck Tavern at Georgetown's West End had restrained oak paneling, subdued lighting, inconspicuous waiters, candle-lit tables and soft conversation. Guests enclosed in private glass booths, combined with superb food and good company, it provided an exclusive setting for something special. He didn't frequent this type of restaurant often, not on an FBI salary, but some things were worth spending that little extra. He loved the sound of her voice, happy in a cloud of satisfying warmth and companionship.

They had dated for more than a year before deciding to take the next step—a somber step. Over dinner one evening at his place—he wasn't a bad cook—gazing into her hypnotic deep green eyes, golden hair falling across her shoulders, slim hand warm in his, he asked her to move in with him. Only five months ago? He remembered clearly how her eyebrows arched as she smiled mischievously, glass of chardonnay held before her.

"Is this a proposal, Tom? A girl likes to be swept off her feet when such a question is asked."

"I'm happy to sweep you off your feet later—"

"I must be slipping, allowing myself to come into your den."

"—but I'm not asking *that* question. Not yet anyway. I want to give you a fair chance to test drive before you buy. How about it?"

Long blond hair framed her delicate round face. Pale blue shadow highlighted her eyes, complementing the restrained lipstick around her small mouth. Lavender perfume hovered around her like a cloud, inviting, but also capable of lightning, which he discovered. She adored the old dances, turning him into an acceptable partner, no longer an embarrassment with two shuffling feet. She dabbled in old English literature, loved South American folk music and appreciated all things cultural. Visiting the Smithsonian, strolling through an art gallery or sitting through a Mozart symphony weren't exactly Tom's ideal pastimes, but to his surprise, his horizons were broadened and he actually relished those outings.

"Is it that you want to enjoy the advantages of living together without the corresponding responsibility of a permanent relationship?"

Melissa wasn't anybody's dummy. With an MBA, holding down a senior assistant position with the FBI Director Patrick Marshal, a brilliant career ahead of her, she could have her pick of corporate jobs. Talking about it, she admitted that she'd had offers, but for now, she appeared content to stay with the Bureau. Never shy to challenge his male chauvinist dogma, as she termed it, in many ways, she was smarter than him. It was due to her influence that he studied for a master's in Criminal Psychology and Terrorism.

"Christ! I only want us to be together without having to dissect my motives. Look, maybe I'm afraid to commit—a little— but you know what life's been like for us so far. The Bureau owns us and neither of us holds a nine-to-five job. What we had so far was great, but I want more. I want to see if being together will work with the Bureau being in bed with us."

She chuckled and shook her head. "You have such a romantic way of putting things." Lifting her glass, she took a sip, her large eyes regarding him over the rim.

Feeling this might be getting out of hand, he wondered if he should have popped *the* question that seemed to preoccupy her mind. His problem, and she commented on it more than once, he was a hard man with little romance in his soul. Given his work, romance played a very small part in his life. He had his flings and enjoyed them—all women love a tall, dashing FBI agent, and he was both. With Melissa, it wasn't a fling and she knew it.

He took a gulp of bourbon from a cut crystal tumbler, placed it down with a click, and returned her gaze.

"If you want the flowers, diamond ring, and the bent knee bit, I'll do it right here and now."

"You don't have the flowers or the ring," she murmured, always practical.

"Christ! You know what I mean."

She patted his hand. "You're a hopeless lug, Tom, and I love you. Okay, I'll try you out, but be warned. There are lots of other models out there."

Beaming, he wagged a finger. "Maybe, but they don't have my slick finish."

She rolled her eyes and sighed.

Her parents being Catholic, they didn't think much of his cohabitation idea, but after visiting them a couple of times, they seemed to accept him. At least they hadn't rejected him outright or condemned his scandalous relationship with their only daughter, although her old man hinted darkly to Tom that he should 'make things right'.

Perhaps it *was* time to make things right.

How fast the months have gone!

"Isn't it awful what happened at La Palma?" Melissa quipped, holding her gold rimmed black coffee cup between her hands.

Tom shrugged. "Tough on those people, but they were living on borrowed time and knew it."

"That's so callous!"

"It could have been much worse—for us—if that tsunami was any larger. Our eastern seaboard would have been devastated, leaving America crippled."

"Strange how the Cumbre Vieja slope simply gave way. According to the papers, the geologists cannot figure out how it happened. No warning at all."

"It just goes to show you, my sweet, the eggheads don't know it all."

She giggled and slapped his wrist. "You're impossible, did you know that?"

"I did. You keep telling me often enough."

"You seem to be enjoying your promotion."

Four months ago, he got a shock when Hancock told him he'd been moved out of his job as Supervising Special Agent heading the Counterterrorism Analysis Section, and would take over Operations Branch I as Special Agent in Charge. Ops I ran two sections: ITOS-I and ITOS-II, responsible for all Al Qaida activities and global terrorist groups in general. At thirty-two, a huge step for Tom, and a mark of trust in his abilities by the Bureau.

His unexpected promotion generated some friction among several older agents who had eyed the position for themselves, but Hancock took care of that, quietly moving two people out. The others kept their mouths shut. There was also some reshuffling of roles within the Analytical Branch, Albert 'Slats' Slater taking over Tom's old section. For Tom, the move meant a very sharp learning curve. After an intense six weeks, he had a handle on all major cases and stamped on his sections how he wanted things run. Fortunately for him, nothing critical had reared its head while getting into harness. As usual, the administrative aspects of his job wore him down, giving rise to thoughts of palms, smooth sands and warm ocean water. It would never have worked. Unless he drove himself until something burst, he would turn into mush.

"It's been a challenge that took me out of my comfort zone just as I settled into the Counterterrorism Analysis Section."

"Your boss speaks highly of you, as does Marshal."

Tom raised an eyebrow. "The FBI Director is spreading unwarranted gossip?"

"I work for him, Tom, and I get to hear things. You wouldn't have gotten this job if the Bureau didn't think you could handle it."

"I suppose, but sometimes though, I wouldn't mind simply handling cases."

"Why, Tom. Do I detect a level of self-pity there? The last thing I expected to hear from you."

"Things get complicated sometimes, that's all."

"Rodney Clavel?"

"The fly in my otherwise tasty soup," Tom acknowledged glumly.

Clavel represented the Bureau at the CIA's Counterterrorism Center as the unit's deputy director. Liaison between the two agencies tight and worked well, especially after Mark Price took over as the DCIA. There were elements of inevitable redundancy, which the president, Patrick Marshal and Mark were looking to eliminate. Too many people were sifting through the same sand pile and getting in each other's way.

An experienced fourteen-year Bureau veteran, Clavel owed his appointment to Hancock's predecessor, Bruce Wellard, who got canned for arranging to have Tom murdered during the John the Baptist scroll affair last year. It was no secret that Clavel wanted Ops Branch I for himself, and resented that a comparative rookie got the slot instead. Tom had a potential discipline issue and still to decide how to handle it.

If he could only swap Clavel for Davenport, it would solve the problem neatly. Davenport was CIA's representative on ITOS-II, serving as the deputy section chief, and one of Tom's major intelligence assets. The CIA man openly said more than once how he liked the FBI. For now, Clavel would simply have to lump it. Fates were funny. When Mark Price received his appointment to head the CIA, he asked Tom to be the Counterterrorism Center's deputy director, but it was too soon. Although working smoothly enough, the Counterterrorism Analysis Section still needed tweaking around the edges. It wouldn't have been fair leaving Slater holding the bag. Had he taken the job, it was likely Clavel would have gotten Ops Branch I.

Tom looked at Melissa and frowned. "You haven't talked about this with Marshal, have you?"

"I don't gossip, Tom," she replied archly.

"Sorry. Clavel is a pain, but he is a problem I need to handle myself." He took a sip of coffee, reached across the table, and stroked her hand. "Let's leave it, okay? I don't want to spoil our evening with shop talk."

# Chapter Four

Julian eased the heavy black Cadillac into Potomac School Road and the engine growled as he applied power. Mark Price hardly felt the turn, gazing absently at the scenery through three-inch tinted armored glass. On the outside the limousine looked like any other car favored by well-heeled moguls, which belied its sophisticated construction and defenses. As the CIA director, he could no longer afford to drive himself to Langley every day from his house in McLean. The very thought made Adam Spiteri, head of Office of Security, turn pale, instantly adding to his existing crop of gray hairs. When he first stepped into the job, Price resented being managed, but understood the need for extra protection and adjusted to the necessity. Besides, the Cadillac was more comfortable than his battered old Chevy, not that he drove it around much these days.

A year into the job and the changes he implemented were starting to show results. He had weathered the Congressional confirmation hearings—several Republicans questioning the competence of someone only forty-five able to manage one of the nation's premier intelligence agencies—because President Walters made it clear that he didn't want partisan byplays. Even before the votes were cast, he was already on the job, something Congress hadn't liked, jealous of their prerogatives.

One of the first things he did was fire his former boss, Leonard Zardwovsky, head of the Clandestine Service Directorate. The man had been a good agent and case manager, but as he ascended the Company ladder, power got to his head and he overreached himself. That wasn't necessarily fatal, but when he started chopping heads to cover his own sins—which incidentally cost Price his position as Deputy Director of Operations—that was unforgivable. His attempt to topple the North Korean regime last year, believing he knew better how to execute foreign policy for the United States than the president, really tipped the scales. Part of the problem, Price's predecessor, retired Vice Admiral Raymond Grant, thought the sun rose and set on Zardwovsky. Well, both were now out of the way, and Mossman had done a creditable job stepping into Zardwovsky's shoes.

With the help of Claire Dobson's encyclopedic knowledge of everything that went on in the agency, Price had cut parasitic departments and sections, drastically trimmed Science & Technology—the thing had grown into a university-sized research monster—emphasizing HUMINT programs. For too long the CIA had relied on SIGINT and ELINT gathering for its intelligence, which was NSA's job, forgetting that the best information came from someone on the spot, not an analyst interpreting photos. He also tackled duplication across the two agencies, finding a sympathetic ear with the NSA Director, Trent Bruster. They had reached a working understanding and information sharing more open now. The fact that Walters threatened to carve up the NSA like he had done with the Department of Homeland Security if Bruster didn't open up, helped oil the process. Inter-agency rivalry wasted billions every year employing thousands in paper shuffling jobs. The lost jobs hurt some, but most had skills readily applicable in commercial enterprises and were snapped up.

Price allowed himself a small smile as he thought about his trim, serious, middle-aged executive assistant. The Steel Lady had seen more than one DCIA come and go, and he hated to think the damage she could do to the Company and United States security in general if she were ever turned, however unlikely the scenario. Her loyalty was to his office and the agency, and Price had no problem with that.

Lots more work needed to be done before the agency regained its focus on intelligence, reliable interpretation rather than mere information gathering and industrial espionage, but Walters seemed satisfied. He often wondered why he allowed himself to be talked into the job, and there were moments when thoughts of resigning became alluring, but he had stuck with it, partly because it was his job and because he had an agenda to set some things right. Ego tripping? He enjoyed the power of his position, but as always, the responsibilities weren't compensated by the few superficial privileges.

The car turned right off Colonial Farm Road and made its way toward the VIP parking lot in front of the original old building. Inside the compound, tall oak provided a break from the expanse of bare concrete. Cars littered the lot, which came as no surprise for an agency that worked 24/7. Morning sunshine glinted off the heavy green-tinted glass cladding that covered the new building. Seven thousand employees worked at Langley, a cutback from nine thousand. The remaining ten thousand were overseas or scattered through various Washington offices. This proliferation of locations and use of parasitic manpower another area Price had begun to rationalize.

Julian escorted him to the reserved elevator that took him to the seventh floor.

"Have a pleasant day, sir," the stocky driver said gravely as he did every morning.

"Thanks for the ride," Price replied with equal formality. Upstairs, he strode toward his domain past glass-walled reception areas guarding wood-paneled enclaves of senior agency executives.

As he entered the outer office, Miss Dobson stood up and patted down her conservative blue business jacket, holding her five-foot-eight frame with composed dignity. Her short light brown hair framed a pleasant face that was actually pretty when she allowed herself a rare laugh. Devoted to her job, it was unlikely that she would be hunting for a husband anytime soon.

"Good morning, sir."

No matter how early Price came in, she was always there, ready to serve him. He didn't know how she did it, but he certainly appreciated her dedication. He wouldn't be surprised if she had his house bugged.

"Anything I need to know?"

"There is additional data on the Chinese *Jing Long* naval exercise on your desk, sir. Mr. Trent Bruster asked you to call him and I have scheduled a meeting with Mr. Mossman for ten."

Price tilted his head. "What's his problem?"

"He didn't say, sir."

"Okay. Put a call to Bruster. Anything else?"

"Mr. Casey Purtell would like to see you at nine."

After a rocky start, the diminutive director of the Intelligence Directorate had turned into one of his staunchest supporters, and enthusiastically implemented changes that improved efficiency and effectiveness.

"Right, that's it?"

"The percolator has fresh coffee," she added dryly.

"Definitely a priority item, Miss Dobson," Price said solemnly and opened the door to his office.

The thirty-by-thirty room had ample light coming from specially made windows designed to defeat microphone and laser eavesdropping devices. Tucked into a corner on his right stood a rectangular conference table surrounded by six padded chairs. Beside the door on his left, a high cabinet/bookshelf stood filled with bound volumes, periodicals and decorative crystal vases. Against the wall in front of him stood a large L-shaped executive desk, its polished dark brown surface holding a phone station, a flat computer screen, a standard keyboard and a wireless mouse. Two soft visitor chairs guarded the desk.

He strode to the cabinet and poured coffee into a silver enameled mug bearing the CIA seal. Adding sugar and cream, he walked behind his desk, pulled back a high-backed black leather chair and eased himself down. It used to be Grant's chair, but that wasn't the chair's fault. Neatly stacked on the desk's corner were extracts from *The New York Times* and the *Washington Post*, including the editorials. Reading them a ritual he went through every morning, keeping his finger on the domestic and international pulse from sources other than the Company's. Sometimes the papers picked up things his own people had missed or paid little attention to. There was also a slim blue folder containing input for the President's Daily Brief. He made it his business to personally review the document before it was sent to the Director of National Intelligence for compilation. This ensured that the president had salient facts on everything that went on around the world, including pertinent analyses and recommendations, pleasant or otherwise.

Glancing at the headlines, his frown deepened. He had watched coverage of the La Palma tsunami and its impact on the American eastern seaboard during breakfast. The Canary Islands were beaten up pretty badly, but everybody else had gotten off lightly. Apart from minor flooding and damage to moored boats, the United States suffered only nineteen fatalities and over sixty injured—idiotic sightseers caught by the tsunami surge. Two of the injured had taken out lawsuits against the city of New York, which made him snort and shake his head. News was still to come in on South America and the Caribbean, but they were off his radar.

Price picked up the *Post's* leading page and skimmed over an article by Professor Shaun Degard from the University of Hawaii's Department of Oceanography. He figured the old boy was probably up all night to get an article out for the morning edition. Data still sketchy, but volcanologists and geophysicists everywhere were scratching their heads over the La Palma event. The island experienced minor tremors every day, but the Cumbre Vieja slump had given no precursor warning. The slope simply gave way. According to Degard, the western flank experienced gradual deformation as trapped high pressure water slowly pushed against the slope, indicating ongoing activity inside the magma chamber. Although possible the southwestern rift zone ruptured under this pressure, Degard found that unusual, since no surface venting was observed prior to the slump.

Price put the page aside, not really concerned with La Palma. Nature flexed its muscles from time to time and people simply had to lump it. The phone rang just as he picked up the *Post* editorial. He pressed a glowing yellow button.

"Mr. Trent Bruster on line two, sir."

"Thanks, Claire." He pressed another button. "What's up, Trent?"

"Hi, Mark. I'm getting sidelined by this tsunami thing. I'm told it could have been much worse."

"That's what the papers say."

"From the intel we're getting, the eggheads are chattering to each other like sparrows, but that's not the main reason why I called. You've been following the Chinese *Jing Long* exercise?"

"Indirectly. There is supposed to be a folder on my desk about it. Your doing?"

"Some phone transcripts we picked up between PLA Navy heavyweights, the Central Military Commission, and several Standing Committee luminaries. It's all encrypted, but we have broken their codes. Routine stuff mostly. They don't bother changing the codes too often, but cracking them is still not easy. You should see what they do to their top level diplomatic and military traffic. A 60,000-character alphabet gives you a lot of maneuvering room to muddy the waters."

"My sympathies, but that's why you have all those fancy supercomputers. So, what will I find when I read the transcripts?"

"Depends on what Purtell's boys and girls come up with when it's all integrated, but I thought you'd like to see the raw stuff for a change."

"You don't usually waste my time sending me raw intel, Trent, and I don't usually have time to read it. What are you trying to tell me?"

"Such ingratitude, especially when I'm going out of my way to be nice. Your analysts will fill in the squares for you, but my sit-guess tells me the PLAN isn't entirely satisfied with the finding that the lost *Shang* SSN suffered catastrophic failure, and Bohai Shipyard can't find anything wrong with those they've already checked."

"What else could it have been?"

"Since they haven't managed to locate any remains, nobody knows. If the sub went over the continental shelf, which is likely, nobody *will* find it. There is some seriously deep water down there and the Chinese don't have the equipment to look for it."

"What makes you think it went over the shelf?"

"NAVFAC Guam picked up a *Shang* on the CHIJAP SOSUS line that sortied from the Yulin Naval Base at Hainan Island on the day the exercise started. The incident was reported to Vice Admiral David Owen, who passed it on to the CNO."

Price didn't have to ask Bruster how he got hold of this information. He knew. The NSA had big ears and listened to everything and everybody. He wasn't sure that he was entirely comfortable with that. Then again, both of them were in the suspicion business, which meant that no amount of eavesdropping was ever enough. He wasn't entirely comfortable with that either.

"I still don't understand why this should concern me."

"My, aren't we dense this morning. It's no secret that Dzhang Qishan and Han Yunshan have it in for the CMC Vice Chairman. They could be using the incident to even out an old score. Rumor also has it that our friend Han might be maneuvering to ease Dzhang out. You know how the game is played over there. Given the recent talks we had with China, anything that could destabilize our relationship with Zhou Yedong should be on your radar."

"I'm not being dense at all, Trent. You threw me off track with that *Shang*."

"It's all linked, Mark, but I'm happy to leave the tealeaf sorting to your guys. I just collect and pass on the data."

"Big of you."

"When Zhou took over as President, we applauded his decision to relinquish control of the Central Military Commission, seeing it as a first step toward internal democratization and genuine distribution of power. It may have been a mistake—for him."

"Institutional inertia, I know. You think the PLA hawks might be circling Zhou?"

"I'll let you decide that one."

"You're a lot of help."

"When you open that folder, you'll also find some intel on the La Palma tsunami," Bruster remarked quietly, but Price sensed a level of tension in his friend's voice. "It might be nothing, but my sixth sense is wiggling its antenna."

"Clue me in."

"The scientists cannot account for it. They all acknowledge that the western slope is highly unstable, but it wasn't *that* unstable to have suddenly given way."

"Unexplained natural events happen all the time. Why should this one concern me?"

"I only pass on the intel, Mark. It's up to your analysts to make sense of it."

"Okay, I'll look at it, but I think you're feeding me a load of stale crock just to watch me squirm. Call me when you get something solid on a possible Beijing coup."

"You'll be the first." The line went dead.

Price took a sip of tepid coffee and leaned against the chair. Internal Chinese politics was beyond unraveling. The baggage of history, of course, and the peculiar Chinese psyche—peculiar to Westerners. Their mentality still family, clan, and village oriented, as were their political leaders. It was the younger, Western educated businessmen turned politicians who were slowly but steadily dragging China into the twenty-first century, to the intense dislike of the traditionalists. Cultural diversity notwithstanding, when boiled down, the universal conflict over power and the desire to hold it were things he understood. The Chinese might play it differently, smiling while they slipped the knife in your guts, but the game had certain rules everybody obeyed.

In Beijing the princelings ruled and the Tuanpai wanted to tear them down; the same old satire, which had nothing to do with the lost attack submarine. Besides, if Chen Teng got marginalized, it would stabilize Zhou Yedong's position, which would be in America's interest. He didn't need his water muddied by talk of internal Party unrest or a lost *Shang*—or a land slip at La Palma.

* * *

Frustrated, Shaun Degard flipped through color printouts looking for some data item to prove him wrong. Staring at the sharp graph peaks, the acoustic trace hadn't changed since he last looked at it. Five seconds of accumulated hydrophone, motion, and laser displacement detector data, crunched into a complex diagram by the computer, dared him to accept what the resulting wave pattern suggested.

He flung the printouts to one side, rubbed his burning eyes, and sighed. Maybe if he forgot the whole thing for a while, looking at it after he had a good night's sleep and felt more human, he would spot the anomaly in the data right away. Unfortunately, that's what he told himself yesterday and he still couldn't spot any anomaly. Enough to drive a man to drink.

Other volcanologists and geophysicists had looked at the same data and found nothing odd. High pressure water had ruptured vents along the rift zones and a slab of the Cumbre Vieja slope slumped into the sea. Not a unique event and it would happen somewhere again. He had studied the 1975 Hilina Slump in detail, using it as a reference case, but its acoustic signature, although similar in many respects, didn't match the Cumbre Vieja slump; not in its first two seconds anyway. Those two seconds gnawed at him, making him doubt himself. Admittedly, instrumentation in 1975 couldn't compare to the sophisticated devices everybody used today, but that still could not explain those damning two seconds. Could he be reading something into the data that wasn't there?

Like any good scientist, he should confirm his hypothesis and have his conclusion validated by an independent party. There were several geophysicists at the faculty he could call on, and there was always Thorne. Johan would listen to him no matter how crazy his interpretation. What stopped Degard from calling his friend was the real possibility that he could be wrong. Not only wrong, but proven to be an incompetent. Over time in some innocent conversation, Johan would let slip a word or two and Degard's reputation would be shredded. In passing, his colleagues would nod and smile politely at him with condescending understanding while laughing behind his back. He could lose his tenure, the university having no wish to be embarrassed by his presence. He would be lucky to teach freshmen physics at some backwater cow college.

But was he wrong?

He had stared at the cursed printouts for two days now, sifting through the source data itself, racking his brain for an alternative explanation, but nothing presented itself. He wasn't an amateur and knew how to interpret data. However, if he spoke to the authorities and they subsequently found he had made an observational error, he would be openly ridiculed. The university would have no option but to terminate him, disgraced. Even that cow college job might not be a choice. Then what? Would Judy take him back?

Idiot! Did he think she would feel any pity for him? Even if by some miracle they did get together again, he would be a clear liability to her career—wife of a nutcase. No, it wouldn't work. Academic politics notwithstanding, he was a scientist first. His discovery had ramifications far beyond one career, regardless how dear that career might be to him. Perhaps he was exaggerating the potential fallout of being wrong.

*That is why you did independent analysis*, he told himself, *to validate a hypothesis*.

Was he that insecure?

He exhaled loudly, reached across the desk and picked up the phone. Punching in the first four numbers, he hesitated, knowing if he went through with this, there was no turning back. Mouth pursed, he stabbed at the keys.

Hunger gnawed at his stomach. Glancing at the digital clock next to the computer screen, surprised to see it showing 2:30 p.m. He came early to work on the cursed slump data and hadn't had much of a breakfast, not having slept well at all. His mouth tasted bitter—too much coffee. Tempted to get a quick bite at the staff cafeteria, about to replace the receiver, a masculine, evenly modulated voice burned his options.

"Doctor Thorne."

"Hi, Johan. It's Shaun Degard."

"Hey, Shaun! How are you? Good job on the symposium last week. Lots of fun."

"Thanks. We had some interesting papers."

"You're telling me. Your dissection of Wilbur's dual magma plume theory that gave rise to the Hawaiian chain was devastating. I almost felt sorry for the schmuck."

"Wilbur and I were never pals and his theory was bunkum. I allowed the paper to be presented simply so he could hang himself publicly."

"He did that, all right. Were you there when Wei Xhulai presented his paper on wave harmonics? Just when I thought I knew it all, this little guy comes and makes me feel like an undergrad."

"It really wasn't Wei's paper, but Chuan Jianbo's."

"Yeah, I know. Too bad. From what I heard, Chuan was a good geophysicist. Are you looking into the Cumbre Vieja slump? It's the topic of the day. I never thought the slope would give way like that. No precursor activity at all, which is very unusual, but it goes to show that we cannot take nature for granted. Tough on those people over there, though."

"As a matter of fact, I *have* been studying it. Have you seen the data?"

"Just a cursory peek. One of my PhD candidates is crunching the numbers for me. Nothing odd so far. Why do you ask? Have you found something?"

Degard gripped the phone hard, his mouth suddenly dry.

"Shaun?"

"Look at the first two seconds, Johan."

"What about the two seconds?"

"You're probably going to laugh at me, but the acoustic trace isn't natural. I wouldn't have given it a thought, but after reading Chuan's paper, the harmonic pattern is unmistakable."

"What pattern?"

"Reinforcing antinode points from standing wave fronts."

Degard didn't have to explain. Johan understood high school physics. For a couple of seconds, he heard nothing but soft breathing. He knew what his friend was thinking. After the initial shock and natural denial reaction, Johan started to work the problem, the scientist in him taking over.

"You ran the numbers?" Johan demanded in his crisp lecturer voice.

"I can email you the printouts."

"Do that. You sure about this?"

"No, I'm not sure, damn it! That's why I called you. I need you to tell me I'm nuts."

Johan sighed. "Yeah, I'd be doubting my sanity as well. You

know what you're implying, don't you?"

"Tell your PhD candidate to mask out all the secondary frequency tonals and concentrate on the high sinusoidal peaks."

"If you're right…"

"It will be a nightmare come true, I know. And Johan? This is under the lid, hear me?"

"Send me the printouts and I'll call you," Thorne said and hung up.

Degard replaced the phone and sagged into his chair, unaccountably relieved. He might still be proven wrong, but he had done the right thing to seek confirmation. Despite what the data told him, he hoped Johan would provide another explanation. In his bones though, he knew he was right.

Turning to the computer, he pasted four attachments into an email and clicked the Send icon. It was done.

He stood up, stretched his arms and pocketed the cellphone. No use gnawing his fingers waiting for Johan to call. Besides, he would be better prepared emotionally for the verdict—good or bad—on a full stomach. His blood sugar must be terribly debased.

Working his way through a plate of lasagna—he'd been neglecting his carbs lately—with a generous helping of assorted salad on the side as a concession to eating healthy, he took a hefty swallow of mixed fruit juice and glanced around the canteen, mostly filled by students. A lot of the faculty preferred to eat out, turning up their noses at cafeteria fare, ungracious as the university provided very good meals. Degard couldn't see any logic in paying three or four times more simply to enjoy a dubious restaurant atmosphere among a noisy, milling crowd.

The meal made him feel much better. He left the tray at a dump station and took the stairs to his office. Hearing the phone ring, he hurriedly unlocked the door and rushed in.

"Professor Degard."

"It's Johan. I thought you skipped town. This is my third

call."

"Sorry about that. I took a break to have a quick lunch. I haven't eaten anything all day. You got something for me?"

"I tried telling myself that you finally went around the bend after losing Judy, but sensor data doesn't lie. Once you told me what to look for, it was obvious. I'm damned if I know how everybody missed it."

Degard exhaled with an overwhelming sense of release and felt like jumping with glee. He shouldn't have worried himself to death, but interpreting raw data wasn't always simple even when you knew what you were doing, especially when more than one conclusion fit the facts. In this case, he'd simply been skirting around those facts, unable to accept them.

"You just took a huge load off my shoulders, Johan. For a while there, I thought I'd get certified for even thinking what this means, let alone talk to somebody about it."

"I don't blame you. What are you going to do?"

"I'm not sure. I'm certainly not going to write a paper about it."

Johan chuckled. "Yeah, I can see your point. To think somebody deliberately set off that slump—"

"Probably aimed at us."

"Yes, that's a reasonable assumption. The obvious question I would want to ask is, how it was done? Considering the mass, it would have taken more than a stick of dynamite to set that thing off."

Shaun frowned, annoyed at himself for not thinking this through. "You're right. We'll have to check for radiation and fast, but if someone used a nuke—"

"I don't want to get upset thinking about it. Let me finish running the numbers to confirm your findings, more to settle my own misgivings than anything else. I'll send you the results and then I'll have a few stiff drinks."

"Johan, when I talk to the authorities, are you okay if I use you as a corroborative reference?"

"I don't mind. After you tell them what really happened, I'd suggest that *you* have a few stiff drinks."

"I hate drinking alone. Care to join me?"

"What's the matter, Shaun?"

"You'll most likely think I'm a fool, but I wanted to call Judy—"

"About getting together again?"

"No, that's not going to work and we both know it. I just want to talk to her, you know. Find out how Rosalyn is doing. Every time I pick up the phone and try to punch in her number, I can't seem to go through with it. Is it me?"

"Have you spoken to her since she moved to San Francisco?"

"Once, but that was about the divorce. If I call her, I don't want to sound like I'm crawling…"

"Do you *really* want to know about Rosalyn?"

Gripping the receiver, Degard clenched his teeth. "No, damn it! I don't know. I'm mixed up. I just…"

"We both made our choices, my friend," Johan said gently. "But I'd be happy to drink with you. Tonight at seven okay? Your place?"

"My place. Thanks, Johan."

As he replaced the phone, he noticed the open door. He got up and closed it, the lock making a soft click. Looking around his office, the stacked books, piles of periodicals, his diplomas and awards hanging on the wall, symbols of accomplishment and acclaim, he wondered if it had been worth it. The Degard residence these days was full of hollow echoes, and he hated the prevailing silence surrounding his house. Like Johan said, he had made his choice.

Sighing, he sat down and pulled the keyboard toward him. He logged on, checked the local phone directory, and dialed a number. He winced when a pleasant and annoying automated system voice answered after four rings.

"Welcome to the Federal Bureau of Investigation. Please select from the following menu. Press one if you want to report a federal crime. Press two…" After what seemed like an eternity the voice said, "Press nine if you want to hear these options again."

If the lady who recorded those prompts were here now, he would have a justifiable excuse to report a federal crime. He pressed six and waited.

"This is Janice. Welcome to the FBI. Please be advised that this conversation is recorded. How may I help you?"

"I am Professor Shaun Degard from the University of Hawaii. I need to speak to Miss Margaret Duval, Special Agent in Charge."

"I am sorry, sir. I cannot connect you without additional information."

"Please inform Miss Duval that I'm calling regarding a case of international terrorism."

"Sir, do you have information relating to a possible—"

"The event has already happened."

"If you could give me some details—"

"I'll speak to Miss Duval only."

"Sir, without more information, I cannot possibly—"

"Janice, I don't know what you're cleared for, but you're definitely not cleared for what I have to say."

After a moment of poignant silence, she cleared her throat. "Just a moment, please."

Degard didn't blame her. The FBI must receive crank calls by the dozen, and it wouldn't do to have just anybody call the Field Office boss lady without some screening. Three minutes dragged by before he heard a click on the line.

"This is Harvey Bennett, Assistant Special Agent in Charge, Professor. My apologies for keeping you waiting." The voice firm, somewhat deep, and totally professional.

Degard had an image of a man in his late thirties, experienced and very competent. If he was wasting the FBI's time, he could expect to be in a bucket of trouble.

"That's all right, Mr. Bennett. I guess you had to check me out."

"We did, and the number you are calling from matches Professor Degard's office. That doesn't prove you're him, but we'll deal with that later. Now Professor, you said something about a terrorist event?"

Degard took a deep breath and wiped his left hand against the trouser leg, knowing that his life was about to change forever. Well, the university wouldn't mind one of theirs suddenly becoming famous.

"The La Palma land slump was deliberate."

No need to get into complicated explanations, not now at least. Judging by the silence at the other end, he figured he had Bennett's attention.

"You must understand the implication of that remark or you wouldn't have called. You have proof?"

"I understand, all right, and I have proof that can be corroborated by a colleague."

"We'll get into that later as well. Do you have any other information?"

"Like who did it? No, but I have suggestions how you can find out."

"Who knows about this, Professor?"

"My colleague and you."

"Keep it that way. If this were to hit the papers—"

"No need for explanations, Mr. Bennett."

"Well, I can understand why you didn't want to talk to Janice about this. She would never have believed you. I'm still not sure that I believe you. We get all sorts of calls here, you know."

"I am sure you do."

"Are you going to be in your office for a while?"

"When do you want to see me?"

"Is half an hour okay? Perhaps a bit later?"

"I'll have coffee waiting."

"I'll probably need it." A click and the line went dead.

Degard sat back and figured half an hour wasn't anywhere near enough to settle his affairs.

\* \* \*

Tom Meecham stared at the last paragraph he had just written and absently groped for the mug beside the keyboard. He took a slurp of lightly sweetened coffee and made corrections with his left hand. Satisfied, he exhaled loudly and sat back against the ergonomic cloth-covered chair. The computer cooling fan whispered to him. He glanced at the watch on his right wrist: 11:20 a.m., and frowned. Could he squeeze in a quick half hour at the downstairs gym and still be ready to pick up Melissa by one?

He had a serious thing going with that girl and now faced a tipping point. After moving in with him, the last five months a unique experience for him and a discovery for both, had intensified what they felt for each other. Never having lived with anyone before—Malena only a short-term distraction—having Melissa in his large two-bedroom apartment in Petworth required some adjustment on his part. It helped that she was neat and liked things tidy. He did too, but he could no longer do some of the things when always alone, not necessarily a bad thing. If those months were his training wheels, he figured himself ready to take them off for the real thing.

She sensed his readiness to take the plunge and appeared willing, waiting for him to pick the right moment. He had it all set up, flowers and diamond ring this time, intending to ask her tonight, the lunch confirming an evening at Georgetown's West End 1789 Restaurant.

Perhaps a brisk workout was what he needed to settle a small butterfly that fluttered in his stomach. After all, one didn't propose to a girl every day. Draining the last of his coffee, he saved the Word document and stood up. The phone rang and he glared at it, not wanting interruptions right now.

"Meecham!"

"Can you come to my office, Tom?" Drake Hancock, FBI Assistant Director, Counterterrorism Division, asked mildly.

Tom had built a solid working relationship with the balding forty-seven-year-old man, only five-foot-ten, liking his quiet, efficient way of doing things. Hancock might be soft spoken, looking like a banker, but there was tough steel beneath his conservative business suit.

When Tom came in this morning, Marsha, the Division's gofer, told him the director didn't want him going anywhere. That was at 7:30, and he wondered what was going on. Perhaps now, he'll find out.

"Be right there, boss."

He hoped this wouldn't upset his lunch plans.

Outside his office, the bullpen cubicles were occupied by an agent handling cases. Most of them were his people.

He strode past Marsha's open cubicle, nodding to her in passing. Reaching Hancock's office, he knocked once on the oak-veneered ceiling-high door.

"Come in," the director's muffled voice answered.

Facing Pennsylvania Avenue, the office brightly lit, spacious without being overwhelming. A wide executive desk stood in front of two small, prison-like windows. The light gray walls on either side held open shelves filled with case files, law manuals, and periodicals.

Hancock looked up and waved a hand at a chair. "Take a seat."

"What's up, boss?" Tom asked, making himself comfortable. The old man was a stickler for protocol and small courtesies, but he seemed to have given up on him. He also looked like he hadn't slept much.

The director leaned back and gave Tom an appraising stare.

"You have settled in well since taking over Ops I, but that's what I came to expect from you." He raised a hand. "You don't have to say anything. You have earned my approval. The work you did with the John the Baptist scroll and cleaning up the scandal Professor Krafter's old skull generated proved to me that you are one of the Bureau's better assets, but this also puts me in a bind. I have something that, frankly, should be handled by someone with more experience. However, I believe you can rise to the challenge, and Director Marshal is of the same opinion."

Tom sat up, not liking where this was going. He hadn't heard anything about a terrorism crisis, for that's what Hancock must be hinting at, falling as it did into Tom's area of responsibility.

"I'm giving you the job, but I want to make one thing unequivocally clear, and I apologize in advance for having to say this. If you get a problem you can't handle, I want to know about it. I won't think any less of you if you ask for help, but I won't be impressed if you dig yourself into a hole and allow pride to cloud your judgment. Is that understood?"

"You got it, boss."

"You'll be working with Mark Price on this. A joint command is inherently vicious, but given your past relationship with him, Marshal doesn't think there will be a problem. Comment?"

"Mark and I get along well, sir, and I don't mind working with him at all."

"I thought that might be the case. You two still playing an occasional round of golf?"

Tom suppressed a groan. When he first started, he resorted to bashing the little white thing when the sucker refused to go where he hit it. Lately, with Melissa providing soothing encouragement, he actually started enjoying himself as his skills improved.

"Are you having us tailed?"

His boss chuckled. "Miss Foster has regaled us on your short game prowess."

"I can imagine what she told you guys," Tom said bleakly, not amused. Mixing it with senior Bureau execs, Melissa had the ear of lots of very powerful people.

"Are you going to marry the girl?"

"As a matter of fact, we're having dinner tonight and the question might come up."

"She'll be good for you. Trust me not to say anything."

"I appreciate that."

"Back to this assignment I got for you. You will have authority far beyond the strict interpretation of your job description, but you'll need it if you're to solve this. Call anyone you think can help, within reason, of course. Local and international intelligence agencies are at your disposal, as are the Joint Chiefs. Mark Price will handle the former, and you will have to work out the protocol with him."

"Christ, boss! What's the job?" Tom exploded, impatient with the rain dance.

Hancock's mouth twitched. "We have information that suggests the La Palma land slump was deliberately induced."

Tom gaped, unable to say anything as his brain went into overdrive. He closed his mouth as the full impact of Hancock's words struck home.

"Somebody set off that slump to target the United States?"

"And possibly Europe."

"How did we find out?"

"Professor Shaun Degard, a geophysicist at the University of Hawaii, called our Honolulu office. After talking to him and examining the evidence, the Special Agent in Charge called me. That was at eleven last night. I've had two hours of sleep since then. The only thing keeping me awake is knowing that a lot of other people haven't slept either, and that includes the President."

No wonder his boss looked a little worn around the edges, Tom reflected. He could clearly imagine what went on during those meetings as different agencies fought for jurisdiction.

"And you convinced the President that this was FBI's job?"

"Marshal convinced him, but Walters didn't need much persuasion. This falls directly within our charter."

"Mark Price didn't fight it?"

"He did, but when he heard who would head the investigation, he folded."

Ordinarily, domestic terrorism events were handled by Operations Branch II, but given the international dimension surrounding La Palma, Tom appreciated why he got this.

"Do we know how it was done?"

"It will be your job to find out, but it wasn't nuclear, if that's what you're getting at. That's been checked. Remember, whatever it takes. If Professor Degard is right, somebody out there is going to have a really bad day."

Tom figured that was putting it mildly. "How do you want to handle communication?"

"You report to me and Director Marshal. Nobody else. The White House promised not to get in our way, but don't be surprised if you get a call from the Chief of Staff or the National Security Advisor. Once the story breaks, the President will be under a lot of pressure to go after somebody, which means *you'll* be under a lot of pressure. If you need military resources, the Joint Chiefs will have operational control, but they work for you. Tell them what you want done, but don't micromanage them. Authorization code is Canary Zulu. If there are problems, deal with them. I don't want to spend my time fighting turf fires, so don't start any."

"Got it, boss." Tom slowly stood up. "What if we can't find who did it?"

"This may be huge, but it's still a crime case. Treat it as such. Don't get sidetracked by the political dimension and you won't be overwhelmed."

Easily said than done, but Hancock was right. Standard investigative and forensic procedures still apply…well, almost.

The director held out a flash drive stick. "Everything we got from Degard is in there. Good luck, Tom."

As Tom grasped the door handle, he looked at the director. "Is it too late to resign?"

"Get out," Hancock growled with a twinkle of amusement in his eyes.

Back in his office, Tom plugged in the flash drive, opened the file directory and started reading Degard's notes. The scientific parts were beyond him, but he understood well enough the summary. Agent Bennett's observations made more interesting reading, providing the human element. Apart from the interview notes, Bennett had attached Degard's detailed profile, including personal and family information Tom wasn't really concerned with, but understood why it was done. With Dr. Thorne's corroborative evidence, there wasn't much doubt what happened, certain last night's sweat session at the White House must have verified. Launching what would undoubtedly be a prolonged and very expensive investigation, only to have it proven a misguided interpretation by a troubled academic, would create more damage to America's reputation than the tsunami.

His planned workout at the gym forgotten, he reached for the phone and pressed a direct dial line button.

"Mark Price," the familiar voice answered after two rings.

"It's Tom. I guess you know why I'm calling."

"I've been expecting to hear from you all morning, but I figured the wheels of FBI bureaucracy turn just as slowly as they do for us."

"They've turned and I was shoved into the gears again. From what Hancock told me, you were briefed."

"The all-nighter generated a lot of heat and position jockeying, but you know the outcome. You want to settle jurisdiction?"

"Feels like old times, eh?"

Tom felt a flash of *déjà vu*, the situation reminding him of the Valero Texas City Refinery incident two years ago when a Mossad black ops team caused some damage, making it look like the Iranians did it. Mossad hoped the United States would bomb the crap out of Iran's nuclear facilities, relieving Israel of a troublesome strategic threat. Working with Mark, the plot was uncovered and Israel was still paying for that blunder.

During the investigation, Mark was Director, National Operations Center, at the Department of Homeland Security. Working out of the Houston office, Tom was placed in charge, given that the act happened on U.S. soil, which meant the CIA wasn't able to mess with it—directly. They had to settle jurisdiction then as well.

"Hancock told me that you'll deal with all things intelligence and gutter crawling, and I'll look after forensics."

"I was told the same thing, but with one additional proviso. This is an FBI case and the Company is providing support for the international end. You're in charge, Tom."

A nice thing to say. Tom was about to voice his doubts and lay bare his lack of experience to tackle anything of this magnitude, then pulled himself up. Hancock was right when he said that he should treat this like any other criminal investigation. A lot of people would be watching, hoping to see him stumble, and he would be under considerable strain to produce results quickly. This was not the time to start doubting himself or voice doubts to others, even his friend.

"Jump in if you see me cocking things up."

"Don't worry, I'll be making a pain of myself, or Keith Davenport will."

"He was told what's going on?"

"We have some ideas where to start looking, but I won't be

doing anything until we settle a detailed framework of action."

"I'll talk to him. Have you spoken to Rodney Clavel?" Tom chewed his lip, not having seen his liaison officer all morning.

"He's been told that you'll be calling him. Last I know, he was on his way downtown."

"You mentioned a framework of action, Mark. You've had time to think things through and I just walked into this. After reading Professor Degard's notes, there are one or two obvious angles you could start looking at right away."

"Method of delivery?"

"The slump was obviously caused by an explosive device, probably more than one according to his notes. Somebody had to plant them, and there are only three ways to do it."

"Air, surface or submarine. The Clandestine Service Directorate has started the wheels moving and we're sifting through our SIGINT and ELINT data. Trent Bruster is shaking the NSA tree hoping something will fall out. Knowing the type of explosive used would help to narrow the field a lot."

"Agreed. I'll talk to the Navy and get them to search every inch of La Palma's western side."

"Let's pray the landslide hasn't buried the evidence."

"You can leave the pessimism bits to me, Mark. I'll get back to you once I have a chat with Davenport and Clavel. And Mark? I better take a rain check on our golf game this Saturday."

"Not a good idea, my boy. A few hours away from your desk is just what you need on a job like this. Take it from me, I know. You won't get this done if you burn yourself out. Let everybody do their job without you hovering over them."

Tom blanched, realizing he was an inch from making a major blunder, and he thought he had learned that lesson.

"Perhaps you're right."

"You would also be depriving me of the pleasure I'd get whipping your ass."

Tom laughed. "Bastard."

"Talking about pessimism, I may have dropped the ball here."

"Oh? How's that?"

"Bruster gave me a heads-up about La Palma and how the whole thing was so improbable."

"Yeah, Melissa and I talked about it. So?"

"Had I listened, we could have had this investigation further advanced."

"Like you said, Mark. Sometimes the bad guys also get to tick all the right boxes. I wouldn't worry about it."

"Talk to you later."

Replacing the phone, Tom chuckled, amused by Mark's confession. The DCIA was a policy maker, not a field operative handling cases. Glancing at his watch, his smile faded. Already 12:20 and far too late for a gym session. He loaded Degard's file directory onto the server, then used Outlook to set up a meeting for two o'clock, attached the directory URL, and sent it off. He wanted to give his ITOS-I and ITOS-II section chiefs and the two liaison officers time to digest the data before he assigned specific tasks. He also needed time to figure out what tasks he wanted done and in what sequence. His section chiefs were both experienced men and knew how to play the game. Like Mark said, they would need minimal guidance and supervision to get them going. Was he over-planning?

He also had a lunch appointment with Melissa, something he didn't want to miss, or his plan for tonight. Mark was right. La Palma won't go away if he wasn't on the job 24/7. The damage was already done. Didn't somebody say that revenge was a dish best served cold?

He picked up the phone. "Marsha, it's Tom. Please get hold of Admiral Wayne Parker, Chief of Naval Operations."

Two minutes later the phone rang and he picked it up. "Meecham."

"Mr. Meecham, this is Admiral Parker. I understand you

want to talk to me, sir?"

Tom blinked. Did a four-star admiral address him as 'sir'? The admiral either had an exaggerated view of his importance or Tom had a profile he wasn't sure he wanted.

"Admiral, this is going to work out much better if you just call me Tom." He heard a fruity chortle at the other end.

"I wasn't sure with whom I was dealing."

"Oh? You mean to tell me that you didn't have me checked out?"

"Guilty. You have some impressive credentials, Mister, but some of the Washington weenies I've come across also had impressive credentials."

"Believe me, Admiral, I'm different."

"So I've been told. What can I do for you, Tom?"

"I am sure you're already doing it."

"Hah! I see we're going to get along famously. I wasn't jumping the gun, Mr. Meecham. Not much anyway, but I knew you'd be calling, and it didn't take much to figure out why."

"Clue me in."

"You want a ship at La Palma with deep water search capability, which means a submersible or ROVs, and I have both. In this case, I'd recommend using an ROV. A submersible is a complex machine and not very versatile."

"Can your ROV operate at 14,000 feet?"

"What I have in mind is the National Oceanic and Atmospheric Administration research vessel, the *Okeanos Explorer*. It's fully equipped to handle this mission and has two ROVs capable of reaching 14,000 feet."

"Where is it now?"

"Naval Station Rota, Spain, as a matter of fact. It just finished a mission in the Mediterranean. At maximum speed, it can be off the Canary Islands in seven days."

This was longer than Tom expected, but ships weren't airplanes, and a special research vessel he needed wasn't available just for the asking. Parker had clearly done his homework, something he appreciated.

"Sounds good, Admiral. I'll take it."

"Most of the scientists on board were flown off to make way for a new contingent, an operation in the North Sea, but we can reschedule."

"Who is left?"

"Two marine biologists and four technicians, but manpower isn't your problem. The ship is equipped with a telepresence facility."

"A what?"

"Live data feeds transmitted to scientists at the Inner Space Center at the University of Rhode Island. It's like being on the ship."

"But not quite. Well, I won't need the biologists."

"I didn't think so. We'll organize a few people for you."

"There is only one person I need and I want to put him on board. This will be a fact finding mission, not an exploration cruise."

"My orders are to cooperate with the FBI, Mr. Meecham, but nobody said we'd be babysitting a landlubber. You tell us what you want done and the Navy will deliver."

"This is no ordinary landlubber. It's Professor Degard."

"The man who blew the whistle? Okay, that's different. How soon can you get him there?"

"Honolulu to Washington…nine hours. Once he's here, eight hours to Rota…He could be there in twenty-four hours."

"Good enough. It will take *Okeanos Explorer* that long to refuel and take on supplies. We'll need clearance from the Spanish authorities to anchor at La Palma."

"Leave that with me."

"It's your show. Anything else?"

"What are the lab facilities like on board?"

"Apart from the mission control room, they have a dry and

a wet lab. They can handle most geological and marine life analysis, but not much else. If Degard finds something, we'll have the stuff flown Stateside."

"I like it. There is one more thing. Everything done on board the *Okeanos Explorer* is classified."

"Don't worry; the captain will be briefed, as will the crew."

"I appreciate your cooperation, Admiral."

"A pleasure."

Tom hung up and wondered how much pleasure it really was, but he didn't mind Parker's parochial attitude. With the fancy toys at their disposal, the Navy naturally resented outsiders messing on their turf. As long as they produced results, he would stay out of their way.

Hancock wasn't kidding when he said he would have authority to call anyone. Having the CIA director and chief of the Navy at his beck and call was heady vapors. This represented raw power, and he could see how a man could get swept up in a balloon of self-importance. Still, no rule existed that said he couldn't savor the experience.

He held the phone next to his ear and pressed another button. "Marsha? Please get hold of the Undersecretary of State for Arms Control and International Security for me, will you? Once I'm done with him, I'll need to talk to Professor Shaun Degard, University of Hawaii. It'll be early in the morning over there and he might still be in bed. Then call Hickam Field. I want them to pick him up and ferry him to Andrews. From there, to the Naval Station Rota in Spain. If they don't have a Gulfstream V that can go the distance, have Andrews get one of theirs ready. Authorization code is Canary Zulu. If anybody gives you a hard time, put them through to me."

Almost five minutes passed before the phone jangled.

"Tom Meecham."

"This is Griffin Hauser, Mr. Meecham, State Department. I understand you wanted to talk to me."

"Thanks for getting back to me, Mr. Hauser. I have been put in charge—"

"I know who you are, Mr. Meecham."

Tom got an impression of a youngish man occupying a comfortable office, hot and cold secretaries fulfilling his every whim, condescending to talk to an FBI underling. He took a deep breath, remembering what this was about. Time to dislike the officious bureaucrat later.

"The Navy has organized an oceanographic vessel, the *Okeanos Explorer*, currently tied up at the Naval Station Rota in Spain, to check out La Palma. The ship will sail within twenty-four hours and should reach the island on June 13. I would very much appreciate if the State Department could take care of the formalities with the Spanish authorities."

"I'll see what I can do, Mr. Meecham. Okay?"

"I'm afraid it's not okay. You can either do this or you can't. If you can't, I'll take this up with Secretary Tanner."

"Leave it with me." The line went dead.

Tom fancied he could hear the phone slam down, but he had no time for Mr. Hauser's wounded feelings. He pressed a button on the keypad.

"Marsha? Put that call to Professor Degard."

After a minute, the phone rang and he picked up.

"Meecham."

"This is Professor Degard, Mr. Meecham. Your sense of timing is abominable. I barely had three hours of sleep, having spent most of the night answering fool questions."

Tom winced, realizing the professor was probably a star witness at the White House meeting. Well, he started it...

"I regret the inconvenience—"

"Never mind, I expected this. Are *you* going to ask me fool questions?"

"Professor Degard—"

"Call me Shaun. It's 6:40 in the morning here, far too early

177

Stefan Vučak

for formalities, and you don't have to introduce yourself. The sternly polite lady who called told me who you are. She reminds me of Canny, our departmental secretary. They both have that top-sergeant manner."

Tom grinned, the description fitting Marsha perfectly.

"Mind if I get some coffee while we're talking?" Degard ventured.

"Get your coffee, Professor, and perhaps a good breakfast while you're at it."

"You're going to tell me something bad, I know it."

"Only following one of your suggestions. We need to collect hard evidence from La Palma and I volunteered you to get it."

After a moment of silence, Degard snorted. "You want me to go there?"

"I don't know anybody better. You know what to look for and how to go about finding it. Giving instructions over the phone or videolink isn't the same thing. By the time you get there, we'll have worked out our action plan. Somebody from the Air Force will pick you up within the hour."

"You can't do that! I have responsibilities at the university."

Tom knew how to handle prickly academics and trotted out his trump card.

"You'll get to write the paper, all by yourself. The university won't mind the limelight coming their way."

Degard laughed. "That's barefaced blackmail and you know it, but I'm glad you didn't roll out the old patriotic song. Okay, Mr. Meecham, what's the deal?"

"The Navy has a ship for you, the *Okeanos Explorer*—"

"The *Okeanos*? A first rate research vessel, but if I remember correctly, she's somewhere in North Atlantic. It will take her forever to reach La Palma. By then, any evidence might be gone."

"She's tied up at the Naval Station Rota in Spain after doing something in the Mediterranean. I'm having you flown there."

"That's good. You mentioned the Air Force. Does that mean

178

I'm not using commercial flights?"

"You'll have an executive Gulfstream V at your disposal, Professor. We don't have time to fool around with commercial flights."

"Does it have a bed?"

"A bed, great food, and a nice flight attendant to tuck you into it. I know."

Tom and Mark Price used one to fly to Tel Aviv and snatch the Mossad operative who carried out the Valero Refinery sabotage. The Gulfstream really was a comfortable way to fly.

Degard chuckled. "I better pack, then. Before you call me about this action plan of yours, be a pal and let me get some shuteye first?"

"It's a deal." Tom smiled, wishing he could talk to Degard face to face. He seemed to be a character.

"Mr. Meecham?"

"What is it, Professor?"

"You may consider this crazy, but there is something I think you need to know."

"Oh?"

"Whoever carried out the La Palma operation meant to inflict horrendous damage against countries along the North Atlantic seaboard, us included. They almost succeeded."

Tom chewed over what Degard said, not liking the taste at all. "You're saying they might try again?"

"It would only take a good sneeze to send the Cumbre Vieja western slope all the way to the bottom. If that were to happen, the United States might cease to be a country. At the very least, we'd be reduced to Third World status."

"Christ! Have you told this to anyone?"

"Last night, I gave the President and his advisors the facts surrounding La Palma. I didn't believe airing unfounded speculation in an already tense situation."

"But you were prepared to lay this on me?"

"I hope I'm wrong, Mr. Meecham. I really do, but you're in a position to follow this up."

"Enjoy the trip, Professor. I'll be in touch," Tom said after a moment and hung up.

Could Degard be right? This needed a bit of lateral thinking, silently cursing the professor for spoiling an already grim day.

Glancing at his watch, he jumped up and rushed out of the office. Two minutes after one, the elevator doors opened to the subdued opulence of the seventh floor. Soft dark carpet and richly paneled walls guarded the executive offices. Melissa stood there, small tan leather bag hanging on her left shoulder, looking regal in a cream business jacket and knee-length skirt. Hair tied in a bun, her face broke into an impish grin.

"Ah, my shining knight finally arrives. I was about to come down and get you, not wanting to be stood up."

Stopping before her, Tom lightly brushed her lips with his.

"Stood up? Never! Shall we go? I'm dying for another gastronomic assault at our fabled cafeteria."

"We'll both die if we keep eating there," she said softly, her fingers stroking his cheek.

Tom didn't mean it, of course. The downstairs kitchen served plain, but good meals. Ordinarily, they went to one of the numerous eateries around the Hoover Building, but today was special, and an elaborate lunch would spoil what he had in mind for tonight.

They took the elevator down, which stopped twice to pick up more lunch goers, and entered the noisy, crowded cafeteria, and Tom looked around to secure an empty table. Spotting one in a windowless corner, he steered Melissa in the general direction. After taking her order, he got into the self-serve queue to load up.

Having satisfied their hunger, chatting about nothing in particular, he sat back and sipped coffee. As she held her orange juice between both hands, her eyes regarded him carefully. Her look always managed to probe his soul, often an uncomfortable feeling. It made him want to confess all, real and imaginary sins.

"Tom, perhaps it's not a good idea about tonight."

He sat up in alarm. "Why not?"

"Your case. You must have a lot of things on your mind."

"You know about it?"

"Everybody is buzzing about nothing else."

"And you're buzzing too, my sweet. Tonight at seven o'clock, your shining knight will rescue you from the slums of Petworth and take you on his trusted steed into the glamour of Georgetown's West End." He stroked the smooth skin of her hand. "There is no escape."

"In that case, kind sir, I am in your hands."

"You will be later tonight," he promised dryly, and she laughed.

"I see my cultural indoctrination still has a way to go. Seriously, Tom. If we postpone—"

"Nothing doing. La Palma isn't going anywhere and neither are the bad guys. They're toast, and they'll be pinning another medal on me when I parade the miscreants down Pennsylvania Avenue."

"You're hopeless. Okay, tonight it is."

"My girl."

He deposited her on the seventh floor and returned to his office feeling refreshed and energized. At exactly two p.m., he walked into the meeting room, quickly sweeping his eyes over the four men. The conversation stopped and they looked at him as he sat at the head of the table.

"You all know what's going on and I won't hash over it again. Rod, you'll have to liaise closely with Keith on this one. Positive feedback only. I don't want to be flooded with negative reports."

"I'm already on it," Clavel said coldly.

"You don't know how relieved I am to hear that," Tom said, ignoring the implied impertinence. This wasn't the time for a family fight. He glanced at Andre Norton, head of ITOS-I, and Isaac Federer who ran ITOS-II. "This will be a tough one, but we have a few things going our way. We can ask for whatever we need and we'll get it. If somebody wants to play inter-agency games, flatten him. Talk to me if you strike a wall and I'll see what can be done. Questions?"

Davenport cleared his throat. "What's been done so far?"

"Under Director Mark Price's direction, the intelligence agencies have started the sifting process. The Navy has assigned a research vessel to check out La Palma. It's tied up at the Naval Station Rota in Spain. Professor Degard is on his way there and will be in charge. Andre…Isaac, we need to establish the method used to trigger the slide. We know it was caused by a series of explosions, but what type of explosive? Degard's data tells us the triggering energy was on the order of two megatons. Scientists at La Palma established that the blast wasn't nuclear, which is good, or this would be even nastier than it already is. Start looking at non-conventional explosives capable of generating such a yield. Once we have that on the table, we'll have an idea if we're dealing with a terrorist group or a foreign power."

Clavel gaped at him. "A foreign power? That would constitute an act of war!"

"Perhaps. Before we start speculating, we need evidence. Rod, the CIA must have done what-if studies into non-military scenarios against the United States. Then again, Europe may have been the primary target. We simply don't know. That's why we need hard facts. The research ship won't shove off for another twenty-four hours, and when it does, it will take it seven days to reach La Palma. It will be at least nine or ten days before Degard can give us some hard data. While we're waiting, concentrate on intelligence leads and ordnance used. Keith, you normally report to Isaac, but given the scope of this investigation, I want you to coordinate with Andre."

Davenport nodded. "That's fine with me."

Tom slowly looked at them. "Don't get in each other's way. If you need intelligence, Keith is your man. Rod, your job is to make sure our requests get processed and everybody gets the information. Remember, our objective right now is to gather credible leads. What we do then will depend on what Degard finds out." Momentarily tempted to voice Degard's suspicions about another attack, he decided not to sidetrack the issue. Time to broach the subject later. "That's all for now."

Tom stood up and walked out, leaving the others deep in discussion. Having Clavel in the loop worked under normal circumstances, but this was not a normal situation and might create a bottleneck for Davenport. His instincts told him to sideline Clavel and use a single pipeline to the CIA, but he didn't want to do that right now. Walking back to his office, he sensed he was making a mistake. Time would tell if he had.

After the La Palma excitement it took some effort to get his mind into gear on other Ops I activities. He could not afford to fixate himself on one case, regardless how important.

Around 5:30, he picked up Melissa and drove home. When they got there, fighting the inevitable evening rush hour jam, there was just enough time to shower and change. Having more things to do, it took Melissa longer to get ready, but he had gotten used to that and no longer fumed impatiently. He wore one of his favorite black lightweight wool suits, black tie, adding small gold cufflinks as his only accessory. When Melissa emerged from the bedroom, he paused and smiled with approval.

Dressed in a long, dark blue satin gown, open at the back, plunging neckline, a necklace of black pearls adorning her throat with matching pearl earrings, hair flowing like golden oil, she looked stunning. A touch of red lipstick highlighted her features without overwhelming them. Tom disliked women whose lipstick clamored for attention, hiding the face.

"My god," he whispered reverently. "You look like a package demanding to be opened."

She waved a hand at him. "I bet you say that to all your girls, Mister."

"What's your name, honey?" he purred, getting into the game.

"What do you want it to be, lover?" She placed one hand on her hip and batted her eyelashes.

"My Venus, my Aphrodite, you're mine forever."

"Uh, I like the sound of that, Mister."

"How about we skip dinner and go straight to dessert?"

"Later, lover. I need to build up my strength," she purred softly, sending tingles up his spine. She was a package he looked forward to opening.

Driving to Georgetown bearable, the traffic having eased off. Valet parking at the 1789 Restaurant saved Tom from the hassle of finding a place to leave his car, almost impossible at this end of town. Located on 86th Street, the heavy stone double-story building looked more like an antique shop than an up-market eatery.

Tom steered Melissa to the upstairs dining room, the white walls plastered with old colonial black-and-white photos. The wood-paneled ceiling crossed with heavy beams added character. Round tables covered with white cloth lay scattered over the floor without crowding each other. The waiter took them to a corner table overlooking the street below. Two other tables were occupied: an elderly couple at one and two men in conservative business suits at the other. Neither looked up as Tom and Melissa entered. Not an exclusive restaurant, it did attract more discerning patrons who relished good food and an unobtrusive ambiance.

A vase at their table held a bunch of blood-red roses, the perfume filling the air. Melissa cooed and sniffed with appreciation. The wine waiter appeared and poured them a white La Grande Dame champagne into tall crystal glasses, 'compliments of the management', he declared, giving Tom a wink. He doubted it was with compliments, otherwise the scandalous prices would be merely outrageous.

Picking up his glass, he held it up. "To my fair lady."

"To my gallant knight."

They clicked glasses and sipped the delicate wine. Looking around, she nodded. "This is nice and I like coming here."

"I could get used to it, provided somebody else paid the bill."

She giggled. "You're hopeless, did you know that?"

"I did. You keep telling me often enough. How are your parents?"

"My Dad keeps making noises about me being your kept woman."

"You *are* my kept woman."

She picked a bread stick out of a glass jar and nibbled. "You know what I mean."

"In that case, I'll have to do something about it."

Before she could reply, the waiter sauntered over and placed their entrée dishes before them. He took the furled napkins, fluffed them out and delicately laid them on their lap.

"Enjoy." He beamed, bowed and left.

The wine waiter walked up wheeling a small trolley with an ice bucket. He lifted out a bottle of Puligny-Montrachet white burgundy and filled their glasses.

Melissa raised an eyebrow. "No menu?"

"Worrying about what to choose only adds to indigestion," Tom told her. "Besides, I have come to know what you like. If the duck confit strudel isn't to your taste, I'll swap you my foi gras torchon brulee."

"Oh, the strudel is fine."

He took a sip of wine and started on his entrée. After a moment, he looked up.

"How's the duck?"

"Good." She reached for a glass of water. "Do you mind if we talk shop?"

"As long as it doesn't rile the stomach."

"I find it incredible that somebody would deliberately cause a natural disaster simply to cripple us."

"That's what they intended, all right, but it didn't work out. It could have been much worse. Imagine thirty-foot waves sweeping the east coast. America would now be in a world of trouble."

"Any idea who might have done this?"

"Too early to tell, but it's simple enough to figure out. My money is on a foreign power. I can't see a terrorist group mounting anything that big, even if backed by somebody, but I'm not saying it's not possible. La Palma took sophisticated technology and logistics to pull off. That's not something Al Qaida or some other fringe group is capable of."

He drained his burgundy and topped up their glasses. She took a sip.

"What will the President do if we find out?"

"I have no idea, my sweet, but I wouldn't want to be in their shoes. Let's leave it, okay?" Looking at her, his heart melted, still unable to believe she picked him. He figured he must have *some* redeeming characteristics. "Did I tell you how much I love you?"

"Not recently."

"Well, I do. Your test run...have you decided to buy?"

"Mmm. I'm still considering the extras I could get for free."

The waiter cleared the plates, glasses, and took away the wine. Another came bearing a bottle of Mangaux red. He poured a little into Tom's glass and waited for Tom to taste it. A smooth delicate wine, it had a faint berry taste and fruity bouquet. He nodded and the waiter poured for them. The main course came, Melissa eyeing her lamb rack with interest. Tom had a roasted pork loin smothered with a mushroom sauce and little fried potatoes on the side. A large platter of chef's selected vegetables made up the salad.

Two more couples showed up, filling the room and the noise

level rose. Tom didn't notice them, his eyes on Melissa. The pork was delicious and the meat melted in his mouth, complemented by superb wine. She chatted about her day, the goings on among the senior Bureau directors, which made Tom chuckle from time to time. Mostly common gossip without revealing any confidences. She was far too professional to divulge any even to him and he didn't pry.

When the plates and cutlery were cleared away, both of them declining dessert, nursing espressos, Tom felt good. Judging from Melissa's bubbling conversation, she was also enjoying the evening. Feeling it was time, he caught the waiter's eye and nodded. Moments later, the waiter came to their table holding a small silver plate on which stood a black velvet box. He placed it in front of Tom and with a bow, withdrew.

Melissa saw the box and her eyes grew round. Her hand hovered on her chest, fingers splayed. Tom opened the box and held it to her. He cleared his throat and swallowed heavily.

"I'm not much good with fancy speeches, so I'll blurt this out in my clumsy way. My heart is yours, Melissa my love, and always will be. I want to make you mine forever. Will you marry me?" He took the diamond-encrusted ring out of its white silk setting, reached for her left hand and slid the ring onto her finger.

Eyes swimming, she studied the ring and bit her lip. When she looked up, she flashed him a radiant smile.

"You're a hopeless lug, Tom. I thought you'd never ask."

"Is that a yes?"

"Yes."

The couple next to them clapped and cheered. Tom beamed at them and nodded. Leaning across the table, he took Melissa's hand, turned it and kissed her palm.

"Your old man will approve," he said gruffly and she giggled.

"He's been waiting for you to make an honest woman out of me."

Squeezing her hand, he brushed her cheek. "Thank you."

"Let's go home," she said softly, eyes shining with happiness.

# Chapter Five

Keung Yang strode briskly down a wide, brightly lit corridor. As he neared the heavy ceiling-high door, two armed Ministry of Public Security guards snapped to attention, their worn AK-47 rifles grounded at their side. One of them opened the door and waited for the Standing Committee chairman to walk through, then softly closed it.

At the sight of the important visitor, the executive assistant scrambled to his feet and hurried to open a polished door leading into the inner office.

"The President is expecting you, sir."

Keung nodded and walked past him.

Watery sunshine dribbled through tall windows, olive drapes neatly tied back. Beyond the trees and manicured lawns, Keung could see the gray waters of Zhongnanhai's Central Sea lake. Summer had struck with a vengeance, as had the June rains, making Beijing a very uncomfortable place. Spacious but simple, the office not overly large. On his left two beige couches flanked a low coffee table inlaid with a traditional mountain setting against a black background. Steam rose from a white porcelain pot.

Zhou Yedong looked up from his computer screen and smiled faintly. On the wall behind him, Mao's pudgy face stared benignly into the room. Zhou stood up and extended a hand.

"Good to see you, Yang."

Keung grasped the proffered hand and squeezed firmly, weighing up Zhou's mood. The president was a year younger, yet looked more youthful. Keung knew he showed his age, but he wore the years with dignity, hoping his demeanor wasn't betraying a tiny flutter of uncertainty. Not an ordinary visit, a lot depended on what happened in the next few minutes.

"I trust you're well, Mr. President?"

"Tolerable. You used to call me Yedong, remember?"

"And sometimes other things," Keung said dryly and Zhou laughed.

"I don't doubt it. Let's make ourselves comfortable."

As Keung sat down, twitching his glasses into place, Zhou poured tea into two pale green jade cups. He mixed in brown sugar crystals and held out the cup. Keung nodded and took a sip, savoring the delicate flavor and aroma. Zhou sat on the opposite couch, arm extended over the backrest looking relaxed, but he had always been good at hiding emotion, keeping a reserve of energy to be unleashed on demand.

"You serve good tea as always," Keung commented, studying the Paramount Leader.

Impeccably dressed, at sixty-two, Zhou was still a striking man. Tall, muscled, a bulbous nose protruding beneath a high forehead, the Communist Party president carried his power well. Retired now, his father used to be director at the CMC's General Armament Department, but not before he saw his son entrenched within the Standing Committee. Born in Quanzhou, Fujian province, Zhou entered politics relatively late in life, devoting his energies into gaining an MBA at Stanford and running a number of state-owned companies. As a rising star in the elitist princeling coalition, he moved to Beijing and quickly installed as Secretary of the Central Commission for Discipline Inspection, a prize posting. Having made his mark, four years ago, he became premier of the State Council. He had an engaging grin, a good speaker, passionate in his convictions, and an expert in economics and international finance. Unfortunately, he was also Keung's enemy.

Zhou didn't display his enmity openly. That would have been beneath him. He dealt with his opponents using subtlety, having learned well the art of character assassination from his father, a minimum skill for anyone who sought power. Keung didn't take it personally. A simple difference of ideologies and vision, and neither of them was prepared to compromise. Not much anyway. Politics was a tiled tapestry of grays, which often confused the ordinary man on the street.

"It's an imported blend and I've developed a taste for it," Zhou said with a disarming smile, his eyes watching everything, gauging his opponent.

*Like your taste for all things Western*, Keung mused, glancing pointedly at the liquor cabinet with its array of European brandies and American bourbon mixed among bottles of local spirits. Zhou's years in America had corrupted him, or merely expanded his horizons. Keung wasn't sure which, but it didn't matter. The man had to be bent to his will or removed.

"The family. All are well?"

Zhou shrugged. "My son made full colonel in the Second Artillery Corps and he's only thirty-six. I'm naturally proud of him, but somebody in the CMC is sucking up to me."

Keung allowed himself a small smile. If anyone was sucking up, it had to be Han Yunshan, the CMC chairman, looking after the Party president's son while greasing his own ambitions. Officially, nepotism frowned upon—when practiced by lower Party echelons, but senior members saw to it that their offspring, family and relatives were looked after. Practiced for millennia, it was part of the Chinese psyche, something Westerners found difficult to grasp, seeing it as blatant corruption, not distinguishing between genuine criminal activity.

"I guess congratulations are in order."

Zhou waved a hand. "A dubious honor, Yang. Your Tuanpai colleagues will undoubtedly exploit this to their advantage."

"Not on something like this," Keung said seriously. "We all seek to advance the interests of our clans."

"True, but that's not going to stop them. Anyway, I have

more important matters on my mind."

"The unrest in Tibet?"

"That's one of them, but I was thinking of growing desertification. We're losing more than 4,000 square kilometers of arable land every year to the Gobi, and that's not the only place. It's not the loss of land *per se*, but displacement of local populations, which in turn puts additional pressure on urban centers and service infrastructure elsewhere. It's a reinforcing cycle without an easy solution."

"The reforestation programs are having an effect," Keung pointed out. "Last year we restored a record of 78,000 square kilometers of land."

Zhou shook a finger at him. "We planted trees, but we haven't recovered land suitable for farming, and our deserts are still growing."

"It will take time."

"Something we might not have." Zhou picked up his cup and sipped.

Keung leaned back. "What we really need to do is clean up our industrial emissions. That's what's killing us. An example or two needs to be made, Yedong, and you know it. We need to enforce our antipollution laws."

"Yes, I know, but you're the Standing Committee Chairman. You should be taking action."

"Things would get done if you and Dzhang Qishan supported me."

Zhou shifted and his face darkened. "We need to develop our economy!"

"Not at any price."

"Let's table this for now. You've been following the news?"

"About La Palma? Whoever did it made a major blunder."

"By not succeeding, you mean?"

"Exactly. A crippled America would have been a clipped eagle. Now we might face its wrath."

"You said 'we'."

Keung reached into his jacket pocket, extracted a folded paper and held it out. Frowning, Zhou took it, opened it and began reading. When he looked up, his eyes were bright with anger.

"So that's why you're here. How did you get this?"

"That's not important. What is important, it looks like Han Yunshan is guilty of treason."

"Only if this is genuine!" Zhou declared, waving the sheet. "You could have had this fabricated. It would be easy enough to do. It's no secret that you don't care much for Han and I know how you operate. Discrediting a senior member of the elitist coalition just as the National Congress is about to convene would undermine my authority, and you know it."

Keung shrugged. "We see things differently, but I don't disagree with everything you have done. If I really wanted to discredit you, I would have raised this at the full meeting of the Standing Committee. However, if those orders are genuine, we face something far more serious than our inter-factional squabbles, or the fact that a senior Politburo member sought to do this. Should America find evidence that we were responsible for the La Palma event, President Walters won't care about our factions. He'll target you and he'll target China."

"I believe you. What I don't believe are these orders. If Han did this, and I cannot see any reason why he would, he couldn't have been so stupid to leave evidence for you to conveniently unearth."

"Even the best of us can make a mistake, and you cannot tell me that Han hasn't been eyeing Dzhang Qishan's job, or yours. If he could point a finger at you as the architect of this monstrosity, some of your *taizidang* princeling supporters might believe him, leaving you in a very unenviable position. As far as I know, you may have told him to do it."

Zhou sat up and glared. "I'd be very careful saying that."

"I wasn't, but others will—if this got out," Keung said softly,

193

the unstated threat obvious.

"What would be his motive? If he sought to advance himself, he wouldn't attack America to do it. It doesn't make sense. No, it wasn't you who fabricated this cheap piece of paper, but your lackey, Chen Teng! He's after Han's job and everybody knows it."

"That doesn't make those orders invalid. Chen stumbled across them and, knowing their importance, brought them to my attention."

Zhou took a sip of tea, shook his head, and chuckled. "You're a top political mechanic, Yang, I'll give you that, and you think you may have me boxed into a corner. I advance your Tuanpai policies or you expose Han on trumped up evidence, but it won't work. This is nothing more than a blatant attempt on your part to protect Chen over the lost *Shang*. All you have is a piece of paper with Han's signature, probably forged. It wouldn't be difficult. You have no real proof that Han ordered one of our submarines to attack La Palma."

Keung nodded slowly. "No, I haven't any proof and I hope I'm wrong. I really do, but as I said, if the Americans find remains of our *Shang* at La Palma, the Tuanpai will be the least of your worries. Think what you will, but I came to see you because China could face disaster."

"Giving you an opportunity to milk political advantage out of it."

"Jin and jang, Mr. President."

Zhou stood up and began pacing, hands clasped behind his back. Eminently satisfied with the proceedings, Keung picked up his cup and drank. Of course he wanted to milk all the advantage he could out of the situation, Zhou was right about that. After all, he wasn't a bad political mechanic himself and knew how to work the system. Watching him pace, Keung almost felt sorry for the man. No matter what he did, Zhou faced possible personal oblivion, the undermining of the entire princeling coalition, and

American retaliation, perhaps even military. They were good at reacting, only afterward considering the consequence of their actions. Like a cowboy shooting from the hip, realizing later that he got the wrong man. Of course, America might not find anything at La Palma, which would leave Keung to deal with the domestic dimension only.

Zhou stopped and glared. "I'll have this investigated. If these orders turn out to be genuine, Han will face a firing squad. If they're a plant, which I suspect is the case, then you and Chen will be shot. That would include all your families. Are we perfectly clear?"

Keung nodded. "Given the gravity of this situation, I took some precautions before coming here. A small indiscretion on your part that would be more than a little embarrassing if it came to light, but never mind that. Should anything happen to me or Chen, or any member of our family, and I mean as much as a sniffle, I won't have the pleasure of seeing *you* shot, but I guess it won't matter to me then."

"You're threatening me?"

"No more than you're threatening me."

Zhou sighed. "The Navy investigation said the *Shang* was lost beyond the continental shelf."

"That's what the report said."

"But you don't believe it."

"I am told that Commander Vang Kai was one of Admiral Fang's best sub drivers. Regardless of any catastrophic failure he might have had, he would have sent up an emergency buoy."

"Not if he went beyond crush depth."

"If he approached crush depth, he would have known his boat was lost and would have launched."

"Mmm. You make annoyingly logical sense. So, instead of meeting his end during the *Peaceful Dragon* exercise, you think he is now at the bottom of the Atlantic off La Palma, ordered there by Han Yunshan."

"I hope not."

"Why seek to destroy it?"

Keung stirred restlessly. "Come on, Yedong. You know why."

"Remove evidence, yes. If there are any remains and the Americans find them—"

"Tell them the truth. It was a rogue operation conducted without your knowledge or authorization."

"And I hang Han out to dry, which would play nicely into your scheming hands. Even if Walters believed me, it would hardly be adequate, and I'd lose anyway. You and your supporters would use this to demonstrate the incompetency of my administration and force a power spill."

"Not if we made a deal."

Zhou looked thoughtful. "All this rests on the assumption the orders you showed me are genuine. For all I know, La Palma might be a natural event and you're exploiting it to further the Tuanpai agenda. I wouldn't put it past you. Not all scientists agree with Professor Degard's interpretation."

"True, but the Americans won't rest until they find out for sure."

"Don't fight me, Yang. Support me! Given time, both of us could emerge winners. An internal power struggle is the last thing this country needs right now, especially if it turns out that Han is guilty."

"You offer a pragmatic solution, Yedong, which I can understand. However, past experience has demonstrated that I cannot trust you."

"What do you want?"

"*The strength of a nation derives from the integrity of the home.* Confucius was wise when he said that. You are driving the country too quickly into a market economy mold, and in the process you're destroying our home. I support your initiative to make China a global power without equal, but not at any cost. Our economic miracle was bought on the back of unsustainable shadow banking. Unregulated credit in America triggered the Global Financial Crisis and ushered in a worldwide recession. Blatant profiteering by regional officials will do the same to us. Millionaires walk Beijing and Shanghai's main streets, while a block away slums show our real face. Your coalition talks about the rule of law, political reforms, economic prosperity for all, democratization of the Party apparatus, but it's only talk. Nothing is done to implement those policies. Where is the promotion of social justice, government accountability, and curbing genuine corruption? I want you and the State Council to balance our leap into a modern society by acting on your rhetoric."

Zhou lifted his chin and glared. "Or what?"

"Or justice will be meted to us by others."

"You know what I think, you son of a bitch? I think *you're* behind all this. It has your stamp."

Keung smiled. "You give me far too much credit. I am merely a humble servant of the Party."

Zhou laughed, but it had a sour ring. "Humble servant? I'm yet to see you humbled, but I don't have time to play games with you. I have a government to run. I'll dig into this, and when I uncover the truth, we shall have another conversation."

"If you want my support, Mr. President, pay the price," Keung said bluntly and stood up. "Thank you for the tea. Can I impose on you for a tin?"

"I'll have some sent to your office."

Keung nodded and walked out, feeling Zhou's eyes burning into his back.

\* \* \*

When the door closed behind Keung's retreating form, Zhou uttered a sharp expletive. Could the manipulating bastard be right

and he harbored a snake in his bed? The friendship he had culti-
vated with Han Yunshan over the last eight years saw both of
them rise steadily within the Party. They had their differences and
debated them like they mattered. As a military man, Han's focus,
although parochial, was firmly rooted in political reality, understanding fully the competing elements of China's tactical and
strategic defense posture: policy, service needs and available resources. Han had spent a career juggling those elements, pushing
a reluctant Politburo into a modernization drive, discarding the
outdated notion that a tactical nuke could replace conventional
power projection.

Keung was right when he said that Han was ambitious and
had sufficient support to possibly topple Dzhang Qishan. From
the State Council premier it would be a short step to president,
and Zhou could find himself marginalized, serving the remainder
of his years in Fujian as another disgraced Party hack—if he were
lucky. He chewed his lower lip, not believing it. With the National
Congress only five months off, he was vigorously networking
Politburo delegates, shoring up his own position and seeing to it
that his elitist coalition supporters were looked after. Nothing in
the wind indicated that Han intended to use the Congress to
launch a move, but then, such things were rarely advertised. A
spill simply happened to the dismay of those most affected. Still,
some rumors always circulated and he hadn't heard anything.

Besides, if Han planned to move, why initiate something as-
inine like an attack on La Palma? A pragmatic military commander, Han didn't harbor fanatic revulsion of all things American. Spouting anti-capitalistic rhetoric was done for domestic
consumption and never entertained too seriously by higher Party
echelons. Zhou suspected the people at large didn't pay much
attention to Party spoutings either. He only had to look at China
embracing a market economy as proof. Working for the fictional
benefit of the state in the name of the people was a bankrupt

ideology, demonstrated all too clearly by the defunct Soviet agricultural collective policy and centralized management. National wealth was created by individuals who were able to count personal profit from their enterprise and benefit from it. By triggering a natural catastrophe, even though it had not seriously damaged America, the aftermath from international retaliation could still sweep Zhou and Han out of office, leaving the way open for the Tuanpai to step in.

Tossing it around, Zhou simply couldn't see it. Han just wasn't that devious, but Keung definitely had it in him. Softly spoken, quietly wise, deeply philosophical, a paradigm of social dialectical reasoning, he sought to steer directional change, not fracture it.

Zhou glanced at the damning paper in his hand, snorted, and shook his head, forced to admire Keung's smooth style. His enemy would never advance further, seemingly content to be the king maker, manipulating the Party, the Politburo, and Standing Committee members with consummate touches. If Keung wasn't after more power, who was he grooming? That shit Chen Teng? Zhou didn't believe it. Chen was capable, but he didn't have the drive, vision and ruthlessness to claw for the top. Another and simpler explanation occurred to him and he frowned, realizing that Keung had already told him what he wanted—promote Tuanpai platforms. The old hack wasn't seeking more personal authority. He had enough already. He genuinely believed that current Politburo policies threatened China's social fabric and future. To change that future, Keung would not hesitate to topple Han Yunshan—if those orders were genuine, which Zhou firmly didn't believe.

If they were not, it meant that Keung and Chen had concocted a fantastic plot straight out of the Sun Tzu manual. Was it Keung, though? As commander of the PLA Navy, Admiral Xhal Shenglai had all the instruments at his disposal to orchestrate La Palma, and his antipathy toward America well known.

Afterward, to divert possible attention from himself, it wouldn't have taken much to pass a set of forged orders to Chen, incriminating Han, then sit back while everybody around him self-destructed.

Zhou needed to find out. Too much at stake for him not to know. He stepped to his desk and pressed a white button on the phone pad.

"Yes, sir?"

"I want to see General Han Yunshan. Now!" he snapped and cut contact.

He sat down and his fingers drummed against the desk. Making up his mind, he pressed a direct dial button. A heavy voice answered after two rings.

"General Lin Jinpan."

"It's Zhou Yedong, General."

"Sir!"

Zhou smiled, clearly picturing the Minister of State Security jumping to his feet.

"I have a job for you, General. Use whatever resources you need, including the Military Intelligence Second Department. I want you on this now and I expect a report within ten days."

"Understood."

"I'm sending you a copy of an order supposedly prepared by General Han Yunshan. I want verification that he in fact signed that order. Once you see it, you will understand the difficulty that order creates for me."

"Sir, verification might not be possible."

"The thought had occurred to me, General. You will therefore initiate a parallel investigation of Keung Yang, Chen Teng, and Admiral Xhal as potential sources."

"Understood."

"And General? These men are very senior Party officials and are not to be approached directly. Do you understand me?"

"Completely, sir."

"Ten days," Zhou reminded him and cut contact.

He ran a marginal risk giving the job to Lin, a known Tuanpai sympathizer, although he supported a number of elitist policies—pragmatism at work. However, given the nature of the investigation and possible repercussions, he felt that Lin would not be so foolish to risk his wrath by sabotaging the assignment. Nevertheless, given the volatile nature of Keung's document, he'll have his assistant make a copy—just in case.

He poured himself a fresh cup of tea, sat behind his desk, and sipped the fragrant brew, feeling himself relax. Hating to admit it, Keung was right about one thing. During the Global Financial Crisis the government had largely shielded China from the worst effects of a stalled world economy by pumping huge amounts of credit into infrastructure projects. When the crisis eased and the credit tap closed, enterprising local officials turned to unregulated shadow banks for financing, running up enormous debts they might not be able to repay if asset values fell below acquisition cost. A lot of them got rich in the process, but it was pure profiteering. Some paid for flaunting Beijing edicts with lengthy prison terms, but the provinces were far away from Beijing and enforcement not always easily implemented.

It would take only a few nervous shadow bankers to call in their loans and China could very well experience a financial crisis far greater than what the Americans went through. The impact on the recovering world economy didn't bear thinking about, but sweeping away the shadow banks turned out to be difficult, entrenched as they were in the Chinese underground economy. Stepping on them too hard could trigger the very calamity the government wanted to avoid. However, something needed to be done to curb their influence. Fiscal policy came from Beijing, not some backyard money shark!

The issue right now though, was to neutralize his populist enemy. Zhou could not ignore the threat to his power, even if it meant sending the country into recession. The supremacy of his coalition within the Politburo must remain unquestioned. If one crack was allowed to widen, the stability of the Party itself might come under scrutiny by the population at large, something far more threatening than any potential economic turmoil. He would expose Keung's allegation for the falsehood it was, and the coming National Congress would see the wily manipulator stripped of power and banished into political oblivion. Time then to stage a public trial and make that banishment more than just political— provided Han's orders turned out to be a forgery.

What if he admitted to Walters that a PLAN attack boat caused the La Palma slump? No, announce it at the UN, offering total reparations to Spain and America. China may not escape total international backlash even if he was believed, but Keung's threat to unseat him might be neutralized. Some heads may have to roll, including Han and Chen's, but it would be a small price to pay. More importantly, Keung himself could be marginalized. Instinct told him that he should do this now rather than wait until the Americans found the *Shang's* remains, if the thing was there at all. Making an announcement after it was discovered would sound too much like ass covering, which would be right. No, he would wait and see, fearing his decision might be destroying a valuable friendship with President Walters.

Damn Keung and all Tuanpai!

Twenty minutes later—that's probably how long it took to drive from the Ministry of National Defense—his assistant knocked on the door and held it open.

"General Han Yunshan, sir."

"Show him in, and I don't want to be disturbed," Zhou growled.

"Yes, sir."

Decked out in a smart uniform, the left side of his chest covered with rows of colored ribbons, Han marched in, stopped before Zhou's desk, took off his braided cap, nodded and smiled.

"Hell of a drive to get here and it's getting worse all the

time."

"So they tell me." Zhou glanced at his assistant and waited for the door to close.

He picked up the creased sheet off his desk and held it out. Looking uncertain, Han stepped forward and reached for the paper. Zhou watched the short man closely as he scanned the page, giving a startled hiss. Face pale, Han looked up, his hand trembling.

"Well?" Zhou prompted mildly.

Han swallowed and flung the paper on the desk. "This is a fabrication! I signed no such order. You think me mad?"

"That's your signature."

"A clumsy forgery! To contemplate something like that is monstrous."

"It definitely is." Zhou sat back and sighed. "Those orders place me in a most awkward position, Han. If in fact one of your submarines was responsible for the La Palma slump, regardless of who issued the order, this constitutes a severe breakdown in our command and control procedures. Do you agree?"

Han's mouth worked, but nothing came out, realizing that whatever he said, he would be damning himself, which is what Zhou's question intended. The Central Military Commission chairman composed himself and straightened.

"The order has an authenticator. If confirmed by the submarine commander, he was compelled to obey."

"I see. Without question?"

"The PLA doesn't question authenticated orders."

Zhou nodded slowly. No, the PLA no longer questioned CMC authority. Deng Xiaoping had seen to that.

"How did you get hold of that paper?" Han demanded.

"Keung Yang delivered it to me."

"Keung! There you have it. He got that creep Chen Teng to prepare it and they're using it to discredit me and damage your position."

"Possibly, but that's still your signature, Han, and I have seen enough of them to tell that it's real. Is it?"

Han's shoulder sagged, his face wreathed in misery. "It looks real enough, but Chen has often signed my name, without permission, of course."

"To oil the wheels of CMC bureaucracy? I know how these things work, Han. However done, it's a grave breach of procedure and abuse of your authority. As the CMC Chairman, it demonstrates a level of incompetency."

Han's black eyes flashed with fire, something Zhou was glad to see. This didn't look like a man trapped in a conspiracy. Of course, Han could be putting up a superb front.

"You want me whitewashed, Yedong?" Han pointed at the door. "How many orders has that man out there signed in *your* name?"

"Take it easy."

"Take it easy? I'm accused of initiating a possible global backlash against my country, a coup against you, and you're telling me to take it easy? If you have proof that I issued those orders, then shoot me. Otherwise, I'd suggest you go after the real perpetrators."

"I already have." Zhou's fingers tapped against the desk. "There is a way to prove your innocence, and I must know that you *are* innocent. The alternative is to relieve you on the spot and place you under close arrest."

"You want to question me under drugs?" Han straightened and glared. "I am a general in the People's Liberation Army and CMC Chairman, not some lowly lieutenant you can frighten. If you arrest me without evidence, you'll split the elitist coalition, giving Keung and his Tuanpai rebels the ammunition to bring us all down. I don't think you want to do that."

"No, I don't want that, but I must know if you wrote that document."

"I didn't, and you can believe me or not."

"And be damned, is that it?" Zhou was almost convinced.

Nothing in Han's writing, speeches and actions indicated he was capable of launching something like La Palma. A traditional soldier turned Party politician, he wasn't a manipulator, not in Keung's mold. Han was what one saw. He was either liked or loathed with no middle ground. Besides, why launch a strike at America through La Palma? It broke all the rules of military doctrine. Zhou simply couldn't see Han capable of such subtlety.

Frowning, he nodded. "All right, I believe you."

"But you'll still check me out, right?" Han demanded looking amused, and Zhou chuckled.

"I will, as you know I must. There is a simple solution to all this. Submit to a polygraph test."

"I won't, and you can't force me."

"Then you leave me no choice but to have you investigated."

"Chen's behind this. I know it."

"But how do we prove it?"

Han shook his head. "Provided he hasn't stored something on his computer or blabbed to somebody, I'm afraid you can't. With something like this, he would be very careful. You'll need to establish a link between him and Keung."

"What about Admiral Fang Youxial? He is Chen's protégé and the lost *Shang* was part of his fleet."

Han waved a hand in dismissal. "He was an innocent go-between. Chen would never have revealed the contents of those orders and leave himself open to blackmail."

"You weren't so magnanimous during the investigation into the *Shang's* loss."

"Fang already had his orders. Any change to the *Jing Long* exercise would have come from Admiral Xhal Shenglai. Fang should not have accepted Chen's orders."

"Under strict chain of command rules, no, but Chen is the CMC Vice Chairman. We both know how the game is played, Han."

"And that's why Fang only got a reprimand instead of getting shot."

"Could Xhal Shenglai have orchestrated La Palma, then forged those orders to frame you?" Zhou asked softly and Han gaped.

"Xhal? He definitely had the authority, but frankly, I don't see it. He is a loyal officer."

Zhou stared thoughtfully at his friend. He had given Han an open opportunity to shift attention away from himself, but the transparently honest response did more than anything to convince him of the man's innocence—almost. He would still have him investigated.

"Yes, that's what I thought." Zhou stood up and waved at a couch where only minutes ago, Keung had sat.

"Pour yourself some tea. We need to talk."

\* \* \*

CONSPIRACY THEORISTS HAVING A FIELD DAY
LA PALMA A NATURAL EVENT, SKEPTICS CLAIM
PRESIDENT SEEKS HELP TO FIND PERPETRATORS
WORLD OFFERS AID TO REBUILD LA PALMA

"Hurrah," Tom Meecham muttered, throwing the *Washington Post* on his desk.

Last night, he watched President Walters address the UN General Assembly. Standing tall, face set in an expression of grim resolve, clasping the lectern sides, he spoke calmly, but with quiet authority. No one could mistake the determination in his voice to track down those responsible for triggering the La Palma event, urging unprecedented cooperation from intelligence agencies everywhere. Faced with the specter that somebody else might be tempted to emulate this experiment, all nations must stand united and exact savage retribution against those responsible. Although the world had escaped devastation, no effort should be spared to repair the massive damage caused to La Palma.

Looking tired, but very presidential, Walters received a standing ovation from the floor. A moving spectacle that for a brief moment united the world against a common unknown enemy, but Tom wondered whether that applause would be translated into tangible action by cynical, self-absorbed governments back home. After all, apart from some minor coastal damage along the eastern Atlantic rim, there was really nothing to get excited about. Some countries may even have secretly regretted that America got off so lightly. As for La Palma, well, people there knew they were sitting on a ticking time bomb that would have gone off sooner or later. The island's western coast should never have been settled, but people lived in the shadow of active volcanoes all over the world. Go figure.

Following the speech, there was inevitable handshaking and back slapping among attending dignitaries. Seeing the broad smiles, Tom keenly wanted to know who among those dignitaries knew the truth. As he thought about it, he decided that no one did. Whoever executed this operation would want to keep it deeper than black, which was perfectly understandable.

He gulped down the last of his tepid coffee, got up and strode out of the office, hoping this afternoon's status meeting wouldn't drag on for too long. He and Melissa were going out and he didn't want to be too tired to enjoy the evening. It shouldn't, as nobody had come up with anything, which caused his boss to frown at him with suppressed frustration. What the hell did Hancock expect? It's only been three days. Then again, Hancock must be feeling the heat from the White House, equally frustrated by lack of progress. In turn, the White House got sandbagged by Congress and the papers. As the point man, Tom was also getting it from all sides. He decided that life in Houston used to be much easier.

He walked into the meeting room, nodded to the four men already sitting, and pulled back a chair at the head of the table. Without bothering with any preliminaries, he looked at Clavel.

"What have you got?"

The older man cleared his throat and straightened a pile of notes.

"The most likely non-nuclear weapon used at La Palma, supported by Professor Degard's analysis, is a series of thermobaric mines. Nothing else could have produced the necessary yield."

Andre Norton raised a finger. "Evidence?"

"The *Okeanos Explorer* will be off La Palma in three days. Hopefully, they'll dig up some evidence then."

Tom waved a hand. "Wait a minute. I thought those things are fuel-air weapons."

"They are," Clavel said, "but we've developed naval variants that can be deployed from a submarine or surface mine layer."

"Christ!" Tom peered at Davenport. "Who has the capability to produce them?"

The CIA man returned his gaze. "Apart from us, it's a pretty small club. The Russians have them, as do the Chinese and the French. The things are infernally complicated and temperamental, at least the submarine launched ones are. A torpedo tube has only so much space. We have a working prototype of a vertically launched variant, but that's designed for atmospheric detonation."

"What about surface deployed mines?"

"They were easier to manufacture as designers didn't face shape and weight constraints."

"So, we're looking for a submarine, right?" Tom looked from face to face for confirmation.

"Probably," Davenport said. "It's an ideal stealth delivery platform."

"I agree," Clavel added. "We're checking shipping movements, but given that deployment close to the shore would have taken some time, and likely done from a large vessel, a ship would be noticed. The National Imagery and Mapping Agency has poured over satellite data and came up empty."

"The mines could have been laid sporadically," Isaac Federer, the ITOS-II boss, commented dryly.

"They thought of that," Clavel said. "So far, they have only looked at a month's worth of data. They'll keep at it until they've gone back six months."

"It doesn't sound like we're looking for a ship," Tom said, rubbing his chin. "Whoever pulled this stunt would want to do it in a single evolution. Messing around over a protracted period would only increase exposure and threaten operational security. Besides, somebody would have commented if they saw a large ship loitering off La Palma's coast. Using the same argument, I would also discount an aircraft. These mines must be pretty heavy—"

"Five to seven metric tons," Clavel said.

"—which might have required a number of drops. Is NIMA checking for aircraft?"

"They are. Nothing so far."

"And I don't expect them to find any. According to Degard, to produce the observed reinforcing wave detonations, the mines had to be positioned at precise intervals and depth. Dropping them from an aircraft wouldn't cut it. The things would hit bottom and roll all over the place."

"I'd go along with that," Norton said.

"Has anybody reported sighting a submarine off La Palma?"

Federer sighed. "If this was done by a submarine, Tom, they wouldn't be foolish enough to surface and risk being seen. They might have stuck up a radar mast or search scope to check their position, but that's about it."

"A submarine, presumably nuclear, had to have come from *somewhere*," Tom insisted. "Do we have any data on foreign attack subs or boomer movements?"

"I'll look into it," Clavel said.

"The Navy may have something," Federer mused.

Davenport shifted in his seat. "Tom, you seem to be gravitating toward a conclusion that a foreign country did this."

"I am, and I'll tell you why. The way I see it, no terrorist group, regardless of how well financed, would be able to acquire the required quantity of mines for the job, let alone commandeer a submarine to deliver them. Do we know how many of those things the Navy has?"

"They're still under development and existing inventory is tightly controlled." Davenport raised a hand. "I know what you're thinking. Russian nukes were supposed to be tightly controlled also and some have disappeared anyway, but they've polished their act."

"You just proved my point," Tom said. "It's unlikely that whoever has these mines would be selling a dozen or so to Al Qaida or some other raghead outfit. No, I'd say this was a premeditated government operation."

"What if it wasn't?" Davenport said softly, and everybody looked at him. "It could have been a rogue black ops, you know. Mossad did the same thing two years ago when they sabotaged the Valero Texas City Refinery."

"You're spoiling a great day with that kind of talk, Keith," Tom growled, which raised some chuckles.

The head of ITOS I shifted in his seat. "You're talking about appropriating an attack submarine with a full weapons load, have its commanding officer sail to La Palma and drop his load without anybody knowing about it?"

Davenport looked directly at Andre Norton. "It occurs to me that all three elements could have been fulfilled quite easily during the recent Chinese *Jing Long* naval exercise."

Federer steepled his fingers. "You're saying that a submarine sailed all the way from Hainan Island? Do their *Shangs* have that kind of range?"

"It's a nuclear boat. Those things can run forever, limited only by how much supplies it can carry."

Tom frowned. "Do we have anybody mad enough at Uncle Sam in Russia or China to do this?"

"You left out France," Norton remarked.

"We haven't done anything nasty to the French lately. Boeing is murdering their Airbus sales, but I don't think that's enough of a motive to bend their Gallic demeanor out of shape. They may not have a motive, but would Russia or China, or somebody in their government, have one? I'm making a concession to your rogue ops idea, Keith."

"I noticed."

"We need this checked out. However interesting, our primary focus right now is to identify method of delivery, which Degard will hopefully provide. Once we have that, it really doesn't matter what kind of weapon was used. Means and opportunity, gentlemen. Once we find out how the weapons were delivered and identify the manufacturer—if we can—we'll be able to turn our attention on possible perpetrators. Profiling some of the Russian and Chinese Politburo movers would be useful. Rod, ask the Counterterrorism Center to dig into it."

"I'll get on it," Clavel said. "If somebody did use a thermobaric mine, we'll never find any evidence. The blast would have vaporized everything and the debris avalanche has most likely buried the submarine, if it was a sub."

"You're probably right, but we won't know until Degard starts looking. If we do find remains of a sub and can identify it, our job will only be partially done. We still need to nail down the perpetrators. Once we can name them, President Walters can handle the ensuing political dimension and he's welcome to it."

Federer exhaled loudly. "We might not be able to find out who planned this, Tom."

"I'm aware of the difficulties. That's why it's important that we get those profiles. Finding a sub will be our smoking gun, but

211

we need to tell the President who pulled the trigger. Anybody has anything else? No?" Tom stood up and looked at them. "Remember. Nothing is too insignificant, no matter how innocuous it might seem. We cannot afford to assume or overlook anything." He nodded and walked out.

*Christ!* He was starting to sound like his boss.

Tom recalled his conversations with Hancock. Without realizing it, he had adopted the same 'carry it out' voice his boss used. He could not believe that he had turned into another bombastic management type, toeing the Bureau line, insensitive to individuals in his sections. No, he was sensitive enough, the simmering problem with Clavel attested to that. Or did it? Clavel didn't get Ops I and Tom did, that's all there was to it. The older agent had to accept how things were or transfer someplace else. Tom could not afford to have Clavel's attitude affect the efficiency of his investigation. Peeling away the HR crap, Tom was in charge and his sections did what they were told or got reamed. He wasn't there to be anybody's buddy, but to get the job done. If somebody failed to measure up, they'd get replaced, as Hancock would replace him if he faltered. The Bureau wasn't a kindergarten.

He paused before his office and smiled. He *did* sound like his boss!

As a junior agent, he had bitched with his colleagues about the stupidity of convoluted procedures, heartless management, and dinosaur bureaucracy, promising themselves when they took over, things would be different. Well, he was in charge now. Did his agents talk about him like he used to moan about his superiors? Those were the good old days, all right, but it was just nostalgia. He wouldn't want to live those days again.

Boiled down, his men were tools, like he was a tool.

After he powered up the computer, he picked up his coffee mug and ambled to the kitchenette for a refill. Trawling through the alarmingly long list of emails, he exhaled loudly, took a sip and opened the first one. The phone rang and he groped for the receiver, his eyes on the screen.

"Meecham!"

"And a good morning to you too," Mark Price said amiably. "Getting grumpier, are we? Things not going well?"

Tom leaned back and relaxed, Mark's sarcasm washing away his concerns. Whatever problems he had were minor compared to what the CIA chief must be handling. Sure, Mark unwound when they had a drink together, but he never complained, always looking for angles how to deal with his problems. Maintain an even strain, his friend had told him more than once.

"You're right, I'm getting grumpier and things aren't going well, but your call has brightened my otherwise dull day. And thanks for getting back to me."

"Hang in there, my boy. I don't always feel bouncy either. Things will break, they always do."

"If they don't, I'll come knocking. Perhaps the CIA can use somebody who was once regarded pretty highly."

"That's the spirit. Remember, it's only been three days."

"Doesn't feel like it. I got a call from Graham Stone last night. He wanted to know if I had anything."

"And…"

"I told him that he would be the first to know and almost hung up on him."

"Doing that to the National Security Advisor wouldn't have been smart."

"I guess the President wants answers and is turning on the heat."

"And you're getting it all. I know the feeling. There is a bright side. This job will polish your diplomatic skills."

"You mean that up to now, I've been rubbing everybody the wrong way?" Tom demanded in outrage, and Price laughed.

"It's an unjust world. You wanted to talk about something or feeling sorry for yourself?"

"Both. I may have a problem with Clavel and I want to nip

it in the bud. What's his performance been like in your Counter-terrorism Center?"

"Funny you should mention him. I popped into one of their meetings the other day to see how the wheels were turning. The impression I got, his mind was on other things. You read his latest evaluation?"

"I did. He looks good on paper, but anyone can shine when things are quiet. Bruce Wellard noted that Clavel needed more field work."

"That's the impression I got. He considers himself a thinker-upper, not a carry-outer. It's no secret that he wanted Ops I."

"You guys have long ears," Tom remarked darkly.

"That's the business we're in. You looking to replace him?"

"I'm tempted, but he hasn't done anything to warrant it. Has anything fallen off the NSA tree?"

"Nobody's saying anything. We're still sifting through stuff from the recent Chinese naval exercise."

"Is that the one where they lost one of their attack subs?"

"That's it."

"Have we offered to help find it? Walters and Zhou Yedong seem to have hit it off when they met. Giving them a helping hand might impress them."

"Or they could tell us to mind our own business. Still, it's a thought. I'll mention it to the President, but I wouldn't be surprised if Stone or Tanner haven't already discussed it with him."

Price's casual mention of the president sobered Tom, having forgotten who his friend was. As DCIA, Price wielded real power and rubbed shoulders with some high-ranking people. The two of them may have an occasional round of golf, but Tom should not presume too much on their friendship.

"You do that," he said absently, remembering something that made his skin prickle. "Mark, that Chinese attack sub. What if it wasn't lost?"

For a few seconds, he only heard deep breathing.

"Well, crap! You're full of bright ideas, aren't you."

"Keith Davenport floated the possibility that La Palma was a rogue ops and I more or less shot him down. I considered the idea too ridiculous. My bad."

"You have a good man in Keith."

"I like the way he thinks."

"And I like the way you connected the dots, my boy. Offering our help to find that boat might be very important after all. We have the technology and it would be a terrific way to evaluate their response."

"Get a feel if this was an official ops or somebody's off the shelf plan?"

"You got it. Or maybe they won't care, knowing the sub was disposed of."

"Lying at the bottom of the Atlantic, buried," Tom murmured.

"What might be left of it. If caught in a cascaded thermobaric detonation, we'll only find slag, if that."

"Mark, it doesn't matter if the ops was official or not, presuming the Chinese did it. That sub had to be disposed of in a way that it would disappear forever, including anybody who might have had anything to do with the plan."

"Wipe the evidence trail, eh? Thin, but it's something we can look into. Somebody may know something. Then again, it could have suffered a plain old accident and is now at the bottom of the South China Sea."

"We won't know if we don't look."

"You got that right."

"I'll have Clavel check it out. If his ship doesn't have a mishap, Degard will be at La Palma in three days and then we'll know."

"If he finds something."

"There you go again, more pessimism. There is one more thing that's got me focused on China, though. Going over the

White House meeting minutes, Professor Degard said something that has me bothered. He said he got the idea to look at the La Palma seismic data from a paper delivered at a recent University of Hawaii symposium by Professor Wei Xhulai from Peking University. However, it wasn't his paper. They slotted him in as a replacement for Professor Chuan Jianbo, who apparently met with an untimely fatal accident."

"Well, crap! Accidents do happen, you know."

"For sure, but think about it. Let's suppose someone in the Chinese hierarchy dreamed up this scenario. He would need expert help to validate the feasibility of his idea. You see what I'm getting at?"

After a moment of poignant silence, Price sighed. "Tom, you're creepy. Did you know that?"

"My last girlfriend mentioned it once or twice," Tom said, grinning broadly, thinking of Malena as they lay entwined in pillow talk.

"I can see why. I'll have someone check it out. Despite some very circumstantial evidence, it might not be China at all."

"I know. I'm simply keeping my options open."

This was probably a waste of everybody's time, but as far as Tom was concerned, the dots were connected. Besides, nobody had anything else. He'll have a quiet word with Clavel, wanting him to be in the loop on this.

"You got any other options open, or you want to bend my ear?"

Tom took a deep breath and made the plunge. The problem would not get resolved if everybody sat on their hands.

"There is something you could look into for me."

"What's that?"

"Professor Degard suggested that whoever did La Palma might try again to finish the job."

"Well, crap! He is one gloomy character, and so are you. Unfortunately, what he said makes a lot of sense; too much to be ignored. I'll look into it. Be calling you," Price said, and hung up.

Tom gently replaced the receiver. The phone immediately rang and he picked up. "Meecham."

"Hancock. Can you come and see me?"

*Christ!* He didn't need more hand holding. "Be right there, boss."

He walked into the assistant director's office and waited. Hancock looked up from his pile of paperwork and waved at a seat.

"How's the investigation?"

Tom ran four cases, but he knew Hancock was interested in only one of them.

"Apart from identifying the likely explosive used, and that's only speculation, we won't have anything until Professor Degard's ship arrives at La Palma."

"Not much to show for three days' work."

"We don't have much to go on, boss."

"Humor me."

"The Chinese attack sub they lost during the *Jing Long* exercise? It could have been the delivery vehicle. We're following it up."

Hancock raised an eyebrow. "Interesting, if true."

"Christ, boss! Don't spread it around, okay? It will get people excited, demanding that we deploy the 7th Fleet. We're just stirring tea leaves right now."

"My ears only, but at least you have a lead, tenuous as it might be. By the way, congratulations on your engagement."

Tom smiled. "Thanks. I'm still not sure I'm doing the right thing."

"No one is ever sure about these things. Anything else?"

Tom locked eyes with his boss. "I want to ask Admiral Parker to monitor likely breakout routes a Chinese submarine might take if it planned to head for the Southern Indian Ocean. I also want elements of the 6th Fleet to sanitize approaches to La

Palma."

Hancock's eyes bulged. "You know what you're saying?"

"It's possible that whoever attacked La Palma might try again. It's also possible that China carried out the first attack."

"You don't have evidence to accuse China or anyone else of anything, and on that basis, you want to deploy a substantial fraction of our naval forces?"

"Until I do get solid evidence that identifies the perpetrator, I'm suggesting that we take reasonable precaution, that's all. The 7th Fleet is already in place, boss. So is the 6th. It's not like we're asking for a major deployment."

Hancock exhaled and his shoulders sagged. "I'll have to take this up with Marshal, and he'll probably take it up with the President. Who knows about this?"

"Professor Degard. He made the observation. I also talked to Mark Price."

"I see. You're a bloody pain, Meecham. Okay, leave it with me. Anyway, the reason why I wanted to see you, Clavel made a complaint about you."

Tom felt anger well inside him. "Oh?"

"He wanted to get a few things off his chest...about you. His lack of leadership, and I'm quoting, is jeopardizing this investigation—"

"And as the CIA point man, I should be in charge," Tom finished for him.

"His words almost exactly. Remember what I told you about fighting turf fires? Clavel is your problem. Deal with it."

"I'm dealing with it."

"You want him moved?"

"I'll try to bring him around first."

"Good. These things will come up from time to time and they'll get more complex as you gain seniority and authority. How you deal with them can sometimes be more important than how you handle your case load. It sucks, but that's how it is. That's all,

Tom."

Closing the door after him, Tom snorted and shook his head. Managing office politics wasn't something he relished, but his boss was right. Could he rehabilitate Clavel?

He walked to Marsha's desk and stopped. "Call Clavel and tell him I want to see him. If he's left for Langley, I want him here tomorrow at ten."

Her mouth twitched. "Will do."

Looking at her, Tom knew that rumors were already flying. He didn't mind. People needed something to gossip about and they had a lot of material to pick over.

The coffee he had left on his desk had gone cold. Nothing for it but get a fresh cup. After filling up, walking back to his office, he saw Clavel approaching. The older man set his mouth and nodded.

"You wanted to see me, Tom?"

"Yes, I did. Come on in."

Clavel closed the door after him and waited. Tom waved at a seat.

"You're going back to Langley?"

"I was just leaving when Marsha called me," Clavel said as he eased himself into a chair, looking wary.

"This won't take long. I had a chat with Mark Price about something Davenport said that La Palma was a rogue ops. I didn't think much of it, but he could be onto something. You know the Chinese lost an attack sub?"

"It supposedly went down off the continental shelf during the *Jing Long* exercise," Clavel said softly, holding himself rigid, hands across his chest.

"That's the point. What if it didn't?"

"You mean—"

"It may have had special orders, like delivering mines. Anyway, Price thinks it's worth looking into, and I wanted you in the loop."

"Okay. If that's all…"

"There is one more thing, Rod. You lodged a complaint about me with Hancock. That's your privilege, but if you have a problem working with me, you should have spoken to me first. You resent that I got Ops I and you didn't, and you're taking it out on me. It's a natural reaction, but you need to get over it. If you can't, apply for a transfer and I'll endorse it. What I don't want is have you walking around with a chip on your shoulder, undermining me and this investigation. Is that clear?"

"Clear enough. Can I think about it?"

"Get back to me by close of business today."

Frowning, Clavel nodded and stood up. Hesitating for a second, he opened the door and walked out.

Tom stared after him and sighed. He had a sneaky feeling that this wasn't going to work out at all.

* * *

Vice Admiral David Owen dashed off his signature on the weekly logistics report, rubbed his eyes, and leaned back against his very comfortable leather chair. It squeaked as he crossed his legs and pushed back the computer keyboard. Reports, that's all he seemed to be handling these days. Life as a cruiser captain used to be more fun. Hell, that's why he joined the Navy, to be at sea! The closest he came to the sea now was watching the Yokosuka harbor from his window as other skippers took their ships out. Damn them all. He had three stars and they only had three or four stripes—and being seasick.

He was the one who told them, and everybody else, what to do and where to go, and they jumped when he barked. It made up for the rest, most of the time. His stars came with heavy responsibility, but he wore his duty easily. Like with everything else, one learned by doing, and he did it very well. Still, if he was that good, why hadn't the CNO given him his fourth star? Was Parker worried that a younger dog would eat him? The thought made him smile. Owen wanted that star badly, but he wasn't after Parker's job. He was a theater commander and liked it that way, reports and all. Besides, if he didn't have anything to sign, somebody might start to wonder if he was needed. Bureaucrats! Bah!

The intercom buzzer went off and Owen pressed a button on his multifunction phone pad. "Talk to me."

"Captain Ronald Briggs to see you, sir," his aide announced briskly, and Owen allowed himself a small smile.

The young lieutenant had grown into his role and wasn't overawed anymore by his position or the 7th Fleet commander. That was good. Owen liked his officers to show spunk, without being insubordinate, of course. There were limits to be observed.

"Show him in."

Briggs opened the heavy door and strode in, pulled back a visitor chair and lowered his impressive bulk without asking permission. The man hadn't bothered to salute either, but he was an intelligence weenie, and all intel types were characters. Clearly, Briggs didn't worry about limits. Owen put up with him because Briggs was the best at what he did, far more important than saluting or having pressed pants.

"You look puffed out, Ron."

"I had to walk all the way from Communications," Briggs declared heavily as he wiped his face. "I almost didn't make it."

"If you exercised more, you wouldn't be out of breath all the time. You should stop shoveling in all that junk food. That stuff will kill you one day."

"We all have to go sometime, Admiral. Besides, normal Navy chow lacks the necessary calories to keep me moving. All those fancy diets and rabbit food they keep giving us to keep us healthy, when in reality—and I got the straight dope on this—it's really designed to slowly emaciate us."

Chuckling, Owen spread his arms in defeat. "Okay, Ron. You're suffering and I'll put you up for a decoration. So, what's so important to make you crawl out of your hole to see me?"

"That Chinese *Qin* fast boomer that sortied out of their Qin-gado naval base yesterday."

Owen looked disgusted. "The one with the magnetic fluid water jet propulsion drive and no screw? Supposed to be able to do 100 knots or some ridiculous thing?"

"That's the one."

"Balls, if you asked me. If that were true, those things make our *Virginia* boats look like Model Ts. For Chrissake, Rod, where was our intelligence while the Chinese were building those things?"

"Alive and well, but it was a case of a need-to-know, Admiral."

"As a theater commander, I didn't have a need-to-know, is that what you're telling me?" Owen demanded, feeling his cheeks heat.

Briggs didn't seem fazed. "I'm afraid so, but you don't have to worry about a *Qin* doing 100 knots. It's more like sixty-five."

"That's enough to give me ulcers. Tell me, Ron. How come *we* haven't developed this new thingamajig drive? Have the Chinese suddenly become a whole lot smarter?"

"Not smarter, Admiral, but better at hacking our research databases."

"Damn it all, I thought we plugged those holes with our contractors."

"They *are* plugged, now."

"After the Chinese have cleaned us out, eh? Okay, what about the *Qin*?"

"It vanished and the North Sea Fleet has everything out there looking for it."

"You're shitting me, right? A month or so ago, they lost one of their goddamn *Shangs*, and now it's a brand new state-of-the-art missile boat? What happened? The thing sprung a leak as it went off the continental shelf? Was Admiral Rochester following it? The Chinese made a lot of fanfare around the *Qin* before it sailed."

"COMSUBGRU Seven had two *Los Angeles* boats trailing it as it left Qingdao, but lost it as the thing entered deep water. That boat is a hole, Admiral, and nobody is going to find it unless it wants to be found."

"*Rochester* should have been given a couple of *Virginia* boats for this work. The *Los Angeles* tubs are way past their use-by date."

"A *Virginia* would have kept tabs on the *Qin*, all right," Briggs acknowledged. "However, this could be more than a missing boat scenario, Admiral. That's why I'm here. We just got word that the South Sea Fleet has also sailed out of Zhanjiang. The Chinese are worried."

"I'd also be worried if I lost a two-billion-dollar asset." Owen stared at his intel officer. "When you say the South Sea Fleet sailed, does that include their subs?"

"They've sortied everything."

"Well, damn. Are we talking about another SAR operation here?"

"It looks like it at the moment. It's an experimental boat and bound to be full of bugs. A new propulsion system may work fine in a test bed, but it's a different thing when you're playing for real."

"First, it's a *Shang*, and now this. They're having an interesting time, aren't they? You have passed this up the line?"

"Pentagon has the dope."

Owen sighed. "I better call Parker and cry on his shoulder. I hope this means more to him than it does to me. Keep me posted, Captain."

"Aye aye, sir." Heaving himself up with a grunt, Briggs headed for the door.

Alone, Owen wondered what the hell was going on.

* * *

Outlined in gold and fire, the Caldera de Taburiente mountain ring stood black against the breaking dawn. Tendrils of steam rose from Cumbre Vieja's southern flank, evidence that equilibrium still wasn't reached after the recent disturbance, punctuated by ongoing minor quakes. The weakened western slope hung precariously, temporarily locked against the island's side, ready to plunge into the deeps if hit by another major shock. It would be a disaster unparalleled in human history—at least it would be for America. The slope would give way one day, probably in a series of slumps rather than a single event. It would happen, but Shaun Degard felt confident it wouldn't happen anytime soon. Of course, there was always room for doubt.

Lying at anchor, the *Okeanos Explorer* hardly swayed as the slow flowing Canary Current swept past on its way to the equator. Relatively deep, almost 500 meters, the current at its strongest during winter months, forming cyclonic gyres along the African coast. When it reached fifteen degrees latitude, it shifted west under the influence of the Equatorial Countercurrent. Right now, running at less than twenty centimeters per second, it provided ideal conditions for underwater operations.

Some 700 meters on the starboard quarter lay the gray shape of a Spanish patrol boat, having motored from Santa Cruz on the other side of the island. According to Lieutenant Diego la Cavella, the boat's commander, there to keep away the curious and the nosy. Given the population's preoccupation with the recent disaster, Degard figured there wouldn't be much time for idle sightseeing.

After seven days aboard the research vessel, he had gained operational familiarity with its equipment. Waiting to sail out of Rota, when the two resident marine biologists were told what was going on, their North Sea mission delayed, they elected to stay on board, as did two lab technicians, both experienced geologists holding master's degrees. Degard welcomed their help and the young women added to the shipboard scenery. They all spent a number of hours studying La Palma's geology and topology. He didn't want to be fumbling around when they got there.

He almost lost the biologists, not that their absence would have mattered anyway. Skully, professor of Oceanography and Applied Physics at Harvard's Department of Earth and Planetary Sciences, and School of Engineering and Applied Sciences, was a stuffy individual in charge of the North Sea mission. The old fossil demanded that he be placed in charge of the La Palma investigation, resenting an outsider messing with his research program. Degard sympathized, but wasn't at all impressed with Skully's formidable credentials, and shot him down citing his authority from the president. This wasn't the time to indulge in turf fighting. Things settled down after that, but he suspected that neither would be exchanging Christmas cards.

After overcoming one problem, hearing that *Okeanos Explorer* was heading for La Palma, the French insisted that they be included. Their Ifremer—French Research Institute for Exploration of the Sea—vessel *L'Atalante* was docked at Brest and could be made ready to sail within forty-eight hours. They wanted the Americans to wait for their ship, thereby making this a truly international effort. Degard was tempted, but Tom Meecham immediately vetoed the idea. The French were welcome to send their ship, but he wanted *Okeanos Explorer* to sail as soon as Degard stepped on board. This didn't go down well with the French, but he understood the urgency. Besides, he didn't need other volcanologists or geologists to confirm what he already knew. This was foremost a forensic mission, not a dissection of a geological event. Once he found what he was after, if he could find anything, there would be plenty of time for pure research and the French were free to join in. Swallowing their Gallic pride, the French gave in with ill-concealed antipathy. They could do nothing to prevent *Okeanos* from sailing anyway.

Working with the crew, he launched himself into the overhaul and preparation of two primary ROVs that would do most of the on-site work, appreciating Skully's help and expertise. What he particularly liked was the 30-kilogram xBot, a penetrating machine attached to the primary ROV, providing access to confined spaces where the larger and more expensive ROV couldn't go.

Although equipped with a satellite dome, the 3.7-meter dish capable of transmitting live data feeds through Internet2 connections to scientists at shore-based Exploration Command Centers, Degard wouldn't need it, but it was nice to know he had that support.

Before dropping anchor off La Palma, the ship steamed along the coast using its hull-mounted multibeam sonar to generate high-resolution 3D maps of the slump boundary. The sonar identified three anomalous returns scattered along the slope some 450 meters down, which were diagnosed as metal. Two more pieces were found at the 620-meter level, but what really set everybody speculating and arguing was a large mass at 2,260 meters. The island's side was littered with all sorts of debris, from sunken boats to snagged fishing nets. Identifying them from possible submarine debris took a lot of time and often heated arguments. Despite previous tests, Degard ran another radiation count, which didn't pick up anything, confirming that the slump wasn't caused by a nuclear explosion, which had been a lingering concern. Degard reported his findings to Meecham, who only wanted to know when they would deploy the ROVs. The man had no poetry in his soul.

The crew *did* deploy the camera sled that evening, the need for data and high mission priority overriding the normally relaxed ship's routine. After all, that's why they were here. Concession was made to entertaining Diego la Cavella and his first officer at dinner, the Spaniards looking around the ship with intense curiosity. Having immigration and customs formalities waived with a torrent of voluble Spanish, it was the least the *Okeanos'* captain could do. The two officers were invited to observe the launch of the ROV, but their guests declined, citing official duties. What duties the two could have anchored off the coast, Degard couldn't tell.

Never having seen deployment of such a sophisticated ROV, he hovered at the stern bathed by bright floodlights as the sled was hooked to a crane and slowly lowered into the water trailing a thick control umbilical, the evolution directed by Skully. It wallowed on the black surface while two operators below conducted system checks in the control room used to run the multibeam and telepresence communications equipment. When the sled sank beneath the waves, its powerful lights fading, Degard rushed below decks to watch the live feed displayed on two flat screens.

As the sled slowly moved along the 120-meter deep boundary line, Degard could clearly see what happened when the section of the La Palma island slid down the slope. There was considerable overburden spillage that created numerous underwater landslides, the main mass jamming itself against a plateau that ran approximately eight kilometers along the boundary. Should the plateau give way under the enormous stress placed on it, the locked section would slide all the way to the bottom some 4,000 meters below.

As the ROV glided along the fault boundary, the cameras failed to show evidence of rock deformation indicative of extreme heat application, but he didn't expect to find any. Whatever triggered the slump would be buried under the massive section of the island's flank. Descending to 450 meters, the operators were not able to locate any metallic object indicated on the 3D sonar map, but this was an exploratory run only and he went to bed tired and satisfied.

Degard leaned against the rail and watched the sky brighten. He turned and studied the raw wound that scarred the island at the base of the central volcanic ridge where the land had split open. Stretching for eight kilometers, the gash looked like a giant rock quarry. Puerto de Navos lay in ruins, the destruction running all the way to El Remo. The waterfront and port facilities were gone, sunk beneath the sea, the surviving buildings badly damaged, waves lapping at their base. Fishing boats clustered the shoreline as locals picked through the ruins in an attempt to salvage anything useful, the dead and wounded already removed with the help of the Spanish army. The towns would never be occupied again—at least not officially, the ground far too unstable—the survivors forced to relocate somewhere else in an attempt to rebuild their broken lives. Brooding over the torn landscape, the Cumbre Vieja Volcano slumbered. Degard shook his head and made his way below to get some breakfast.

At eight o'clock precisely the stern crane lowered the primary ROV and support sled. The sled was equipped with HD cameras to image the main ROV, also equipped with lights and cameras, as well as manipulator arms to collect samples. The objective for the day was to locate a metal object that might be from a submarine and bring it to the surface for initial analysis. Navigating from the 3D sonar map, Morris piloted the ROVs down while Joe monitored the data feeds.

Degard watched the display screens and chewed his lip as the primary ROV scanned the slope in a grid pattern where one of the metal objects of interest was supposed to lie. Overcoming his pique, Skully came down and hovered in the background, eager to observe the proceedings.

"Look at that!" He pointed at the screen.

The ROV stopped and Degard stared at a slab of smooth rock, not daring to hope. The surface suggested melting, but it could equally be simple stress cleavage. Morris maneuvered the ROV into position and Joe extended a grasping manipulator arm. It took him only a moment to clamp the arm to the slab which kept the ROV steady, and bring the powerful cameras into play.

"I think it's only a piece broken off a larger section," Degard said after a while. "I can't see any melting."

Skully frowned and shook his head. "No! Look at the right edge. That's evidence of melting."

Degard didn't really want to spend too much time on this, but since the ROV was already in position...

"Okay, we'll get a sample."

Joe extended the drill and extracted two cores, depositing them into a sample basket for analysis in the dry lab.

After three hours of frustrated scanning, finding nothing, at 454 meters the camera sled spotted a twisted black shape protruding from the debris face. The edges were jagged, suggesting the piece was torn from a larger section. Positioning the main ROV, Joe grasped the two-meter-long plate with the manipulator arm. He gave it a tug and the plate moved, stirring some sediment. A firmer tug dislodged it and the image wavered as the heavy plate dragged the manipulator arm down. Undeterred, Joe moved the left arm and clamped it on the plate. Maintaining a firm hold with both arms, he glanced at Degard.

"No rust or algae buildup, doc."

Degard nodded. The piece could not have been there for long.

"Raise it a bit."

The ROV strained, but it couldn't lift the plate. Degard wasn't surprised.

"The thing is too heavy, Professor," Skully declared impatiently.

Staring at the screens, Degard agreed. "Can we cut off a section?"

They had talked about finding a piece of possible submarine hull plating last night, and made sure the ROV had a diamond saw attachment for the day's operation. Joe extended the cutter, positioned the blade below the manipulator arm and the saw whirled. It took almost ten minutes to cut through the three-centimeter-thick plate, but they had their sample, more than enough needed for analysis.

As the ROV glided over the cluttered debris bed in a gentle descent, the radiation counter started chirping. Morris immediately stopped the vehicle.

"What's the reading?" Degard demanded.

"I wouldn't want to handle it with bare hands," Joe declared.

"Pull back!" Degard ordered immediately.

"What do you think it is?" Skully asked.

Degard looked at him. "I'd say it's the remains of a reactor casing. Perhaps the core itself."

It made sense. If a submarine was caught in a thermobaric explosion, the reaction wouldn't be hot enough to vaporize the tough reactor vessel or the enriched uranium fuel pellets. As the section of the island slumped, the submarine's remains were buried, along with the ruptured reactor vessel. Did the reactor vessel itself rupture during the explosion? If it didn't the fuel rods would have melted in absence of a coolant, and they found the spot where a pile of fissioning uranium was boring its way into the island's side. Had the debris avalanche continued to the bottom, it would have swept the entire slope clean, wiping all traces of a submarine.

"What do you want to do, doc?" Joe asked.

"Dive to the 620-meter level and see if we can locate another hull piece." Degard wasn't anxious to mess with radioactive material, happy to leave the cleanup to somebody else.

"You got it."

Morris took the ROV down, following the slope of the island's flank. Cutting through impenetrable blackness the powerful lights revealed snatches of a scoured landscape. At this depth, Degard did not expect to see coral colonies or swarms of colored fish.

As the vehicle approached the 620-meter mark, Morris began a search pattern for the metal object the 3D sonar map said lay there. It looked easy on the map, but it took almost an hour to find the thing, the ROV's lights providing a restricted view. Morris was sure he went past it more than once. Finally revealed, Degard stared at the torn torpedo cylinder protruding out of the rubble, the twisted propeller making it clear what the thing was.

"Get close-up shots," he ordered.

"We've got ourselves a sub, doc," Joe muttered. "You want a souvenir?"

"Definitely. A section of the casing will do."

With the evidence in the sample basket, the ROV angled down and Morris applied power. Descending at three meters per second, nine minutes later, they were at the 2,260-meter level. Following the sonar map, it took some twenty minutes to locate the wreck. The mangled section of hull looked like crumpled tissue paper. Whatever interior structure might have been attached to it was ripped away as the hull section rolled down within the debris avalanche.

Degard tried not to think of the trapped men as their boat was torn to shreds around them. In the final moment before death came, what were their thoughts? Expecting a leisurely voyage home after a successful mission, looking forward to seeing their family and sweethearts, did they have time to feel outrage, betrayed by the state they served? Did they even know why they had to die?

Morris maneuvered the ROV, allowing Joe to film everything.

"Get a couple of samples then bring her up," Degard ordered and stood up.

Without looking at Skully, he strode out of the control room. Thrusting the haunting images out of his mind, he scrambled up the companionway that led to the bridge. Inside, Captain Truscot and the watch officer looked up as he walked in.

"How's the dive, doc?"

"I have what we came for. It was a submarine. No way to tell whose until we analyze the samples."

"That was quick work. I thought we'd be here for at least two or three days."

"So did I, but the 3D images we took last night helped a lot, as did Professor Skully's expertise. Any way that we can fly the samples out of here in a hurry?"

Truscot scratched his left ear and pushed back his hat. "The Spanish have a helicopter battalion at Santa Cruz. I could ask them if they can pick up your stuff."

"And me."

"I thought you wanted to hang around until *L'Atalante* got here?"

"I did, and still do, but now that our job is done, I doubt that Uncle Sam would be willing to pay for my extended stay."

Truscot chuckled. "You won't know if you don't ask."

"No, I won't."

"Does this mean I can pull up anchor and return to Rota?"

"The ship is all yours, Captain, and thanks for the service."

"You're welcome, Professor."

Degard felt somewhat deflated—he hadn't expected to get results this quickly—he went below to his cabin. He pulled back a chair beside his work table, sat down, and reached for the phone. Punching in numbers, he peeked at his watch, leaned back and waited for the satellite connection to put him through.

"Meecham!"

Degard smiled, picturing the harried young FBI man having to answer another phone call, and it was only 8 a.m. in DC. It couldn't have been easy for him, fielding questions to which he had no answers. Well, he would have a few answers now.

"And a good morning to you, Mr. Meecham. It's Professor Degard."

"Ah, Professor, just the man I want to talk to. What have you got for me?"

Degard sighed and shook his head. The man had no grace,

but what could he expect from a starched government issue personality.

"Actually, some good news. I can confirm that a nuclear submarine delivered the explosive used to trigger the slump. We came across a radioactive patch on the western slope, probably from the reactor vessel. There is no way to tell for sure as everything is buried, and we don't have the special gear required to go after it. You will have to notify the Spanish authorities and organize a cleanup."

"We figured it had to be a sub, Professor. You got hull samples?"

"Several. Captain Truscot is arranging for a Spanish Air Force helicopter out of Santa Cruz to pick them up."

"Great work! I'll arrange to have them analyzed. The Navy's Research Laboratory in DC is good at this sort of thing. If anyone can identify the material, it's them. Were you able to get a handle on the type of explosive used?"

"Everything is buried under the debris avalanche, Tom, but I did get two rock samples. We'll be able to check them out on board. One of the marine biologists thinks they show melting, which would support your theory that the weapons of choice were thermobaric mines, but I think they are simple stress fractures. Anyway, we'll know once we take a look at the rocks."

"Don't worry about it, Professor. Identifying the submarine is far more important. I didn't think you guys would come up with something so quickly."

"To be honest, neither did I. If it weren't for the special *Okeanos* 3D sonar, we'd still be scrambling over the bottom."

"Then you're done over there?"

"What we have here is a unique geological event, regardless of the fact it was man induced, and I'd love to do more research, but *L'Atalante* won't get here for another three days and Captain Truscot wants the ship back at Rota. I am sure the Spanish authorities would let me stay with other scientists crawling all over

La Palma, but I'm interested in the event's underwater geology. Unfortunately, nobody has the equipment I need for my research."

"If you want to stay, Professor, I can have *Okeanos Explorer* wait for *L'Atalante*."

Degard blinked. Perhaps the FBI man had some redeeming qualities after all. "It's a tempting offer, Tom, but *Okeanos* has a bunch of scientists cooling their heels at Rota. I'm sure they're anxious to start their North Sea mission."

"A few more days won't matter, but I understand. Can you upload all your videos to the Inner Space Center? The Navy can start looking at them right away."

"I'll see to it."

"Get yourself to Santa Cruz, Professor, and we'll have you back in Honolulu by tomorrow."

"Sounds good. Do you have any leads on who may have done this? There hasn't been much on TV except wild speculation by chair experts."

"Until the Navy completes its analysis of your samples, we're also speculating. However, you did give me something to think about."

"Oh?"

"At your university's symposium held a couple of weeks ago, you said that Professor Wei Xhulai presented a paper written by Chuan Jianbo, who met with an accident. What if it wasn't an accident?"

Degard frowned. "Someone picked his brains and didn't want him to talk?"

"That's it."

"Mmm. Knowing how to set off the slump would take an expert, all right, but connecting it with Chuan is a wild leap of imagination, Tom, with nothing to support it."

"You're right. Still, it's an interesting coincidence."

"That would mean the Chinese are behind this."

"I have no evidence one way or another, but we should know soon."

"Ah, about that other possibility we discussed…"

"I'm following it up. Talk to you later, doc."

Replacing the receiver, Degard sat back and exhaled loudly. *Quite a feather in your cap, eh, Professor? Feeling proud of yourself?* Damn it all, he did feel a measure of pride. He risked his career on evidence others had dismissed, and he would deserve any accolades the university cared to heap on him. The PR limelight won't do them any harm either.

"I hope you're satisfied," Judy's hollow words echoed in his head.

\* \* \*

Meecham hung up and reached for the coffee mug. He took a long sip, leaned back, and stared absently at the daunting list of emails displayed on the screen. At last things were moving. With solid evidence, the investigation could now shift into a more interesting phase, and he wanted to be part of it. Strictly speaking, nosing around a foreign country was more in CIA's line, but the Bureau did have legal attaché offices in most countries, attached to the American embassy. If the FBI could send in a Fly Team, he would have to find a way to be on it—once they found out where to send one! His ITOS I and ITOS II guys hadn't come up with anything to suggest that the Russians or the Chinese were behind this. Once the hull samples were analyzed, he would know and could move.

He picked up the phone and pressed a button. "Marsha? Please get me Admiral Wayne Parker." Glancing at his watch, just after 8:30, and the CNO might be in. If not, he would leave a message.

A minute later the phone rang.

"Meecham."

"Morning, Tom. It's Parker. I wanted to talk to you, but you go first."

"Thanks for calling back, Admiral. I just had a chat with Professor Degard—"

"I know. Captain Truscot sent me an email saying Degard found submarine remains and is arranging to have them flown to Santa Cruz. I'm organizing an aircraft to pick him up and his samples."

Tom blinked. "It's a pleasure doing business with you, Admiral."

"That's how I like my Navy to operate, Tom. Who did you have in mind to do the analysis?"

"I'm open to suggestions, but I hear the Navy Research Laboratory in DC would be a good bet."

"They're the ones to call, all right. You want Degard flown back to Honolulu?"

"I would appreciate that."

"And so will he, I am sure."

"Admiral, I asked Degard to upload all the ROV video footage to the Inner Space Center. You may want somebody to start looking at it."

"We'll do that. Thanks, Tom. My turn now. Two days ago, the Chinese sortied one of their new *Qin*-class boomers, supposedly to test new inventory and give the sub driver a chance to play some war games."

"Don't tell me. The sub disappeared."

"I heard about your theory that La Palma might be attacked again."

"Degard deserves the credit."

"So I understand, but you pushed the idea along, which by the way caused some people at the White House to question your sanity."

Tom laughed. "Christ! The number of times people questioned my sanity…"

"I know the feeling. What I wanted to tell you, we're moving assets into place to find the *Qin*. We're also setting up a sensor net around La Palma in case somebody has evil plans about that place. It might not be China at all, you know."

"I am very aware of that possibility, Admiral."

"It's been interesting working with you, Mr. Meecham."

Tom replaced the phone and shook his head, amazed how events happened to turn. He opened Outlook's meeting planner, booked a meeting room for 10:30 and sent invitations to his team. He hadn't had a status check for two days now, and with the latest developments, it was important to keep everybody in the loop. He had lunch organized with Melissa for 12:30, but he figured it shouldn't be a hassle making it.

He needed to make one more call, and reached for the phone.

"Marsha? Please get the National Security Advisor for me."

Calling high-powered people had lost some of its initial grandeur, leaving him bemused by the whole thing. Still, he appreciated having some pull, even though for him only temporary power.

"Hold on," she said, switching him into some background music.

"Mr. Meecham?"

"Yes, sir. I have an update for you."

"Glad you called, son. I know these things take time, but we were starting to get anxious here. What have you got?"

"Professor Degard has secured hull samples from a nuclear submarine. They'll be flown to DC for analysis."

"That is good news. Anything else?"

Tom wasn't sure he wanted to sound off to Stone about China, but the man had a need-to-know.

"Nothing solid so far, sir. Mark Price is following up a couple of leads that might point to China."

"China, eh? Specifics?"

"They lost one of their attack subs during the *Jing Long* exercise—"

"I know about that one."

"—or so they claim, and we may have found its remains at La Palma. Late in April, one of their prominent geophysicists met with a fatal accident. It's thin, but I think the two are connected."

"It's thin, all right, but it's something. I'm meeting with Price today and I'll talk to him. That idea you mentioned about offering to help the Chinese locate their sub had merit, but we already sounded them out. We haven't heard anything from Premier Dzhang Qishan. If those samples you recovered are from their sub, we'll have a few more things for Dzhang to think about."

"I dare say. I also want to express my thanks to Admiral Parker. Without his cooperation, we'd have nothing."

"I'll pass that on to the Chairman of the Joint Chiefs. Thanks for the heads-up, son."

"We're not done yet, sir."

"But you're making things happen and that's what counts. Before you mention it, I know about the Chinese *Qin*. Has Admiral Parker talked to you?"

"He did, and I hope I'm wrong, sir."

"That makes two of us. Good work, Mr. Meecham."

Tom felt some of the load shift off his shoulders and started tackling his email list.

At 10:30, he walked into the meeting room, noting Clavel's conspicuous absence. Taking a chair at the head of the table, the door opened and Clavel burst in.

"Sorry…traffic."

Tom waited until the grins faded.

"Some progress at last, gentlemen. Professor Degard has several submarine hull samples for us. They'll be flown to Washington for analysis. I'll go into the details later."

"We needed a break," Andre Norton growled.

"Any hint on the type of explosive used?" Isaac Federer

asked.

"We have a couple of rock samples, but nothing conclusive as yet. From what Degard tells me it's unlikely that we'll find anything."

"A long shot at best," Clavel mused. "The slump would have buried everything."

Tom pictured an eight-kilometer section of land breaking loose and sliding into the sea. It must have been a nightmare out of hell for those caught in it. Degard was lucky to have found anything.

"Getting those hull samples is far more important," Davenport added.

"Agreed," Tom said. "While we're on the subject of submarines, I must apologize, Keith, for dismissing your theory that this was a rogue ops."

Davenport shrugged. "A shot in the dark, Tom."

"Perhaps, but in absence of evidence to the contrary, it's a valuable lesson that we cannot discount anything. There is something else, and I'm also shooting in the dark here. It doesn't matter whether this was a rogue ops or sponsored by some government. Whoever planned this needed a lot of scientific input on how to go about doing it. You recall how Professor Chuan Jianbo met with an untimely accident?"

Clavel looked up and frowned. "Chuan?"

"It was in the White House meeting minutes," Tom said and gave Clavel a hard stare. "You haven't read them?"

"I skimmed through them…"

"Read them!"

"You think Chuan may have been the scientific expert?" Davenport said, breaking an uncomfortable interlude.

"And perhaps canned for his help."

"A lost Chinese sub, and now Chuan," Norton mused. "You're stacking a shaky house of cards against the Chinese, Tom."

"Ask me again once we have the hull samples analyzed. Anyway, Mark Price is going to look into it. Before we get to Professor Degard, have you guys got anything?"

Davenport glanced at the others and cleared his throat. It looked like he was elected as the group spokesman.

"Nothing we know so far points to the Russians or the Chinese. Both have internal factions who would love to slit each other's throat, and ours, but neither is dissatisfied enough with us to do something drastic about it. Clavel is digging into this. President Walters has a scheduled meeting with President Kurov in September, and he recently walked away from a successful one with President Zhou Yedong. The fact that Zhou was all smiles and cordiality doesn't mean he wasn't plotting something behind the scenes. China is becoming more dominant on the world's stage, and America isn't the power it once was. At least that's how Zhou may perceive things, and he could have sought to add to our problems. They are firm believers in Sun Tzu's philosophy to misdirect an enemy. Defeating him without having to fire a shot would be something they'd relish. I admit that this scenario applies equally well to a rogue ops."

Tom studied the CIA man fondly, liking Davenport's quiet, competent manner, his thinking, and preparedness to look outside the obvious.

"I didn't expect that you were about to give me the culprit's name." This generated a few chuckles and some grins. He looked at Clavel. "Profiles on Russian and Chinese Politburo luminaries who may have a grudge against us?"

"Still working on that one, Tom."

"Christ! How much time do you need? Light a fire under somebody. I want a report on my desk by tomorrow morning. You were also going to check out foreign submarine movements. Anything?"

"Nothing from our Navy, but…" Clavel shifted in his seat, clearly stung by Tom's remark. "A piece of trivia, really. About a week before the La Palma event, a South African frigate spotted what it claimed to be a Victor III off Cape Agulhas."

"Source?" Tom demanded.

"NSA ELINT. The information was passed to the Counterterrorism Center four days ago."

"Four days ago? Why didn't you bring it up?"

"As I said, it's trivia; a Russian boat taking its bearings."

"Or a *Shang* doing the same thing," Davenport said slowly. "It's basically a Victor III hull design."

Tom exhaled slowly, wanting desperately to jump over the table and pound Clavel.

"Rod, you're relieved. Wait for me outside."

Clavel gaped. "What? You can't do this!"

"I just did. Out!"

Clavel turned red and glared. "We'll see who's going to be out," he grated and stomped from the room.

Embarrassed, Federer cleared his throat. "I apologize, Tom. He works for me and I should have monitored him more closely."

Tom didn't blame Federer. Clavel was supposed to be a professional and should have known better than to withhold information, especially after he reminded everybody that nothing was too insignificant, no matter how innocuous it might seem.

"Forget it, Isaac. He's had a chip on his shoulder ever since I took over Ops I. I thought he had gotten over it, but apparently not."

"It could have been a simple oversight, you know."

"You don't believe that any more than I do. You saw his reaction." Tom chewed his lip. "For the duration of this investigation, I would like Keith to liaise with the Counterterrorism Center. He'll still keep his job as your deputy section chief. Are you all right with that?"

"I don't mind if Keith doesn't."

"I can handle it," Davenport said calmly and Tom nodded.

"Good. There has been a development that might be related to our investigation. The Chinese have sortied one of their new *Qin*-class Type 097 boomers, and it has disappeared. It might not mean anything, but then again, this could be a follow-up mission to finish the La Palma job."

Davenport stared at him. "After failing the first time, this would have taken some organization."

"Which would make the perpetrators very sneaky," Tom agreed. "If China did this."

Federer bit his lip and gave Davenport a sour grin. "Keep an eye on this, okay?"

Tom stood up. "If it's okay with you, we'll meet this afternoon at two and go over Degard's mission."

"Fine with me," Norton said, and the other two nodded.

Tom hated doing this to them, but he had to take care of Clavel and they knew it. Walking out, he looked around and frowned when he spotted Clavel talking to Marsha. He marched to him and glared.

"My office."

He waited for Clavel to close the door, keeping a tight rein on his emotions. Nothing would be gained by recriminations.

"I want you to go to Langley and clean out your desk. You're not the Counterterrorism Center deputy director anymore. I'm having you transferred. I am also placing a reprimand in your record."

Clavel went pale, seeing his career in the Bureau trashed. He would never be offered a senior position again. It wasn't necessarily a career showstopper, but it came close.

"I'll take this to Hancock!"

"We can both see him right now if you want."

Clavel clamped his mouth and seethed. Without saying anything, he turned and walked out. When the door closed, Tom stared at it for a few seconds.

"Christ!"

This had been inevitable really, but he hated seeing a potentially good agent shaft himself. He closed the door after him and headed for Hancock's office. Pausing, he knocked and heard a muffled 'Come in'.

He stepped inside and leaned forward. "Got a minute, boss?"

Hancock waved at a chair, his eyes probing. "What happened?"

Tom's mouth turned up. The man was very good at reading emotions and body language.

"I just fired Clavel for withholding information."

Hancock exhaled slowly and sat back. "Was it really necessary?"

"A pattern of behavior, boss. I thought I had things settled with him, but…"

"I'll want a full report, Tom, with your recommendation."

"On your desk before end of the day."

"Anything else?"

Tom quickly summarized Degard's find and skimmed over Chuan's death. When he finished, Hancock nodded.

"Lots of speculation there, but like you said, we'll be in a position to act once those hull samples are analyzed. I'm glad you updated Graham Stone. I understand that Admiral Parker talked to you about the Chinese *Qin*."

"I just updated my team, boss."

Hancock shifted his bulk and managed to look uncomfortable. "After our discussion last time about your follow-up attack theory, I was tempted to have you relieved, but you were doing your job, and doing it well. I must tell you, not everybody thought so. I'm glad you proved them all wrong, and that includes me, even though we still don't have any solid evidence one way or another. Good work."

"Thanks, boss," Tom said and stood up. "About Clavel—"

Hancock raised a hand. "He is part of your team and your responsibility. That's all, Tom."

As Tom walked back to his office, certain that it wasn't all. Hancock would undoubtedly talk to Norton and Federer, but he wasn't concerned. Like his boss said, it was his responsibility. One thing he would never do was pass the buck. Still, he preferred handling cases than getting involved in greasy office politics, recognizing that Bureau politics was likely to consume more of his time as his career developed.

He glanced at his watch and smiled. Lunch with Melissa would wash out the bad taste in his mouth left there by Clavel.

\* \* \*

President Samuel Walters rested his elbows on the dark, matte brown table, leaned forward and looked pointedly at Price. "Your evaluation?"

The DCIA returned his gaze, eyebrows furrowed in concentration. There was some criticism when he announced the appointment of such a young man to take over the Agency—Price was only forty-five then—but after almost a year in the job, Walters had no complaints. Even Congress, on both sides of the aisle, came to appreciate the man's deft handling of intelligence, defense and appropriation committee members. Efficiency savings, eliminating redundant functions and duplication of inter-agency intelligence gathering, especially with the NSA, shaved the fiscal year's budget to both agencies by close to three billion—a remarkable achievement.

Using Price as a model, Walters had removed four of his departmental secretaries, replacing them with younger men driven by vision. The old hands were adept political mechanics and Hill manipulators, but they spent too much time turf fighting and point scoring rather than implementing policies. He told his Cabinet more than once that they were appointed, not elected, and appointments can always be withdrawn. Congress had to be stroked, but that was merely an itch, not a full-time job. The four he replaced didn't get it, seeing their insider expertise more valuable than doing their jobs, not believing it when shown the door. He had his eye on the Education Secretary as the next to go, unless the lady picked up her skirts.

"Frankly, Meecham has done more than anyone had any right to expect in such a short time. He needs polishing—"

Walters suppressed a smile, recalling how Price had stormed through the establishment.

"—but he gets results. He knows how to get the best out of his people and he hasn't abused his temporary authority. Wayne Parker was highly complimentary."

Walters peered at his national security advisor. "Graham?"

The retired admiral shifted in his seat and cleared his throat. "I like the way he does business, Mr. President. I had misgivings when Marshal appointed him, but I'm happy to see that they were unjustified. He would have made a good naval officer."

From Stone, high praise indeed, Walters reflected. He had met Meecham twice after he and Price uncovered Mossad's Valero Texas City Refinery clandestine operation. In many ways, Meecham was a younger version of Price. Both men were self-starters and high achievers, shunning protocol and stifling procedures when that stood in the way of getting the job done, a practice often frowned upon by superiors. Unfortunately, as Walters learned after three years in his job, becoming a political operator would increasingly dominate both their lives. He hoped it wouldn't become an overriding preoccupation.

Larry Tanner glared at Price. "Mark, you know him well. Do you have any idea why we're all here?"

Price grinned. "I do, but I don't want to spoil this moment for Meecham."

"Humph!"

The door to the Situation Room opened and a marine guard in full dress uniform snapped to attention as Thomas Meecham walked in. Walters rose and extended his arm.

"Good to see you again, Tom," he said warmly as they shook hands.

"It's a pleasure, Mr. President," Meecham replied, looking quickly around the room.

Subdued lighting from ceiling cornices and down lights focused on the long table. Apart from three speakerphones, the dark surface bare. A giant LED screen behind Stone, showing a color map of China, took up most of the wall, flanked on either side by smaller screens. A communications console stood tucked against the right corner. The room pleasantly warm without being stuffy.

"Take a seat and let's get on with it," Walters said briskly, his morning packed with other engagements, but Manfred always loaded him with more things to do than he had available hours to do them in.

According to Manfred, Meecham didn't want this meeting, preferring to relay the information through Stone, but the White House chief of staff insisted that he make the presentation in person, and Walters agreed. His impression of the younger man hadn't changed. This was someone he wanted to keep an eye on.

Meecham nodded to Tanner and sat beside him. He looked at Walters, not at all flustered.

"It's China, Mr. President," he said simply.

Walters felt a lead weight settle on his shoulders and gave a soft sigh. The possible repercussions of Meecham's simple statement were daunting, but he needed facts, which explained the reason for this meeting.

"Go on."

"Three days ago, Professor Degard retrieved hull samples at La Palma, which the Navy Research Laboratory identified came from a *Shang* nuclear attack submarine. How they managed to do that, they didn't say. Degard also recovered several rock samples, but they didn't show signs of extreme heat exposure indicative of a thermobaric-type reaction, the only explosive I'm told is powerful enough to have caused the slump. When the slump triggered, the resulting debris avalanche buried everything, including evidence of the submarine, and it almost worked.

"It is clear what happened, Mr. President. The Chinese sought to induce a collapse of the Cumbre Vieja's western flank and trigger a massive tsunami that would have devastated the American eastern seaboard and our economy. I surmised that there are several strategic reasons why they might have wanted to do this. The foremost in my opinion, was to gain an overwhelming political and economic advantage, but that's not necessarily the driving motive. However, this is outside my terms of reference and not looked into in depth. Strictly speaking, determining whether this was officially sanctioned or a rogue operation wasn't part of my job either, but we did look at several scenarios."

"Yes, I know. Mark told me," Walters said mildly, understanding perfectly what those scenarios were. "Including the disappeared *Qin*, which now makes a lot more sense."

"Your response, sir, will depend on knowing who executed the La Palma operation. That part of my investigation is still in progress, supported by Mr. Price and his agency."

"I applaud your enthusiasm, but why are you continuing with this, Tom? The political dimension is not part of your job."

"With respect, Mr. President, within strictly narrow parameters, it is. Treating this event as a criminal case, although we have identified means and opportunity, I don't have a clear motive or a perpetrator, and you need that information. The case is still open, sir."

Walters frowned. Meecham had done his job, but identifying the perpetrator, as he put it, wasn't something he could do. Or could he?

"Why do I need that information?"

"Because, Mr. President, if Zhou Yedong organized the

247

strike against La Palma, your response will entail more than enacting economic sanctions."

Nodding, Walters chuckled. "Finding out who organized this, official or not, might not be possible and the Chinese aren't likely to help you."

"This is where some push from you would be useful, sir."

Biting his lip, Walters looked at Tanner. "Any response from Premier Dzhang Qishan on our offer to locate their *Shang*, not that it matters now."

"Nothing as yet, but my sources tell me that our communiqué caused a small stir with President Zhou and the Premier. They could be looking at our offer in any number of ways. We're meddling in their internal affairs; they have already established that the sub was lost during the *Peaceful Dragon* exercise; they suspect that we know they sent the sub to La Palma, or we have uncovered an internal plot. Any of these scenarios could be valid. With Meecham's evidence, I'd say it's imperative that we find out."

Walters turned to his national security advisor. "Graham?"

"I concur, Mr. President. We cannot consider a response until we know one way or another. We need to force the issue."

"Tell President Zhou what we have?"

"Yes, sir. We have to tip his hand."

"He might not know anything about it."

"Which would make it an internal plot and in his interest to find out who was behind it, and would leave him obliged to us."

Cottard glanced at Meecham. "There is one scenario you overlooked, Tom, which could explain why this may have been done: an internal power struggle. Zhou and his elitist coalition, the *taizidang* princelings, hold power right now, but it's no secret that the populist faction, the Tuanpai, are after his scalp. La Palma may have had two objectives."

Tanner nodded. "Or Zhou could have orchestrated the whole thing, telling everybody it was a Tuanpai operation. The

Chinese are good at that kind of convoluted thinking and misdirection."

Walters grunted in frustration. "Damnation! This is more tangled than a bowl of spaghetti." He looked at Meecham. "I wish you told me it was the Russians. Nothing gets done over there without Kurov knowing about it. I'd bomb his ass and that would be the end of it."

Meecham shrugged and smiled. "Sorry about that, Mr. President."

"Don't worry, I won't shoot the messenger."

"There is another possibility," Tanner mused. "Zhou might know or suspect who did this and chose to sit on his hands, hoping we wouldn't find their *Shang*. He may not have wanted to talk to you, fearing you'd overreact and do something drastic. That is not necessarily duplicity on his part, merely a holistic reflection that life is full of contradictions without a simple solution which the West often tries to implement."

"Walk the middle ground, right? The thought did occur to me, Larry. We won't get to the bottom of this by hashing over it. All right, I'll talk to Zhou. Manfred..."

Cottard looked at his watch. "It's ten p.m. over there, Mr. President."

"I'm sure Zhou won't mind being disturbed."

Grinning, Cottard picked up the phone and pressed a button. "Unice? Please get hold of President Zhou Yedong and patch it to the Situation Room."

Meecham cleared his throat. "If you don't need me anymore, Mr. President—"

"You're in a hurry to go, Tom?"

"Of course not, sir. Having—"

"Sit back and relax. This is the fun part and may help you, although it might not be fun for Zhou."

Smiling, Price gave Meecham a nod of encouragement.

Walters understood Meecham's discomfort. Apart from having the president stare at him, he had some of the most powerful people in the country around him, and he naturally felt out of place. Being part of these proceedings would mature the young man. Or at least give him a glimpse into the workings of realpolitik.

The phone rang and Cottard picked up. "Thanks, Unice." He pressed the speaker button and replaced the receiver.

"President Zhou, this is Samuel Walters."

"Good morning, Mr. President. I trust you're having a productive day," Zhou said in perfect American English.

"And good evening to you, sir. My apologies for the late call, but I have information regarding the recent La Palma event that might be of interest to you." Walters could clearly see Zhou wincing at this abrupt statement, made without any preliminary small talk so cherished by the Chinese. Right now, he couldn't be bothered with diplomatic dancing around.

"The affairs of state never rest, Mr. President. What is this information?"

"We found your missing *Shang*," Walters said simply and waited. After what felt like an eternity of silence, he heard a heavy sigh.

"At La Palma. I feared this day would come, and now it has."

"After our meeting in April, I thought we had an understanding. Tell me, Yedong. Are you responsible for this?"

"Mr. President, I assure you, this was not done by my hand. I was appalled as you must have been when I saw the TV footage."

"But you know who ordered this done?"

"We're looking into it."

"Damnation! Why didn't you tell me? You hoped that we would never find the submarine and you'd be off the hook, is that it? You broke trust, Yedong, and severely compromised my options. When this breaks, Congress and the people around the world will demand that I retaliate. What am I supposed to tell them? That you're sorry and you'll shoot the bastard who did this—once you find out who it is? Nobody will believe you and I'd be impeached."

"Mr. President—"

"You used to call me Sam."

"Thank you...Sam. It was in error of judgment not telling you, I admit that. This is intensely embarrassing, and it's true that I hoped you would never find our submarine. Although devastating for La Palma, the event caused relatively little damage to the United States. I hoped to resolve this without generating an international incident."

"Well, you have an incident now. How can I trust you again? You used this disaster to pursue an internal agenda, knowing that you were compromising relations between our two countries and the world, for that matter. Everybody would applaud if I lobbed a tactical nuke on your head."

"Are you prepared to do that?" Zhou demanded with a touch of frost in his voice.

"I might be, you son of a bitch, and you better give me a good reason why I shouldn't. Regardless of who is responsible, China carried out a covert attack not only against the United States, but on the free world. I cannot let that slide. Everybody would demand that I do something about it, and I will."

"A military response would not be in our mutual interest, Mr. President."

"Perhaps not in *your* interest, but you attacked us. That's how the people will see it. It would only be the truth. They won't care about your internal squabbles. They will see a ruthless, oppressive regime prepared to commit genocide to achieve its ends. You only had to pick up the phone and call me!" Walters snarled, wanting to strangle the scheming bastard.

"There is nothing that I can say to undo what has happened—"

"No, there isn't."

"—but perhaps I can salvage something from this shameful episode. I offer your investigators and your intelligence services my full cooperation in identifying and apprehending the person or persons responsible."

"You want to throw us one of your political enemies and conduct a show trial? That's not nearly enough."

"You're understandably skeptical, Mr. President, but I also might lose my head over this. I can only tell you again that I had nothing to do with this. We have our differences, but I would never seek to resolve them by employing something hideous like La Palma. Despite Western propaganda, we're not fanatics and don't seek to conquer the world. I don't deny that we want to expand our influence on the world's stage, but that is no less than you and your European partners seek to do."

"Your full cooperation, Yedong? Talk to anybody we want? See anybody we want? Total disclosure by your security apparatus?"

"Inasmuch as it relates to the investigation. I will not allow blatant intelligence gathering."

Walters chuckled. "I never expected that you would, and I did not imply that I want to compromise your internal security organs. I only want to help you find out who was behind this and have them dealt with. If it turns out to be you…"

"Then we have a mutually compatible objective, Sam."

"Satisfactory as that is, and I accept your offer—Larry Tanner will be in touch with Premier Dzhang Qishan to work out the protocol—but that is still not enough. I need something substantive to tell the world."

"I expected that. China will offer Spain full reparations for material damage to the Canary Islands, rebuilding of La Palma, and compensation to those who were affected. This will not help the dead, but perhaps the lives of those living can be made better. We will also provide full reparations to the United States and every country affected by the tsunami. We will accept legitimate claims, but I'll not condone rapacious profiteering. I want a UN body set up to administer the claim process, with acknowledgment that any settlement is made without further liability."

"Acceptable. I'll call for a special session of the General Assembly for seven p.m. New York time. Your ambassador can announce your offer then—after I finish my address. I will acknowledge that the attack on La Palma was carried out by a dissident element within your government, which should serve to reduce the international temperature somewhat. However, I will also announce the imposition of immediate economic sanctions and I'll revoke China's most favored trading nation status. What sanctions Europe and others will seek to implement will be up to them. One more thing. The United States will block your application for an additional seat on the IMF Executive Board. Is that clear, Mr. President?"

"Are these measures really necessary, sir?"

"I can have the 7th Fleet parading up and down your coast, blockading your shipping."

"That would be a technical declaration of war, Sam."

"Yes, it would, and I'd have the world behind me."

Walters clenched his right fist. Zhou was only offering what he had to, nothing more. With China's bulging foreign currency reserves of more than four trillion dollars, reparation payments would amount to petty cash. They must be made to feel real pain as a reminder that regardless who planned this operation, Zhou and his government were ultimately responsible. He suspected that even this measure would be seen by some as not going far enough. Damnation, he couldn't and wouldn't go to war over this. That would be compounding madness with lunacy.

"I will need to ratify our respective responses with the State Council."

"You do that, but this evening, I talk to the UN. I'll also tell them about another of your submarines that's missing. We know about the *Qin*. The two disappearances are remarkably similar. Let me make my position clear, Yedong. We're looking for it, and if we find its remains at the bottom of the South China Sea, we'll tell you where it is. On the other hand, if we find it transiting toward the Cape of Good Hope, it will be sunk without warning. Do I make myself perfectly clear?"

"Are you suggesting—"

"I'm not suggesting anything. I am simply telling you how things stand. Recall that submarine. Good night, Mr. President."

Walters nodded to Manfred who cut the connection.

"You hung up on him!" Tanner stared in disbelief.

"Zhou Yedong needed to know that I'm pissed, Larry. This isn't a photo shoot where we glad-hand each other. Despite what I told him, I plan to deploy the 7th Fleet."

"I wouldn't advise that, Mr. President. China will see it as needless provocation, and they'd be right. Your proposed sanctions are a measured proportional response, even though some Republicans may demand blood. With control of both Houses, you don't need to be drastic, and you can rely on the Europeans to exact their revenge."

Walters studied his SecState. "Can we, Larry? Sure, they will fulminate and make rousing public speeches, but will they really do anything? Treading on China too hard would hurt every one of their multinationals that have manufacturing plants or financial services over there, including ours. What would happen if stores run out of Nike shoes and TVs? People will howl, forgetting that only yesterday they howled with righteous indignation, wanting China nuked. Like Zhou said, the tsunami devastated La Palma, but elsewhere, we have a handful of deaths and minimal infrastructure damage, hardly worth going without my Nike. In a week, this will be page ten news, if at all. He knows this, hoping to mitigate any backlash by handing out bags of cash. A person's indignation is quickly stifled when he sees dollar signs."

Cottard laughed. "I cannot believe that you've become so

cynical, Mr. President."

"You all made me that way," Walters told him bleakly and Cottard's smile vanished. "You heard me, Larry. Get hold of Dzhang Qishan and start hammering out the protocol details. Mark…Tom, you two work out how we're going to do this. Zhou hasn't found the people responsible or may be reluctant to cause an internal flap, preferring us to do the dirty work for him. I don't care, but I want to show him how real business is done. Manfred, get hold of Granger. I need him to get his press gaggle together and make an announcement. I also want him to work on my UN speech. Oh, and call the UN Secretary General about tonight. Tell SecDef to prepare the 7th Fleet for immediate deployment. Make a slot for me to update the Vice President." He turned to Meecham and nodded. "Good work, Tom. That's all, everybody."

# Chapter Six

Zhou Yedong placed the receiver in its cradle and sighed. Night shrouded the Zhongnanhai compound in darkness that even the city's lights could not penetrate. Soft rain blurred everything, reflecting his chaotic thoughts. He should have gone to bed earlier with orders not to be disturbed, he reflected moodily. Refreshed after a restful sleep—he hadn't been sleeping well for some time now—he would have confronted the American president in a better frame of mind. Staring at the blackness outside, he felt the crushing weight of events pressing down on him.

It hadn't been a good day.

After a light lunch, impatient for some positive news, he summoned General Lin Jinpan. He had given the man ten days to uncover the truth behind those damning orders supposedly signed by Han Yunshan and heard nothing. How hard can it be to disprove fake orders? Strictly speaking the orders themselves were not fake, printed on genuine CMC stationery with all the right seals and authentication code…and Han's incriminating signature. The nagging thorn Zhou wanted pulled from his side was ascertaining whether Han issued them, despite the man's assurance that he hadn't, but he would say that as a matter of course. Friend or not, if Han did this, he would face a firing squad at dawn.

The sun hugged the skyline on its way down, dribbling out feeble light over a cloudy city. Lin Jinpan finally deigned to see him. Dressed in a working khaki uniform, wearing an impressive collection of ribbons, the swarthy army officer stood stiffly at attention as Zhou looked him up and down.

"Your ten days are up, General. I expected a report without

having to summon you. Well?"

Lin swallowed hard, clearly uncomfortable. Zhou could read the signs and braced himself for bad news.

"Mr. President, I didn't report because I have nothing to report."

Zhou slowly nodded. "With all the resources available at your disposal, you have nothing to report?"

Lin's mouth worked, but nothing came out.

"Have you found *anything*?"

"Sir, your directive not to approach Chairman Keung Yang, Vice Chairman Chen Teng, and Admiral Xhal severely restricted our options. Unable to interrogate them, we had to employ covert investigative techniques. Our efforts to date are negative," Lin concluded miserably, then thrust out his chin. "We shall redouble our efforts!"

"Yes, very commendable. Tell me what steps were taken?"

"Chairman Han Yunshan's movements, telephone and cellphone traffic, people he met, were vigorously prosecuted for the period leading up to deployment of the *Jing Long* exercise. The others were subjected to the same treatment. Forensic examination of Han's signature has determined that it is genuine. Comparison with documents on file signed by Han, including those produced from Chen Teng's office, could not establish that Vice Chairman Chen forged the signature."

"What tests were applied?"

"Computer matching, microscopic examination, and testimony from a subject matter expert."

Zhou glared, forcing himself to stay calm. "What else?"

"Ah, that has been the extent of our investigation, sir," Lin said weakly.

"Have you checked into their movements?"

"Apart from official business meetings, my sources have not identified any unusual interaction between them."

"Has your investigation addressed movement and communication by these men *following* the *Jing Long* exercise?"

Lin blanched, genuinely surprised. "No, sir. Your instructions were to authenticate whether Chairman Han Yunshan signed that order. My investigation was constrained by those parameters."

Zhou snorted, looking disgusted. "You're an idiot, General. A junior officer carries out orders without question. I expected someone of your rank and position to exercise initiative and look beyond the obvious."

"If you want me to expand our investigation—"

"Yes, General. I do want you to expand your investigation. You have five days. And General? If I have to summon you again for a report, it won't be a comfortable meeting…for you. That's all."

Lin Jinpan clicked his heels and stomped out, leaving Zhou glaring at his retreating back. The man *was* an idiot, but was Lin being deliberately obtuse by sticking to the letter of his instructions, or did his Tuanpai leanings influence the investigation? No way to tell, but knowing he had a spotlight on him, Lin would not have risked Zhou's wrath by sabotaging any findings.

From there, the afternoon only got worse.

Utterly weary, ready to retire, President Walters called, really topping off his day.

Sitting in his comfortable soft leather chair, slowly rocking back and forth, Zhou contemplated a new world tomorrow. His instincts warned him to call Walters following Keung's revelation, but he had been too clever, underestimating American technology when he should have known better. Two years at Stanford made him familiar with all things American. Lin wasn't the only idiot.

His offer to pay reparations a throwaway gambit, through which Walters saw immediately and announced his sanctions. They would hurt, but the severity of pain inflicted on China was questionable. Curtailing business activity could hurt the West more, having just recovered from the Global Financial Crisis. Would America and Europe be prepared to trigger another crisis merely to punish China? Would the G20 countries follow the Americans? Walters must know all this, but the comedy had to be played out by the rules.

China would ride out the international backlash and sanctions, but denying it an additional seat on the IMF Executive Board was bad news. Getting that seat was a critical element in his Go Global Strategy to gradually assume control of the world's financial systems and bond markets. The nation that controlled the world's stock exchanges also controlled its economic decision making machinery, and with it, the political landscape—his ultimate objective.

Was Walters serious about blockading China's shipping? Listening to the younger man, he sensed resolve to act beyond diplomatic rhetoric. La Palma, after all, was a direct attack on America, something Walters could not ignore, and Zhou understood why his people would insist that he retaliate. However, by choosing to compromise, to take a more conciliatory stand, recognizing that a military response could escalate beyond the ability of both leaders to control, Walters had demonstrated remarkable tolerance. It had a flavor of Chinese thinking. Of course, that might not stop Walters from retaliating militarily. It was the form of that retaliation that nagged at him. Dark clouds hovered on the horizon and Zhou wasn't sure of weathering the coming storm.

With two quarters of declining GDP, the yuan still to find its level after being floated—it would probably take a savage hit following the UN announcement—with a corresponding reduction in the balance of trade, although that would not be felt for some time. Increased unrest in Tibet and the Xinjiang Uyghurs demanding more autonomy, clashing with the Han Chinese, was making the State Council scratch their heads, debating what to do. He faced environmental problems without having a neat solution, for which there wasn't one, and reforms ignored by provincial officials, or given token notice only. Compounding his domestic problems was the growing complexity managing China's international relationships. Zhou wondered if the long days and sleepless nights were worth the effort of having power.

He glanced at the city's lights, picturing the streaming traffic winding its way along wide boulevards and towering skyscrapers, proclaiming growing industrial prosperity, which in turn has produced a measure of international respect, he decided it was worth it. The job might kill him, but he would leave a legacy of reform to be proud of.

What if Lin couldn't nail Keung or Chen? The two of them *had* to be involved! Should he concede defeat in this round and entertain partial implementation of select Tuanpai policies? Were their objectives so divergent from the elitist coalition to be rejected outright purely on the basis of ideology? It wasn't the lack of merit in those policies that rankled, but the erosion of Politburo authority should he accede to Keung's demands. In time perhaps it might happen, but not in the conceivable future, not until there was a generational change.

He took a deep breath and exhaled loudly. He should have remained in the finance business, but no. His father wanted him in the center of power, shaping policy, not merely implementing it. Looking around his spacious office, he *was* shaping policy, but he wasn't sure the personal cost really made a difference. Straightening, he clamped his mouth. So, things were getting a bit tough, eh? He longed for a simpler life without decisions, is that it? Become a peasant, where the only thing he needed to worry about was weather and getting the crops in.

He allowed himself a small smile and chuckled, feeling better. Morbid introspection had no place in his life. It is not as though he had resisted his father's guidance. He knew what he was getting into. In the meantime, he had work to do. Contemplating another long night, he reached for the phone.

"Yes, sir?"

"Get me Dzhang Qishan." If he was going to lose sleep, he saw no reason why the premier shouldn't either. He needed to know more about the missing *Qin*.

\* \* \*

Wearing a concerned frown, Keung Yang watched Chen Teng pace around the office. Chen paused, passed a hand over his bald head and touched the scar on his left cheek, a characteristic gesture of tension and anxiety. Instead of wearing his impressive 180-centimeter frame with dignity, his shoulders were stooped, the expensive London suit propping him up. It wasn't something Keung expected to see.

"Lin Jinpan's goons followed me everywhere!" Chen raged. "And they weren't subtle about it either. Their Volkswagen Jetta's were easy enough to spot. I had my office and phone bugged, and my computer was hacked! They haven't dragged me off in the middle of the night for a cellar and lights session yet, but it's only a matter of time, I tell you. Zhou grilled me for an hour wanting me to admit that I forged Han's orders."

"Take it easy, Teng," Keung said mildly. "You knew this would happen."

"Take it easy? He knows!"

"He doesn't know anything. If he did, both of us would be under arrest. Without proof, all he has are suspicions, and the only proof is against Han, which he cannot ignore. Things are working out as planned. Trust me."

He was aware of the not so covert surveillance by State Security operatives. Lin Jinpan told him all about it over tea, but this was not something Chen needed to know. Lin didn't know anything, didn't want to know, wanting only to sink back into anonymity of his sinecure position. With Zhou breathing down his neck, he had to go through the motions, skating on thin ice if he tried to sideline the investigation in any obvious way, deciding to stick to the letter of his instructions, accepting the attached risks.

Chen stared at him. "Were you harassed? Of course you were, stupid of me. I told you it wasn't wise to confront Zhou with that document, but you wanted to play your game." Sighing, Chen lifted his right hand. "I'm sorry, my friend. I didn't mean that. It's just—"

"Sit down, Teng, before you wear out the floorboards," Keung said sharply and waited for the CMC vice chairman to settle down. "We discussed what would happen. So far, Zhou and the Americans have ticked every box, even to the announcement of sanctions. Zhou and his faction are squeezed and I aim to squeeze harder. He's got a raft of national problems on his hands and we can help him solve them, but under our terms. We don't need to push too hard. He'll come around. He'll have to."

"He'll send the country into recession before caving into Tuanpai demands."

"No, he won't, and I'll tell you why. He may be a princeling swine, but he is the President and Communist Party General Secretary. As such, he is accountable to the State Council, the Standing Committee and the National People's Congress. He is not the CMC Chairman and doesn't hold absolute power in Deng Xiaoping's mold. Our focus has globalized and the people are starting to enjoy the benefits of that shift. Zhou will adopt our policies, some of them anyway, because he must, and he'll deal with me or I'll bring him down."

"Your grand vision has a glaring flaw. Han Yunshan hasn't been removed from his post."

"He will be. Those orders make him damaged goods. Zhou won't have any choice but to remove him."

"Han won't go quietly. He's got very powerful friends in the PLA. If it comes to a push, they might support him rather than

Zhou. After all, Zhou is a civilian, an opportunist who worked to diminish their influence."

"The State Council is no longer a mere constitutional figure-head, Teng, and rightly so. The PLA is subordinate to civil authority for a good reason. Lin Jinpan's investigation will flounder and Han will be gone."

"And I step into his shoes, right?"

"That was the deal we made," Keung said, evaluating his friend's character cracks.

His initial assessment had turned out to be uncomfortably accurate. Chen Teng was a smooth water sailor, but under pressure, he lost objectivity and perspective.

Chen bit his lip. "You make it sound so simple, but there is one item you overlooked, my friend—Zhou's invitation to allow American investigators to snoop around, and there is a small matter of the missing *Qin*."

Keung waved a hand. "A gesture to placate President Walters. If our security apparatus couldn't expose us, a bunch of foreigners certainly won't. They'll wander around looking busy, poke into things and find nothing. Your original orders went down with the *Shang*, and the link to the Wushiht'ala software engineer was dealt with. The *Qin's* commander hasn't broken EMCON, and it looks like he won't until his mission is completed. When completed, there won't be any remains for the Americans to find. They'll be too busy salvaging what is left of their country."

"I wouldn't underestimate the Americans. We have twenty days or so before the *Qin* can get into position and the American navy has already started looking for it. They'll have La Palma protected."

"The *Qin* is stealthy, better than their *Virginia*-class boats. You told me that yourself. It will do its job."

"I wish there was a way to recall it."

"The *Qin* is not a problem, I tell you. If the Americans find it and sink it, nothing points to us. It will be Zhou's problem."

"What about the American investigators?"

"You've been watching too many of their crime shows. This isn't a CSI program. Short of using invasive interrogation techniques, Zhou has a bare cupboard."

"And if he hauls one of us in and shoots him full of babble juice? He might, you know. The stakes we're playing for..."

Keung smiled. "Oh, I'm sure the thought had crossed his mind, but I have taken steps and made certain he knows it. We won't be touched. Hold your nerve and everything will fall into place."

"Easy for you to talk. I have two daughters to worry about and a bitching wife. I may not love her, but that doesn't mean I want to see her or my daughters executed for high treason."

"I also have a family, Teng: a son, two brothers, and a sister. I don't relish the idea of having them executed either."

"I'm sorry, my friend. I spoke out of turn. It's the waiting for something to happen that's wearing me down." Chen shook his head. "You're sitting there, calm and composed, and I don't know how you do it, Yang. You were set to devastate the United States without blinking, and you played Zhou like he was a political amateur."

"It's a question of perspective, Teng. Almost every politician and senior military officer's foremost concern is how to further his career. Everything else is subordinate to that overriding objective. I don't seek more power, which allows me to use what I have to further Tuanpai's policies. If a gambit fails, there is always something else. Just relax, will you?"

Chen stood and nodded. "I have work to do, and my security tail is probably wondering why I'm talking to you. Take care, my scheming friend."

"And you," Keung said softly.

When the door closed, he sat back, swiveled his chair and gazed at Zhongnanhai's lush landscape. He needed to get out and stretch his legs, smell a flower, gaze at a snowy mountain, breathe fresh air. Instead, he played high stakes politics, wondering if that made up for everything else missing in his life.

Chen was a nervous woman and a growing security risk. Should he do the obvious and send Chen to join his illustrious ancestors? Tempted, Keung rejected the idea. Chen appeared twitchy only because he felt free to unburden himself to a friend. It did not necessarily mean he would collapse under the strain. After all, he survived a session with Zhou, and the president could be a formidable interrogator at times.

Keung absently adjusted his glasses, turned the chair and reached for the pipe resting beside the crystal ashtray. Priming it with fresh tobacco, he lit up and puffed, his thoughts racing each other, security uppermost on his mind. One item he really should take care of…

Shen Lei wasn't merely chief of his bodyguard detail, but a genuine friend and confidant. Friend or not, Shen represented a vulnerability, one that could potentially unravel everything. He was surprised that Lin's interrogators hadn't hauled him in, which would have been a disaster. Perhaps it was only a matter of time. Keung's logical mind told him what he needed to do, but his emotional side shunned that option. Some lines cannot be crossed simply because of pragmatism. Nevertheless, a dangerous security risk did exist.

A Confucius saying bubbled to the surface, which he thought apt. *It is more shameful to distrust our friends then to be deceived by them.* He reminded himself that in his position, he could not afford friends.

He took a puff and pressed a glowing white button on his multi-function phone station.

"Yes, sir?" his assistant queried politely.

"Have Shen Lei report to me."

"Right away, sir."

Turning to the computer, Keung began reading his emails.

Some minutes later, a knock on the door made him look up. It opened and Shen strode in. He stopped before the desk and stood at attention.

"You wanted to see me, sir?" he rasped through a mangled throat.

"I'm having lunch at Da Giorgio's. Pick me up at 12:30."

Shen raised an eyebrow. "Ravioli and gnocchi?"

Keung smiled, permitting his friend this familiarity. "You know me too well." Making a decision, he rested his crossed arms on the desk and leaned forward. "We have known each other for some time, Shen, and I'd like to think that we have something more than a bodyguard/client relationship. You exercised your special skills with exemplary efficiency whenever I had the need to call on them, and your last two jobs were no exception. Do I have to explain further?"

"No, sir. I saw what happened at La Palma."

"Then you understand what I'm getting at."

"I am a security risk you must eliminate."

"A security risk to be mitigated, not eliminated!" Keung snapped. "I have no wish to see you dead. If you wanted to betray me to your Ministry of State Security handlers—don't look surprised, I've known about it for years—you had ample opportunity to do so. You still do. I am sure they would pay you handsomely for my head. What I wanted to tell you, the Americans are sending investigators. They will sift through your past and recent activities, and will almost certainly want to talk to you."

"There is no evidence trail to uncover, sir." Looking embarrassed, Shen swallowed. "I apologize for thinking—"

Keung waved a hand. "I would have thought the same thing, were I in your place. I don't do business that way. However, should it become necessary for you to disappear, make your preparations now. Understand?"

"Yes, sir, and thank you. Regarding Vice Chairman Chen..."

If Chen's health suddenly turned for the worse, it would be

extremely difficult to explain under current circumstances, no matter how natural. Attention would turn to Keung, something he did not want. He had enough attention already.

"He is a friend...until proven otherwise. Have a contingency measure in place, just in case."

"Of course, sir."

"I'll see you at 12:30."

\* \* \*

WORLD SHOCKED AT CHINA'S REVELATION!
EUROPEAN UNION IMPOSES TRADE SANCTIONS
CONGRESS DEMANDS RETALIATION
STOCKMARKETS TAKE A DIVE!

As they lay side by side, gauze curtains hardly stirring, cradled in night's shadows, Tom stared at Melissa's barely discernible features. Left arm thrown across his chest, her fingernails traced random patterns that made his skin tingle. Smelling faintly of wild flowers, her flowing hair cascaded across her shoulder, hiding the curves of her body. He reached with his finger and traced the outline of her cheek and jaw, bemused that she agreed to marry him, and just a little concerned that he wouldn't be up to it. At least the announcement made her father's stern face crack into a smile of approval.

"About time, my boy," he said gruffly when they visited to tell her parents the news, handing him a tumbler of bourbon. "She'll take care of you or break your bones trying."

Tom didn't like the sound of that, but knowing his darling girl's fierce determination when she set her mind on something, he believed it, the images making him wince. She never said she wanted to change him; liking him just the way he was, but in her opinion, he did need some domestication. What, vacuuming the floor and taking out the rubbish? He did that already. As a long

267

standing bachelor, he told her, he could take care of himself, in-cluding the washing up—and then went and did it, to her vast amusement. He didn't mind the daily chores, but having some-one around all the time sharing his space took getting used to. Some things he used to indulge in were simply off the list now. Once she moved in with him, he made several adjustments, but his experience with Malena had given him a heads-up. Anyway, those adjustments were far more pleasant than onerous.

"I would rather have a simple civil ceremony and get away, only the two of us," he murmured, stroking her bare arm.

"A church wedding, I'm afraid," she said dreamily.

He could imagine her and her mother, huddled together, go-ing over the arrangements and the reception afterward, and flinched.

"We elope and my parents, not to mention some of my clos-est friends, would never forgive me. You'll like it," she told him comfortably. "Anyway, you don't have to do anything. I have it all in hand."

He could picture her old man going after him with a shotgun if he attempted a Las Vegas-style ceremony. He still needed to find a best man, the list of people he cared to ask alarmingly short.

"How many people will be at this clambake?"

"Clambake?" She giggled. "Tom, you can be such a square, you know."

"How many?"

"Nothing fancy. Mother is talking about 100 to 150 people, and that includes those from your side."

"Apart from my parents and sister, there aren't that many on my side. When I left Seattle, I also left my old friends behind. The only people I really know are my Houston colleagues and I don't like them well enough to invite to my wedding."

"What about Malena?" she purred maliciously.

"Oh, that's droll. Christ! If I got you two together, one of you wouldn't be walking out."

She chuckled, her fingers marching across his chest. "Then you'd take the one who's left standing."

"Nothing doing. She was an interesting chapter in my life, but I want the rest of my book to be with you, my sweet."

"Why, Tom. You're sweeping me off my feet."

"You *are* off your feet."

Melissa grinned. "You randy old thing. Is that all you think about?"

He ran his palm down to the swell of her hips and caressed her thigh. Her every curve known to him, having explored them over endless nights, but he never tired of touching her, marveling at the silky smoothness of her skin, loving every inch. He planted a lingering kiss on her bare shoulder and stared into her captivating eyes.

"I'm thinking how nice it will be to spend the rest of our days together," he said softly.

Sighing, she leaned against him. "The thought does have some appeal. Your parents are okay coming to Baltimore for the wedding?"

"No problem," he assured her. "It will give them a chance to do some east coast sightseeing, and September is a nice time of year. Sis and her brood are in New York, a short hop to DC."

"You get to see your parents a lot?"

"Not too often. I moved around when I joined the Bureau and was too interested in my career to worry about what my parents were doing. I try to see them for Christmas, that's about it."

"Sounds like you don't have much of a relationship."

"It's a live and let live proposition. We get along."

She stirred, snuggled closer and rested her head in the crook of his arm.

"Tom, why do you want to go to China? I know you said the case isn't closed, but you're not a field agent anymore. If something were to happen to you, I'd simply die."

"Nothing is going to happen to me, my sweet, and I won't be doing anything dangerous."

"Being in China trying to catch someone who is probably high in the Politburo isn't dangerous? This is a risk you don't have to take. What with the wedding and all, I feel like you're running away from me. Are you?"

He stroked her shoulder, thinking that perhaps he shouldn't have told her, but he didn't want to load it on her when it was a done deal. He pictured the ensuing scene without any trouble, including the unpleasant consequences for him. Besides, he wanted to share everything in his life with her—well, almost everything. Anyway, it wasn't a done deal yet.

"As far as I'm concerned, until the perpetrator or perpetrators are uncovered, the case is still open. President Zhou is bending over backward to cooperate, but that could be a blind play. President Walters cannot act until we find out who pulled this off, and he's under a lot of pressure to pound the Chinese."

"I don't blame him, but why does it have to be you?"

"I could give you a dozen Bureau issue answers why I shouldn't, but the bottom line is; I want to because it's my job. I'm good at this kind of thing. Anyway, Hancock might not let me go and he'll also trot out all those Bureau reasons why I can't." He brushed her cheek. "You don't want me to go?"

Silence crowded the dark room.

"I won't hold you back. I know enough not to try and tie you down. It's only—"

"I know, but this is important, and I'll be careful."

"That's spin talking and you know it. This may be your job like you said, but you have people who work for you. Field agents."

"You don't want me to go," Tom said flatly, tension building in his stomach.

"I want a husband in my bed, not a hero. A posthumous medal won't keep me warm at night."

The problem was, he appreciated her point of view, and that's what made it painful. Was it hubris and he simply didn't want to let go, knowing she was right? He wished it were that simple.

"I'll make you a deal. This will be my last field job."

"Don't make promises you can't keep, but if you get hurt, I'll…I'll never speak to you again."

"Who's making promises now?"

He gathered her in his arms and she threw a leg over him. Stroking her back, he stared into darkness. After a while, her breathing became slow and even, leaving him wondering if he was doing the right thing. Even if right, it didn't mean he should be the one going, and Melissa had a point. His field days were behind him now. Because he was now an executive, would the rest of his Bureau days be spent chained to a desk, sending others into the firing line? Grim as the idea was, it probably reflected his career path. He would have to resign himself to playing at a different level. No, resigning himself wasn't quite right. He enjoyed his work, interacting with powerful people, making decisions that count.

*Save it for the mind benders, Tom. You're a power addict and you know it.*

*Christ!*

Breakfast a rush affair as always. He drove downtown aggressively, but took care. Getting injured or worse to save a few lousy seconds didn't balance the books. If he hurt somebody by being an idiot? It wasn't worth the trip.

After dropping Melissa off, he got out of the elevator and strode toward Marsha's open office. Seeing him coming, she smiled.

"Oh, Tom. Mr. Hancock wants to see you."

"Good, because I want to see him."

It hadn't turned eight yet, but most of the floor already occupied and humming. Stopping before Hancock's door, he knocked and stepped in.

"Morning, boss."

The older man nodded and waved at a chair. "Sit down, Mee-cham."

Tom made himself comfortable, crossed his legs, and waited.

"I had a chat with Graham Stone about your meeting with the President. You made a favorable impression on both. That's good, because the Bureau needs that kind of stroking. Then you went and soured the cream by telling the President you haven't finished your job. In case it slipped your mind, your terms of reference were to find out who attacked La Palma. You did that. The political dimension surrounding the case is not the Bureau's concern, or yours."

"In my book, telling the President that China pulled the trigger and leaving it at that isn't what I'd call finishing my job."

"You think I was found in a shopping bag, Tom? I'm the one who told you what you had to do, remember? The fact that we don't know whether this was a rogue ops or a government sponsored deal isn't our business!"

"Whose business is it? Leave it to the State Department and the CIA? You told me to treat this like any other criminal case, and that's what I've been doing. Perhaps you and the Director didn't intend to push it this far, but that's the job you gave me, boss."

Hancock sighed and nodded. "Well, whether we did or we didn't, President Walters has taken this out of my hands. Stone told me how he wants you and Price to put together a plan that will hopefully nail the bastards. Have you talked to Price about it?"

"I have a meeting with him at ten this morning." Tom shifted in his seat. Might as well get this over with. "I want to go to Beijing."

"Out of the question. You have a stack of people at your disposal. Use them."

"And I'd like to take Keith Davenport with me. I'm sure Federer won't mind. As a CIA operative, Keith will represent the Agency."

"Which part of the no wasn't clear, Tom?" Hancock asked softly, his eyes glittering in warning.

"Boss, this isn't a case for a Fly Team and it's not something we should leave to the CIA alone, despite President Zhou's invitation that we can send anyone. You know what they'll think if we do that. The CIA people are spies and Zhou invited them in to spy. Our guys won't get any cooperation and won't find a thing, leaving us none the wiser."

"I didn't say the Bureau wouldn't be sending a contingent," Hancock countered. "It's just that you won't be on it."

Tom leaned forward. "We send one of Federer's boys, right? How will that look to Zhou? La Palma has created a major national crisis for him and the Bureau sends him an ordinary agent and a snoop. The way it will look to him, we can't be taking this very seriously, or President Walters is only going through the motions, having already decided on a course of action. I was there when he spoke to Zhou, threatening to send in the 7th Fleet. If Zhou hasn't sanctioned La Palma we must show that we believe him, and we do that by giving him senior people who can interact at ministerial level and still know how to run a ground operation."

Hancock frowned. "Okay, I'll buy that, but you don't go and that's final. Federer is capable and he is senior enough."

"It's my show, boss."

"Who is running this Division? You or me?"

"Boss—"

"Shut the hell up. You're a bloody pain, Meecham. Did you know that?"

Tom grinned. "Yeah, so I've been told."

"I'm not surprised. I'll run this past Marshal and get back to you. One question. If you don't want the responsibility of being a Special Agent in Charge, I can move you back to field work, which you seem to prefer. Promoting you too quickly could have been a mistake, but it's one I can correct."

Tom felt his mouth go dry and slowly stood up. "This isn't an ordinary investigation and we both know it. If we don't get this right, President Walters could end up making a wrong move, escalating what is already a tense situation. As head of Operations I, my concern is to close this case, political dimension and all. This has nothing to do with being a field agent. I know how to close this and I'm the best person to do it. If I have given you any other impression, relieve me."

"Get your feathers down, my boy," Hancock growled. "You have given me the reaction I wanted. As you pointed out, this isn't an ordinary case, and whether we like it or not, it does have a political dimension. Come and see me after you've had your chat with Price. By the way, *do* you have a plan?"

Cooling down from Hancock's stinging remark, his response more vehement because it held a grain of truth, Tom sat down and refocused his thoughts. Damn it all, he liked field work, but he liked planning, organizing and managing far more.

"President Zhou hasn't said so outright, but I gather that his investigative efforts to pin down the perpetrators weren't entirely successful."

"Not surprising," Hancock added musingly. "Given the factional byplays over there, whoever was behind this would have covered his ass."

"That's what I figured, boss. I don't know much about how their Ministry of State Security runs things. They're probably more comfortable doing direct arrests and aggressive interrogation than genuine detective work and following forensic procedures. I have asked our Beijing legate office to give us a heads-up on them. When we get there—whomever you send—we'll go over everything that's been done so far and start from scratch. To avoid possible local stonewalling, our Quantico labs will process any evidence we find. There are lots of details to work out, but that's what my meeting with Mark Price will essentially cover.

"To understand the background over there, Price is digging up profiles of all major State Council and Politburo Standing Committee members, identifying their affiliations with the elitist princeling *taizidang* or populist factions. The problem we'll face from what I have learned, most of those guys have a foot in both camps, which might mean the La Palma campaign could be personal."

Hancock pursed his lips and nodded. "I guess you can't have things pinned down until your team is over there and gets its bearings. You have considered the security angle?"

"According to Larry Tanner, Zhou will have us covered, but we'll have to watch our backs anyway. If we dig up a suspect and he knows we're after him—"

"He probably knows that already."

"—there could be consequences."

"To put it mildly."

"Of course, if Zhou is behind this, I doubt that we'll find anything, and he'll make sure he's covered. However, every crime scene has a clue, even if it isn't immediately obvious. We'll just have to find it."

"In this case, all the clues are at the bottom of the Atlantic at La Palma."

"Perhaps, but there has to be a trail we can follow back to the source, and the submarine remains have given us one to follow. *Somebody* ordered it out."

"See me when you get back from Langley. That's all, Tom."

* * *

Parked on the taxiway, the sleek twin-engine Air Force Gulfstream spooled up its engines, impressive with its coat of white and blue belly. Four F-16 Falcons stood parked side by side on the flight line. An open 'Follow Me' pickup rounded the corner and sped toward the fighters. The Andrews Air Force Base seemed otherwise deserted.

A light breeze stirring his hair, Tom turned from the open hangar where mechanics fiddled around another Gulfstream, his heart heavy. Looking at him, Melissa's mouth curved up in a stilted smile before curving down again. With the smell of jet fuel clogging the air, he opened his arms and she stepped into his embrace. He squeezed her tight, brought his mouth down on her soft lips, and she hugged his neck. He came up for air and smiled as he brushed a lock of golden hair that hid her right cheek.

"No visitors while I'm away, okay, my sweet?"

Grim, eyes serious, she nodded. "I'll be counting the hours."

"Me too. Love you," he said softly, swallowing a lump in his throat.

"Take care."

"You know me, always prepared." He glanced at the executive jet ready to roll, flashed her a small smile and disengaged her arms.

Four yards away, Keith Davenport hugged his two little girls, his pretty brunette wife trying hard to keep her emotions under control. Tom knew how she felt.

"I'll call you every day," he said and waved to Melissa.

"You better, or I'll have one of Mark's people rough you up," she declared.

Wanting badly to stay with her, he clamped his mouth, nodded and strode toward the aircraft. The master sergeant standing beside the boarding steps saluted as Tom climbed in. Inside the luxuriously appointed cabin, the flight attendant beamed at him, smart in her blue Air Force blouse and skirt.

"Welcome aboard, sir."

"Thank you," he growled and made his way toward the beige portside calf leather seat. A moment later, Keith stepped in and took the other seat, squeezing past a small table.

"I hate saying goodbye," he said gruffly.

The sergeant dogged the hatch and went into the cockpit. The attendant grinned at them.

"My name is Stefanie and I'll be looking after you during this flight—with some help from Master Sergeant Ricardo. On behalf of Major Weber and copilot Captain Cardy, I want to welcome you on board, gentlemen."

The Gulfstream wound up its engines and slowly began to move.

"Our flight time to Beijing will be 11 hours and 35 minutes, cruising at 51,000 feet. Our airspeed will be 600 miles per hour. Scheduled arrival time at Beijing Nanyuan military airport is 10:05 a.m. today." She smiled as she said that. "Beijing is exactly twelve hours behind DC. Lunch is in two hours, and I'll bring coffee and snacks once we're on course. Don't hesitate to call on me or Ricardo if you need anything."

Tom grinned at the pert kid. "Thanks, Stefanie. I didn't know a Gulfstream could reach Beijing in one hop."

"We're in a long-range G550 version, sir. It has a cruising range of 7,500 miles, which will get us there easily. If you would strap in please, we'll be taking off shortly." She flashed them an advertising grin and made her way to the rear.

Tom got a better view of the base facilities when the jet turned onto the East Perimeter active runway. The pilot walled the engines and he sagged against the seat as the aircraft accelerated. He saw Melissa waving and he blinked a couple of times. Thinking about her, he was grateful for the relative silence in the cabin, spared the annoying preflight safety spiel passengers endured on commercial flights.

The wingtip came up as the airflow strengthened and the nose pitched up. A thump as the gear sagged in the wells and they were airborne. The flaps wound in and the aircraft turned west. This was his second time in a Gulfstream. The first two years ago when he and Mark Price flew to Tel Aviv to snatch a Mossad operative who organized the sabotage of the Valero Texas City

Refinery. He enjoyed that flight and service, and he planned to enjoy this one, despite being a ball busting long haul. Still, it was better than having to stop over at Seattle's McChord Field for refueling.

He vaguely wondered what happened to the cute attendant he had on that flight. He dated Nancy a couple of times, but both knew it wasn't going anywhere. She was a career Air Force girl and he belonged to the FBI. It simply wasn't meant to be.

Still climbing, the Gulfstream began to eat the miles, the landscape below starting to lose definition under the pervading brown smog haze as they gained altitude.

Stefanie walked up carrying a tray, a home-grown smile lighting her face. She unloaded a steel pot of steaming coffee, cups and sundries, and a dish of fried Chinese finger foods. Tom wondered if this was a gag, then decided not. The Air Force had no sense of humor.

"Enjoy," she said brightly and strode down the slightly sloping aisle.

Keith turned his head to look at her.

"Dirty old goat," Tom muttered with a broad grin. "And you a married man."

Chuckling, Keith reached for the pot. "And you're about to be married. I saw how you looked at her."

"My interest is purely platonic."

"So is mine. Just checking her landing gear."

"I'll bet you were." Tom reached for a golden spring roll and popped the hot finger-long morsel into his mouth.

Chewing on the delicious tidbit, he looked forward to some VIP treatment. Keith poured coffee into their cups and Tom stirred in half a teaspoon of sugar. He sniffed the fragrant brew, took a sip, and nodded in appreciation, reminding himself to ask Stefanie if he could buy the blend somewhere. Taking a miniature dim sum, he sat back, allowing the comfortable seat to mold itself around him.

"Eleven and a half hours, she said. My butt is already killing me," Keith remarked dryly.

"They could have put us on a commercial flight, you know," Tom told him callously.

"Yeah. By the way, Tom. Thanks for letting me come along."

"No one I'd like better."

"I'm surprised Hancock let *you* go. You're a pretty senior guy to be getting your hands dirty."

"Can't have the CIA hoard all the fun. By the way, the Beijing station chief, Paul Rogan. What do you know about him?"

"Supposed to be reliable, a self-starter. However, he's become domesticated, too many diplomatic functions, and may resent us messing in his veggie patch."

"Well, we'll deal with him as necessary. I know I said this before, Keith. We have a clear objective on this trip. If you or Price have another objective in mind and I find out, you'll be flying back the same day."

Keith chuckled. "Don't worry. The Company has no hidden agenda to push. Anyway, we have specialists looking at China. I won't spoil this trip by pulling a beginner's trick."

"You've got nice kids," Tom said, having made his point.

They would be operating on Chinese sufferance and he didn't want to get them offside by nosing around where they weren't wanted. There would be enough local resistance to their presence as it is.

"Now that I'm no longer in the field, I get to see them more, and Karelina likes it that way. So do I, for that matter. Undercover work isn't all that dashing anyway. The movies got it all wrong and gave us a bad name. As an FBI man, you'd know."

Tom nodded. "I do. I must admit, I enjoyed my field days until I remembered all the dull parts. What I'm doing now is far more consuming and satisfying," he added, realizing it was true. "Have you ever considered a career in the Bureau? Norton is moving to the LA office at end of the year. With your experience and attitude, you'd be ideal to take over ITOS-I."

Smiling, Davenport crossed his legs. "Funny how these things come around."

"Funny how?"

"I've been offered to head our Counterterrorism Center at the end of my tour with the Bureau."

"So, come December, I'll be losing another good man."

"If Raymond Grant was still the DCIA, I'd probably take you up on that offer, but I like what Mr. Price has done with the Agency, although not everyone welcomed the spring cleaning."

"Yeah, he told me. If you change your mind, let me know."

"I'll do that and I appreciate the offer."

Tom nibbled on another spring roll and sipped his coffee, feeling completely at ease, the engine hum providing a soothing background. Disappointed at Keith's rejection, but not altogether surprised. Men like him were valuable commodities and the Agency would naturally want to hang onto them. It meant that he would have to scrounge a replacement for Norton from somewhere else, and Hancock would probably have a say in it anyway.

Davenport surveyed the cabin's wood-paneled layout and nodded. "The Air Force knows how to travel. I could get used to this."

"So could I," Tom agreed. "Unfortunately, there isn't time to enjoy it. Still, it's nice to have one of these at your beck and call when you need it."

Davenport leaned over the snack dish and frowned, fingers hovering before deciding on a sesame seed morsel. When he finished, he wiped his fingers on a cloth napkin.

"You want to go over the profile sheets?"

"After lunch," Tom said. "I want to enjoy the ambiance for a while."

Keith smiled, sat back and stretched out his legs. "Yep, I could definitely get used to this."

"It's a pity your guys couldn't come up with anything on Professor Chuan Jianbo," Tom mused. "It would have helped."

"We didn't have much to go on with," Davenport said apologetically. "He slipped in his office and cracked his head."

"Inconvenient."

"You think he's involved?"

Tom shrugged. "It's possible. He is a small piece of data that I don't want to discard just yet, and somebody I want to look at more closely. We have few enough leads as it is."

"We're not going in entirely empty-handed."

Tom raised his eyebrows. "Minister Lin Jinpan's report? Everything done correctly and it doesn't tell us anything. No, we do have something. His profile sheet says Lin is a Tuanpai. If he is also Chairman Keung Yang's buddy, he wouldn't want to compromise him."

"True, but the report does give us three solid leads to follow," Davenport pointed out. Tom wagged a finger at him.

"Four leads. You forgot Zhou."

"You're right. Just because he asked for our help doesn't mean he wants us to find anything. Unraveling Chinese corner politics could derail our entire investigation."

"Frankly, I don't care about their politics, or who did what to whom and who got paid. Not entirely anyway. Understanding their psychology will help us nail down the motive. If we can establish a solid link between any of these men, we'll be able to wear one of them down."

"Or he'll wear *us* down if we get too close—terminally. All these guys are senior Politburo luminaries. They've got to be tough to have climbed that high. We do have a solid link: Keung and Chen Teng."

"It's a link only because Zhou says it is and because both are Tuanpai. That's not enough to damn them, although I'm not discounting the possibility that they're our men. Others could be involved, like Admiral Xhal Shenglai. There is talk he'll be the next minister for National Defense, and his hawkish anti-American views are well known. As commander of the PLA Navy, he would have been in an ideal position to order the *Shang* to sail. Talking about orders, the one Han Yunshan is supposed to have written, we need to get our hands on that paper."

"According to Lin Jinpan, it's genuine," Davenport said.

"Perhaps, but I want our guys at Quantico to go over it. Including other documents Han and Chen have issued. I don't know how the Chinese go about doing their forensics, but I know how we do it. If we can nail down who actually signed those orders, we'll have our man without having to make ourselves too unpleasant."

"If Han did issue those orders, knowing how toxic they were, why make a copy?"

Tom chuckled. "Beats me, Keith. That's why I want to have that piece of paper analyzed."

"Even if it appears Han wrote that document, it could still be a forgery. It wouldn't be difficult to cut and paste his signature, run a photocopy, and there you are."

"I know, but a copy is all we have."

Davenport sighed. "I hope they meant it when they said we can nose around anywhere."

"If we get tangled in local protocol, Larry Tanner will hear about it."

Davenport blanched in surprise. "The Secretary of State?"

"He's been laying the groundwork for our visit, making sure Zhou spreads the word to everybody that we're not to be messed with."

"That's nice. I hope the people we're after paid attention."

Tom smiled broadly and placed his cup on the small table. "We'll find out, won't we. By the way, Mark Price promised that his CIA guys won't get involved. I hope that's true, Keith. I don't want them getting tangled with Chinese security. Somebody fumbles and we could have a major diplomatic flap on our hands."

"Don't worry, Tom. Paul Rogan received the word. However, they *are* available if we need extra support."

"We'll play it by ear," Tom murmured.

He exhaled softly, sat back, and glanced out the window. Unbroken by any cloud, the deep blue sky faded into haze as it straddled the horizon. Far below, the ground looked like a satellite map, a fuzzy mosaic of browns and greens. He had no regrets coming, giving a mental sigh of relief when Hancock told him the FBI director, Patrick Marshal, had approved the trip. Procedurally, Hancock was right to veto his plan and Marshal could be working a deeper game. He had the White House to deal with, and Walters wanted answers. The way Hancock explained it, Tom had the big picture and understood all the threads wound into it, including the nuances and different interpretations of available facts. It would be impossible to pass all that to someone else. Tom didn't argue with him. Of course, having bullied his way into the trip, everybody up to the president would now be demanding results. Failure might very well see him out in the field again, or managing the Anchorage office.

Looking at the sky, he listened to the hum of the engines.

He wasn't aware that he had dozed off until enticing smells drifting through the cabin made his nostrils twitch.

"Tom…" Davenport prompted, and Tom looked up to see a young black officer smiling at him.

"Mr. Meecham, I'm Major Weber, your pilot. I trust everything is satisfactory, sir?"

"Fine, Major. Stefanie is taking good care of us."

"I'm glad to hear it. We'll be crossing the Oregon coast in about two hours. Since we're moving against the Earth's rotation, it won't be long before we're into night. We have a wide selection of entertainment and news channels we can patch into. Just tell Stefanie or Sergeant Ricardo what you want."

"Thanks for the service, Major."

The young officer's demeanor became grave. "Sir, find out

who attacked us and I'll be paid in full."

"Is the Air Force keen to pound on somebody?"

"We've been screwed over by the Chinese for some time, Mr. Meecham. This latest incident is merely another link in their policy chain to bring us down. It's time we stopped taking it and dished it out. If you'll excuse me, sir, I'll get back up front."

When the cockpit door closed after the fire-eating major, Davenport pointed a finger at Tom.

"You know, he's got a point."

"You've been eating raw bran for breakfast, Keith?"

"I'm serious. The man on the street is sick and tired of seeing us shafted by everybody. If it's not our own financial institutions, it's the politicians. People out there don't care if La Palma was officially sanctioned or not. All they see is China attempting to cripple us. Zhou might not have authorized it, but he wouldn't be shedding any tears if the plan succeeded. They are our ideological enemies, and whoever pulled this off proved it."

"I read the papers," Tom said. "I agree with your sentiments, but it's not that simple and you know it. The papers and the networks sensationalize everything."

"La Palma and the tsunami weren't sensational?"

"They were for La Palma, but the tsunami hardly touched us. The headlines don't necessarily reflect genuine public opinion, regardless of the polls. The polls only ask questions that will support whatever outcome the pollsters want. Sure, corporate greed brought on the Global Financial Crisis, which almost killed us, but President Walters isn't taking this lying down. He wants to hang the bastards responsible for La Palma, but he needs to know who they are, and that's where we come in."

"Well, we had the guts to slap sanctions on them. That's something," Davenport growled.

"If we do our job, I hope to see Walters do more than that," Tom shot back.

Stefanie walked up the aisle carrying a tray with two small

wine bottles and glasses. Beaming at them, she unloaded the stuff on the table, opened a bottle and poured for them.

"Krug Grand Cuvee champagne, gentlemen. You'll find it different," she told them warmly. A moment later, she came back with two bowls on plates. "Spicy pork rib soup with croutons."

Tom sniffed at the steamy concoction and his mouth watered. He picked up the champagne glass and raised it in a salute to Keith. Taking a sip of the fragrant white wine, he nodded in appreciation at the delicate fruity flavor.

Davenport tried it and sighed. "You'll have to dream up more jobs, Tom, where I can wine and dine like this."

Laughing, Tom tried the soup. It certainly didn't come out of a can.

After soup, they had shredded slices of roast beef served with a mixed salad. The main course of honey-glazed duck breast, golden potatoes and warm vegetables, accompanied by a French merlot, went down well. Both of them had a slice of baked cheesecake with a sour cherry sauce. Over coffee and a snifter of fine Otard cognac, Tom felt pleased with himself and the world. He would have relished a nice cigar to top off the meal, but sadly, Stefanie ruled that out. He didn't complain.

High in the sky, the sun lit the smudgy landscape below, making the massed cloudbanks look like popcorn. From the flat desert in the east, overflying the Cascades, the terrain turned into forests and checkered farmland. Snow covered the higher peaks. The aircraft crossed the coast and headed over the open Pacific. As he looked out the window, it hardly seemed real that they were only a third of the way into their journey.

Before getting down to business with Keith, he walked up and down the short aisle, smiling at Stefanie and Ricardo, both buried in a book. Tom took his seat and gave Keith a nod. The CIA man opened a slim briefcase, took out a sheaf of stapled papers, and held them out. Tom flipped quickly through the pages, spending a bit of time over the photographs, building an impression of each man. He had gone over the documents in detail yesterday, but apart from dry statistics, career summary and political leanings, nothing stood out to give him a handle on anybody.

"You want to go over each one from the top?" Davenport asked, rifling through his copy.

Tom sighed and sat back. "Frankly, Keith, I'm a little disappointed with this stuff. I'd have thought the Agency would have something more substantive on these men. All I have here are resumes. I wanted to know what makes these guys tick. Motive, remember? The psychological profiles don't tell me anything apart from the fact that they're determined, ruthless and overachievers, borne out by the positions they hold. I knew all that already."

Davenport frowned. "It's my fault, Tom. I should have debriefed Clavel before he cleaned out his desk."

"Never mind. I already spoke to Mark Price. He'll look into it and email our Beijing legate office if he finds anything." Tom peered down and tapped a sheet. "Chen Teng, Central Military Commission Vice Chairman. President Zhou suspects him of forging Han Yunshan's orders in a possible frameup, but I don't see Chen gunning for Han's job or planning an attack on us through La Palma. Why would he want to strike at us? He just doesn't seem the power hungry type. It's the one thing that's had me scratching my head from the beginning. See why I want to get into the heads of these men?"

"I wondered the same thing," Davenport said. "There is a scenario though, that could explain everything."

"Oh?"

"Ordinary politics. Keung Yang is on record criticizing Zhou's headlong rush to embrace a market economy, and vocal at identifying the United States and the GFC for damaging China's economy. They weathered the GFC by pumping billions into a national infrastructure building program which has left them financially vulnerable."

Tom shook his head. "I don't buy it. China has over four trillion dollars in foreign reserves. How are they vulnerable?"

"Not the national treasury, but local provincial and city officials. When Beijing turned off the funding tap following the GFC stimulus, those officials turned to what's known as the shadow banks—private lenders—borrowing hugely to fund their building programs, inflating property values to unrealistic levels. Should this bubble burst, a lot of people over there could get seriously hurt and plunge the economy into recession. Keung could be blaming the United States for driving China into this mess, and used La Palma to cripple us in retaliation."

Nodding, Tom pulled at his chin. "If he could blame Han Yunshan for the attack, he would also be striking a blow against a *taizidang* enemy, and indirectly against Zhou. I like it, and it would give us a motive."

"A possible motive," Davenport said. "Like you said, Zhou could have engineered the whole thing himself in an attempt to rid himself of two Tuanpai troublemakers."

"By launching a sneak attack on us? From what I read in the papers and what the TV chair experts said, Zhou and Walters had a chummy meeting in April. If Zhou wanted to rid himself of Keung and Chen, he could have done that without striking at us. What would he gain?"

"China is our enemy and a growing world power. Perhaps Zhou wants it to be the only power."

"You're paranoid," Tom told him. "Even if Zhou did engineer this, he wouldn't have issued those orders. Much too dangerous. What if Han did in fact write those orders and arranged for Chen Teng to conveniently find them, then blamed the whole thing on Chen?"

Davenport scrunched his face. "Convoluted, but possible, I suppose. We're just going around in circles, you know."

"The tangled web we weave…" Tom chuckled.

"Han could clear himself if he submitted to a polygraph test."

"Perhaps, but the test wouldn't be conclusive. We'll do this the hard way, by the numbers. We get our facts, spread 'em around and put the jigsaw together until a picture emerges."

Davenport smiled. "You're pretty methodical how you do business. I noticed that about you, as have others."

"I'm a detective, Keith. Your training at The Farm must have given you a similar background."

"With an emphasis on dirty tricks," Davenport said wryly, and Tom laughed.

"Had any hairy experiences?"

"A couple of moments in Iraq and Afghanistan got my asshole puckered. Most of the time though, it's been boring surveillance work, sifting through documents and files, trying to fit it all together. These days, it's not so much political espionage, but keeping an eye on commercial developments and weapons intelligence. Maintaining a national competitive advantage automatically feeds into a national defense advantage. You only have to look at China as a classic example of that philosophy. The advances they made modernizing their military weren't done through original research and innovation. They stole it from us and the Europeans."

Tom nodded. "I've seen video footage of their new air superiority fighter, a copy of the F-35."

"And it has all the bugs we have in ours," Davenport said. "Security at Lockheed Martin was lousy, and you'd think they'd know better. They've beefed it up, but the damage is already done. The Chinese probably got our plans for the *Virginia*-class attack boat, but don't have the technology to produce it. The corollary to doing commercial spying is preventing foreign agencies from doing it to us. You don't need to have a costly nuclear weapons program if you can cripple your opponent's civil services systems. Unfortunately, a lot of our corporations, and others around the world, fail to recognize this as a serious threat, more interested at maximizing short-term profits. Cyber security simply isn't on their radar."

"Unless they want to hack into a competitor's system," Tom pointed out.

"You got that right. The other thing Price is tuning up is threat assessment. With a ten billion annual budget, the NSA and the CIA never saw 9/11 coming, wise after the event."

"I can see why you'd be interested at running the Counterterrorism Center."

"It's not about Al Qaida at all, although we're keeping an eye on them just as you are."

"I wondered why it took twelve years to nail Bin Laden."

"We had to find him first," Davenport deadpanned with a straight face, "even though he lived in a house a stone's throw from a Pakistani military base. Nobody's taking any bows over that one."

Not in the mood for more shop talk, Tom ordered coffee. Sipping, he allowed his thoughts to wander. Feeling drowsy, he reclined the seat and closed his eyes. Images chased each other in his mind of a giant tsunami sweeping up the Potomac, inundating everything in its path. The wall of water raced up Pennsylvania Avenue, carrying away cars, people, and anything loose. As he watched the catastrophe unfold, he flinched as the wave reared up, heading straight for him. Towering over him, he wanted to run, but his legs were stone. He wanted to scream, waiting for the wave to smash him...and waited, but it just hung there as terror built inside him. He could hear the hiss of tumbling water, the cries of people trying to scramble to safety, the blare of car horns, the grinding and tearing of trapped debris, yet everything was frozen. Somebody called his name and he thought of Melissa. Was she caught up in this monstrosity? The thought of losing her sent him into wild panic.

"Mr. Meecham?" The soft voice made his eyes snap open.

Stefanie's smiling face bent over him, a slim hand on his shoulder. "Are you all right, sir? You were moaning."

Blinking, the nightmarish images still vivid in his mind, he nodded. "I'm fine, thanks. Bad dream."

"If you'd like to pull up your seat, I'll be serving dinner."

Tom glanced out the window and saw darkness. "Wow, I must have really dozed off."

"A couple of hours," Davenport told him, nursing a glass of red wine.

While Tom got his seat upright, Stefanie cleared the table. "And what have you been up to?" he asked Keith.

"Watched a couple of documentaries. The movies didn't interest me, but I might give one a go after dinner."

Tom looked at his watch: five hours to go. Downhill from here in, the flight no longer a daunting prospect. The inviting smells coming from the galley got him primed, and he wondered what culinary delights awaited him.

*  *  *

A thick grayish-brown blanket hung over the horizon, obscuring the landscape. Tom couldn't believe it. They were supposed to breathe that soup? He looked up and inclined his head at the window. Davenport raised his eyebrows and shrugged.

"I'm sure they'll give us oxygen cylinders."

Tom could only shake his head. Beijing's twelve million people and unchecked industrialization did that, and they had to live in it, day after day. As he took a sip of coffee, he wondered if his health insurance covered this.

According to Stefanie, they'd be landing in ten minutes, which was okay with him. He slept surprisingly well in a bunk stowed against the aircraft's side, forward of the kitchenette bulkhead. Keith had the opposite one. Refreshed, greeted by a new dawn over what he expected to be a very strange country, both went through their morning toilet routine, emerging to a simple, but appetizing breakfast of mixed fruit juice, scrambled eggs, fried chicken sausages, button mushrooms and sliced potatoes. Accompanied by a basket of mixed pastries, bread and spreadable sundries, with good coffee to wash it all down, it was more than enough to quell his appetite. After all, how hungry could he get sitting inactive for eleven hours?

It wasn't until the Gulfstream sank into the smog layer itself that Beijing came into stark relief. Looking down, nothing distinguished it from any other city sprawl. With a brief apology, Stefanie cleared the hardware from the table and asked them to strap in. Tom was actually surprised to see blue sky, all traces of smog gone, but that was only an illusion. If this was as bad as it got, he could handle it.

Traffic moved steadily along a two-lane highway cutting through suburbia crowding the airport boundary. Evidence of industry lay visibly everywhere. The aircraft overflew a fuel tank farm and seemed to drift as it sank. Four twin-tailed fighters lay parked beside a hangar. Two large wide-body aircraft painted drab gray stood next to them. Cargo or fuel haulers, Tom figured. Well, Nanyuan *was* a military airport. The Gulfstream touched down with a squeal of tires and everything speeded up as it rushed down the runway. The pilot engaged reverse thrust and Tom sagged against his seat. As the aircraft turned onto a taxiway, he got to see houses built dangerously close to the airfield.

It felt somewhat surreal seeing China for himself, and exciting. Apart from a trip to Hawaii and Florida, he hadn't traveled much. Playing the tourist enthralled him. Although this wasn't a holiday trip, he hoped there would be time to see some of the sights.

The aircraft stopped some hundred yards from the terminal building and the engines immediately wound down. According to Stefanie, the crew would have a twenty-four-hour layover before heading back. When Tom finished his job, another Gulf-stream would pick them up.

Ricardo cracked the hatch and warm, moist air flooded the cabin, accompanied by a smell of burnt jet fuel. An aircraft somewhere spooled up its engines and roared down the runway. Tom wondered what it was and where it was going. Major Weber emerged from the cockpit and waited. Tom hung on a smile and walked up to him.

"Thanks for the flight, Major."

"It's been a pleasure, sir. Watch your back here."

"I intend to." Glancing at Ricardo and Stefanie, he nodded. "Thank you both for looking after us."

"You're welcome, sir," Stefanie said, smiling broadly.

Two trim men, a Chinese and a Westerner, both dressed in dark blue conservative suits, stood beside a black saloon parked on the apron. A heavyset individual wearing a stiff face that might have been nailed on leaned against the hood. The bouncer type stance told Tom he was their security. He took a deep breath and climbed down. The Chinese official strode toward him wearing a broad grin and extended his hand.

"Mr. Meecham, welcome to the People's Republic of China. My name is Weng Leijang, personal secretary to Premier Dzhang Qishan. You will meet him over lunch."

Tom nodded as they shook hands. He would be meeting the country's premier? It looked like Zhou was serious about this investigation or this may be merely slick PR.

"Thank you, sir. I am pleased to be here."

"Just call me Leijang, okay? We have a suite for you and Mr. Davenport at the Diaoyutai State Guesthouse. That's where we house all our important international visitors. Located in the center of the city, downtown as you call it, you will find it convenient." Weng turned toward the man beside him. "May I introduce First Secretary Hayes Lipson. He is from your embassy."

"Good to see you, Mr. Meecham," Lipson said briskly, an

important diplomat doing an underling a favor. As they shook hands, he tried for a crusher grip. Tom squeezed back, not giving an inch.

"I dare say we'll be talking to each other, Mr. Lipson."

After an uncomfortable moment the diplomat cleared his throat and released his grip. "We certainly will. The Ambassador is keen to see you. Dinner will be at the embassy."

Tom introduced Keith and there were more handshakes.

Looking apologetic, Weng clasped his hands. "Immigration formalities are waived, but I trust you're not carrying any weapons, gentlemen?"

"We're not armed, Leijang," Tom assured him.

"Excellent. I see that your luggage is loaded into the car, we might as well be going."

Weng insisted that his guests get into the limo first. Tom and Davenport took the rear-facing seat. The security guy slammed the door shut, opened the front door and slid in. The engine purred and the car moved off.

"I hope you had a pleasant flight?" Weng asked, settling his bulk into the soft seat.

"It's a long way to come, but they made us comfortable," Tom said and inclined his head at the window. "I thought it was the rainy season this time of year."

"It is, but we do get an occasional break in the weather," Weng commented, looking vastly amused. "We also get an occasional break from the smog, Mr. Meecham. It's one of the evils of industrialization, I'm afraid, and I'm not sure the benefits are worth the price. Don't look surprised. We *are* allowed to voice constructive dissent."

Tom studied the official. "You will have to forgive me if I make an inadvertent *faux pas*, which is due to my ignorance rather than any intended disrespect."

Lipson snorted and glared at Weng. "This barbarian wouldn't know the difference, Mr. Meecham."

Wincing, Tom expected an angry retort, but Weng merely laughed.

"Hayes has an oblique sense of humor, which I have learned to ignore. Pay no attention to him." He turned serious and folded his hands in his lap. "For the duration of your stay, Mr. Meecham—"

"Just Tom, if you don't mind."

"Thank you…Tom. As I was saying; for the duration of your stay, I shall act as your guide. This is not to watch you or prevent you from going anywhere or seeing anyone in the course of your investigation. My function is to open doors which under normal circumstances would be locked, especially to a foreigner."

"I appreciate that, Leijang," Tom said and meant it.

Without active cooperation from the Chinese government, he might as well go on a sightseeing tour. That didn't mean Weng couldn't also fulfill his duty as their official minder, something he did not resent. Were the roles reversed, the Bureau would have done the same thing.

"Given the delicate nature of your visit, Premier Dzhang does not want anything preventing you from achieving a successful outcome."

*Successful for whom*, Tom almost blurted, realizing that such a crass remark would alienate Weng and probably derail his investigation. He would have to tread carefully here.

"May I speak bluntly? And forgive me if I am breaching some protocol."

"Perhaps I can answer your unspoken question, Mr. Meecham," Lipson grated. "The United States is keen to uncover the people responsible for La Palma, as is President Zhou. Identifying these men is vital to formulating an appropriate response by the United States, regardless of any personal interest pursued by President Zhou. That interest is an internal matter which we're happy for him to deal with."

Tom clenched his teeth to stop himself from gaping. Judging

from Weng's wooden expression, Lipson's words were inflammatory in the extreme. There had clearly been some energetic discussions behind the scenes regarding his visit. Tom wasn't sure he wanted to know the details. Still, Lipson didn't have to rub it in so hard.

Weng noted his discomfort and gave a stiff smile. "Your countryman treads heavily, Tom, but given the circumstances, understandably so."

Weng was trying to make the best of it, but clearly looked annoyed. If this was the pinnacle of American diplomacy, Tom felt that someone in the State Department should tell Lipson to take a refresher.

"I am certain that Mr. Weng and Premier Dzhang wish only to preserve a mutually beneficial relationship between our two countries, Mr. Lipson."

"Well said!" Weng chortled and slapped Tom's knee. "I knew right away that you were a cultured man. We shall get along well," he said and turned slightly. "Is he always this diplomatic, Mr. Davenport?"

Smiling, Keith shook his head. "I'm afraid not, sir, but I have learned to live with it."

"Hah! Two unique individuals. Well, well."

Looking keenly out the window, Tom marveled at the profusion of cottages, large houses, small shop fronts flashing by, all brightly colored, traditional concave roofs with rounded red tiles and gargoyles at each corner. Clusters of slim residential towers farther back provided a contrasting backdrop, poignant evidence of China's transformation. Heavy traffic packed the two-lane highway, but moved steadily. He expected to see lots of bicycles and quaint little three-wheeler jeepneys, but all the cars appeared new and were a mixture of recognizable Western models. The modern look and feel of the city dispelled images of slums, narrow alleyways and oddly dressed peasants roaming about. This was a fully developed country and it would not do to underestimate the sophistication of its leaders.

"Our twenty-four-hour rush hour," Weng said wryly, and Tom grinned. He believed it.

Large neon signs mounted on most buildings advertised company names and decadent capitalist products. The other thing that struck him, all the signs were either in English or had English subtitles, including road boards, something he hadn't expected to see. What surprised him the most, every spare yard of space had lush trees, some very old, evidence that this wasn't done to impress visitors during the 2008 Olympics. The government clearly recognized it had a pollution problem and was doing something about it.

"Not so different from America, Tom?" Weng asked with a smile.

"Buildings are buildings, Leijang. It's the people inside them that make the difference."

"You don't fit my image of a typical Westerner. Most of them I meet are starched diplomats, so I suppose that doesn't count. Wouldn't you agree, Hayes?"

Lipson sucked in his breath. "As your guest, I would not presume to argue with my host on etiquette."

"Wise."

Recognizing that Tom and Keith wanted to play tourist, Weng left them to take in the sights as the limo wound its way deeper into the city. The sheer profusion of people everywhere somewhat daunting. Some twenty minutes later, driving past a sprawling park protected by a high brick fence, the car turned onto a driveway guarded by two uniformed armed soldiers. The heavyset guy up front got out and had a brief chat with one of the guards, who nodded and smartly presented arms.

"We have a small cottage placed at your disposal, Tom," Weng said as the car moved down a narrow lane lined with towering trees hiding several ancient buildings. "I trust it will be satisfactory."

"I am sure we will have no complaints," Tom said.

"Excellent!"

The car stopped beside a wide doorway flanked by two thick wooden posts. A red lion stood sentinel in front of each post. Weng opened his door and got out. Tom waited for Lipson to alight, then followed. Subdued city noises assaulted him immediately, but more like the sound of receding surf. The humid air had an unusual smell, a mixture of smog and blooming flowers. Looking around the immaculate lawns, the cathedral-like atmosphere made Tom feel he had stepped into another world. A large black BMW stood parked a few yards ahead of them. He noted the U.S. embassy markings on the number plate and figured it was Lipson's ride.

A diminutive elderly man emerged from the house, bowed and shuffled to the rear of the limo where he proceeded to extract the suitcases and carry them inside.

"That's Joseph," Weng said. "Make your wishes known to him and he'll look after you. He speaks passable English."

Tom glanced at Davenport. This was unexpected patronage indeed.

"I shall give you and Mr. Davenport time to freshen up, and I'll pick you up at 12:30," Weng said.

"Thank you."

"A pleasure, Tom." After shaking hands, Weng climbed quickly into the limo and it whispered off.

Joseph appeared and gave a small bow. "If you would please come inside?"

A tastefully decorated library opened on his left as Tom stepped into the cool house. Joseph stopped beside frosted glass sliding panels and waited. The room turned out to be a large lounge elegantly furnished with soft cloth divans. Ornately carved French chairs surrounded a heavily polished round wooden table, laid out with a coffee set and a plate of finger foods.

"I shall take your luggage to your rooms, gentlemen. Should you need anything, please pull the cord beside the door."

"Thank you, Joseph," Tom said.

The little man nodded and closed the panels after him. Lipson immediately strode to the table and poured himself a cup. He added cream and sugar, pulled back a chair, and sat down.

"You'll enjoy this place," he said after taking a sip. "Weng was right when he said they'll look after you—smiling while slipping in the knife. Don't be taken in by his charm. He is hardboiled as they come and will see to it that his interests aren't compromised, whatever they might be. Although relevant to your investigation, the political dimension shouldn't concern you too much. That'll be my responsibility. You do your job and the State Department will owe you big time."

Taken aback by Lipson's blunt declaration, Tom walked to the table, helped himself to some coffee and gazed pointedly around the room.

"Is it safe for us to talk here?"

Lipson snorted. "Do you mean, have they got the place bugged? Probably, but we'll discuss important stuff at the embassy." He took two quick gulps and stood up. "I'll want a full report on your meeting with Premier Dzhang."

Tom frowned at the diplomat's top-sergeant manner and bridled. "What exactly is your function in this investigation, Mr. Lipson?"

"Seeing to it that you find the bastards who attacked us, using whatever facilities are available at the Ambassador's disposal, which are considerable."

Tom looked hard into Lipson's granite eyes. "I'm happy to provide you feedback on any progress we might make, including requests for information or resources we may need, but I don't report to you. I just want that clarified."

"Without me, Tom, you won't find your way out the front door. As an interested party, I wanted to attend your luncheon with the premier, but that shit Weng vetoed it. You report to me because *anything* they say could have serious diplomatic implications, which you, as an amateur, might not recognize or appreciate. I also wanted to be there to stop you blurting something that could be counterproductive for everybody. You and Davenport were not invited to that lunch because Weng or Dzhang want to be pals. Am I painting the picture for you, Tom?"

"I get the picture, all right, except that you're painting the wrong one, Hayes. You don't have to tell me why I'm here or what is at stake. I know exactly what I have to do. As for reporting to you, forget it. I have my instructions from President Walters. If you don't like that arrangement, send Larry Tanner an email. Now if you'll excuse me, I need a shower. By the way, what time is dinner?"

Coloring, Lipson opened his mouth, then closed it. Exhaling loudly, he shook his head and smiled, but his eyes remained cold.

"Okay, hotshot. We'll sort this out later. I'll send a car for you at 6:30." He strode briskly toward the sliding panels, opened them and stomped out. The heavy front door slammed shut after him.

Davenport chuckled and hooked a finger over his shoulder. "We're going to have fun with that guy. If all our embassy staffers are like him we could be in trouble."

"One more minute and I would have pasted him one," Tom growled. "Still, he does have a point about the political nuances we'll face."

"Right now, I really don't much care for political nuances. That shower you mentioned? Sounds good to me."

Tom sighed and nodded. Lipson was on his home turf and didn't appreciate a couple of Washington weenies messing in his pond. As long as Lipson didn't attempt to throw his weight around, Tom was happy not to get in his way. He had enough on

his hands without having to patch up wounded sensibilities.
*Christl*

# Chapter Seven

Cottard frowned and rubbed the underside of his bulbous nose. "I would advise against it, Mr. President," he said heavily, clearly uncomfortable having to openly dissent. "Your UN address went down well and the retaliatory measures you announced were seen as measured and responsible. President Zhou is cooperating with our investigation. This will only risk unwarranted escalation of tension."

Walters understood Manfred's reluctance to take this to the next level. With a popularity rating of sixty-four percent, it looked like he would win a second term without having to conduct a major primaries fight, the Republicans lacking a candidate who could touch him. Raising public temperature over what many commentators interpreted was his vacillation to strike at China risked that rating, and Manfred didn't think the plan was worth it, especially as a negative outcome carried with it the real possibility of military confrontation. However, Walters looked beyond the next election campaign. Being president meant that sometimes he needed to take unusual action when American domestic and global interests were threatened.

He nodded and looked at his SecState. "Larry?"

Tanner thrust out his chin. "I have to agree with Manfred on this one. There is no percentage sending in the 7th Fleet. Despite heated editorial rhetoric from some papers and right-wing groups who are really only pushing their own ideological agenda and using this incident as a suitable vehicle to do so, the people don't want us pursuing a military solution. We only have to look at results of past Administrations—"

"Republican administrations," Walters added wryly, keenly

conscious of the fact that his Secretary of State was a Republican.

"—when they employed that option. We failed to achieve our objective every time, embittered our allies and wasted American lives and resources in the process." Tanner gave a small smile. "And yes, this was done by my Party, but you guys didn't protest much when we did it. The point I want to make, President Zhou will see the 7th Fleet loitering off the Chinese coast as provocative and he'll be right. We're picking a fight you don't want and can't win. You cannot launch a strike even if we had defined targets, which we don't, and risk a major retaliatory response. Everybody is still enraged and wants to see China pounded, but not if it embroils the United States in a major war or damages the world's economy. They're not Iraq whom we can roll over with a couple of tank brigades."

"A good analysis, Larry," Walters acknowledged and turned to his national security advisor. "What about you, Graham?"

Hands clasped behind his back, standing on the great seal, Stone showed little emotion as he glanced at Tanner.

"I think you're wrong, Mr. Secretary. The threat of a response doesn't necessarily mean that there will be a response. We announced trade sanctions and the European Union followed suit. It is interesting though, apart from the British, the French and the Germans made only token protests. Both have significant commercial interests in China, interests important to their economies, which bears out what you said."

"Important to their multinationals, you mean," Tanner snorted.

"Those multinationals provide employment and revenue that keeps those countries prosperous," Stone countered evenly. "Look at other major global players. India reported the event, but they hardly said a negative word. They're trying to patch up and expand their relationship with China. Why risk diplomatic gains simply because the United States is morally outraged and wants to strike back. Brazil made a tepid protest for local public consumption, but they're not keen to alienate a vital trading partner because they lost six people in the tsunami with negligible infrastructure damage."

"You seem to be defending my position, Graham," Tanner said with satisfaction.

"I'm merely demonstrating that the world isn't interested in following the United States into a military response, when such a response would clearly be damaging to everyone's strategic economic position. La Palma was an attack on *us* and everybody is happy for us to handle it. The world is prepared to give us diplomatic support, but you can bet that vested interest lobby groups are already exerting pressure on their respective governments not to overreact, as has already happened here."

"He's right about that," Cottard acknowledged glumly. "I've had more than a dozen calls from Congressmen crying the world will cave in if commercial ventures in China are compromised." Looking like he was in pain, he cleared his throat. "Perhaps I unconsciously reflected their concerns when I disagreed with your proposal, Mr. President."

"Go on, Graham," Walters said softly.

"Sending in the 7th Fleet, Mr. President, will be seen by many as another example of American knee-jerk reaction, abandoning the diplomatic process in favor of a quick military option. You will probably get that reaction from the very people who only a few days ago demanded that you take that very action. As I said, the threat of a response doesn't mean there will be a response, although I would recommend a limited strike.

"China sought to annihilate us, regardless who over there initiated the plan. Impact on other countries was merely collateral damage. Implementing economic sanctions was a measured proportional response, which I supported, but does nothing to punish the regime. Keep in mind that it's their regime who chose to strike at us, not their companies or people who will bear the brunt of our sanctions. Now, that regime may have sent another submarine to finish what they have started. If they succeed, the world will face a nightmare. The 7th Fleet is the face of your Administration, Mr. President. It is *your* face and you need to show President Zhou your displeasure at a national level rather than merely an economic one."

Walters nodded slowly. "You summed up my feelings well, Graham. If I don't do this, China and everybody else will see us for what we really are—capitalists who will not risk their precious dollar no matter what. I don't have your foreign policy experience, Larry, but I can read people. So far everybody has reacted predictably. After the initial indignation and enthusiastic applause to my UN speech, feelings have cooled and governments everywhere are now in the second phase: reflection. They have the wellbeing of their voters in mind, as do our Congressmen. I have no problem with that, but who speaks for America? I'm talking about the third phase: national conscience. I agree that people on the street don't want us embroiled in another war, a serious war, and I don't want to start one, but soon they'll begin to think. Is the Administration going to let China get away with this, slapping them on the wrist by applying sanctions? Where is the punishment for a gross criminal act, because that's what La Palma was. Having the 7th Fleet steaming down their coast will show them that we haven't lost our sense of justice or resolve to act. The presence of those ships won't be a hollow gesture either. What's more, like I told Zhou. Should we find their *Qin* steaming into the Indian Ocean, it will be sunk." He looked at each of them in turn. "But I intend to do more than that. I want a surgical strike against China's Qinggir Lop Nur test site, regardless of Meecham's investigative efforts."

Tanner gaped. "You intend to detonate an atmospheric nuclear warhead?"

"That's right."

"You can't mean that, Mr. President! That's against every

treaty we signed and the world will treat *us* as the pariah!"

"I already consulted with Congressional leaders of both Houses and obtained their support."

"You made a major policy initiative without consulting me?"

"Damnation! You *are* consulted. That's why you're all here."

"If you do this, Zhou will retaliate. He won't have any choice and he's not likely to bomb Nevada."

"He does have a choice, Larry. He can choose to do nothing, acknowledging that ultimately what happened at La Palma his responsibility. If we detect that his Second Artillery Corps are fueling their ICBMs, Zhou will get one call from me before I launch a full strike."

"Mr. President, if he does nothing, he'll be overthrown—"

"That will be an internal matter for their Politburo."

"—and whoever replaces him *will* strike back!"

"Zhou knew about the attack on La Palma and chose to sit on his hands, hoping we wouldn't find his missing sub, knowing full well he was compromising the relationship between our two countries. However, we did find his sub and he ended up severely embarrassed. As you pointed out a number of times, China is seeking to become a dominant political, economic and military world power. Keeping silent about La Palma confirmed that policy. I intend to demonstrate to Zhou and everybody else over there that being a player on the world stage also has obligations."

Tanner wagged a finger. "That's all very well, Mr. President, but you're talking like a Westerner. The Chinese don't look at things the same way we do. Zhou was educated here and understands us, but his philosophy is totally Chinese. To him, we are uncultured barbarians and pretenders. They have a proud and rich history, which the Western powers shamed during the 19th century opium wars. They regained a measure of that pride through a period of painful modernization and industrialization after the Mao era. Your military strike won't be seen as punishment for a criminal act, but as another attempt by the West to humble them again, denying their right to be equal. By apologizing, Zhou and his government lost a lot of face. Your response will aggravate that feeling, forcing them to respond in kind, regardless who might be in power. You're proposing a reckless course of action, Mr. President, one that could have grave consequences not only for us, but the world at large."

"I appreciate your candid evaluation, Larry, as always," Walters said, smiling faintly. "Ordinarily, I would not question your input or advice. However, this time, I must." He raised a hand to forestall a protest. "Hear me out. The world at large is already facing grave consequences, especially if that *Qin* manages to reach La Palma. Zhou may not have had anything to do with the attack on La Palma, but he won't grieve if a much larger tsunami wipes us out, leaving China the dominant world power. That, people, is a scenario I'm not prepared to tolerate. However, I won't be totally reactionary. I'm sending in the 7th Fleet with a clear objective not to intimidate or engage Chinese forces. Their presence is for public consumption only."

"That's intimidation enough." Tanner shook his head. "A nuclear strike against Lop Nur? I don't know…"

"I'm not sending our ships to pick a fight, but I don't want the Fleet taking any crap from the Chinese either. Normal ROE will apply." Walters turned to Cottard. "What do you think, Manfred?"

"If we leaked to Premier Dzhang—"

"Absolutely not!" Walters grated harshly. "Zhou and his whole Politburo must see that I'm serious when that mushroom cloud goes up over Lop Nur."

"Mr. President, if the United States launches a nuclear missile, radicals around the world will crawl out of the woodwork denouncing us as warmongers, even some of our allies perhaps. They'll point out that despite our high moral ground about nuclear nonproliferation, we're the only country who used that weapon in anger, and we're doing it again."

"Our allies didn't have a tsunami unleashed against them, Manfred. Anyway, we're not going to bomb a city or anything. Call General Jason McDonald and tell him to deploy the 7th Fleet into the East China Sea, tasking order to follow. Not a full deployment, but enough to do the job in case of trouble. Do we still have any AGM-129s around?"

Graham Stone shifted his bulk and cleared his throat. "The Air Force was supposed to have all of them decommissioned in 2012, but I believe there are still a few serviceable units left in the inventory."

"Can the Chinese air defense systems track it?"

"Mr. President, those things are stealthy. Their systems won't see it."

"Good. Manfred? Ask McDonald to have a B-2 Spirit loaded with an AGM-129 cruise missile equipped with a tactical warhead, something like a W80 set for a five kiloton yield, and stage it at Osan Air Force Base ready for deployment."

Cottard nodded. "Since you already decided on a course of action, and I gather you've been thinking about it for some time, what was the point of sending Meecham to Beijing?"

"I was giving President Zhou the benefit of the doubt that he wasn't responsible for La Palma, and Meecham just might find those who are responsible. If he does, it will bolster Zhou's administration and place him in our debt. We have a serious international situation on our hands now, but when things settle down, and they will, everybody will continue doing business with China. However, they won't have it all their way. The United States must demonstrate to Zhou our displeasure without forcing him into a position where we remove all rational options."

Tanner smiled and shook his head. "You don't need me to formulate your foreign policy, Mr. President. You seem to be doing well enough on your own."

Walters nodded. "That's all, everybody...Manfred, stay a moment."

When Stone and Tanner filed out, he confronted his hard-bitten chief of staff.

"Larry is a diplomat and doesn't like solutions—"

"You call this a solution?"

"—that challenge his sensibilities. You, on the other hand, don't mind dishing it out to me. Go ahead. Tell me I'm wrong."

Cottard sighed and scratched his chin. "Frankly, Mr. President, listening to you, I was dismayed by your proposal. Not only at the idea of executing a nuclear strike, but being prepared to launch an all out attack? You're acting like a boy who's about to pull off a prank, hoping his parents won't find out."

Walters sat back and laughed, relieving the tension in the room. As usual, Manfred had cut through the fog to the issue at hand.

"Actually, you're not far off the mark. However, this is not a prank. We must send China a tangible message other than economic. Like you said, I've been thinking about doing this very thing when I spoke to Zhou. Announcing sanctions won't cut it. It's too remote and clinical. Graham was right when he said that we must hurt the Chinese leadership and not their people."

"The sanctions *will* hurt their people, Sam."

"Unavoidable, but they will do more than that. It will get them mad at Beijing and perhaps usher in further freedoms."

"You're dreaming, and asking Zhou to sit back while you nuke his country...I don't know. Even if there is no loss of life from the blast, there will be fallout."

"Lop Nur is a hundred thousand square miles of nothing, which should mitigate the problem, and if we do a high altitude detonation, there won't be any fallout. The province is practically deserted. I want to make a point, not an attack, and I think Zhou will play ball. He must, and what's more, he knows it. In time the sanctions will be relaxed and the people will forget them. What will not be forgotten by anybody is that taking on the United

States means feeling major pain, and that's why this strike is necessary. Call McDonald and tell him the bad news."

"Mr. President, is La Palma worth a possible nuclear exchange?"

"Where do we draw the line, Manfred?" Walters rubbed his eyes and sighed. "I sometimes wonder if I have the right to sit behind this desk. Everything is so complicated these days and getting more so all the time. I look at the pace of technological innovation and I'm frightened. We're inventing powerful tools to improve our standard of living without fully understanding their impact on the social fabric."

Cottard cocked his head and gave a wry smile. "Feeling sorry for yourself, Sam? It's not fun anymore? Don't tell me you didn't know what you were getting into."

"I knew, all right, and I have seen what this office has done to my predecessors. What I never appreciated fully was the level of partisan infighting, the bureaucratic inertia, and the power of the Military-Industrial Complex to influence policy. I control both Houses, but I sometimes wonder whether that's an illusory power. Behind the scenes, Congressmen and Senators dance to the tune set by lobby groups to preserve their seats, ignoring serious national issues in the process. It's amazing we ever legislate anything, and when we do, the concepts are so watered down, the laws are totally ineffective."

"Sam, if you're intent on pushing those reforms to the Foreign Corruption Practices Act, half the Democratic party will quit Congress."

"Damnation! That's exactly what I'm getting at. Our armaments industry is out of control, overcharging us for weapons systems that don't work, and we end up subsidizing them when programs go over time and budget, which only encourages rapacious business practice. You only have to look at the F-35 fiasco. What's worse, the oversight systems that Pentagon is meant to enforce don't work because those monster corporations we helped create have our generals and admirals in their pocket. It's got to stop, I tell you."

"Inertia, Sam. You said it yourself. Those corporations know what they want and how to get it, and they're prepared to fight anyone, Democrat or Republican, who stands in their way."

"You're telling me it can't be done?"

"I'm saying you'll have a fight on your hands."

"Then I'll have a fight. Our current annual military budget is 650 billion, more than Russia, China, Japan and the rest of Europe combined; all driven by the Military-Industrial Complex. No one can explain to me why we need such a buildup. Where are the threats that warrant such expenditure? I want this to be one of my reelection platforms, Manfred."

"You're sure you want to do this?"

"I'm sure."

* * *

As Meecham gazed at the unbelievable landscape of the State Guesthouse grounds, he found it difficult to accept that he was actually in the middle of a large city. Small villas nestled among tall trees, surrounded by flowerbeds and rolling lawns. Clearly, the Chinese government wanted its official visitors to feel comfortable and at ease, sheltered from the mad bustle outside. He certainly felt comfortable as the limo approached a stately building crowded by ancient conifers. A lake opened on his right, its bank dotted with white and yellow water lilies. The narrow road turned and the car slowed as it approached the old building topped by an elaborately carved concave roof. It lost none of its grandeur flanked by the official ultramodern conference center. Tom felt that he had stepped into a fairyland.

"The Fang Fei Yuan villa," Weng remarked. "This whole complex used to house the imperial palace and is more than 800 years old. Premier Dzhang often entertains his guests here and is keen to meet both of you."

"We're having lunch here?" Tom asked as the beefy security guy up front got out to open the door for them. He thought this was merely a stopover, allowing him to look at some old architecture.

"As a secure location, it's convenient, as foreigners are not allowed into the Zhongnanhai compound where the State Council has its headquarters."

Weng led them into the building, the interior covered with elaborate tapestries, paintings, and what Tom presumed was genuine jade sculpture. He doubted that anything here would be fake. History was loud in this place and he felt like tiptoeing. Stopping beside an elaborately carved door, Weng knocked and entered. Taking a quick scan, Tom reflected the room didn't look all that different from the lounge at their residence. Standing beside a ceiling-high window, hands clasped behind his back, the short portly man smiled. Tom recognized the tastefully dressed premier from his profile sheet.

Only fifty-nine, Dzhang was young for his position, but Tom was told that this had been the general trend in recent years, appointing more vigorous people into senior government positions as old reactionaries either retired or were eased out. Born in Urumqi in the Xinjiang Uyghur Autonomous Region, the premier came from a harsh province, only 4.3% of its land fit for habitation. Although the largest administrative division in China, Uyghurs and Hans made up most of the twenty-two million mainly Muslim population, the province did have extensive oil and gas reserves. It was also a serious sore for Beijing, the Uyghurs constantly fighting to achieve greater autonomy, which the central government suppressed in the most brutal fashion. Well, America also had its share of problems.

Thoroughly briefed by a State Department weenie on Chinese philosophy and thinking, Tom hoped he would be up to it. One thing to talk about it and read dry briefs, but his exposure to this unique country made him think that no amount of preparation could adequately make him ready to face these people. Well, he'll just have to wade in and see what happens. He took a deep breath and stepped into the room.

"Mr. Meecham…Mr. Davenport, I am so pleased to meet you," Dzhang said smoothly as he strode toward them.

"It is an honor, sir," Tom said with feeling as they shook hands, not fooled by the premier's silken smile. The black eyes regarding him missed nothing. The smaller man had a forceful personality, radiating from him like heat. A wrong word here and Tom could be sent packing home in disgrace. "I genuinely did not expect such a welcome."

"I dare say. However, the nature of your visit precludes going through normal diplomatic channels. You will have to make your own determination, but President Zhou and I want your investigation to be successful; not only to forestall any, ah, adverse response by President Walters, but because we also have a vested interest to uncover those responsible."

"Keith and I will be relying heavily on the cooperation of your law enforcement services to get the job done, sir."

"And you shall have it, without reservation. Leijang will see to that." The premier looked keenly at Tom and tilted his head slightly. "Pardon me for saying this, but I expected President Walters to send us a larger contingent."

"Reading Minister Lin Jinpan's report, a lot of background investigative work appears to have already been done. Keith and I will build on that, pursuing additional avenues, and our legate office has adequate resources."

"Yes, of course. Speaking personally, Mr. Meecham—"

"Please, call me Tom, sir."

"Tom, I wouldn't place too much reliability on Lin's report. As you no doubt know, the minister is a populist, a Tuanpai, and Chairman Keung Yang's friend. If, as we suspect, Keung is involved, Lin would make sure his investigation did not compromise him."

"We already surmised that this might be the case."

"I am sure you did," Dzhang said dryly. "Presumably, you also considered the possibility that President Zhou might be responsible. Don't be alarmed. As an investigator, you would have to explore that likelihood."

Studying the premier, Tom nodded. "Yes, sir. We considered it. We're also considering who might have sent out that *Qin* missile boat."

"Ah, the *Qin*. I fervently hope it's at the bottom of the sea due to a mishap, because if it isn't, your Navy will have a very hard time intercepting it. Before you ask the obvious, there are no forged orders to follow up. The *Qin* sortied officially under close security."

Smiling, Tom shrugged. "Once we find who sent out the *Shang*, sir, we'll also know who sent out the *Qin*, covert orders notwithstanding."

"Indeed." The premier turned to Weng and waved a hand at a small liquor cabinet holding a variety of bottles. "Please serve our guests some *San Hua*. I think they will find it delightful."

As Weng walked to the cabinet, Dzhang steered Tom toward a round table covered by a black tablecloth elaborately embroidered with cloudy mountains and misty waterfalls. Translucent white china bowls sitting on broad plates, folded black napkins, accompanied by usual cutlery, completed the setting. Tom noticed a set of white chopsticks beside each plate.

"I want to introduce you to genuine Chinese cuisine, Tom, unlike what you may be normally familiar with back home. Please don't feel embarrassed if you're uncomfortable using chopsticks."

"Chopsticks are fine, sir," Tom said, "and I enjoy Chinese food, even though we have Westernized it back home."

"You will now be able to tell your compatriots what authentic cuisine is like." Dzhang sat down and fiddled with a carved crystal goblet as Tom and Davenport took their seats.

Weng walked up carrying a smoky dark bottle and poured half a glass of clear yellow liquid for everybody.

"*San Hua*, or three flowers, is an ancient rice wine with a long history that goes back more than a thousand years," Dzhang explained. "The fragrant herbs which are added during the fermentation process give the wine its unique bouquet and flavor." He picked up his goblet and held it up. "To your success, gentlemen."

Tom returned the salute and took a cautious sip. The premier was right when he said the wine had a fine bouquet and flavor. He could not compare it to sake, almost flavorless, but this stuff left a pleasant aftertaste on the palate and a warm glow as it went down.

"Superb," he said seriously as he placed the goblet on the table.

"I knew you would enjoy it. Mr. Davenport—you don't mind me calling you Keith?"

"Not at all, sir, and I agree with you. The wine has a unique zest, Mr. Premier."

"I shall see to it that both of you leave home with a bottle."

"That's very kind of you, sir," Tom said.

As though on a signal, two black garbed individuals came in, one pushing a loaded trolley. They placed a small soup tureen on the table and a basket of mixed rolls. They filled everyone's bowl, moving around the table as required, bowed and left.

"Bread is not our usual fare, Tom. We don't grow much wheat in our country, but I have developed a taste for it, as have many of our people. A product of your decadent Western influence," Dzhang added and chuckled.

Smiling, Tom looked for a hidden meaning behind the prem-

ier's words, then decided he was overanalyzing. If he started sec-
ond-guessing himself before saying anything, this conversation
would die. He picked up a traditional curved broad spoon and
tried the soup, a mixture of various vegetables, black mushrooms
and chicken. Somewhat spicy, but excellent.

"If you don't object to discussing business, and I apologize
in advance for this rudeness, the Premier and I would like to
know how you intend to conduct your investigation," Weng
asked between mouthfuls.

Swallowing, Tom placed the spoon beside the bowl. "One of
the first things we need to obtain is Chairman Han Yunshan's
orders. I understand Minister Lin had the paper analyzed and the
signature proven genuine. However, given his relationship with
Chairman Keung, I acknowledge that the finding might be
tainted. I propose to send a high resolution scan of the document
to our Quantico laboratory for detailed analysis. As a photocopy,
its value is diminished, but we can overcome that problem by
scanning original papers signed by Chairman Han and Vice
Chairman Chen for comparison."

Dzhang leaned forward, holding his spoon above the bowl.
"I respect the sophistication of your forensic techniques, Tom,
but Lin's finding seems conclusive."

"With respect, sir, our facilities are pretty advanced. Normal
computer signature matching techniques are quite reliable, but
we need a very high level of confidence in this case. We'll look at
a number of elements to identify whether Chairman Han has in
fact signed that document. Every time we write something the
writing is not entirely identical, but there are patterns unique to
every individual: amount of pressure applied to each letter, the
slant of each letter, direction of movement as the words are written, the height of each letter. There are other components, but
simply put, no matter how superficially accurate a forged signature might look, the forger cannot completely suppress imparting

some characteristic of his natural writing onto the forgery. By analyzing genuine signatures made by both individuals, we will determine if Chairman Han signed that document."

"You sound confident, Tom," Weng said.

"We have some experience with this."

Dzhang gave a wan smile. "You understand, just because Han Yunshan's signature appears on that document does not mean it's genuine."

"Correct."

"Leijang will provide you with whatever documents you need."

"Thank you, sir."

"But that's not all, is it?"

"No, sir. We have two other leads, both tenuous, which we feel need to be run down." Tom wondered whether he should divulge anything more, given Dzhang's relationship with Zhou, then decided it was ridiculous. If Zhou was involved in any way, the investigation was already doomed. Holding back might also alienate the one person in a position to help him. "In late April, Professor Chuan Jianbo, a geophysicist from the School of Earth and Space Sciences at Peking University, met with a fatal accident."

"Your point being?" Weng asked.

"Whoever planned the attack on La Palma needed accurate technical data, which only a scientific expert in the field could provide."

"And once this Chuan provided the information, you believe he was disposed of to eliminate a potential security breach," Weng mused, and Tom nodded.

"That's our conjecture. Once he secured the necessary data, our planner had to obtain a submarine to deliver explosive charges to La Palma, then arrange for its disposal. Can you tell me if the *Shang* was equipped with thermobaric mines, the weapon we think used to trigger the slump?"

Weng glanced at Dzhang, who gave a minute nod. "The *ChangZheng 4* carried sixteen advanced torpedo tube launched thermobaric mines."

"That gives us our second lead," Tom said.

Dzhang laughed at Weng's puzzled expression. "The mechanism used to dispose of the submarine, right, Tom?"

"Exactly, sir. Regardless of how dedicated or loyal to the Party, I doubt the *Shang's* commander would destroy his submarine or crew merely because he may have been under orders to do so."

"You're right. No one would issue such an order."

"I suggest, sir, the trigger that set off the mines was also used to destroy the submarine. We need to identify the person who could have set up such a trigger, but more importantly, find out who told him to do it."

Dzhang looked pointedly at Weng. "Talk to people at Wushiht'ala."

"That's their submarine weapons research facility," Davenport added to Tom and Dzhang shrugged.

"The existence of that facility is not classified, Keith."

"There is another avenue that our investigation will focus on, sir," Tom said, not wishing to enter into a discussion of U.S. surveillance capability.

Dzhang snorted. "You don't need to tell me. You want to establish a link between Keung and Chen, as I do. That fool Lin never bothered looking into that, at least not in enough depth to matter."

"With respect, sir, they are not the only link we must pursue. As commander of the PLA Navy, Admiral Xhal Shenglai is also a person of interest."

"Of course, and we have discussed that possibility. I must say, Tom, I was skeptical when President Zhou told me the Americans will be sending us investigators, but you convinced me. Your reasoning is focused and consistent, and connects events in a way we haven't considered. You make me feel much more optimistic." He took a spoonful of soup and grimaced. "The damn thing has gone cold. Get us fresh bowls, Leijang."

Weng looked up and clapped his hands. The door immediately opened and the two undertaker types hurried in. Weng spoke to them rapidly and the bowls were quickly replaced and refilled. Alone again, tasting the soup, Dzhang smiled approvingly.

"I am being remiss as your host with all this weighty talk. We're supposed to be enjoying our lunch."

Tom found the steaming soup delicious and the premier steered the conversation into pleasant generalities. Having visited Washington once, Dzhang had glimpsed something of the American way of life, albeit a distorted view, being chaperoned everywhere. He admitted that Western television shows gave him a better insight into its society than the sanitized tours, although a somewhat surreal one.

"Our entertainment programs hardly do us justice, sir," Tom remarked, shuddering to think the impression they left on any sane individual.

Dzhang chuckled. "As ours don't to foreigners visiting our country. However, they do reflect our psyche to a degree. Some of our historical drama for instance, sprinkled with magic and flying warriors, must seem ridiculously stylized, and they are, but they serve as a window into our cultural philosophy, in the same way that your cowboy and Indian films gave me a glimpse into yours."

Tom regarded the premier with growing respect. This was not a fanatical communist determined to rule his people with an iron hand simply to maintain personal power. Dzhang was cultured, sophisticated and worldly-wise, doing his best to usher change and promote material prosperity to a country that had known only oppressive rule for millennia. Given that environment, China's emergence as a modern world economy was even more remarkable. Of course, modernization did not automatically mean embracing democracy or allowing unfettered freedom of expression. Given time perhaps, but Tom figured it would probably not be in his lifetime. After all, there *was* significant cultural divergence between them.

"I have seen some of your historical films, sir. Their depth and social density often got me thinking. Disregarding the obvious differences portrayed by our shallow productions, a common thread does run through both."

"Oh? And what would that be?"

"All those films, yours and ours, are about people; how they love, fight, face adversity, overcome injustice and manipulate each other. There are many more things that make us the same than those that divide us."

Dzhang and Weng exchanged looks, and the premier looked at Tom with genuine warmth.

"To have someone so young say such a thing is truly remarkable. I think you may have missed your calling. America could benefit having someone like you in the State Department."

"If you're referring to Mr. Lipson, I can only apologize," Tom said, feeling his cheeks heat.

Weng laughed. "There is no need to be embarrassed. Hayes and I play mental games. The episode you witnessed today is typical of the First Secretary. He really is a skilled diplomat, despite his predilection for plain talk."

The soup was replaced with fresh plates. When the finely cut slices of duck, chopped vegetables and light crepes were served, Dzhang licked his lips, clearly relishing the dish. One of the waiters poured them tall glasses of rich amber beer and withdrew.

"The finest Peking duck. I doubt that even the most authentic restaurant in Washington serves anything like it."

Tom sprinkled vegetables onto a crepe, placed two long slices of exquisitely smelling roasted duck on top, rolled the crepe and bit into it. Whatever spices were used to prepare the duck, the meat delicious and not at all stringy. Chased down with ale, it made an excellent dish.

"I had something similar when I was in Hong Kong, but this is extraordinary," Davenport said, nodding in appreciation.

"I am pleased that you find it palatable, Keith," Dzhang said. "We haven't heard much from you. Tell me, what is your involvement in this investigation?"

"I am here to support Tom in whatever way necessary to achieve our mutual objective, sir. That includes using all the resources available to the CIA. I'm not one of their field operatives, although I used to be, and I will not attempt to compromise our investigation or abuse your hospitality by engaging in any covert intelligence gathering. Tom and I have complementary skills to bear on this case, that's all."

"I appreciate your frankness and I did not imply that you're here on a spying mission."

"That is perfectly okay, sir. Even if I had any such inclination, I doubt that I'll be in a position to indulge in it."

Dzhang laughed. "Well said! I love people who are totally unpretentious and utterly pragmatic."

Deep fried pork ribs followed the duck, replaced with shredded beef served with hot vegetables. Tea came with a variety of sweet yum cha dumplings and cigars. Lighting the fragrant leaf, Tom sat back, completely satisfied.

"A product from our Cuban friends," Weng explained after exhaling a perfect smoke ring. "A decadent indulgence, I admit, but life without some pleasures is reduced to tedious existence, don't you agree?"

Tom nodded. "Completely. It's what makes living endurable."

"I knew you would understand."

Dzhang rolled the cigar in his mouth and took a puff. "What do you want to do first, Tom?"

"Have a long sleep." The premier and Weng laughed. "I

would like to talk to one or two of Minister Lin's investigators to establish a baseline. I don't want to cover the same ground twice. Getting hold of Chairman Han's orders is a priority, as are the supporting documents. I want them analyzed as soon as possible."

"Leijang will be at your villa at 8:30 tomorrow morning. Make your wishes known to him and he'll do the rest. Under the circumstances, I don't see any reason for you to personally interview Keung or Chen."

Dismayed, Tom sat up. "Sir, without direct access—"

"Unless your signature analysis proves inconclusive." Dzhang placed his cigar into the ashtray and stood up. "When you meet Ambassador Sawyer, please extend him my respects. It has been a genuine pleasure, gentlemen." He nodded and walked out.

Startled by the abrupt departure, Tom looked at Weng. "Christ! I hope I haven't said something to offend him."

"On the contrary. Both of you have made a favorable impression on the Premier, and he has given you a generous amount of his time. There is a development and he needs to deal with it. President Walters has ordered the 7th Fleet into the East China Sea."

Tom gaped at him. If the president had already decided to act, what the hell was he doing in China? Did his investigation really matter in the larger scheme of things? If it didn't, surely the president would not have sent him here. His moment of indignation passed as he realized that he was not in position to pass judgment. There were any number of reasons for Walters to send out the Fleet.

Weng smiled knowingly. "The news caught us by surprise as much as it has you. However, we did anticipate this as one possible reaction."

Tom collected his thoughts and nodded. "May I ask what will be China's response?"

"That, my friend, is something the Premier is yet to decide. However, this in no way diminishes the importance of your investigation."

Tom wondered how true that really was.

Weng escorted them to the car waiting outside, and after a round of handshakes, returned into the building.

Listening to the whisper of tires as the car made its way to the villa, Tom stared at the magnificent gardens, a world out of place and a different time; an illusion that hid a harsh reality. Surrounded by stately buildings from an era of mysticism in an island of quiet tranquility, it would be easy to lose perspective and objectivity. By housing him here, was the Chinese government extending genuine courtesy or attempting to lull him into a false sense of security? He had read up on Chinese philosophy, their awesome history, dynastic rule and a penchant for playing mind games. Nothing could be taken at face value and first impressions were usually a façade designed to mislead. At lunch, Dzhang appeared genuine, and as far as he could tell, hadn't tried to be subtle. Of course, a face can have many veils, and he could also be overanalyzing.

The tires whispered on the road.

Walters had deployed the 7th Fleet? He still felt the shock reverberating through him. Knowing this, Dzhang could have been cold and formal, but he hadn't shown any sign of displeasure. Tom wondered whether this would impede his investigation in any way, then decided he couldn't worry about it. He may be a mere pawn on the global chessboard, but he'll play his part—provided he wasn't gobbled up by a bishop or something before he got to the other side to claim his prize.

The limo pulled up to their villa and Tom got out. Feeling the fine meal working on him, combined with the aftereffect of a long flight, he wanted to go for an invigorating run, a steaming shower and a few hours of sack time in a real bed. Why not? He still had some time before the embassy dinner. The thought of wading through another formal engagement made him wince. He decided that life as an FBI agent was hell.

He reminded himself to call Melissa or he *would* catch hell.

Grave as always, Joseph greeted them as Tom and Davenport walked in.

"There are two gentlemen waiting in the lounge, sir," he told Tom.

"Oh?"

"From your embassy."

"Thank you."

Joseph nodded and withdrew. Tom exchanged glances with Davenport, shrugged and walked to the sliding panels. He pulled one back and paused before entering. The two men inside stopped talking and looked at him. Both were tall, easily six-foot-three, dressed in conservative dark suits that were almost government badges. One had a pencil mustache, a hard square jaw, pepper hair cut short, and cold blue eyes. The other, fractionally shorter, had a softer face, but the brown eyes were just as cold. Hard customers both, Tom mused.

"Mr. Meecham," Blue Eyes said briskly and extended a hand. "I'm Paul Rogan, CIA station chief."

"A pleasure, Paul," Tom said cautiously as they shook hands, not sure he liked the man's take-charge attitude. First Lipson, now this guy.

"Neil Fuller, Special Agent in Charge of our legate office," the other man said, a cautious smile creasing his face.

Tom shook hands and nodded. "I look forward to working with you, Neil."

"You must be Keith Davenport," Fuller said.

"I must be," Davenport acknowledged, and there were more handshakes.

Tom extended an arm toward the table. "Let's get comfortable."

After some pushing of chairs, everybody settled in. Instead

of feeling pleased at seeing his visitors, Tom sensed an undercurrent of unease. Then it hit him. His presence was resented, at least by Rogan. If there was any investigating to be done, the two men may be resenting having strangers messing on what they considered their legitimate turf. Well, that was tough cookies.

"What brings you out here, gentlemen?" Tom asked, taking in the subtle play of expressions from the two men.

Rogan inclined his head at the large brown envelope on the sofa and his mustache twitched.

"Delivering some background information on your persons of interest. I expected that you'd be fully briefed before coming, Tom, but no damage done. When I heard that you and Keith were on your way, I started things rolling."

Fuller shifted in his seat and cleared his throat. "Preliminary review of Minister Lin Jinpan's report, to bring us up to speed, you know."

Tom ignored him, leaned forward and stared at Rogan. "You have men on the ground checking on Chairman Keung and Vice Chairman Chen?"

"Validating Lin's report. It's tainted, of course, as he is Keung's pal," Rogan said offhandedly. "Something you would have known if you'd been properly informed. Never mind. I'll make sure that we get to the bottom of this."

"Who authorized you to do anything?" Davenport demanded.

Rogan looked surprised. "My instructions came from the First Secretary, Hayes Lipson. This investigation has serious diplomatic implications and he wanted to make sure we didn't compromise our relationship with China over what is essentially an internal matter and a short-term international aberration."

Tom snorted and his mouth firmed. "I would hardly call it an aberration. For your information, Lipson has no authority here and you take your instructions from me and Keith. Is that clear?"

Rogan clamped his teeth and his eyes narrowed. "You may have been sent by the President, but you don't know the setup here and neither does he. If it hasn't sunk in yet, you're a public relations exercise. I don't mind if you get the limelight, but my men will do the real work around here. Is that perfectly clear to *you*?"

Before Tom could give Rogan a blast, Davenport pointed a finger at him. "You received your brief from the Counterterrorism Center? My brief?"

After a moment, Rogan gave a stiff nod. "I did."

"And you appear to have disregarded it."

"Given Mr. Lipson's authority—"

"You disregarded my instructions!"

Rogan glared at Davenport. "Things look different in Washington, Keith. The CIA desk isn't an independent body. I have to work with Lipson."

"I want you to suspend whatever you're doing," Tom said quietly. "I admire initiative when it's properly channeled, but you should have given me and Keith the benefit of the doubt that we just might know what we're about. I'll be relying on your support, and Neil's, during this investigation, but let's get one thing straight. This is my investigation, not Lipson's, and not yours. I have enough grounds to have you dismissed, but I don't think that will be necessary, unless you prove me wrong. Well?"

Terrible things went on behind Rogan's eyes. After a moment, he nodded.

"Understood."

"Good." Tom turned to Fuller. "Do you have a conflict of interest, Neil?"

Fuller smiled broadly and raised both hands. "You're the man in charge here, Tom. Whatever you want done, the legate office is at your disposal."

"Now that we have jurisdiction sorted out, there is something both of you can look into. I want you to pull the postmortem report on Professor Chuan Jianbo. He was a geophysicist at the Peking University's School of Earth and Space Sciences."

Rogan frowned. "Chuan? What's the connection?"

"He could be the subject matter expert who advised whoever planned the attack on La Palma how to go about doing it."

"And may have been disposed of to plug a security hole," Fuller murmured thoughtfully.

"Exactly," Tom said. "His death supposedly an accident, but I want to make sure."

"When did he die?"

"April, a couple of weeks before deployment of the *Jing Long* naval exercise."

Fuller raised a finger. "Tom, if the authorities found the cause of death resulted from an apparent accident, they wouldn't have conducted an autopsy. Digging up the postmortem report won't tell us anything."

"If they haven't done an autopsy, I'll request Weng Leijang to exhume the body and have one done."

Rogan's eyes narrowed. "You met Premier Dzhang's personal secretary?"

"Keith and I just had lunch with him and the Premier."

Rogan exhaled slowly. "It looks like I owe you an apology, Mr. Meecham. It seems I may have been a subject in one of Lipson's games."

Tom recalled the first secretary's earlier attempt to shanghai the investigation and wasn't altogether surprised. However, he expected someone in Rogan's position to have seen through the ploy and not allowed himself to get sucked in so easily. On the other hand, he could be making an attempt to retrieve something from an untenable position, realizing that pissing Tom off might not be conducive to his career, and he would be right.

"Whatever Lipson is playing doesn't concern me and it

shouldn't concern you. Neil? Can you get hold of the postmortem report?"

"There is a powerful bureaucracy operating here, Tom, and they won't cooperate willingly, if at all. Especially not with a Westerner."

"Tell whoever is putting up a stumbling block to call Weng. I think you'll find that they'll be anxious to cooperate."

Fuller chuckled. "It will be a first. Anything else?"

"Weng will dig up Han Yunshan's orders and comparative documents signed by Han and Chen. I want our Quantico lab to go over them, which will hopefully nail down who really signed those orders. I'll take care of that personally tomorrow."

"Tom, if President Zhou is right and Keung and Chen are behind this—"

"We need to establish a connection, I know, Paul. That's something you can continue looking into, but overtly. I want your people to be open when dealing with Ministry of State Security investigators. I want them to know we're looking into everything and everybody."

Rogan blinked. "If Keung and Chen are involved, they could take direct action against my guys, you know. These are two very powerful people you're dealing with. If they want you to disappear, you'll disappear, and Zhou won't be able to do anything about it."

"I know, but I want to provoke a reaction from one of them."

"Not if it's a terminal one."

"Christ! You don't have to remind me of what's at stake here, Paul."

Rogan nodded and stood up. "If there is nothing else…"

"I want you to run a check on Admiral Xhal Shenglai. While everybody is running around looking at the big fish, he could have planned and executed the whole thing. He had means and opportunity…and motive—he is a hardline hawk."

Stefan Vučak

"If that's all…"

"I'll let you know," Tom said, not bothering to stand.

Fuller smiled sheepishly, stood, and patted down his jacket. "I'll get onto Professor Chuan. A pleasure meeting you Tom…Keith."

Tom nodded and Davenport escorted the two visitors out. When he returned, he sat down and exhaled loudly.

"Rogan could be an impediment. I can ease him out if you want."

"He's a pain, but I think he understands now which way the wind is blowing. You were right about him. He has turned into a diplomat, forgetting what his job is all about. The real problem is Lipson."

Davenport chuckled. "I suspect dinner tonight will be lively."

Tom grinned back. "He was a former Second Secretary at our London embassy. Getting posted to Beijing was a major career step. He can't be as dense as he appears."

"All those endless cocktail parties and caviar may have gotten to him."

"As long as he stays out of our way, he can have all the caviar he wants."

"Deployment of the 7th Fleet could make our investigation difficult," Davenport ventured.

"Perhaps, but I doubt it. I admit being startled by the development, but Walters is playing on two levels. He has a domestic and international dimension to consider, and it's in his interest to find out who orchestrated La Palma. Our objective for being here hasn't changed."

"What now?"

Tom bit his lip and glanced at his watch: four o'clock, which made it 4 a.m. in DC. "Remind me to call Melissa before we turn in for the night. I think I'll get some shuteye."

Davenport nodded. "Not a bad idea, and I'll have to call

Karelina or I'll get my balls busted." He stood up and waved. "Catch you later."

When the sliding panel clicked shut, Tom walked to the liquor cabinet and poured himself a slug of Wild Turkey bourbon, noting with interest an assortment of local wines ready to be sampled. It appeared that Weng wanted to make sure their every desire was catered for. Gulping down the last of the whiskey, he yawned, figuring the nap wasn't a bad idea at all.

At 6:30 precisely, Joseph knocked on his door, poked his head in and announced that the embassy car was waiting. Tom finished the Windsor knot in his tie, gave himself a quick once-over in the mirror, and decided he was presentable enough to be called into the ambassador's presence. From his fact sheet, he knew that Macey Sawyer was a former California senator, and one of the longest serving. During his lengthy career, he held chairmanships in a raft of committees, including the vital Appropriations Committee. After a brief stint in the California House of Representatives, the ambitious Sawyer served one term as a Congressman before moving to the Senate.

An expert on international trade and finance, with a bachelor's degree in economics from Princeton and a law degree from Harvard, the former senator did much of the footwork to warm the relationship between Walters and Zhou. Sawyer wasn't tall, only five-eight, but his thin frame and elongated bald head made him appear taller. His photo showed a reserved smile and a friendly twinkle in his eyes, but PR boys were known to touch things up. Tom looked forward to meeting the person behind the image.

Davenport waited for him downstairs. Joseph wished them a pleasant evening, bowed and closed the door after them. The serious individual dressed in a black suit got out of the dark car, murmured something into a wrist mike and hurried to open the back door.

Tom nodded to him and slid onto the soft leather seat. Davenport climbed in, fastened his seatbelt and sighed.

"That nap was just what the old body needed."

"If Joseph hadn't woken me, bowing most apologetically, I'd still be snoring," Tom agreed with a grin.

"He'll make somebody a good wife," Davenport said cheerfully as the car eased off.

Traffic along the way heavy, noisy, and people rushed everywhere. Tom could not see anyone simply standing and talking. He wondered what the hell everybody did. Hugging the city skyline, the sun shone bravely through a thin cloud layer, or it could have been smog.

The car slowed as they neared a cluster of embassies: Malaysian, Indian, Brunei and Korean. The imposing eight-story box clad in reflective green glass sitting on priceless ten acres of land, the U.S. embassy dominated the landscape. The car turned off at Dong Fang East Road and stopped at the heavily guarded entrance on Liangmaqiao Bei Xiaojie Lane. The marine guards opened the steel gate and the car whispered in.

Their minder said nothing as he escorted them past a security point inside the building to what appeared to be a reserved elevator. Stopping on the eight floor, he nodded as the doors slid aside, but didn't get out. Tom saw the first secretary and put on a brave smile.

"Mr. Lipson."

"Welcome to our little piece of United States, Tom…Keith," Lipson said breezily. "We'll see the Ambassador in his private office before getting down to dinner. If you gentlemen will follow me?"

This high up, the city sprawled to the horizon, an unbroken vista of low buildings and clusters of towers. The sheer size of the place slightly overwhelming, Tom wondered how people got from one end to the other. Probably didn't, he decided. Given the traffic, despite the city's extensive public transport, such an attempt would likely take all day.

Lipson strode quickly across the soft gray carpet, paused in front of a highly polished wooden door, and knocked. Without waiting for a response, he walked in. Tom and Davenport filed in after him.

The individual behind a standard office desk, flanked by poled American flags, smiled and stood up.

"Ah, the President's investigators. Welcome to Beijing, gentlemen."

Lipson made the introductions. After a round of handshakes, Sawyer had everybody sit on two couches guarding a low coffee table. Tom stared at the black surface intricately overlaid with mother of pearl. The exquisite detail and workmanship astonishing, representing a lakeside scene, bowing willows, a moored rowboat set against a misty mountain.

Sawyer smiled. "A little gift from President Zhou. Enchanting, isn't it?"

"It must cost a fortune," Tom murmured reverently.

"Priceless. So, what do you think of Beijing?"

"Frankly, sir, it's a bit daunting. There is no end to the city."

Sawyer laughed. "Yes, it takes some getting used to, but your State Guesthouse residence will shield you from the worst this place has to offer, and it does have a dark side."

"As every city does, I imagine."

"Quite right, Tom. Quite right. We'll go to dinner shortly and I'm looking forward to catching up on the latest gossip, but Lipson here has some concerns regarding your brief and I wanted to hear your side of it before I got involved."

Tom suppressed a smile. The first secretary hadn't wasted any time making his pitch, thereby having the ambassador form those vital first impressions.

"I don't have a side, sir. Hayes is under the impression that I am subordinate to him and should coordinate my movements through him. He already instructed Paul Rogan to undertake some investigative work, which contravenes a brief from Keith, the DCIA Mark Price, and the President. For the duration of my mission here, the CIA station chief and the head of the FBI legate office report to me. I welcome Lipson's support, but I don't report to him and he has no authority to order any action related to our investigation."

Scowling, Sawyer turned to Lipson. "You ordered Rogan to conduct a surveillance mission?"

Lipson firmed his jaw. "He reports to me, sir. I was preempting something Mr. Meecham would have ordered anyway."

"I see." Sawyer turned and smiled. "A misunderstanding, Tom, for which I apologize. Hayes is at your disposal, as are the resources of this embassy. You got that, Lipson?"

"Yes, sir."

"Good! Don't mind him, Tom. He really is a good executive. It's just that his enthusiasm gets the better of him sometimes."

"I understand, sir."

Tom understood that Sawyer was covering up for Lipson, and he suspected that there would probably be a fatherly talk later, but he didn't care. Any hint to the Chinese of divided authority and his investigation would be in the hopper. They would sense this immediately, which could cause untold diplomatic damage.

"There is one thing, Tom, where I have to agree with Hayes. Your lunch with Premier Dzhang. If you don't mind, I would appreciate your feedback. The fact that you were with him is highly unusual in itself, and suggestive. Dzhang is an extremely powerful figure, and anything he says is important."

Tom smiled. "He asked me to extend you his greetings."

Sawyer chuckled. "Bastard. Never play mahjong with him. He'll take you to the cleaners, but I don't suppose you'll ever play with him."

"I suppose not, sir. He was extremely friendly and I was impressed with his candid attitude."

"Yes, he is a sophisticated politician, and what's more important, a pragmatic one."

"I outlined the approach I will take with my investigation—"

"Was that wise?"

"Sir, if he and President Zhou are involved, we won't find anything. If they're not, it's in their interest that we identify who planned the attack on La Palma. Without their genuine cooperation, Keith and I might as well take in the sights."

"Yes, you're right, of course. Presumably, you have leads to follow?"

"I'll keep Hayes informed of our progress." Tom crossed his legs. "Sir, is it true that President Walters ordered the 7th Fleet into the East China Sea?"

Sighing, Sawyer nodded. "I'm afraid so. They should be on station tomorrow. How did Dzhang react to this?"

"It never came up. Weng told us after lunch."

"Mmm, interesting. There is something more serious that nobody here knows. The President intends to launch a nuclear strike at China's Lop Nur proving ground."

Tom gaped at him, but recovered quickly. "I am not entirely surprised, and I understand what the President is doing. He is sending China a message."

"China and everybody else," Sawyer agreed solemnly. "I only hope Zhou gets it, but enough serious talk. We're having dinner in my private lounge. We'll talk afterward. I'm sure Dzhang served a superb table as always, but I think you will welcome a genuine Texas steak."

His stomach still processing lunch, Tom did not relish the idea of stuffing himself with a heavy steak, but he really had no way to avoid it. Putting on a resigned smile, he nodded.

"It will be a pleasure, Mr. Ambassador."

Judging by Sawyer's laugh, Tom wondered whether this was a little payback for having embarrassed Lipson. He glanced at

Davenport, the same thought apparently having crossed his mind.

* * *

USS *George Washington*, CVN-73, a *Nimitz*-class carrier, plowed through the long swells, its 1,092-foot length not swaying at all. Powered by two Westinghouse A4W reactors, its four shafts left a creamy wake in the following seas. July heralded the start of the typhoon season in these waters, which would challenge any operation Task Force 70 may be called upon to execute. Forty or fifty-foot swells wouldn't bother the carrier, but such seas would wreak havoc with the group's destroyer and cruiser screen.

Patchy cloud hugged the horizon, their bellies dark, and the sky had a sullen gray look that meant a squall in the afternoon. There were always afternoon squalls this time of year. It would make flight operations uncomfortable for those on deck, but Captain Brian Ormond didn't mind the weather, any kind of weather; nothing like a crisp blow to get the crew and pilots frosty. Not having sortied for over six weeks, everybody had gotten a little too comfortable enjoying the highlights of shore life.

He enjoyed those highlights himself. Still holding her trim figure after seventeen years of marriage, his wife didn't mind the prolonged layover at Yokosuka, knowing that once the carrier sailed, it might not return for three months or more. Japan wasn't home, but if the scuttlebutt ran true to form, he was due to get his two stars in December and relocation to USPACFLT at Pearl. In the meantime, both of them made the most of the time the Navy gave them and didn't question their luck. She gave her love without reservation, occasionally reflecting how their life would be complete if they had children. They tried, but his unusually low sperm count made it almost impossible for her to conceive, and she had ruled out IVF or adoption. If she couldn't have one with him, she didn't want someone else's. What astonished him, she still chose to stay with him and make their marriage work. He wouldn't have blamed her if she left him, and strived to make it up to her as best he could.

Wedged into his comfortable leather chair, Ormond watched the Air Boss manage the morning's flight evolutions, keeping tabs on VFA-27, the 'Royal Maces' F/A-18E drivers going through their day carrier qualification landings, commonly known as traps. Last night as they cleared the Japanese coast, VFA-115 and VFA-195 went through their night quals—always a hair-raising business. Tonight, VFA-27 and VFA-102 boys would be showing the other two strike fighter squadrons how business should be done.

Ormond didn't mind healthy competition among his pilots and actively encouraged it, something Commander Adrian 'Duke' Varnecky fully supported. The XO had finally gotten his fourth stripe and an *Arleigh Burke*-class guided missile destroyer, and Ormond would miss his rake-thin friend. Varnecky ready to transfer to his new command when the 7th Fleet got priority orders to deploy. Going out on active deployment with a brand new executive officer would have been a major fubar. Fortunately, the deputy fleet commander, Rear Admiral Rick Haddon, agreed to delay Varnecky's transfer until Task Force 70 completed its current mission, whatever that was. Putting the Navy's interest above any personal consideration, Varnecky hadn't raised an eyebrow when Ormond told him the bad news, which earned him a fat 'attaboy', and a pat on the back. After all, the XO had his stripe and ship in the bag. He didn't need to sweat it.

Primary Flight Control, Pri-Fly, 140 feet above the four point-five acre flight deck, a busy place with officers and ratings, mikes dangling in front of their faces, milled around directing flight operations. The Mini-Boss, a junior commander, kept track of what was going on deck: refueling, armament, aircraft relocation, and a score of other tasks needed to maintain combat readiness. This deployment could actually see combat, something Ormond didn't relish. The Chinese had a modern navy and acceptable aircraft, and were not at all bashful showing the world what they had. Whatever the job, he was confident his ship would be up to it. A deck above in flag country, hardass Haddon would make sure that was the case.

After serving under Kenneth Pacino, Ormond initially found Haddon a cold character, strictly regulation. However, once the ice thawed, the rear admiral turned out to have a sharp sense of humor, which took some time getting used to, and a fair but strict command style. Every deployment was executed under wartime conditions as though the admiral expected to be attacked by submarines, ships and aircraft spewing missiles as soon as he cleared the harbor. His training program drove people to thoughts of murder, but once the Fleet achieved the desired level of proficiency, Haddon had eased off, expecting his ship commanders to maintain the set standard. It was a program Ormond didn't mind working with at all.

He glanced at the flat LED screen showing a Super Hornet coming in for a trap and bit his lip. The fighter wallowed, clearly underpowered as it came in below the glidepath. The LSO, Landing Signals Officer, waved him off and the Hornet barely cleared the stern, both engines in afterburner as it roared across the flight deck in a bolter, the noise shaking the armored glass in Pri-Fly.

"Who was that joker?" the Air Boss blared, eyes flashing with anger. He peered at a screen and turned to a lieutenant standing beside him. "Have Boomer report to his squadron commander as soon as he traps. That was, by God, the lousiest approach I have seen in a while. Boomer better get his shit together or he'll be flying weather kites off the stern!"

"Aye aye, sir," the lieutenant responded crisply and spoke urgently into his mike.

Ormond smiled. The Air Boss took no prisoners, not where

flying was concerned, and Lieutenant 'Boomer' Holace was supposed to be a first rate driver. At the ragged end of day quals, it was getting to everybody, not that Ormond had much sympathy for the young pilot. Should his ship engage for real, everybody would have to be crisp for the duration, and weekend drivers would be weeded out. His carrier did not haul passengers.

Captain Fraser 'Pike' Malone sucked on his pipe, shook his head, and sauntered over.

"The boys are tired, sir. You need to ease up a bit."

"No excuse, CAG," Ormond grated. "If they're tired after making a few lousy traps and flying simple racecourse patterns, air refueling and maintaining CAP, they'll fall apart on me if action starts. What the hell were you doing while nesting at Atsugi?"

When USS *George Washington* was tied in port at Yokosuka, Carrier Air Wing 5's fighter squadrons were based at the Naval Air Facility Atsugi. They were also meant to maintain their flying status there while waiting to sail.

"As air group commander, Malone, you should have been exercising them to maintain desired proficiency. Instead, judging by today's performance, they've been hitting the bars."

"That's not fair, Captain. You're giving a downcheck to the whole wing based on one crummy trap."

"It's not my job to be fair, Pike, but combat ready. Too many of your boys are hooking the two and four-wire. I want them hitting the three-wire every time. They got their birds down, but they're not following proper landing procedure, and it's worse with night quals. Get them sharp, Pike, or I'll start chewing stuff on somebody."

"Aye aye, sir," CAG answered glumly, clamped his teeth around the pipe stem and strode to the outward sloping windows overlooking the deck.

Ormond sighed. He *had* been pushing the squadrons hard, exposing weaknesses, which was the whole idea. According to the flight stats, Malone's boys had done fairly well, but Ormond wanted perfection. If that meant pissing off his friend, he would wear it, and Pike shouldn't have been bitching.

When some Washington weenie changed the air wing's nomenclature from Carrier Air Group to Carrier Air Wing, the whole Navy groaned. Calling the captain in charge of the carrier squadrons CAW wasn't likely to enhance the miscreant's career track. In its wisdom, although the name had stuck, people always called the Wing's boss, Commander Air Group. Ormond sometimes wondered what the hell went on in the Pentagon. In his view, the place was a retirement village for officers who simply couldn't hack it.

A Hornet came barreling in holding steady on the glidepath as though glued. It cut power at the last minute, came down with a crunch, and hooked the three-wire. The pilot immediately engaged afterburners, the orange-blue flames belching from the twin pipes, ready to do a bolter if he failed to snag a wire. The exhaust died and the arrestor wire pulled the aircraft back slightly, releasing the hook. The pilot retracted it and, following directions from a yellow shirt handler, moved the Hornet to the starboard side of the deck in front of the island. The arrestor wire slithered across the deck as the tension mechanism on either side wound in the slack, making the wire ready for the next aircraft.

A black phone beside Ormond buzzed and he picked up. "Captain."

"CVIC, sir, Tactical Action Officer. Sentry reports an element of four J-15 Shenyangs inbound. Range, 120 miles. CAP is intercepting."

"Are we being painted?"

"Nav and weather radar only, sir."

"Warn them off if they cross the fifty-mile exclusion zone," Ormond ordered crisply. "Light them up at thirty."

"Aye aye, sir."

Ormond replaced the phone and frowned. Flying a racetrack pattern twenty miles portside of the carrier, the E-2D Hawkeye sentry provided long range radar coverage for the task force. In battle it also acted as a coordinator of all air activity in the theater. In any engagement the Chinese would seek to eliminate the slow and vulnerable turboprop aircraft, but he did not believe this was an engagement. The Chinese were naturally nosy and wanted to pull his chain.

The Shenyang J-15 was a carrier-based multi-role fighter, the design copied from the Russian Sukhoi SU-33, which many said was an F-14 offshoot. Deployed in 2012, the J-15 was rumored to be a match for the F/A-18 Super Hornet, something Ormond discounted as Chinese propaganda. Intelligence said that although the J-15 possessed superior thrust-to-weight ratio and lower wing loading, it was weak in its electronics and combat systems. Its lack of air-to-air refueling capability also meant restricted operating range, which in turn meant the Chinese carrier *Liaoning* might be prowling around the neighborhood. However, with a maximum reported range of 2,150 miles, the J-15s could have sortied from Shanghai or Qingdao, the North Sea Fleet home port, only some 300 miles from his position. Anyway, the *Liaoning* was supposed to be tied up at Qingdao, although the PLAN liked to move it around, exercising their carrier doctrine.

Regardless where the fighters came from, he had to honor the threat.

A few minutes later the phone buzzed again.

"Commander Varnecky, sir. The J-15s have entered the exclusion zone. They were warned off and I have them illuminated with the Mk 91 NSSM and Mk 95 radars to let them know that we aren't fooling. Missile cruiser *Shiloh* has lit off its AN/SPG-62 fire control radar."

"Any reaction from the J-15s?"

"They're still boring in."

"I'm on my way down," Ormond said and climbed out of his seat. "I'll be in CIC," he told the OOD and headed for the hatch.

The marine standing guard snapped to attention. "Captain is

off the deck!"

Ormond made his way down steep gangways one level below the flight deck, and entered the darkened, fully manned Combat Information Center, officially known as the Combat Direction Center, but old salts like him had little patience with constantly changing nomenclature. Varnecky looked up from his large-scale electronic display map, flanked on either side by two tactical repeater screens from the covering Aegis missile cruisers, and nodded.

"The J-15s just crossed the twenty-mile circle, Captain."

Ormond took the command seat overlooking the manned combat stations and picked up a red phone.

"Haddon," a heavy voice answered immediately.

"It's Ormond, Admiral. Four J-15s just crossed the twenty-mile line."

"I know. I've been watching the development from here. Have they lit off their targeting radars?"

"Negative. It could be a Kodak run, sir."

"Wanting to take some pictures for their albums? It's possible. Keep tracking them, Captain. If they get a missile lock, engage countermeasures and issue a final warning to break off. Otherwise, let them have their fun."

"Aye aye, sir." Ormond replaced the receiver and bit his lip.

Fun could turn out to be pretty hot, but he wasn't particularly concerned. The PLAN had pulled this stunt before, wanting to observe American naval doctrine in action, and always pulled back at the ten-mile line. That didn't mean he would not blow up their ass should they activate their attack radars. Four fighter-bombers wouldn't give his task force any trouble at all, but he didn't want the messy paperwork afterward, should somebody start shooting.

In the plot, keeping a perfect diamond formation, the four red triangles edged closer to the screening destroyers. At ten miles, the element swung north and headed toward Qingdao.

Varnecky exhaled loudly and smiled.

"That's about as close as I want them, Captain."

"If the Chinese meant business they'd have launched shore-based cruise missiles. Sending in vulnerable fighters was a game of nerves," Ormond said with a smile.

"Well, they got on *my* nerves!"

Ormond chuckled. "You worry too much, Duke."

"Guilty."

"Anyway, why would they want to tangle? They're just being nosy."

"Nosy or not, I don't like them buzzing us. Any idea how long we're going to be out here? Lillian is packing everything up ready for San Diego."

"Haddon hasn't told me, Duke, but I doubt that we'll be prowling around for long."

"If we're a retaliatory strike package, it's not like the Admiral to keep our mission under wraps."

"I'm sure he'll get around to telling us." Ormond got up and stretched his arms. "I'll be in Pri-Fly."

As he walked up the companionway, he wondered what game the Chinese would play next. He figured he could expect to see ships from their East Sea Fleet, and Shanghai a bare 200 miles on his port quarter. Was Task Force 70 a retaliatory package?

At least President Walters had the balls to finally show his displeasure in a substantive way. Making speeches at the UN and announcing sanctions may have pleased the boardroom types, tickertape running out their ears, but national outrage demanded a positive response. Ormond didn't want an all out confrontation, but a limited strike at some disused military facility—if the Chinese had one—would get the point across that you don't mess with Uncle Sam.

This business that La Palma was a rogue ops executed by some Politburo heavyweight pissed off at America was, in his view, a load of crock. The Chinese wanted to cripple the United

States without getting their hands dirty, simple as that. Walters couldn't take that lying down. Like Duke, Ormond wondered what Admiral Haddon had in mind for his task force. Of course, Haddon might not know, unlikely as that was.

\* \* \*

Rain fell steadily from bleak clouds, obscuring the Zhongnanhai grounds in fine mist. As he stood beside the tall window, hands clasped behind his back, Zhou Yedong's thoughts wandered down memory alleyways of a time when playing the politics game used to be an intellectual exercise of brinkmanship, where failure was met with a shrug and a polite smile of acknowledgment to a skillful opponent. Faced with a dangerously real situation, he could only nod in acknowledgment to an underestimated adversary—always fatal in any game—and he thought he had learned that lesson. Complacency and overconfidence? It did not matter. What mattered now was to retrieve the current situation from escalating into a confrontation, saving some pride for his country along the way.

Turning, he studied his friend with interest. Legs crossed, Dzhang Qishan sipped tea from a delicate blue porcelain cup, apparently unmoved. Zhou allowed himself a faint smile, admiring the premier's calm composure. Then again, Dzhang could afford to be composed. Whatever happened, he would emerge appearing the resolute statesman, a person the Party could turn to in time of crisis. Dzhang was a genuine friend and a fellow *taizidang*, but the premier was also a political rival who would not hesitate to step up should Zhou falter. It was the way of things; something Zhou understood well and did not resent. One cannot resent falling rain or the sweeping wind.

Dzhang took a sip of tea and glanced out the window. "I know it's supposed to be the wet season, but does it have to be this wet?"

Zhou chuckled. "A portent of darker things to come?"

"I wonder how much this is our doing."

"The rain?" Zhou sat down and poured himself a cup of tea.

"That too, but I was thinking of unchecked development, which gave rise to unchecked pollution, which in turn resulted in desertification and loss of productive land."

"You've been talking to Keung?"

"He may be a populist worm, but his concern for the welfare of our people and the environment is genuine. Maybe we're pushing too hard."

"Don't tell me you're swayed by his alarmist rhetoric, Qishan. We're making progress to curb industrial excesses."

"Yes, we have impressive environmental regulations. The problem is, we're not enforcing them, and there lies our dilemma. Keung may be right when he says we're driving our economy too hard. If we don't pause and reflect, spend some of our resources to address environmental degradation, when the situation becomes critical the problem may no longer be tractable."

Zhou leaned back and nodded. "Yes, he and I talked about that before he confronted me with that damning document Han is supposed to have signed. He's playing us, you know that. He's playing all of us."

"The FBI investigation may yet thwart him."

"Perhaps, but Walters is already moving. He has the 7th Fleet parading up and down our coast, inviting us to dare something. If we paraded one of our fleets off San Francisco, he would have it blown out of the water, but I'm supposed to swallow my indignation and take it?"

"That's right. Swallow it and give thanks that Walters hasn't done something more drastic."

"We offered reparations and we even apologized at the UN! What more does he want?"

Dzhang gave a gentle smile. "Yedong, you're avoiding the issue, and what's more, you know it."

Weary of the whole sordid thing, Zhou nodded. "We committed a technical act of war, agreed, but if the 7th Fleet starts anything, I will be forced to respond. If I don't, Han Yunshan and his generals would depose me or have me shot."

"You have him shot instead," Dzhang retorted mildly and raised a hand to forestall a rejoinder. "Getting rid of him would remove a festering problem for both of us. My sources tell me he's been counting numbers, bolstering support for a move against me at the upcoming National Congress."

Zhou frowned. "I haven't heard anything about that."

"You wouldn't. He's been very careful, but some of his friends are also my friends. The investigation you launched against him hasn't exactly endeared him to you."

"That couldn't be helped, and he should know that it wasn't personal. Even if what you say is true, I cannot move against him on mere innuendo."

"You have more than mere innuendo."

"Those orders, you mean? I still think that shit Chen forged them—at Keung's urging."

"Probably, and the FBI team just might prove it. Whether they do or not is really irrelevant in the larger scheme of things, although of more than academic interest to you and me. Their investigation is a PR exercise to help us expose Keung and Chen—if they're guilty—and everybody knows it. Han is a different matter. He wants the Central Military Commission dictating policy for the government in Deng Xiaoping's mold. A lot of generals and admirals aren't happy having the CMC subordinate to the State Council—"

"They *are* on the State Council!"

Dzhang waved a dismissive hand. "A technicality. Han is your friend, but that's not going to stop him from usurping your authority…or mine. Unless he submits to a polygraph test denying he wrote that document, you must make an example of him. Others will think twice before risking their careers or lives."

Studying the quietly spoken premier, Zhou wondered whether his colleague had another motive for getting rid of the CMC chairman. Han was ambitious and made no secret of it, but was he actually working to bolster support for a power spill? As CMC chairman, Han wielded considerable authority. In many ways, he was more powerful than the State Council Premier. Was he seeking to become premier *and* retain chairmanship of the CMC? Now there was a nasty thought. If he succeeded, the position of Communist Party president would be effectively marginalized. Although a possibility, he simply couldn't see it. There was, of course, a simpler and more plausible explanation.

By urging him to depose Han, in one stroke, Dzhang would rid himself of a potential rival and weaken Zhou's hold on the presidency. He might also be considering grabbing the CMC chairmanship for himself, a very dangerous combination. Dzhang's clear black eyes and placid features revealed nothing, but Zhou did not expect to see anything. Inscrutability was a minimum requirement in their respective positions.

"You have a ruthless streak, Qishan. Did you know that?" Zhou murmured, certain that Dzhang would not discern the double meaning of his words.

"And so do you, Yedong. Are you surprised?"

"I would be surprised if you didn't have that quality." Zhou said softly, deep in thought. Whatever plot his friend might be hatching, the situation could still be turned to his advantage. "Attractive as the idea is, the State Council would not tolerate having Han removed in such an exemplary fashion. I would be forever looking over my shoulder waiting for a State Security goon squad to come after me. I cannot move against him without irrefutable evidence, and that means waiting for the FBI team to complete their investigation." Taking a sip of tea, he shook his head. "To think we that have descended into gutter politics by plotting against one of our own."

After a moment, Dzhang shrugged. "It has always been like

this, my friend. Even if the FBI team clears Han, Keung and Chen have caused the elitist princeling coalition a lot of damage. There is no way to expose them?"

"Not without hauling one of them in and subjecting him to rigorous interrogation," Zhou said, "which is really not an option. I try something like that and *I'll* be hauled in. There are limits to my power. I still haven't completely discounted the possibility that Xhal Shenglai might be behind this."

"He is very competent, but he doesn't have that kind of strategic thinking." Dzhang uncrossed his legs and placed his cup on the coffee table. "Getting back to Keung, he might not be invulnerable as you think."

"Oh?"

"For the sake of argument, let's say Keung hatched this thing. He would need some very technical information on how to go about doing it. This is not something he could get off the Internet."

Tantalized by the thought, Zhou's eyebrows climbed. "He would consult a subject matter expert."

"That's what Meecham said. It just happens that late in April, a geophysicist at Peking University met with a fatal accident. Let's suppose he was the subject matter expert. After getting his information, Keung would want to eliminate a grave security risk."

"Agreed. Your point?"

"Keung wouldn't do that himself."

Zhou smiled, but it wasn't with humor. "He would have somebody do it for him. Somebody he would trust implicitly. I should have seen this myself."

"A forgivable oversight. You don't operate at that level."

"Yes, I have others who do my dirty work."

"We all do, my friend," Dzhang said softly.

"You have someone in mind who is close to Keung?"

"Shen Lei, head of his security detail. My sources tell me that Shen has been Keung's shadow for a number of years. I wouldn't be surprised if they had more than a bodyguard/client relationship."

"All security detail personnel report to State Security," Zhou pointed out sharply and Dzhang chuckled.

"Loyalties can shift, you know. Don't tell me you don't exchange confidences with your security chief, or have him carry out a special assignment from time to time?"

Zhou allowed himself a faint grin. "Unfortunately, I do. Talk to Lin Jinpan. I want all security detail personnel re-vetted and rotated on a twelve-month basis. Starting now."

"In this case the damage may already be done."

"Perhaps, but this will remind everybody where their loyalty lies."

"I know what you're thinking, Yedong. We haul Shen in and interrogate him. However, I wouldn't advise it. We do this now and Chen is found innocent, Keung could make a lot of trouble for us."

Zhou snorted. "Over a bodyguard?"

"Not because of Shen, but the precedent. There are a lot of old skeletons rattling in many people's closets that are better left undisturbed."

"Including yours? Never mind. Have Shen hauled in. We're not facing normal circumstances here."

"Very well, but I'm still worried about the precedent."

"Leave that one with me. What is your impression of the FBI team?"

"Meecham is nobody's fool, and his shadow Davenport is another capable operator. If anyone can validate who really signed those orders, it will be them."

"American technology…we have a right to fear it."

"With the FBI here, do you want Lin Jinpan to continue *his* investigation?"

"It won't do any harm. Call a meeting of the State Council. While you're at it, have a quiet chat with everyone and explain why we cannot retaliate against the American fleet. Han Yunshan and his generals won't like it, but if he protests, I'll wave his orders in front of everybody, fake or not. You may care to pass that to him."

"He'll construe this as lack of confidence and he'll remember this as a personal slur."

"It's good that he'll remember. The CMC is subordinate to you and me."

Dzhang chuckled. "Someone needs to remind them of that."

Zhou nodded slowly. "Perhaps. Damn Keung! I *know* he's behind it all. It has his trademark stamp, but this is not how we execute our foreign policy."

"You're upset because his plan didn't work, not that he may have directed it."

"You're right, of course. An economically crippled America would have been a broken force. Now we're facing a global backlash and an emboldened U.S. President who won't hesitate to clamp down on us."

"You made a mistake not voicing your suspicions to him."

"I know and we're paying for it. All we can do now is tidy up the mess and repair the damage as best we can." Zhou pursed his lips. "You have the FBI team protected?"

Dzhang nodded. "They're covered, but any man can be eliminated. However, I don't see that as a high risk. What would be the percentage? The Americans would simply send someone else. Besides, the only incriminating evidence we have points to Han. If Chen forged those orders and the FBI manages to prove it, I'd get worried, but by then it would be too late."

"Those orders, Qishan. Make sure the document doesn't disappear."

"Lin Jinpan wouldn't be that foolish. You *do* have a copy, don't you?"

"Of course."

"Make sure *it* doesn't disappear," Dzhang murmured.

* * *

Meecham took a sip of coffee, placed the cup on the table, and looked at Davenport.

"How are Karelina and the kids?"

"Wishing I were home. You?"

"The same, and we haven't been here two days yet."

"I told her not to worry, but you know how women are."

Living with Melissa, Tom had learned. "Yeah. I'd like you to stick with Paul Rogan today, if you don't mind, Keith. Go over all source material Lin Jinpan's investigators compiled. Talk to them. Find out how they went about their business. Somebody at the embassy will be able to translate the stuff for you."

"You want to establish a baseline?" Davenport queried, pursuing a piece of fried egg with a toast remnant.

"We need to know what they've done before deciding on our move. Another thing. I want all communication transcripts between Keung and Chen."

"That might not be easy to get. The two of them would have handled a lot of classified material and they wouldn't have been foolish enough to discuss La Palma over an open cell or landline phone."

"No, they probably didn't, but they must have met once or twice before and after the event. I want to establish a possible inconsistency in their movement pattern."

Davenport smiled and shook his head. "We're not dealing with amateurs here, Tom. If those two are involved, they wouldn't have left any trail."

"There is always something. Check with their drivers. If they visited each other, their office may have a record."

"Okay, so we establish that they met and had fireside chats. That's not evidence supporting a conspiracy. There are lots of perfectly legitimate reasons why they'd meet."

Smiling, Tom raised a finger in admonition. "I'll do the pessimistic bits here, and you have forgotten your sleuth training. We're playing a psychological game with them. We probably won't unearth anything incriminating, but one of them may start to wonder if there is some little detail he overlooked that could trip them up. It could provoke a reaction."

"Like Rogan said, as long as it's not terminal. I want to enjoy the years I have left. Pity that we can't haul them in and shoot one full of babble juice. It would save everybody all this footwork."

Tom chuckled. "This isn't the CIA, you know, and I'm certain the thought had already occurred to Zhou and Dzhang."

"If we cannot prove that Chen signed those orders—"

"They'll probably both walk. I know." Tom took another sip of coffee. "If Keung is involved, he must be getting a *little* nervous now."

"You mean, he may want to remove Chen?"

"To keep his neck, what do you think?"

"I don't know. It's too convenient and the timing would stink. You seem to be focused on Keung and Chen as the culprits."

"Actually, I'm trying to rule them out. President Walters would have an easier job on his hands if Zhou in fact orchestrated this. If one dissenting group can pull off La Palma, what's to stop somebody else from emulating them? Next time it could be a suitcase nuke in Manhattan."

Davenport winced. "You have a convoluted mind, Tom. Did you know that?"

"Just looking at angles. Dzhang said something yesterday that got me thinking."

"Somebody at Wushiht'ala must have cut a CD to synchronize the firing sequence for the thermobaric mines," Davenport mused. "Probably a software patch for the sub's firecontrol computer."

"Exactly."

"Another loose end, perhaps?"

"Only someone with a lot of authority could have got that done—and removed any evidence behind him. I'll ask Weng to check if there were any untimely deaths at that facility. Who knows, something might come up."

Davenport sat back and crossed his arms. "I wonder if it was wise coming here. I understand why you want to see the case closed and the perpetrator found, but when Weng told us the President had sent in the 7th Fleet and intends to carry out—"

"Watch it," Tom said, mindful of possible bugs listening in.

"Does our presence make any difference?"

"I've been thinking about that. If Zhou's government set up La Palma, we're just a PR exercise as Rogan said, but if Keung or Han pulled it off and we uncover them, Zhou will owe President Walters a rather large favor. That will be one substantial chip in the poker stakes they're playing for."

"As long as we're not thrown in as change."

"I just don't see Zhou doing it. If he wanted to rid himself of two Tuanpai headaches, there are easier ways of going about it than setting off an international incident."

"Either way, Tom, we need to be careful. I wouldn't be walking around alone at night. Hear me?"

"If Chen signed those orders, he's in for some tough explaining and he knows it. Getting rid of us won't make any difference."

"It would to us! We could be shot out of pure spite."

"Christ! Leave off the pessimistic bits, okay?"

"What if those orders have disappeared, with Lin Jinpan's help?"

Tom chewed his lip and nodded. "That's possible, but I doubt it. Even if Lin disposed of them, Keung probably has a copy. He would be foolish handing Zhou the original, and if I were Zhou, I'd have made one for myself. I'm more worried that

351

Chen might disappear."

Before Davenport could respond, the sliding doors to the lounge slid open and Joseph entered.

"Pardon the interruption. Mr. Weng Leijang requests a moment of your time."

"Of course. Please show him in," Tom said and glanced at his watch. It was exactly 8:30.

Weng strode in wearing a broad smile. "Good morning, gentlemen. I trust I am not intruding?"

Tom swept a hand at the table. "Please, won't you join us for some tea?"

"Thank you. Perhaps another time. You are sure I am not intruding?"

"Just finishing breakfast," Tom assured him, pulling back a chair for his visitor.

"Excellent." Weng sat down, holding his frame straight. "Following our discussion with Premier Dzhang, I managed to procure a copy of Han Yunshan's orders—"

"But not from Minister Lin Jinpan?" Tom prompted, chuckling as Weng's eyes widened.

"How did you know?"

"Keith and I were discussing that possibility just now. Who provided the copy? Chairman Keung?"

"No, it was President Zhou. I'm afraid it's only a photocopy reproduction, which might diminish its value."

"Mmm. The resolution will certainly be degraded, but we'll get a high rez scan done and have it computer enhanced."

Weng reached into his pocket and held out a silver flash drive stick. "JPG and PDF images scanned at 1,400 dpi."

Frowning, Tom reached for the stick. He would have preferred seeing the document for himself and have it scanned at the embassy, but saying so would not be diplomatic.

"You understand, having lost one copy, President Zhou was not keen to lose another," Weng said apologetically.

"That's all right, Leijang. I understand. Do you know what happened to Lin Jinpan's copy?"

Weng's mouth twitched. "According to his office, it was misfiled somewhere. The person responsible will be disciplined."

Tom was about to tell him not to worry about it, but refrained. It wasn't his business how the Chinese ran their bureaucracy, wondering what disciplined meant for the luckless individual.

"Neil Fuller from your legate office met with some resistance when he requested a copy of Professor Chuan Jianbo's death certificate, but I am glad to say the matter has been resolved. Having read the document, I'm afraid it doesn't tell us much. Anticipating your request, I ordered the body exhumed and a full autopsy carried out."

Tom exchanged looks with Davenport. This was good news, but Weng was rushing things. Being handled was something new for him, and he wasn't sure he liked it. Did Weng intend to keep him and Davenport in the villa, stopping him from doing any footwork? The Chinese might be concerned for their safety, but this could also be a soft coverup under the guise of open cooperation.

"Thank you. Fuller has a copy of the death certificate?"

"Certainly. I knew you would want to see it for yourself and have it independently translated."

"I do. When can we expect the autopsy report?"

"Within twenty-four hours. Tom, I am curious about something. Even if the autopsy shows that Professor Chuan's injury was not the result of an accident, which might be hard to determine anyway, how does that help your investigation?"

"It will confirm that he was the subject matter expert our perpetrator or perpetrators used, and will provide a critical link in the evidence trail."

"And if the autopsy is inconclusive?"

"We'll follow another possible lead. Does Peking University

have a surveillance system?"

Weng frowned and pulled at his chin. "I believe there are cameras covering the parking lot and various entrances. I'd have to check. Why do you ask?"

"If Professor Chuan was murdered, the tapes might show if he was accompanied by someone on the day of his death. Someone linked with the four persons of interest. Minister Lin Jinpan's report stated that Chairman Keung Yang frequented Da Giorgio's at the Grand Hyatt from time to time, and it just happens that he was there on the day Professor Chuan died. This could be perfectly innocent and I may be clutching at straws, but if the Hyatt has surveillance cameras…"

Weng chuckled and shook his head. "You have an intricate way of thinking, Tom. I'll look into it."

"Do that. Yesterday, Premier Dzhang mentioned Wushiht'ala."

"I already spoke to the facility director. Nothing out of the ordinary has happened there during the period of our interest."

"Have you asked him if there were any deaths in April or early June, particularly in their IT department?"

Weng's eyes narrowed. "No, I haven't, which is unpardonable. I shall take steps to remedy that omission."

"Can you keep Keith in the loop, please?"

"Of course. May I ask how long it will take the FBI to analyze Han's document?"

"We'll know by tomorrow morning."

"The computer in your study has a high speed Internet facility."

Tom smiled. "Thank you, but since Keith and I need to see Fuller and Rogan, I'll transmit the files from our embassy."

"As you wish. Tom, Mr. Rogan made a request for all paperwork from the Ministry of State Security relating to Chairman Keung and Vice Chairman Chen's movements and electronic communication; including information on Admiral Xhal Shen-glai. They will be provided, but we need to sanitize them first. The documents may not be available until sometime tomorrow."

"And tomorrow we might not need them," Tom said, and Weng chuckled.

"It will be an interesting day, whatever the outcome of your analysis. Was there anything else?"

"An entry in Minister Lin's report said that Commander Vang Kai signed a receipt slip when he received Vice Chairman Chen's orders."

Frowning, Weng nodded. "That is normal procedure."

"Yes, we do the same thing," Tom mused. "What is odd, there is no mention of a receipt slip for Chairman Han's orders."

"Because Commander Vang never received them?" Weng ventured slowly. "An interesting observation. I'll look into it. Should you and Mr. Davenport need to go anywhere, a car is now at your disposal. An MSS security officer will accompany you everywhere you go. He'll also act as your interpreter. If either of you want to travel separately, he'll arrange for another car. Now, if you will excuse me, I have some calls to make." Weng stood and smiled. "I wish you a productive day, gentlemen."

"Pretty efficient guy," Davenport remarked after Tom saw his visitor out.

"Too efficient, perhaps," Tom muttered darkly. "Christ! Do you get the feeling that we're in a gilded cage?"

"So you noticed that. I wouldn't read too much into it, though. That's how business is done here."

"Maybe. I'm just not used to running an investigation chained to a desk."

Davenport laughed. "You're not?"

Startled, Tom chuckled. "Yeah, I guess I *have* been running this case from my desk."

"And don't expect things to change either."

"Right. Let's take a ride and see Lipson. While I have a chat with Fuller, you talk to Rogan. Afterward, I think I'd like to see Peking University."

# Chapter Eight

Afternoon shadows filtered through the window, casting a gray blanket over Zhongnanhai. Keung watched torn clouds cling to the horizon, bathed in blood by the setting sun. Nothing stirred outside. Expecting to have a straightforward day of work, the sudden State Council meeting had soured his mood. Meeting locations were rotated, supposedly a security measure, which was ridiculous. A hangover from Mao Tse-tung's days, a tiresome ritual that should have been abandoned years ago. Perhaps he should raise the matter at the next Standing Committee meeting. Fortunately, Dzhang had this one scheduled at the convention room two floors above him.

Debating the proceedings with Chen Teng, they retired to Keung's office, enjoying a glass of fine *Hua Diao* wine. Half listening to his friend's chatter, his mind on the meeting, Keung suddenly sat up, took the pipe from his mouth and stared, not believing what Chen said.

"You what?"

The CMC vice chairman shifted his stocky frame and touched the ragged scar running down his left cheek. Looking relaxed, he smiled.

"I said we should remove the FBI team from the picture. By the way, I was glad to see your security chief doing his job."

"Shen Lei? He sweeps the office every time I come in. Why the sudden concern?"

"My minder found two bugs in mine."

Keung waved the pipe. "Forget the damn bugs. Why would you want to do a stupid thing like making a hit on the Americans? They have nothing!"

"Getting rid of them would make sure of that."

"The FBI would simply send someone else and you'll be introducing a needless risk factor into an already tense situation."

"They may send somebody else, but whoever they send won't have Meecham's background knowledge and the web of threads linking everything."

"Irrelevant. He probably passed whatever he had to Weng Leijang, and the only thing he has is Lin Jinpan's report and Han Yunshan's orders."

Chen leaned forward, his black eyes searching. "Are you sure about that?"

"He may have suspicions, but there is no trail to follow. I made sure of that. The FBI will authenticate Han's signature and Zhou will have no choice but to remove him, which will shake the whole princeling coalition. The last thing we want right now is to add another dimension to their investigation. Anyway, how would this implicate Han?"

"It doesn't directly. The Americans will have two bodies on their hands with no answers and they'll be pointing their finger at Zhou. He may have *his* suspicions, but he won't have any answers either."

Keung chewed on his pipe, working the problem. "Perhaps removing them might not be such a bad idea after all."

"Talking about risk factors, what about the person you used to clean up after us?"

"That's been taken care of."

Chen nodded. "I am glad to hear it. I don't want us going down because of misguided sentiment, my friend."

Keung ground the pipe stem between his teeth. He took a couple of puffs, savoring the rum-flavored tobacco, and stared at Chen. "I have been accused of many things, but never for being sentimental."

"I know. You're a hardnosed, calloused bastard."

Keung chuckled. "Zhou told me that more than once."

"And he is right. What do you make of President Walters sending in the 7th Fleet?"

"It was a logical and expected move. What surprised me, despite the threat of exposure, Han didn't mince words when he slammed Zhou for allowing China's territorial integrity to be violated. I could see he wanted to say more, but those fake orders placed him in an invidious position."

"Which you intended. Having me cut and paste his signature rather than signing the thing myself was clever and may yet hang him."

"Signing that document yourself may have been good enough to fool Lin Jinpan's forensic people, but the FBI is more sophisticated."

Chen stared. "You thought that far ahead when we dreamed this up?"

"I try to think of everything. All we need to do is sit tight and we'll emerge clothed in power. Whatever leads the FBI team might be following are dead ends. Zhou will be forced to remove Han, fatally fracturing the *taizidang* elitist coalition, paving the way for us to move in. Zhou will work with us or he'll be the next to go."

"I noted that you sided with Han," Chen pointed out.

"Of course. It would have been out of character not to. My motion demanding that President Walters withdraw the 7th Fleet failed along factional lines, but Han's proposal to shadow it aggressively was adopted. Zhou didn't like it, seeing it as needless provocation, and he is right, but he is in a bind. After all, China launched an attack on the United States and they are responding in kind. Had there been significant loss of life and infrastructure damage, I dare say it would have been an altogether different response. Having the 7th Fleet parading up and down our coast weakens Zhou's authority, which plays nicely into our hands."

"Mmm. If we push the Americans, there could be an incident."

"Which would further weaken Zhou's position."

"You *want* Zhou removed?"

"I want him and the princelings destroyed! He is driving China into a social crisis, a price he appears willing to pay to modernize the country. I consider the price too high and there are those who agree with me. I cannot see the Tuanpai marginalizing the princelings anytime soon, but we could work with Dzhang in a more even partnership. He is a pragmatic politician. Besides, he agrees with many of our policies."

"Dzhang, eh? And who would step into his shoes? You?"

Keung smiled without mirth. "I am quite content where I am, but there are others better suited."

He peered out the window. Dark clouds were still sliding across the sky. He wanted to go home and luxuriate in a steamy bath with a snifter of cognac at his side. He needed to wash the stink of intrigue out of his nostrils, suspecting that it would take more than one bath. Perhaps he had played the game for too long.

Following his glance, Chen grunted as he pried himself out of the chair. "I better be going and get some work done. It's not wise being with you, not right now."

Keung escorted his friend out, then sprawled into his chair. He bit his lip, reached across the desk, and touched a glowing white button on the phone keyboard.

"Yes, sir?"

"I want to see Shen Lei immediately."

"Yes, sir."

It took only a few minutes for his bodyguard and trusted confidant to appear. Shen never went home until he saw Keung safely at his residence for the night. Closing the door softly, he marched into the room and stood at parade rest.

"You wanted to see me, sir?"

Making a decision he knew he had been avoiding, Keung sighed. "Remember the conversation we had about mitigating risk?"

"Yes, sir," Shen replied woodenly.

"You must disappear...today, and you have to do it in a way where no one would ever consider looking for you. Is that clear?"

"Sir..."

Keung raised his hand. "I shall miss you, but I'll sleep better knowing that I have not betrayed your trust."

"You have always been very considerate, Mr. Chairman," Shen rasped from his mangled throat.

"There is one last thing I need you to do. I want you to eliminate the two American investigators."

"I shall take care of it, sir."

Keung rose and extended his hand. "Goodbye, my friend."

Startled, Shen stepped forward to grasp the proffered hand. "Goodbye, sir," he said softly and swallowed. Snapping to attention, he saluted and quickly walked out.

When the door closed, Keung sat down and turned to gaze at the rolling clouds. After a while, he pressed a glowing button on his phone pad.

"Yes, sir?"

He squared his shoulders and took a deep breath. "I want you to place a call to Commander Keung Meng." There was no need to elaborate. His aide knew who Meng was. Everybody did.

"Commander Keung. Yes, sir."

He sat there, puffing out clouds of smoke. After almost ten minutes, the phone finally jangled, momentarily startling him. Why should he be so jumpy for wanting to call his only son? Nevertheless, he was jumpy and somewhat apprehensive. He pressed the speaker button.

"Yes?"

"Commander Keung, sir."

"Very good...Meng?"

"Hello, father," a deep, confident voice answered, and Keung relaxed. He shouldn't have worried. In the background, he could hear the hum of ship's machinery.

"Hello, my boy. It's good to hear your voice."

"Is something wrong, father?"

"Nothing is wrong. I only wanted to chat. I hope I'm not calling at an inconvenient time." Keung sat back and reached for his pipe. Everything was all right.

* * *

Shen Lei turned from Fucheng Road and drove along the narrow roadway toward the elaborately carved hanging entrance that led into the Diaoyutai State Guesthouse grounds. The heavy traffic noises faded behind him He had to show his fake ID to an unsmiling guard before being allowed in.

He did not anticipate any problems removing the two Americans, and his source told him that both targets were in their residence. Two quick shots from his silenced semi-automatic and he would return to his apartment to pick up a few things necessary for his disappearance. His plan absurdly simple and eminently workable because it would not be questioned. He would literally disappear, leaving everything he owned behind, including his battered Honda Civic. He'll miss the little car, but he could not risk taking it. Keung's enemies were bound to mount at least an elementary search for him, but they wouldn't do it very hard. After all, everyone expected the chairman to have him killed to remove a genuine security risk—Keung had been right about that. Under the circumstances, disappearing would fuel everyone's suspicions, but that was all they'd have.

After taking care of the Americans, he would make his way to the Gansu Province and settle down somewhere along the Yellow River. Gansu was known for its hot summers and sometimes very cold winters, but also a land where a man can lose himself and have a new life. Perhaps he'll find a wife there, the women having a different temperament than those trawling the big cities.

Shen drove past the small double-story cottage, noting the wide doorway flanked by two thick wooden posts guarded by red lions. Checking the area, nothing stirred. He turned the stolen car, slowed as he approached the cottage, and stopped. He flexed his fingers, the black leather driving gloves feeling like second skin.

He took out the Narinco Type 77 semi-automatic from the glove compartment, screwed on the silencer, and chambered a round, leaving the safety off. From his pocket, he dragged out a brown balaclava with cut eye holes and pulled it on. Leaving the engine running, he climbed out of the car and partially closed the door.

He strode up the paved path, stopped before the wide door and knocked with the barrel of his gun. When he heard footsteps, he lifted the weapon. The door opened and Shen glimpsed a small elderly man, his eyes widening in astonishment. Before Shen could fire, the man attempted to slam the door shut, but Shen barged in, pushing open the door with his shoulder.

He immediately fired two shots at the figure running down the corridor toward the stairs. He heard a cry of pain and the figure sprawled onto the polished floor. Shen strode quickly toward frosted glass sliding panels. Pulling one back, the two men inside gaped at him. Without hesitating, he fired, seeing both of them fall. About to make sure by giving each a head shot, a gun cracked and he gasped as pain seared his left side. Another crack splintered the doorframe above his head.

The American minder!

Shen loosed two quick shots at the prone figure in the corridor and ran through the open doorway. He jumped into the car, engaged first gear, and tore down the road, slowing as he rounded a bend. He didn't want to attract any unnecessary attention that might prevent him from getting away. Wincing, he glanced at his side. There wasn't any blood, but he felt the familiar wetness. His shirt and jacket were soaking it up. Nothing to be done about it until he cleared the Diaoyutai grounds.

When the guard at the entrance saw him, he waved him through and Shen turned right onto Fucheng Road. Two blocks later, he entered a side street and parked behind his Honda. The police would eventually find the stolen car, but it wouldn't do them any good. Nothing in it could possibly incriminate him. He slapped on an emergency bandage patch against his side, then drove quickly, but carefully, into the Zuojiazhuang residential district. He smiled as he reached his apartment building and left the Honda in its designated underground parking spot.

Inside his condo, he stripped down and bundled the bloody clothes into a black plastic bag. Showering, he properly dressed his wound. Regarding the gaping, weeping flesh with distaste, he should really have it stitched, but he had lived with worse. He could not tell if the two Americans were dead, but his carelessness at failing to dispose of the minder with his initial shots meant that he might have failed his mission. Karma.

The chairman can chew him out, he reflected with a smile.

Shen locked up for the last time, carrying a small suitcase and plastic bag. He walked down the deserted corridor and paused before the garbage chute. He shoved the bag into it and listened as it bounded down. Satisfied, he walked toward the two elevators serving the building.

A soft *ting* announced the arrival of the elevator. Shen got in and pressed the upper basement button, not wanting to leave through the main entrance and risk being seen. When the elevator door opened, he stepped out.

Light exploded in his head.

* * *

Meecham was in the shower nursing his bruised side when Sam, their new minder, came upstairs, apologizing profusely for intruding, announcing the arrival of the U.S. embassy courier who demanded that he sign a receipt before handing over the package. Wrapped in a towel, dabbing delicately at exposed parts, Tom stood in the open doorway as the embassy car pulled away and quickly tore open the wrapping. Coughing discreetly, Sam placed a terry robe around his shoulders.

"I trust it's good news, sir?" he queried politely.

Tom closed the folder, looked up, and smiled. "It depends on how Premier Dzhang will respond."

"I have found, sir, that unsettling news is best delivered through a third party," Sam said gravely, bowed and shut the front door.

Dressing, Tom gingerly prodded the wide bandage taped to his right side. The encounter with his would-be assassin left him with a collection of twelve stitches below his ribcage. He had been lucky. Had he faced a younger, more agile man, he and Keith wouldn't have needed any stitches. Both of them would have been in a box. Keith got shot through the fleshy part of his right thigh, which thankfully missed all the vital arteries. He would hobble for a while, but he'll live to enjoy his retirement.

Unfortunately, the encounter cost them Joseph. Tom hadn't known that the little man carried a gun, otherwise they'd all be dead. That weapon had been the tipping factor, something the assassin hadn't anticipated, fleeing after Joseph shot him. With Joseph disposed of, Tom was surprised the assassin had not finished his job. Not that he was complaining.

At 8:00 a.m. precisely, Sam showed Weng into the lounge. Tom greeted his visitor and pointed to a chair. Davenport poured him a cup of tea.

Seating himself, Weng stirred in sugar and took a sip. "Ah, that was good." Looking at them, he raised an eyebrow. "I trust you gentlemen are recovering from your unfortunate encounter?"

"Nothing that a few days of rest and female companionship won't fix," Davenport growled and Weng smiled.

"You Americans find humor in everything, and perhaps that is just as well."

"Speaking of humor," Tom said, "I hope you will keep yours after you read this." He handed Weng a slim blue folder, glad to have the thing finished, but wary of the reaction it might provoke. "The FBI forensic report."

The Chinese bureaucrat hesitated before taking the folder. Giving Tom a speculative look, he quickly rifled through the three sheets. Frowning, he shook his head and sighed.

"So, Minister Lin Jinpan's investigators were right after all. Han Yunshan did sign those orders. This is unwelcome news indeed."

"That's not what our report is saying at all," Tom corrected him firmly as he sat down.

Weng tapped the folder, looking annoyed. "Your analysis confirms the document was signed by Han," he said, pulling back a chair.

"The report says the document bears Chairman Han's signature. That's not proof that he wrote it or signed it."

"To use your quaint American idiom, you are splitting hairs, Tom."

"Leijang, do you want to whitewash Han or get at the truth?"

"Of course we don't want to whitewash the Chairman. He is a senior *taizidang* coalition figure and his dismissal would be very disruptive for the government, but this report seems conclusive."

"I'm not saying that he didn't prepare and sign those orders. What you must keep in mind, without the original document, we cannot prove it conclusively one way or the other. Unfortunately, the original might be at the bottom of the Atlantic."

Weng stared at him. "After all this effort, you mean we have nothing?"

"The copy Chairman Keung gave to President Zhou isn't admissible evidence. It is still possible that Chen Teng forged it. There is simply no way we can establish that with information currently available to us, but we haven't exhausted our leads yet."

Frowning, Weng squinted, his forehead furrowed in concentration, and took a sip of tea. "The Wushiht'ala software engineer?"

"The police report you sent Keith said that he died from head trauma caused by a blunt instrument, and his body was found in an alley behind a supermarket. The metal rod used to kill him right there beside him. A *prima facie* case of simple mugging."

"That's what the report said," Weng confirmed with a nod. "Even if the man was deliberately murdered and the autopsy shows the body was moved from the crime scene and dumped in the alley, how does that help us?"

*Christ!*

Tom could not believe that Weng wasn't able to connect the dots, but given the environment in which he lived, perhaps it wasn't altogether surprising. He kept forgetting that this country operated without the rule of law, at least not in the Western sense.

"Listen. If Professor Chuan's autopsy report shows that he was also murdered, we'll have a pattern. Whoever ordered one hit may have ordered both. Not always true, but it's symptomatic. In cases where collaborators are able to expose the principal perpetrator, a single hitman was usually employed to get rid of them."

"Ah, that's why you asked about surveillance tapes from the Grand Hyatt and the School of Earth and Space Sciences."

"That's right. The same face could appear in both locations. Do you have anything so far?"

"We only secured the tapes yesterday, Tom, but we have some bad news. This morning, a man's body was found in a basement parking lot of an apartment building in the Zuojiazhuang residential district. That's less than two kilometers from here. He died from blows to his head and face, which suggests more than one assailant. I am told the first blow was delivered from behind.

The police identified him as Shen Lei."

"And how is that significant?"

"He was Chairman Keung's chief of security. We planned to haul him in for questioning."

Tom glanced at Davenport. "This is not good."

Weng looked from one to the other. "It is clear what happened. Shen is our hitman and Keung had him removed to plug a security risk."

"You're assuming he was the hitman. Anyway, you now have a face you can match against the surveillance tapes. Even if you do find a match, that doesn't necessarily implicate Chairman Keung." Tom reached for the coffee carafe. "Shen's death could have been a case of plain bad luck."

"But you don't think so?"

"A man trained in unarmed combat surprised by a mugger? I don't believe it. Somebody like that would be *aware*! Still, it's possible he was caught unawares. Did that basement have surveillance cameras?"

"The police report didn't say, but I'll look into it. I will also direct our analysts to expand their search to include known underworld figures who may have been used to execute Shen Lei."

"While you're at it, include security personnel from all four parties of interest," Davenport added, munching on an apple Danish pastry. "Chairman Han may yet prove to be the perpetrator."

Startled by the notion, Weng gawked. "Why would Han seek to remove Keung's security chief?"

Tom chuckled and patted Weng's arm. "Misdirection, my friend. Everybody suspects that Keung and Chen are behind this. What better way to reinforce that perception than to eliminate Keung's most trusted operative. Of course, we may be building a house of cards here and the simplest explanation that supports all the facts is usually true. Nevertheless, given the political ramifications of this case, we cannot afford to overlook anything."

Weng grinned. "A house of cards…an apt analogy. I must remember that."

"I just had a nasty thought," Tom mused. "Shen Lei, do you know if his body had a bullet wound on the left side?"

Weng's eyes widened. "As a matter of fact, it did. It appears that he was your assailant yesterday, which bears out what I was saying. Keung wanted you two out of the way, and had Shen eliminated to cover his tracks."

"Possibly, but it's all circumstantial, and is not evidence that Keung is guilty."

Weng sat back, his face serious. "Not in your country, perhaps, but under our system it's enough for us to question him…rigorously. Looking at your report, I felt dismayed and disappointed, but you have given me new hope that we will solve this case after all. Premier Dzhang will be pleased."

"It won't be your fault if we come up empty."

"Unfortunately, he may not see it in that light. America is viewing La Palma as an attack by China against what you call the free world, and from a certain perspective, you are right. You don't care much if this was an internal dissident plot. You see an oppressive communist regime bent on your destruction and you retaliate."

"You're referring to the incursion by the 7th Fleet?"

"Premier Dzhang understands why you need to respond, and he is grateful to President Walters for the restrained nature of his response, although this view is not shared by the whole Politburo. We have our hawks also. It is dangerous for your President to parade his ships off our coast. When you have two forces eager to engage, an incident is almost inevitable, and the outcome difficult to predict."

Tom regarded Weng with interest. Did he just get a friendly warning, an unofficial message to communicate to Walters? Perhaps, but he was sure the president was aware of possible repercussions before he sent in the Fleet. He had advisors who would spell out every scenario for him. If not a warning, then what? An oblique hint that if Walters pushed too hard, he risked alienating a friendly—at least not openly belligerent—Chinese regime? This was something Ambassador Sawyer needed to know.

"I don't pretend to understand all the political nuances of this case, Leijang, but speaking personally, if we catch those responsible for La Palma, I wouldn't shoot them. I would want to make them suffer like the suffering they caused to the survivors of this monstrous act. They played a political chess game, and the death and misery they caused was to them merely collateral damage. While China and America are posturing, let's not forget the real victims.

"You are right when you say that America doesn't care who plotted this act. At least the person on the street doesn't, and you can count me as one of them. If President Zhou wants to make amends, he needs to do more than merely provide monetary compensation, whether the perpetrators are found or not. Your Politburo must make a fundamental policy shift in how you view the West. That shift probably won't happen in my lifetime, but it will need to happen if you want to be a credible and accepted player on the world's stage."

Weng pursed his lips and nodded thoughtfully. "Premier Dzhang was right when he said that you missed your calling. I have been involved for too long with diplomatic doublespeak and word fencing, which provides intellectual stimulation, but tends to avoid resolving an issue, always seeking workable compromises instead. It is refreshing to hear plain and honest talk for a change."

Tom gave a weary smile. "I'm afraid my diplomatic suit would be a tight fit."

Weng laughed and slapped the table with his hand. "I would enjoy playing mahjong with you. You would play hard, but fair. Seriously, Tom. Whether you believe me or not, President Zhou would never sanction something like La Palma. It is not how we execute our foreign policy. However, like the rivalry between your Democrats and Republicans, we also have our divisions. Unfortunately, under our system, concentration of power that's not subject to the rule of law allows individuals to act outside the accepted policy framework. This is why we're keen to identify those responsible for La Palma and deal with them, and why your presence is so appreciated."

"All right, you have internal problems like the rest of us, but tell me this. Had the tsunami devastated our eastern seaboard, would President Zhou be as accommodating?"

"You must know the answer to that. That policy shift you mentioned? Regrettably, it goes all the way to the top."

"I thought so. If you don't mind me saying, and this is a personal view only, I hope your Navy does try something against us. Tell them to bring a shipload of body bags while they're at it."

Weng let out a heavy sigh. "Perhaps we deserve a reminder that money is never adequate compensation for an act of war. When everything is added up we may have gotten off lightly." He pushed back his chair and stood. "Thank you for your unstinting effort to pursue this case to its end. I have a lot to discuss with Premier Dzhang." Hesitating, he extended his hand. "I have come to have a lot of respect for you, Tom, and I would be honored if you considered me a friend."

Tom immediately stood and grasped the proffered hand. "We are driftwood in our respective political streams, Leijang. We can only hope that turbulent water doesn't wait for us around the bend...my friend."

Smiling, Weng nodded. "Perhaps one day those streams will meet, joined into a single river. Now, you must excuse me."

As if on cue, Sam opened the sliding doors and stood aside, allowing Weng to pass, then closed the panels after him. Was he listening? Probably to every word. Sitting down, Tom refilled his cup. Davenport peered at him over some orange juice.

"Interesting conversation you two had. I wonder who

pumped whom?"

"Rack off, Keith. We were just talking."

Davenport laughed. "Maybe it started off like that, but Weng came as close to an apology as he dared."

"Perhaps, but you know what? I don't really give a crap, and I did mean it when I said that whoever pulled off La Palma should be made to suffer."

"I'm sure Weng got the message. I think we need to have a quiet chat with Lipson and Ambassador Sawyer. I don't know about you, but our Chinese friend was sending us a bucket of telegrams."

"That's years of CIA experience talking?" Tom ventured with a lopsided grin.

"It is," Davenport deadpanned. "Weng hoped that our report would nail Chen Teng, and when it didn't, he was left floundering. He, and perhaps Dzhang, is working from a fixed premise, and when the chips fell the wrong way, he couldn't think outside the box. You gave him a lifeline so to speak, and he is grateful. We still have a case, regardless of any internal political machinations going on around us."

Tom lifted his cup in a salute. "To the case."

Davenport grinned and clicked his glass against the cup. "The case."

\* \* \*

Brakes squealing, the jeep slowed as it neared the open rounded hangar and slid to a stop beside the B-2 Spirit's portside wing. Actually, the whole aircraft was one giant 172-foot wing, but Lieutenant Colonel Randal 'Luke' Johnson wanted to call things by their proper name. Unsmiling security guards, rifles held ready at port arms, maintained a vigil around the entrance, showing no sign that they noticed the two airmen. Glancing at his co-pilot, Major Gibbs 'Flea' Shorten, looking ungainly in his green Nomex flying suit, Johnson grunted as he eased himself out of the open vehicle. Helmet in one hand and a thin briefcase in the other, he sauntered toward the entry hatch outboard of the front landing gear well.

Pausing, he punched in the access code into the keypad and opened the entry hatch. He climbed up the steps built into the hatch and made his way up the vertical square passage. On top, he opened the inner pressure door and made his way to the cockpit on his left, automatically slipping into the command seat. He heard Shorten clamp the pressure door and looked up as his partner stared vacantly at the cockpit layout before climbing into the mission commander's seat.

After stowing their helmets, they strapped on their harness and began the pre-flight check, the clear morning light streaming through the window helped light the large interior. Satisfied, Johnson clicked on his mike connecting him to the tug tractor driver.

"Chief? You can wheel us out."

"Copy that."

The orange-painted flat tug tractor reversed and slowly extracted the B-2 out of the hangar. The driver disengaged the pull bar and gave clearance to start engines. Johnson glanced at Shorten and nodded. The co-pilot started the four F118-GE-100 turbofans, running them up to their full 17,300 pounds of thrust, making the bomber tremble, before easing down to idle. He turned and grinned.

"Power nominal, Luke."

"Let's go home, Flea...Tower, this is Designator Charlie Able, requesting permission to taxi."

"Designator Charlie Able, you are cleared for runway 9L-27R."

"Thank you, tower. Rolling."

Mounted on the front instrument panel dividing the two seats, Johnson eased the port and starboard thrust levers a tad forward. The B-2 Spirit moved smoothly over the apron and he steered it toward the taxiway that circled the two runways of the Osan Air Base, Korea, part of the Pacific Air Force's (PACAF) command, home of the 51st Fighter Wing. After four days waiting for the order to go, both men were relieved to be out of here. Not that the F-16 drivers didn't welcome them, but the local pilots considered anyone not strapping on a fighter for a day's work didn't have the right stuff. Johnson took it in stride, pointing out gently that if he and Flea didn't have it, why was there such high competition to be accepted into the B-2 program, rivaling applications for NASA? After such a comment, things got somewhat boisterous.

Finally pulling its thumb out, the National Command Authority issued the Go order. This was the first tactical mission for the B-2 since Afghanistan, although a milk run. This time, nobody was going to get excited and start squirting missiles or triple-A at them, which was okay with Johnson. Dodging flack and riled up interceptors keen to close out his insurance wasn't at all glamorous as the movies made out.

The Spirit reached the end of runway 27R and rocked to a stop.

"Tower, Designator Charlie Able, ready for departure," Johnson declared.

"Designator Charlie Able, you are cleared for immediate takeoff. No traffic within fifteen miles. Visibility unlimited. Maintain flight level 420. Good luck, Colonel."

"Thank you, tower. Rolling."

Johnson stirred the stick, feeling the control surfaces respond through the fly-by-wire feedback system, and pushed forward the four thrust levers. The ungainly bomber raced down the runway. With unlimited visibility it would be a great day to fly, provided they didn't catch a squall, common around here this time of year.

"V1," Shorten called, committing them into the takeoff.

"V2…rotate."

Johnson pulled back the stick and the lumbering aircraft gently lifted itself into the air. Under full power, Shorten retracted the gear as the B-2 banked to port. As they broke through 16,000 feet, Johnson eased off power, the expanse of the Yellow Sea glinting before them through the two wide cockpit windows.

As mission commander, it was Shorten's responsibility to execute the missile run. He carried out a quick instrument check of the specially equipped Raytheon AGM-129A Advanced Cruise Missile mounted in the weapons bay. The stealthy bomber steadily gained height, reaching toward its designated altitude of 42,000 feet.

"All set?" Johnson queried.

"Ready to toast them," Shorten confirmed. "Just say when."

With the mercury waters beneath them, Johnson nodded. "Good a time as any. Deploy the weapon, Flea."

"Copy that."

The huge bomb bay doors swung down, making the aircraft vulnerable to radar detection as the internal weapons bay lay exposed. Shorten pressed a button on his control stick and the sleek twenty-foot, ten-inch black RAM-clad missile dropped from the rack. The computer immediately closed the bomb bay doors and Johnson breathed a little easier. They weren't in a combat zone, but he disliked having his ass hanging in the breeze. He glanced at the radar displays and grinned at Johnson.

"We're clear. Nobody is painting us."

Johnson immediately selected a preset radio channel. "Home Plate, this is Designator Charlie Able. Package deployed. I say again. Package deployed. RTB."

"Designator Charlie Able, Home Plate copies. Out," came the reply from the chairman of the Joint Chiefs, General Jason McDonald, in the White House Situation Room.

His job done, Johnson swung the B-2 hard to port on heading 060. This would take him toward the Lewis-McChord joint

Air Force Base near Seattle and a rendezvous with a KC-135 Stra-totanker, giving them enough fuel to get them the rest of the way home to the 393rd Bomb Squadron, 509th Bomb Wing, Whiteman AFB, Missouri, home of the Spirit.

He expected to have a ball busting flight before they touched down, a total of 6,600 miles, just over thirteen hours of flying, including time spent taking on their fuel load. His butt already felt flat. The bearable part of this flight, once set, the advanced Electronic Flight Instrument System computers would do all the maneuvering, the two sacked out pilots protected from intruders by the aircraft's Defense Management System. Not as good as riding business class in a commercial bird, but it wasn't a bad way to fight a war either.

* * *

When the AGM-129A dropped out of the bomb bay, the onboard computer waited two seconds, powered up the Williams F112 turbofan engine, and deployed its forward-swept wings and hanging tail. It quickly reached its nominal speed of 500 miles per hour, the computer steering the cruise missile slightly to star-board toward mainland China. The GPS would provide final cor-rection when the missile closed to sixty miles off its target in four hours' time. With a range of more than 2,300 miles, the cruise missile would easily reach its target from the middle of the Yellow Sea.

The low-visibility weapon, built from special radar absorp-tion materials to reduce specular and traveling waves, equipped with a horizontal flat exhaust nozzle and low radar cross-section wings, settled on its course and headed toward land. Maintaining an altitude of 35,000 feet, the PLAAF 27th Radar Regiment based at Xuzhou, part of the Chinese Air Defense Identification Zone that linked military and civilian air traffic control systems, failed to establish contact with the missile.

Reaching the desolate desert landscape of the Lop Depression extending from Korta eastward along the Kuruktagh—Dry Mountain—range to the Tarim Basin in the Xinjiang Uygur region, the AGM-129A angled down when the computer determined it was sixty miles from its designated target, the Qinggir nuclear proving ground, and armed the W80 low yield thermonuclear weapon. The missile bored in at 500 mph and descended to 8,000 feet. When the GPS signal said it had reached 41' 15" N, 88' 35" E, the five kiloton suppressed yield warhead detonated.

The blast generated a lethal stream of highly energetic neutrons, x-ray and gamma rays that slammed into the bleak desert below, raising the background radiation slightly above numerous tests carried out by the PLA well into the 1990s. After four seconds of intolerable brightness the three-hundred-foot fireball faded to dull orange and disappeared within two minutes. Effects of the electromagnetic pulse were insignificant. The expanding shockwave hit, sending a wall of sand racing across the desolate landscape. No one heard the furious hiss of its passage.

* * *

USS *California*, SSN-781, a Block II *Virginia*-class fast attack submarine, glided silently through the Indian Ocean deeps some 370 miles northwest of Diego Garcia. Its sister ship, USS *Minnesota* trawled thirty miles west of it. Both were point ships for Carrier Strike Group Ten, part of the U.S. 5th Fleet operating in the Persian Gulf and the North Arabian Sea. The group's flagship, aircraft carrier USS *Harry S. Truman*, CVN-75, was hunting an enemy, as were the subs.

At 7,800 tons, 377 feet long, powered by a single S9G reactor, armed with Tomahawk cruise missiles and torpedoes, it was a powerful ship to go in harm's way. Captain Garry Hewat thought so too as he stood beside the sonar operator watching the large port and starboard display screens that filled the control room one level down below the Operations Compartment under the sail. Apart from background machinery noises, everything was quiet.

"There it is again, Captain," the chief sonar operator announced from his portside station, pointing at the BQQ-10 sonar display screen. "I have it also on the wide aperture lightweight fiber optic array. Depth, 730 feet. No turn count from his screw. Contact tentatively identified as a *Qin*-class missile submarine powered by a magnetic fluid water jet propulsion drive running on course two zero five at sixty-four knots indicated."

Hewat frowned. "Sixty-four knots?"

"That's a confirm, Captain."

He had heard rumors about the Chinese *Qin* and its fancy magnetic propulsor drive capable of doing 100 knots, which he thought a load of whale shit. Still, powering along at sixty-four knots wasn't to be sneered at. The damned thing was about as fast as his ADCAP Mk-48 Mod 7 torpedo. With such a narrow speed gate, to shoot the bastard meant he needed to be close— very close. Close enough for the *Qin* to squirt off a salvo at him. However, his orders didn't say he had to survive the encounter. Well, if the CNO was happy to see a 2.7 billion dollar asset scrape the bottom, Hewat wasn't about to argue the point. He could...

"Very well, sonar. OOD, designate contact as Target One."

"Aye aye, Captain."

"What's the range, Quincy?"

"Showing 7000 yards."

*Ouch!* That was close. The thing was fast *and* stealthy. Could it have detected *California?* Probably not, or it would have tried to evade or engage. The thing might be fast, but the Chinese still had a way to go to match Western electronic countermeasures. The thought didn't give him much comfort. From his ops brief, the Chinese boat had a mission to complete, which meant it would probably try to evade rather than attack. If cornered though, he was sure to receive a hot welcome.

He turned to face Commander Tucker. "What do you think, XO?"

"We found what we were looking for, Skipper. I say let's finish it before the thing finishes us."

Hewat chuckled. Tucker was a charger and wanted one of the new Block IV *Virginia* boats for himself. A positive fitness report from Hewat would get him one, which he was happy to write. Running an ultramodern attack boat and managing fifteen officers and 120 ratings took skill and a deft touch, which the XO seemed to do with ease. By comparison, a surface command was a cakewalk.

"We're still in the thermocline?"

"Our depth, 380 feet. Positive sound speed gradient."

When hunting or being hunted, especially by another submarine, every advantage counted. By drifting within a gradient of warmer surface water and the denser, colder deep water, any transient noise generated by his boat would be reflected upward, while active sonar pings from a submarine below the layer would be reflected down. It did not make *California* invisible, but it helped. In this scenario, Hewat was grateful for any help he could get.

"Weapons status?"

"Tubes one to four loaded with Mk-48s and spun up. Outer doors open. We're ready to do business, Captain," the duty officer declared from his starboard side Weapons Control station. "The *Qin* won't know a thing until it hears our units closing."

"Or we're at the business end of one of their Yu-10s," Tucker growled. "It's rumored that in drift mode, it has a MAD capability."

"You trying to cheer me up?"

"Just giving you the facts, Captain."

"Just for once, I could use less facts, okay?"

"Con, sonar. Target One not showing any Doppler. Speed

constant. No transients indicated."

Hewat chewed his bottom lip. At 7000 yards, with a mutual closure rate reducing that distance every second, he had expected the *Qin* to have acquired him by now. Maybe that fancy propulsion system of theirs interfered with their sonar sensors at high knot rates. Interesting if true.

"Weps, confirm settings for tubes one to four," he ordered.

"Weapons are warm, Captain. Immediate enable set. No active snake set."

"Firing point procedures, tubes one to four," Hewat ordered quietly.

"Ship ready," the Officer of the Deck announced.

"Weapons ready."

"Solution ready."

Hewat could shoot now, but he wanted the *Qin* at point blank range. He could not risk having it slip away. No one knew if they could acquire it again. No, that wasn't quite true. If the thing was really heading toward the Canary Islands as per his brief, they could try cutting it off at the Cape Aghulas waypoint. The whole thing was stupid as far as he was concerned. There was no need to prosecute the sub now, exposing everybody to unwarranted danger. It would be far easier to ambush it once it reached La Palma. Once there, unable to use its speed advantage to maneuver, they could box it, destroy it or force it to surface, parading to the world Chinese treachery. He was only a dumb sewer pipe driver and nobody asked his opinion.

"Con, sonar. Range to Target One now 5500 yards."

"Very well, sonar."

Hewat listened to the small ship noises as he waited for the range to close. He clenched his moist fists and set his mouth to prevent himself bellowing out the fire order. He wanted the *Qin* in his lap before he dished it up.

"Con, sonar. Range is now 3200 yards. Detecting transients. It's possible Target One is opening its tube doors."

Hewat decided he'd come close enough for government work.

"Snap shoot on generated bearings!" he commanded.

"Fire!" the weapons officer snapped and pulled the trigger. "Tubes one to four fired electrically. Running time is 78 seconds."

"All units normal launch," Quincy reported.

"Let's get out of here!" Hewat growled. "OOD, blow ballast. Blow everything!"

"Con, sonar. Two torpedoes in the water!"

A lead ball materialized in Hewat's stomach. At this range, he hadn't a prayer of outrunning the incoming torpedoes. His only hope of saving the boat and his men was to surface where the incoming torpedoes couldn't see *California*.

"Close all watertight doors!" Holace bellowed, his legs buckling as the submarine started to rise like an elevator.

"Captain, ship's units now in active mode. Impact against Target One in fourteen seconds," Weapons announced. "Enemy units still in search mode. Showing decreasing Doppler. Enemy units have acquired."

"Con, sonar. Detecting two explosions. Target One is in terminal descent."

Hewat nodded with satisfaction. He got the *Qin*, but it looked like it was his turn now.

A high speed screech filled the control room—the terrifying sound of a homing torpedo.

"What's our depth?" he demanded.

"Two five five feet," the OOD replied quietly, his face showing resignation.

*Too deep, damn it*, Hewat fumed. They'll never make it up.

The screeching sound became louder.

"Con, sonar. I have transients from Target One. It has gone beyond crush depth."

And we'll be joining it soon, Hewat mused. "Fire noisemakers!"

Two canisters were ejected from either side of the bow, emitting a stream of air bubbles accompanied by a sliding frequency noise pattern designed to defeat a torpedo's acquisition sonar. It was a last ditch desperate measure, and sometimes it worked.

"Con, sonar. Showing a change in Doppler from one incoming unit!"

"Brace for impact!"

Two seconds later, a crash shook the boat and the lights flickered. Almost immediately, another crash rocked *California*. The boat staggered, paused and hovered momentarily. Then it began to settle.

"Damage report!" Tucker shouted.

The OOD pushed back his mike, face ashen. "One torp decoyed. We took a hit from the other aft of the upper mess deck spaces. Maneuvering reports reactor is still online. The pumps are holding, and we have hull integrity."

Although sluggish, the submarine resumed its upward drift.

Hewat reached for the 1MC mike, amazed to see his hand perfectly steady. "This is the Captain. It's bad, but we're on our way up. Damage control parties, report to the XO."

He replaced the mike and exhaled slowly. His wife and two sons would see him again, and that was all that mattered. Unfortunately, that could not be said for the crew of the Chinese boat. The shitty parts came with the territory. He didn't blame the *Qin* crew for the attack, but the unfeeling bastards in Beijing.

# Chapter Nine

PRESIDENT'S APPROVAL RATING RISES 6 POINTS!
CHINA CONDEMNS U.S. NUCLEAR STRIKE
WORLD REACTION MIXED
STOCK MARKETS FEARFUL OF CHINESE BACKLASH
RUSSIA ISSUES UNEXPECTED APPROVAL

Chin in hand, Captain Brian Ormond's frown deepened as he studied the four three-foot by three-foot tactical screens. Unless the Chinese ships altered course, they would close the triangle with Task Force 70 in one hour and forty minutes. Tempted to pick up the red phone linking him with Admiral Haddon, he refrained. The task force commander could see what was going on in his flag bridge repeaters. Within the last hour they had two flybys of four J-15 Shenyang fighter bombers, and they weren't Kodak runs either. Flying three hundred feet above the deck, everyone saw the white warshot missiles hanging from their wing hardpoints. It didn't make Ormond feel better seeing the J-15s shadowed by six VFA-27 squadron's F/A-18 Super Hornets. Overflying USS *George Washington*, the J-15s banked hard and peeled north toward the Chinese carrier *Liaoning*, which had sortied from Qingdao, supported by two *Luzhou*-class and two *Luhu*-class destroyers. The Chinese never did things by halves, and probably had one or two *Han*-class SSNs prowling the deeps for good measure.

At 7,100 tons displacement, armed with SA-N-20 surface-to-air and anti-ship missiles, including torpedo tubes, the Type 051C *Luzhou* was a modern badass customer. Not in the same league as a *Ticonderoga*-class guided missile cruiser, but definitely a handful for any *Arleigh Burke*-class destroyer. To counter the Chinese force, Haddon had two cruisers, three destroyers and two *Los Angeles*-class attack submarines. By now, Ormond figured the subs had acquired the *Hans* and were keeping an eye on them. Still, he didn't like this concentration of forces and wished the Chinese would stop making a nuisance of themselves by going someplace else. It would only take one rash action from somebody—on either side—and instead of being a game of nerves, he could have a shooting situation on his hands.

Ormond wanted to sound off with Haddon, suggesting that Task Force 70 pull back, but the admiral continued to maintain his taciturn demeanor, ordering the fleet to remain on course. Was the admiral pushing a deliberate strategy to intimidate the Chinese? If so, he had succeeded. Ormond had checked the admiral's service record when he took over from Pacino. A first rate administrator and organizer, Haddon had never served in battle. As Ormond found, playing war games was different to being on the receiving end of a real missile. He fervently hoped that Haddon had all his shit together today.

Commander Penrose, the Tactical Action Officer, swiveled his seat and looked up. "Captain, USS *Mustin* reports a positive contact with a *Han*. Distance, 13000 yards on our line of advance. It's just sitting there."

"Very well. Instruct *Mustin* to give the *Han* a ping and sit on top of it."

"Aye aye, sir." After a moment, Penrose smiled. "Sir, *Mustin* reports two contacts. One is USS *Buffalo*. It looks like our sub screen is doing its job."

"Mmm." Ormond wasn't surprised. A *Han* was a first-generation nuclear attack boat and not suited as a tactical platform, but a launched torpedo didn't know that. Old technology or not, he didn't want the *Han* loitering in front of him.

"Sir, *Mustin* reports the *Han* got spooked and is heading

west."

Ormond nodded. That was better.

His XO wanted to be in CIC when the two fleets came together, but Ormond ordered Varnecky to con the carrier, a dirty trick as the XO might spend the rest of his career without seeing action. However, as captain, it was Ormond's prerogative to be in CIC, providing tactical guidance should action precipitate. Besides, it was his damn ship and Varnecky was able to monitor the situation on the bridge repeater screens.

Penrose turned to face him. "Captain! An element of J-15s is closing on the E-2D Hawkeye. Range, forty-three miles."

The red phone gave a harsh jangle and Ormond picked up.

"It's Haddon, Captain. Warn off the J-15s. If they get a missile lock or close within ten miles, splash them. Advise *Liaoning* of our intention. Out."

The Northrop Grumman E-2D airborne early warning (AEW) aircraft, with its crew of five, was the task force's long range eyes and ears. Powered by two turboprop engines, it was also slow and vulnerable. For that reason, when in the air, it was always shepherded by two F/A-18s to discourage visitors. Given the range of modern radar and infrared air-to-air missiles, should the J-15s decided to take it out there wasn't much Ormond could do about it, except exact revenge. Allowing the Chinese fighters to approach within ten miles cut the E-2D's safety margin dangerously thin. This was a peaceful sortie, wasn't it?

If this were a for-real confrontation, the E-2D would be placed well outside the Chinese missile envelope, and the J-15s would be suitably dealt with when they crossed the 100-mile exclusion zone. Right now, everybody was simply having a bit of fun. Glancing at the Cooperative Engagement Capability datalink screen, he hoped the Chinese realized this.

He chewed his lip and nodded to the comms officer. "Lieutenant, warn *Liaoning* if the J-15s close to ten miles or establish a missile lock on the Hawkeye, they will be shot down without warning."

"Aye, sir." A few seconds later, he looked up. "No response from the carrier, Captain."

"Well, they've been given the word," Ormond grumbled, not really expecting the courtesy of a reply. "Alert the covering CAP they have weapons free. Tell them on GUARD."

"Aye, sir," the lieutenant responded with a smile.

Using the open GUARD channel, the Chinese would pick up the transmission, hopefully taking appropriate notice. If they started something, Ormond did not want any misunderstanding who fired first. Not that this would help the E-2D and its crew.

He watched the two red triangles close to the dotted ten-mile exclusion zone. Just as he thought they would cross it, both fighters lit off their active phased array targeting radars. The F/A-18s responded with their AN/APG-79 AESA radar, but the J-15s were already turning to port after shutting down their radars. Ormond gave a loud exhale and smiled at Penrose.

"The boys having a bit of fun."

"If you say so, sir. Two more seconds and nobody would be laughing."

"Position the CAP at forty miles off our port quarter in case our friends want to repeat this gag," Ormond ordered, not in the mood to play anymore.

"Aye, sir."

The red phone rang. "Yes, Admiral?"

"The Chinese surface force will intercept in seventy-four minutes, Captain. No matter what they do, you hold our course. Ignore them."

"Admiral, if they interpenetrate our line, we could be risking a collision."

"The safety of your ship is your responsibility, Brian," Haddon said and hung up.

*Great!* Ormond was free to exercise initiative, provided he didn't deviate from his course or bend his ship. Taking a deep breath, he glanced at the comms officer.

"Lieutenant, advise all ships to maintain course and ignore the approaching Chinese force, consistent with ship safety."

"Aye, sir."

It wasn't long before the Chinese carrier and its four escorts heaved themselves over the horizon. At a combined closure rate of forty-eight knots, the distance between the two squadrons diminished rapidly. Ormond glad to see that nobody actively radiated, which made him very happy. He was prepared to blow them out of the water, political repercussions notwithstanding, but only as a last resort and on Haddon's direct order. The situation between China and the U.S. was tense enough, and he didn't want to give the Chinese a reason to make things even more tense.

He had seen, as had all the crew by now, the TV aftermath of the Lop Nur strike, marveling that President Walters had the balls to take it to them. In typical Gallic fashion, the French expressed grave concern at this latest example of American aggression against a country that had already acknowledged innocence for the attack on La Palma. Promoting nuclear nonproliferation, the United States still chose this heinous device to enforce its foreign policy.

Ormond didn't think much of the French leftist government or its response when the news of the Lop Nur strike broke, certain that their rhetoric would have a different tone had the tsunami swept through their coastal cities with greater force. Well, it had, but without any substantive effect. Then again, this may have been a message for local consumption only. He didn't really give a rat's ass. What did surprise him was Russia's lukewarm approval. Lop Nur was a message to everyone who thought to emulate China's action. The next missile wouldn't be against a barren patch of sand. He hoped the Chinese got the point.

One of the display screens had a real-time view of the approaching PLAN ships, now almost within touching distance. If everybody held their nerve, computer-projected course tracks showed the two fleets passing through each other with a comfortable safety margin—except USS *Shiloh*. If the advancing *Luzhou* destroyer maintained its course, it would intersect *Shiloh's* position. The cruiser's captain was clearly aware of his predicament and wisely increased speed. Biting his lip, Ormond saw the *Luzhou* do the same, apparently determined to ram the American ship.

CIC was tensely quiet as the two ships closed. Unless one of them did something within the next two minutes, Ormond would see his first mid-sea collision. The 508-foot Chinese destroyer, white foam creaming off its bow, trailing a frothy tail, held its course. With seconds to spare, *Shiloh* turned hard to starboard and executed a crash stop, the 567-foot cruiser scraping against the smaller Chinese ship. The *Luzhou* maintained its speed, apparently unconcerned by the incident.

Ormond stared intently at the approaching 60,000-ton *Kuznetsov*-class carrier, its clean lines and bow angled flight deck crowded with parked J-15 Shenyangs and Z-8 Changhe fighters. Although half the size of his ship, the Chinese carrier was nevertheless a powerful weapons platform, and he doubted that he would get another opportunity to see it this close. Steaming at twenty-five knots, the carrier's deck packed with onlookers, it crossed USS *George Washington's* bow and followed its escorts.

Ormond imagined he could hear them shouting into the wind, *'This is our sea, Yankee!'*

The comms officer looked up. "Sir, *Shiloh* reports some bent guard rail and scraped paint, but they're in one piece."

"Tell Captain Teller, well done."

"Aye, sir."

"Captain! We have four J-15s inbound!" Penrose announced. "Range, fifty-five miles. Altitude, fifteen thousand. We're being painted by acquisition radars!"

Ormond groaned. *Gods! If he hadn't had enough excitement already.*

"Advise CAP and portside screen to light 'em up. If the J-15s fire, splash them." This order went against Haddon's 'go soft' directive not to engage Chinese aircraft, but he would rather face a court-martial than risk his ship. "Make ready the countermeasures suite."

"Aye, sir."

When lit by powerful AN/SPG-62 fire control radars, three J-15s immediately stopped radiating and turned away, but the fourth fighter maintained missile lock on USS *George Washington*. When it closed to fifteen miles off the screening destroyer USS *Fitzgerald*, twenty-five miles from the carrier, it released a super-sonic fire-and-forget YJ-12 anti-ship missile. Equipped with a 205 kg warhead, anything it hit would sink or be badly damaged. The J-15 immediately peeled to port, dropping down to hug the deck as it fled.

The solid-rocket booster ignited, sending the missile past Mach 3 to 3,900 feet per second in four seconds. When the booster fell off, the missile's liquid fuel ramjet kicked in. It angled toward the sea where it would skim at a height of twenty feet toward its designated target.

Ormond immediately ordered activation of the SLQ-32A countermeasures suite, jamming the incoming missile's radar and infrared seeker, and readied the Phalanx CIWS. With less than thirty seconds to impact the Aegis Combat System in the portside destroyer and cruiser screen responded by launching two salvos of two RIM-162 Evolved Sea Sparrow defense missiles and chaff rounds, filling the sky with tiny flecks of aluminum foil to confuse the incoming missile's targeting systems. Two Sparrows overshot the incoming YJ-12, but the remaining two merged with the target, obliterating it in a spectacular orange and brown detonation 3000 yards off *George Washington's* port side before the screen's Phalanx close-in weapons system could engage the threat. The enhanced CL-20 explosion was like seeing a tactical nuke going off, rocking the 104,000-ton carrier. As per the agreed

Rules of Engagement, the screening ships allowed the fleeing J-15 to depart, trailed by evil thoughts from Ormond.

The red phone jangled and he picked up. "Yes, Admiral?"

"Brian, warn *Liaoning* that next time, her aircraft will be shot down."

"We should have shot *this* bastard down!"

"Now, Brian, I like to think it was only a misunderstanding."

"A misunderstanding? If you say so, Admiral, but a missile has no sense of humor."

Forcing himself to relax, he tried not to think what might have happened had the Chinese missile struck his ship. Realistically, USS *George Washington* was never in any real danger, the layered defenses of his screen more than capable dealing with a single threat. The question, of course, was the Chinese pilot acting under his own initiative or was he ordered to test American defenses? If it were up to him, he would have blotted the J-15 out of the sky as a positive warning. On reflection, perhaps it was better to have let the J-15 pilot live.

Ormond watched the Chinese ships fade into a black squall line and wondered who would make the next move.

\* \* \*

"Mr. President…Sam, withdraw your fleet. The incident today should serve as a vivid demonstration of what might happen if my forces are provoked further. I will not allow my country to be humiliated."

Zhou clenched his teeth. When he authorized aggressive shadowing of the 7th Fleet, he had not meant to initiate a confrontation, although the possibility of one always there. Fortunately, the incident caused only minor damage to the American cruiser and no loss of life. Had the American admiral prosecuted the threat fully, which he was justified doing after being fired upon, Zhou would be having a different conversation now.

# PROPORTIONAL RESPONSE

Sitting across the desk, Dzhang Qishan had his arms folded in his lap, looking calm and composed. A flash of resentment stabbed through Zhou that the premier could appear so unconcerned. Part of his anger was directed at himself for being placed into a position that would diminish his power regardless of any outcome his talk with the American president might achieve. He had stifled a heated State Council protest for not mounting a retaliatory response against the American nuclear strike, albeit only on a patch of barren desert. Han had seized the moment to demonstrate his control over the military apparatus. In many respects, this was a direct challenge to Zhou's authority, something he could not ignore.

*May whatever gods exist feed for eternity on Keung's bloated carcass!*

"Your destroyer attempted to ram our ship," Samuel Walters countered, then sighed. "Very well, Mr. President, in the interest of both our countries, I will order the 7th Fleet to withdraw. However, Yedong, stand warned. Should China, and I don't care if it's done by your government or a disillusioned reactionary, entertain a repeat of the La Palma scenario or destabilization of the global bond market or stock exchanges, you will have more than a symbolic strike on your hands. America has no problem if you exploit the free market system to maximize your competitive advantage—we all do it—but subverting the system in pursuit of a political objective will not be tolerated. We can all prosper if we play by the rules, Mr. President."

Dzhang chuckled and Zhou raised a finger in warning.

"I understand those rules, Sam, but you cannot blame us for the evils inflicted on you by your own system."

Walters laughed and Zhou allowed himself a small smile, feeling some of his tension easing. The American president, although a cultural degenerate, had a firm grasp of global economics and geopolitical currents. He would probably make a fine mahjong player. Zhou made a mental note to introduce Walters to the game next time they met.

"If you're referring to the GFC, I cannot argue with you there," Walters said, "and I'm addressing the underlying problems that allowed the situation to develop. On a different note, has Meecham made any progress to identify those responsible for La Palma?"

"I'm expecting an update later today, Sam."

"Your internal affairs are your own, Yedong, and I have no business telling you how to handle them. We have our ideological differences, but there is also a lot of commonality, which we can exploit to our mutual advantage. I suggest we work on that rather than polarize our positions beyond retrieval."

Zhou raised his eyebrows in appreciation of this astute observation and nodded. "That was well said, Mr. President."

"Until next time, sir," Walters said and cut contact.

Zhou reached across the desk and switched off the phone speaker.

"We may have underestimated this American President," Dzhang murmured thoughtfully. "He seems to understand us well or has a very good advisor."

"Larry Tanner?"

"I am sure Walters has others."

"I am sure he has. La Palma was an unfortunate incident, which does not change our Go Global Strategy or objective to dominate the world's geopolitical landscape," Zhou declared firmly. "We will play by the rules, but they will be our rules. The multinationals will simply have to get used to the idea that there is one more predator among them, or they'll end up on the menu. In time, Walters must accept the fact that America is no longer the economic driver it once was."

"Not an economic driver, perhaps," Dzhang countered, "but they are for the moment the military one, which they demonstrated with Lop Nur and the sinking of the *Qin*."

"Walters hasn't said they sunk it, but we'll probably never see that submarine again."

"No, he hasn't said because officially, it never happened. Our line must be that the *Qin* was lost with all hands off the continental shelf during the exercise."

"Agreed. This makes it imperative that we also acquire the capability to project power on a global scale," Zhou said. "Until that objective is achieved we will continue to exploit our economic advantage. The West has created its free market system to maximize profits and control their political organs. Walters can hardly complain if we use those same tools to help the system along."

"Enabling *us* to control their political organs?" Dzhang queried whimsically.

Zhou smiled. "Of course. We must identify and eliminate dissident elements within the Party. If we fail, we could end up like the American Congress, a dysfunctional institution that has paralyzed America's ability to be a truly dominant global power. I accept the need for greater personal freedoms and application of the rule of law, but only if the Party maintains control over the national decision-making process."

"With Shen Lei dead, so is the FBI investigation and our case against Keung and Chen."

"They might still unearth something."

Dzhang chewed his lip. "What are you going to do about Han Yunshan?"

Zhou stared at his friend, his eyes hard. "I made a mistake relinquishing the chairmanship of the Central Military Commission, but it's a mistake I intend to correct. At the next State Council meeting, I will announce that I am resuming the chairmanship of the CMC, and I'll nominate Han as the next Minister for National Defense, effective immediately."

*And that, my friend, will sideline any ambitions* you *might have!*

Dzhang allowed himself a small smile and nodded. "Neat. Very neat. You realize, of course, he'll fight you. This will mean a demotion for him."

"He's lucky I don't have him arrested. I can still wave his orders in front of everybody, fake or not, but I don't think he'll risk a confrontation."

"You'll be making an enemy."

"He won't be the first."

"What about Xhal Shenglai? He was promised that ministry."

"If the FBI investigation clears him, he'll be taken care of."

Dzhang grasped the armrest and heaved himself out of the chair. "I have to be going. Take care of yourself, my friend."

\* \* \*

As the black limousine approached the high perimeter fence topped by three rows of razor wire, Meecham saw a twin-tailed fighter roar down the runway of the Nanyuan military base and take off, immediately going almost vertical. The pressure wave of its passing made the air tremble. Two armed soldiers hurried out of the guardhouse when the limo stopped. After a clipped exchange with the security minder up front and flashing of papers, the soldiers snapped to attention and presented arms. The heavy steel gate slid back with a hiss and the limo surged through, angling toward a sleek Gulfstream V waiting on the apron, flanked by four guards.

Tom stepped out, took a deep breath of air tainted by the smell of jet fuel, squinted at a watery sun struggling to break through the smog, and turned to the man standing beside him.

"This has been a unique experience, Leijang, and changed many of my misconceptions about China."

Weng smiled broadly and offered his hand. "It was a pleasure watching you work."

"I hope Premier Dzhang will approve sending a team to Quantico to review our procedures," Tom said, shaking hands, wincing slightly at the pain in his side. It could have been far worse.

Lipson went orbital when Tom told him of his offer to Weng, but after some pondering, Ambassador Sawyer saw merit in it. Any avenue that promoted cooperation and cultural exchange would help pave the way for a closer relationship between the two countries, especially now when China was regarded with hostility by everyone. It was never too early to start mending fences, and whether they liked it or not, China was an important political and economic entity to the West.

Anyway, it was up to the White House and FBI Director Marshal to pick up the bat and field the ball Tom had lofted. At least *something* might be salvaged from his failure. Even now, the memory of his meeting with Weng three days ago burned bright.

Tom rifled through the 6" by 6" photos, sat back, and slid the glossies across the table.

"You have nothing," he declared flatly, understanding fully the impact this would have on all parties concerned. The Chinese government could make his life ugly if they wanted to, and shit always traveled downhill.

Weng's eyes grew round. "Nothing? Shen Lei was identified entering the Grand Hyatt with Chairman Keung!"

"Where the Chairman had lunch at Da Giorgio's," Tom said patiently. "That's been established. Shen had a legitimate reason for being there. He was Keung's bodyguard. If you had a shot of Professor Chuan Jianbo and Shen at the Hyatt, we'd have something to go on with. There are no identifiable shots of Shen at the university, and there is no evidence he was ever at the Wushiht'ala facility. With Shen conveniently removed, unable to talk, we have no links to follow."

"What about the meetings between Keung and Chen, and the encrypted calls?"

"They can say they met on official business. As for the encrypted calls, there is no way to tell that any of them dealt with La Palma, and you cannot decrypt them."

"And Commander Vang's missing receipt slip? This clearly shows that Han's orders were a plant."

"Not necessarily. Given the sensitive nature of his orders, Chairman Han could have bypassed normal procedure. Wouldn't you?"

Looking dejected, Weng's shoulders sagged. "I thought...What do I tell Premier Dzhang?"

"Leijang, sometimes the bad guys cross all the right boxes and there is nothing you can do about it." Tom bit his lip. "Except..."

"Except what? At this point, I am willing to entertain any idea."

Tom waved a hand in dismissal. "Forget it. It would never work."

"What wouldn't work?"

"Write two confessions and confront them, but you will need genuine signatures on original documents, and that's something I don't believe you'll be able to get. On the other hand, you could simply haul each one in for a chat, telling him he's been betrayed. Who knows, one of them might crack. They must be feeling some pressure."

Weng gave a wintry smile. "An interesting notion, but it would be a transparent ploy that Keung and Chen would recognize immediately. They are not men easily frightened."

"You're probably right," Tom said nodding. "In that case, my friend, our job here is done, and my apology to Premier Dzhang for letting him down."

"As you said, sometimes the bad guys get it right," Weng acknowledged, deep in thought.

Tom raised a quizzical eyebrow. "You're onto something?"

"Perhaps. I will need to look into it." Brightening, Weng slapped the table with an open hand. "An arrangement will be made to have you and Keith flown out. In the meantime, you must allow me to be a proper host and show you some of Beijing's highlights, your wounds permitting."

"That is most gracious of you, Leijang, but unnecessary."

"Nonsense! It's the least I can do."

As he stood on the open apron, looking at Weng's clear black eyes sparkling with an inner secret, a transformation from the gloomy figure three days ago. Tom wondered what mischief his friend was up to. Well, it was out of his hands now, grateful for the escorted tour he and Davenport enjoyed during the last two days.

The Great Wall at Badaling, fifty miles from Beijing, was a highlight, of course. Weng assured him it would be unthinkable to leave China without seeing the ancient wonder. It was a wonder, the structure snaking over smog-tinged hills—the smog rolling in all the way from Beijing, something Tom found incredible—the restored walkway crowded with tourists. He didn't even mind the souvenir stalls vying for attention. Lost in history as he strolled along the ramparts, he marveled that any empire could build a structure stretching 5,500 miles across this wild country. It staggered the imagination, and gave him another small insight into the character of these enigmatic people.

After seeing the Wall, their personal guide took them to the Yongsheng Jade Carving Factory, a state-run enterprise that processed and produced an astonishing variety of jade ornaments and decorative sculptures. During lunch, as a token of appreciation from the Chinese government, Tom and Davenport were given an elaborately wrapped package, the contents to act as a reminder of their stay here.

On the way back to Beijing, they had a quick tour of the Summer Palace, a retreat for Qing Dynasty emperors only seven miles from the capital. After a leisurely cruise on the enchanting Kunming Lake, back to the Diaoyutai State Guesthouse. For dinner, Weng treated them to a gastronomic delight at the Flagship Restaurant, the premier Peking duck establishment in the city.

After wading through courses of mustard duck web, boiled liver, seasoned gizzards, hot and spicy shredded wings, quick-fried duck heart and an assortment of dry-fried delicacies, Tom was bloated.

Yesterday, taking pity on them, Weng maintained an easier pace, showing them around Tiananmen Square, the Nine-Dragon wall in Beihai Park, and walked them through the Forbidden City, concluding the day with a visit to the Beijing Huguang Guild Hall for an exclusive performance of classical Chinese opera. It would not have been Tom's first pick as entertainment, but after exposure to Melissa's influence in the arts, he found the performance enchanting, further expanding his understanding of China's culture and rich heritage.

Two months could not have exhausted the wonders of this inscrutable country and its people—inscrutable to him and many Westerners—but the two days he had gave him a wondrous glimpse few Americans got on any terms. Congress politicians would do well to see China for themselves. The corollary of course, applied equally to Chinese politicians. A visit to Quantico may be a first tentative step.

Weng shook hands with Davenport, glanced at his bodyguard, and nodded. The unsmiling heavyset individual reached into the limo's trunk and extracted three packages. Weng took two wrapped in brown silk and held them out.

"Compliments of Premier Dzhang, gentlemen. He promised you a bottle of *San Hua*. We hope it will give you pleasant memories of your stay."

Tom took the proffered package, marveling at the flowing color hues of the fine silk and smiled. "Thank you, Leijang. I wish I had something equally impressive to share with the Premier."

"Nonsense! Although your investigation has not concluded in a definitive manner you would like, rest assured, it has been very revealing, and that is reward enough for us."

"This will definitely be a reminder of *my* visit," Davenport said, a broad grin splitting his face as he fondled the wrapping.

Weng held out a package swathed in blue silk to Tom. "This is for President Walters with thanks from President Zhou."

Tom nodded solemnly and took the package. "I am certain he'll appreciate the gift."

"China will welcome you both should you care to return one day. Until then, I bid you goodbye and a safe flight home." Weng turned abruptly and stepped into the limousine. His bodyguard slammed the rear door shut after him.

Tom watched the black car speed through the heavy gate, then exhaled loudly and glanced at Keith.

"Another productive day at the office."

"For him or for us?" Davenport quipped amiably as they walked toward the waiting executive jet.

"I know. Weng had that pleased look about him. I suspect he might not be finished with Keung and Chen just yet. Did you notice it?"

Before Davenport could answer, Stefanie walked down the steps and gave them a warm smile.

"Good morning, gentlemen. If you would please board, we shall be taking off directly."

"Stefanie! What an unexpected surprise," Tom remarked with a broad smile.

"Somebody in the White House thought you would like to see a familiar face on the way back, sir. I trust your mission was successful?"

"That remains to be seen."

Noticing Davenport's crutch, her eyes widened. "What happened?"

"I'll tell you over lunch," Keith said.

As the Gulfstream broke through the brown smog layer into a crystal blue sky, Tom wondered how Hancock would regard his mission.

* * *

President Zhou Yedong fondled the innocent-looking piece of paper, looked up from his desk, and slowly shook his head.

"This is not going to work, you know that. Chen isn't a political mechanic or schemer like Keung, but he has character and commands a strong following in the Army. He is not the operational head of the Central Military Commission for nothing. What makes you think he'll crack?"

Premier Dzhang Qishan sat comfortably in the visitor chair and shrugged. "Nothing, but consider this. To reach for power we hold, we employed some drastic measures to eliminate an opponent, and nobody is blushing. That's how things are done. La Palma, on the other hand, was a conspiracy and few people have the mental fortitude and temperament to run one. The problem with conspiracies, they suffer from one fatal flaw: betrayal. It's inherent in the organizational structure. As a likely participant, that makes him vulnerable."

"And Keung's security chief was eliminated because of that possibility."

"It could have been a case of simple mugging," Dzhang admitted. "We have no proof one way or another. However, I don't believe it. The timing too convenient and was perhaps Keung's only mistake. Not that he had much of a choice. He allowed emotional attachment to override a logical decision he should have made immediately the *Shang* sailed—if we continue with our thread of suppositions that Keung masterminded the operation."

"If Chen is a coconspirator, he must have considered the likelihood of being the next target," Zhou murmured.

"Exactly. Intellectually, he knows Keung would never betray him or try to have him eliminated—"

"But he could not be certain."

"That's right. Until things settle down, the nagging thought that one day he might be joining his illustrious ancestors must still be lurking, eating at his resolve. La Palma wasn't a simple case of blackmailing or disgracing a political opponent."

Zhou hissed and waved a hand. "I know how these things work, Qishan."

The premier gave a thin smile. "I am sure you do."

"You're saying the FBI investigation has nothing on Xhal Shenglai?"

"He is ambitious, yes, but he is a technician, not a politician. For now, that is."

Zhou made a decision, reached across the desk and pressed a white button on his phone station. "Show the Vice Chairman in."

"Yes, sir."

The door to Zhou's private office opened and Chen Teng strode in, his tall figure impressive in an elegant dark blue wool suit and pale yellow silk tie. His eyes flickered briefly at Dzhang, but his face remained impassive.

"Good afternoon, Mr. President."

"It hasn't been a good afternoon so far, Teng, and I don't expect that it will get any better," Zhou growled and waved at an empty chair. "Sit down. This will take a while."

As Cheng eased himself into the chair, he nodded to the premier. "I trust *your* afternoon isn't veiled in gloom?"

Dzhang chuckled. "There may be one or two bright spots in it yet. That flu of yours still bothering you?"

"I've shaken it off."

"Result of a clear conscience and clean living?"

"Nothing so noble, I'm afraid. It simply ran its course."

Zhou cleared his throat to get everybody's attention, suddenly impatient to get his done. Ordinarily, he relished a moment of light banter with his victims, dropping subtle hints at the disaster about to transpire, seeing them squirm. With Chen, that would be a waste of time.

"You have undoubtedly been informed of the FBI's departure and apparent failure of their investigation."

Chen's forehead creased. "Apparent failure?"

"Apparent in the sense that they could not categorically identify the parties responsible for the La Palma event."

"With respect, sir, my understanding is that Han Yunshan's orders were validated. You have your guilty party."

"Yes, his signature was validated, but it doesn't mean that he wrote or issued those orders. We both know what can be done with a word processor. It's over, Chen. I know all about you and Keung Yang."

Zhou waited for any reaction; a twitch of an eyebrow, change in posture, coloring of cheeks, anything that might compromise him. All he got was a wry smile.

"We had this conversation before, Mr. President, and I resent your baseless slur on my character. Now, if you don't mind..." Chen grasped the armrests, but Zhou waved him down.

"I am not finished. You may consider it a slur, but it is definitely not baseless. Have you heard of Professor Chuan Jianbo at Peking University's School of Earth and Space Sciences? He was a geophysicist. Unfortunately, he met with an untimely death. Murder. Then there is the case of a young software engineer at the Wushiht'ala weapons research facility. His body was found in an alley. Death by misadventure, according to the police. The odd thing about his case, forensic examination established that the body was dumped there. That's not something a mugger would normally do."

"I don't see what this has anything to do with me," Chen declared flatly, his chin thrust out in defiance. Zhou ignored the interruption.

"While we're on the subject of muggings, we had another one a few days ago. This one very interesting as the victim was Keung's security chief."

"Misfortune stalks all of us, Mr. President."

"Indeed. Ordinarily, the three incidents would be dismissed, but the FBI team managed to establish a connection. You see, Chen, their investigation was not a total failure. I don't need to rehash events with which you're intimately familiar. Do I?"

Chen touched his scar and shrugged. "If you have proof that I was in any way involved with La Palma, act on it. Otherwise, sir, I don't appreciate being a political scapegoat in a campaign designed to discredit the Tuanpai coalition."

Zhou's eyes blazed. "Whatever campaign I might be running against the Tuanpai does not extend to setting off a natural disaster aimed at crippling the United States, which in the process cost us two nuclear attack submarines and their crews. We were fortunate that President Walters' response was limited to Lop Nur, and we're still to feel the aftermath of economic sanctions." He reached for the paper on his desk and held it out. "You wanted proof of your duplicity, you have it."

Showing uncertainty for the first time, Chen leaned forward and took the document. Scanning it, he looked up and laughed.

"Chairman Keung's signed confession? Really, Mr. President, you're not confronting me with a forgery?"

"Why do you say it's a forgery? Keung's signature is there. You have seen enough of them to recognize it."

Chen flung the paper on the desk. "All you have is a copy. Show me the original. For all I know, you could have pasted his signature."

"Like you pasted Han's?"

Chen stood up and straightened. "Sir, if this is your proof of my involvement, I want to hear it from Chairman Keung."

"What makes you certain that he wants to see you? Half an hour ago, he sat in that same chair reading *your* confession! And I would not be so foolish to hand over the original so you could tear it up."

Color drained from Chen's face and he suddenly looked a different man. "You forged my confession?"

"You were the weak link in his operation. He always under-stood that you might succumb under pressure."

"He would never..." Realizing what he just said, Chen's mouth sagged in shock.

Zhou smiled with satisfaction. "He would never betray you? No, he wouldn't. You had to do that to yourself, which you have just done."

Chen composed himself and sneered. "I haven't admitted to anything. All you have is hearsay."

Zhou shook his head and reached across the desk for the pocket recorder hidden behind his wife's picture. He switched it off and raised it.

"This says different and will be enough to convict both of you for high treason against the State." He smiled and pressed a button on the phone station. "Send them in."

"Yes, sir."

Almost immediately, two Ministry of State Security agents, dressed in black, strode in, stopped and stood at attention. Zhou waved at Chen.

"Get him out of my sight."

The shorter agent turned to Chen. "Mr. Vice Chairman, if you please."

Chen took a deep breath, clamped his mouth and stomped out. When the door closed, Dzhang gave a couple of slow nods.

"A slip of the tongue, amazing. I didn't think you'd be able to pull it off."

"Frankly, my friend, neither did I. Weng's suggestion bril-liant. You have a good man there."

"He is capable," Dzhang acknowledged. "We need to get a genuine confession out of Chen before he realizes how thin our case against him really is."

"We'll get that confession, and then we'll get the indomitable Keung Yang."

"You know, regardless of his motive the plan to strike at

America was inspirational," Dzhang mused.

"And he'll be punished because it didn't work."

"With Chen removed, it occurs to me that Xhal Shenglai would make a fine replacement."

Zhou raised an eyebrow. "As Vice Chairman? Yes, he would. Have a talk with him. I'll announce the appointment at the next State Council meeting. Care for some tea?"

Smiling, Dzhang shrugged. "I wouldn't mind, but I think this occasion calls for something more potent."

\* \* \*

The snow-capped Cascades emerged out of the dawn's gloom as the Gulfstream V left the Pacific deeps and Meecham had a sudden rush of emotion. He grew up in Seattle before joining the Bureau. These mountains and the endless hiking trails he traversed in his boyhood days were home. They may have been home a long time ago, but he no longer belonged there. Still, seeing that landscape as the aircraft crossed the range into desert brought with it poignant memories.

His parents did not exactly approve when he told them of his plan to join the FBI when he got his degree, but they didn't stand in his way either. Not that they could have done anything about it. Tom had learned a long time ago that he had a willful streak, something he inherited from his mother, his dad used to tell him when he refused to listen. His father was a partner in a management accounting firm and it was tacitly understood that Tom would make his career there, which explained his study in accountancy and business law. What Tom did not count on was being waylaid by a campus FBI recruiter. After listening to career opportunities in the Bureau, the idea of pouring over balance sheets and profit and loss statements suddenly didn't seem very exciting or challenging. Apart from paying lousy money, working for the FBI could also get him shot. That was his dad's argument.

For Tom, it only validated his decision. Some things were worth more than merely money.

Anyway, he figured his father's firm would take him on if he ever got tired chasing the low life. Both of them knew it would never happen. About to walk the aisle with Melissa and a promising career ahead of him—provided he didn't screw the pooch somewhere along the way—Tom's loyalty belonged to the Bureau. Nevertheless, watching the mountains slip into haze, it was nice to catch a glimpse of something pleasant from his past.

There was another thing those ranges unexpectedly invoked—a sense that the whole country out there was home. He had never been fervently patriotic in the sense that he wanted to serve in the military, taking life in America with all its shades of gray for granted. In some indefinable way, China had changed all that, making him appreciate what many around the world could only dream of having. With all the rotten things that went on here, he wouldn't want to swap it for any other place.

Stefanie walked up carrying a fresh carafe of coffee. She placed it on the small table and beamed.

"Some exciting news from China, sir. Major Weber just got it over the radio. It seems that the Chairman of the Standing Committee, Keung Yeng, and Vice Chairman of the Central Military Commission, Chen Tang, are under arrest for treason and will face the Supreme People's Court. Your doing, gentlemen?"

Davenport grinned at her. "So, they got them after all, but it wasn't any of my doing. Tom deserves all the blame."

Tom glared at him. "Thanks a lot, ex-partner! Seriously, Stefanie, this comes as a surprise."

"You two had a hand in it somewhere. President Walters will be delighted. Have you heard?"

"Heard what?"

"The 7th Fleet has pulled back."

"Well, the President made his point with Lop Nur. There was no need to keep annoying the Chinese further."

"What an exciting adventure you two had. I'm going forward. Please buzz if you need anything."

Tom saw Keith looking at Stefanie's trim figure and shook his head. "I don't know how Karelina puts up with you."

Davenport chuckled. "I don't do this when *she's* around, but beauty should be admired whenever one comes across it. Broadens your horizons."

Laughing, Tom filled his cup and added cream and sugar. "To beauty," he declared.

"Everywhere," Davenport agreed heartily and bit into a fruit pastry. After swallowing, he shook the pastry at Tom. "I wonder how they got them. Do you think Weng pulled your dummy confessions gag on them? If he did, it would only be poetic justice."

"We may never find out, but Stefanie is right about one thing. Walters will be pleased."

"And so will Hancock. You must admit, we went there knowing our chances of getting to the bottom of this were slim to nonexistent."

"It would be amusing to find out which one of them caved in."

"They got 'em, that's what matters." Davenport grinned. "I'm still getting over the jade we got. I can't wait to pin that necklace around Karelina's neck...and wait for her to be suitably grateful."

Tom settled into his comfortable seat after takeoff, coffee steaming from the steel carafe, bright sunshine slanting through the small windows—it was startling to see crystal blue sky after days of smog and gray drabness—life seemed good. He was pleased to be going home; back to his work, back to Melissa.

Putting the adventure behind him, Tom asked Stefanie to drag out the packages they got at the jade factory. He tore off the plain blue wrapping, revealing a polished box of rich dark wood, carved with a lake and mountain scene. Stefanie cooed with delight, urging Tom to open it. The box itself would have made a valuable gift. He unlatched the hook, slowly lifted the lid, and stared at the flat 6" by 6" dark red satin jewel box. He reached in and picked it up. After glancing at Stefanie ready to snatch the thing out of his hands, he smiled and opened it. She gasped and clamped her small fists against her mouth.

Resting on a bed of white satin was a necklace of blue-white jade, made out of exquisitely carved hexagonal stones. Beneath the necklace were two pinned earrings, the stones suspended from gold mounts. In the center of the necklace was a solid green jade wristband. Tom didn't know anything about jade, but these pieces looked expensive.

"Oh my," Stefanie whispered, her eyes glued on the necklace. "It looks simply gorgeous. Miss Foster will love it."

Tom was about to ask her how she knew about Melissa, realizing it wouldn't be hard to find out, and Stefanie was naturally curious about her two important charges.

"It's a nice collection," he agreed and turned to Keith, who was studying his gift.

"We need to find another excuse where we can do the Chinese government a favor," Davenport affirmed as he closed his case.

He reached into the box and lifted out a smaller box wrapped in purple silk. Under the wrapping was a plain unpolished wooden container. Shrugging, he opened it and extracted a bundle of more silk. Untangling the silk revealed a dragon curled around a shallow bowl. The whole thing seemed to be carved from a single piece of green jade. It was an extraordinary example of precision craftsmanship.

Hesitating, Stefanie held out her hand. "May I?"

"Of course," Davenport said.

She took the bowl and slowly turned it in the palm of her hand, eyes shining.

"It's almost transparent," she breathed reverently. After a moment, she handed it back.

When Tom unwrapped his little box, the carving inside identical, except it was made from blue-green jade. They were extraordinary gifts and he reminded himself to write a thank-you note to Weng.

Keith wore a beatific smile, probably picturing the look on his wife's face at the gift. Tom wondered if Melissa would be equally appreciative. It was something worth looking forward to.

As the Gulfstream V arrowed its way east, he stopped his reverie and turned his attention to the mundane elements of his job. There would be a long report to write, debriefings, and picking up the threads of his cases. It all suddenly felt drab and humdrum. He realized that he was coming off a high and reaction was setting in, he tried to put a positive spin on it. He had little reason to moan. His work demanded a lot out of him, but it also rewarded. Wasn't China an example of that? And he had Melissa...

He smiled wryly and wondered what wedding arrangements she made while he was away, not there to dampen her plans. He was sure to find out.

They watched CNN chair experts dissect the latest events in Beijing, the aftermath of the Lop Nur strike and the economic sanctions still hot topics. Right then, Tom couldn't be bothered. His job done, others can now pick through the pieces. He just wanted to get home, have a long shower and crawl into bed for ten hours, preferably with Melissa's arms around him. Although he slept well on the bunk Stefanie made for him, it wasn't the same thing.

With Washington DC filling the landscape below, the Gulfstream breaking through the brown smog layer on its way down to Andrews, he perked up. He tightened his seatbelt and watched as the aircraft settled, seemingly drifting. Then they were over the outer marker and everything rushed by. The tires scraped and the pilot initiated reverse thrust, pressing Tom against the seat. As the aircraft turned onto the taxiway, he unclipped his seatbelt. When they finally stopped, the engines immediately wound down. Stefanie emerged from the cockpit and opened the door. Warm moist air drifted in and Tom sighed. It was good to be on solid ground again.

"Made it in one piece," Davenport grunted as he stood up and stretched his arms.

Tom glanced at Keith's leg. "Almost in one piece."

Davenport chuckled. "You should talk."

Stepped out of the cockpit, Major Weber extended his hand.

"Thanks for the ride, Major," Tom said as they shook hands.

"Any time, Mr. Meecham…Mr. Davenport."

Tom turned to Stefanie and Master Sergeant Ricardo. "And thank *you* for looking after us."

"A pleasure, sir," she said, wearing her best flight attendant smile.

In the doorway, Tom paused and the sight out there made his heart skip a beat. Standing beside the black FBI Chevy, dressed in a smart navy blue business jacket and tight skirt, Melissa broke into a smile and fluttered her fingers at him. He stepped onto the apron, opened his arms, and she was there: smiling, crying, hugging his neck. Their hungry lips met and nothing else mattered. After a timeless moment, he pulled back and brushed aside a strand of her golden hair.

"I've missed you," he growled, his throat tight.

"I should hope so!" she replied tartly then broke into a radiant smile, her eyes shining. "And how I missed you. Welcome home, Tom."

Turning, he saw Keith surrounded by his two girls, Karelina's arms held possessively around him. Tom decided they were both two lucky men.

He brushed Melissa's cheek with a finger, happy with the world.

"Let's get out of here, my sweet."

* * *

Watery sunshine dribbled from a pale sun hanging low in the sky. A fitful breeze stirred the branches of trees scattered through the Zhongnanhai compound. Keung Yang stood before the tall window, hands clasped behind his back. The pipe stem clamped firmly between his teeth, he allowed the aromatic smoke to leak between his nostrils, taking solace from its soothing presence. He wondered how long he would be allowed to enjoy this luxury, wanting badly to walk through the grounds and sit by the Zhong Hai Lake one last time, observing the ducks, swans and geese feeding among the white lilies and swaying reed beds. Under close house arrest, deprivation of personal liberties perhaps the hardest burden to bear, patrolling armed guards making sure he did not stray or have visitors. His computer and phone were disconnected and cellphone confiscated, but he was allowed to watch television. Not that he cared for what news commentators said about him and Chen. As for watching mindless popular entertainment, he no longer had the inclination for shallow escapism.

At least Lian remained caring and attending, not commenting in any way on his current predicament. In many ways, she was more attentive, almost attuned to his wants, but she did not intrude, understanding his need for solitude and reflection.

Chen...

He didn't blame his friend, not really. An innocent slip of the tongue undid everything, Zhou told him. Karma. Was Chen allowed the freedom of his house, the comfort of his family, or was he held in some basement annex in the soulless Ministry of Defense building undergoing intense interrogation by unsmiling, shadowy State Security figures? Why would they bother? They had all the facts, unless they were after something else, like inside information on Tuanpai followers? The Communist Youth League and its members was an open union. Like him, he suspected that Chen was also staring out a window wondering what the fates would serve next.

At least they wouldn't be quietly murdered to remove two political enemies. Keung's file on a piece of incriminating action by Zhou's chief of security ensured their lives. Like him, Zhou had developed an inevitable attachment with his personal body-guard. In hindsight, a fatal flaw for both of them, but something very human. They needed someone in whom they could confide; someone who would be obedient and carry out orders without question—be totally loyal. Keung shook his head at the irony of it. In a system where disobedience was subject to immediate and harsh punishment, he and Zhou still sought and expected loyalty. The wonder of it, they both actually got it.

He missed Shen, his quiet competence and unquestioning service. After everything the man went through and survived, to be felled by muggers? Yet, to achieve something monumental, everyone must pay a price, and Shen had paid his.

Keung knew what would happen next. He had dealt with too many opponents and understood how the system worked. There would be a trial, public humiliation, loss of power and oblivion back in Hefei, to live out his days in disgrace. At least he would have those days. Ordinarily, what he and Chen had done would merit a firing squad, or at least lifelong imprisonment at some unpleasant correctional facility, but the compromising infor-mation he had on Zhou meant they would escape that. Once Zhou was swept from power, and that day might come sooner than he expected, the next Paramount Leader may choose to ex-ecute him and Chen, unlikely as that was. It would be raking over old wounds without any political gain.

Keung exhaled a cloud of white smoke and sighed.

*Be not ashamed of mistakes and thus make them crimes*, Confucius said.

In any operation involving more than one person, there was bound to be a mistake made somewhere. However, Keung firmly believed what he and Chen did was not a crime. Lives were lost, yes, but protecting the state and its people always demanded sacrifice.

He keenly regretted not being able to call his son. Right now though, he figured Meng wouldn't be all that anxious to talk to him. Keung hoped his fall from grace would not harm his boy's career. Having gotten him back briefly, it looked like he was about to lose him again. Still, the moments of intimacy they had shared were warming and he found solace in that.

Perhaps a lengthy rest back home was what he needed. He had been involved for too long with the cut and thrust of high Party politics, neglecting his roots with ordinary people who shunned all subterfuge and government obfuscation. He'd had his setbacks before and always managed to rise above them. The gods may yet smile on him again.

Keung stepped away from the window, sauntered toward the bookshelf, and gazed at the bound volumes, considering which one to sample. He had wanted to catch up on his reading for some time, and now, he had time.

The smell of crumbling chrysanthemum leaves were ashes of disillusionment in his mouth.

# About the author

Stefan Vučak has written twenty-one novels, which include eight SF books in the Shadow Gods Saga. His *Cry of Eagles* won the coveted Readers' Favorite silver medal award, and his *All the Evils* was the prestigious Eric Hoffer contest finalist and Readers' Favorite silver medal winner. *Strike for Honor* won the gold medal.

Stefan leveraged a successful career in the Information Technology industry, which took him to the Middle East working on cellphone systems. Writing has been a road of discovery, helping him broaden his horizons. He also spends time as an editor and book reviewer. Stefan lives in Melbourne, Australia.

To learn more about Stefan, visit his:
Website: www.stefanvucak.com
Facebook: www.facebook.com/StefanVucakAuthor
Twitter: @stefanvucak

# More Books by Stefan Vučak

https://www.stefanvucak.com/Books/

www.ingramcontent.com/pod-product-compliance
Lightning Source LLC
Chambersburg PA
CBHW030647120726
47905CB00001B/97